REBEL CONSPIRACY

A YOUNG ADULT DYSTOPIAN SCI-FI ADVENTURE

THE KASEATH CHRONICLES
BOOK 2

JACKIE MCCARTHY

CURLING TEA PRESS

CHAPTER 1

My first taste of cake was at my sister's ninth birthday party in suburban Cookham East. I was used to celebrating milestones with dense, black-market bread with a dash of sugar. But this version was real fluffy sponge slathered in icing so thick it required carving with a wooden spork.

'Spork' was another luxurious word. The cutlery wasn't a spoon or a fork. It was both. Then, it was thrown away after a single use. To me, it was a perfect object, a treasure. That was the scavenger in me, not wasting a single resource.

I didn't think about where the discarded spoils would end up—on Trash Mountain, beside the shacks in my former neighbourhood. I had plenty now. But we'd left people behind.

A fierce afternoon sun burned in the sky like the smoky air was ablaze. The scorching breeze ruffled the balloons stuck to the garage beside the 'Happy Birthday' sign. Scents wafted from dishes of seared meats, piles of fried rice, leafy salads, and my neighbour's speciality—Goan fish curry.

Kids roamed and played games on the lawn, just for the heck of it. Nobody required us to dig through a pile of filth or trade on the black market.

Couldn't the afternoon sun hang on longer, extending this moment with my family and friends?

I left the front yard, where the guests chatted, winding through the cooler house. Past the open-plan living room and the kitchen's island bench. Past that obvious luxury—a dining table littered with food platters. Enough to feed the shacks of Northies for an entire year.

My sister Imogen stood in the backyard, staring sadly at the memorial tree planted for my other sister, lost to the Snatchers. Balloons swayed in the wind, taped to the tree's spindly branches. Lavender daisies from our back garden mingled with the smoke like sweet incense. Kids raced around, playing tag and running amok. Imogen stood apart without the energy to give chase.

Imogen was small for her nine years. She looked less emaciated since we'd moved here, less bony. She had even grown taller, catching up to her classmates. Now, she attended school. Her thin face and dull eyes reflected her plague symptoms. She was part of the unlucky twenty per cent who never recovered from the global plague. Eventually, she would succumb to her symptoms—unless we could find a cure.

Not even my unique hybrid human-alien powers could help. For whatever reason, my healing abilities didn't work on the plague. I was training for the next best thing—a space mission to obtain the cure to save humanity.

Imogen's cheeks were flushed rosy, and my heart fell.

My skinny little sister resembled an old lady rather than a carefree kid.

"Hey, Limpet," I said, using my nickname for her. She followed me like a symbiotic creature, always with me. The name had... stuck?

"Ofelia!" she squealed.

"How is your fever?" I noted her flushed appearance. My tummy fluttered as I waited for her reply.

"Aren't you going to wish me a happy birthday?" She grinned.

"Sorry—happy birthday!"

"I wish you weren't leaving." Imogen kept a brave expression on her face, but the corners of her mouth wobbled.

My heart heaved with guilt. "I'm getting your cure. Nothing's more important."

She unknotted her brow. I wrapped my arms around her shoulders, not wanting to let go. My symbiotic sister. She felt bony and angular and folded in, seeming to fit.

I'd already lost one sister. I couldn't lose another.

My two best friends burst into the backyard, kicking a soccer ball that banged against the fence. They knew how to ruin a moment...

"Oh, hey, Ofelia," Mousie said, her close-cropped hair almost grown in now. It feathered against her temple, a far cry from her matted locks during our time in Northies. Mousie's face had filled out, because of decent suburbs food. Despite her stunted growth, she could hold her own. She was twelve years old.

Aze was a couple of years older than Mousie. She no longer wore her decorative eye patch to appear meaner to the heavies back on Trash Mountain. That was unnecessary here, and she didn't need to hide. We were all safe—for now.

Aze kicked the ball to me, and I caught it deftly in the arch of my bare foot.

She grinned. "There's still time to back out."

"Unfortunately, no." I arced the ball over Mousie's head. "Oops, sorry."

A child's shriek pierced the air like overloaded speakers on an audio feed.

"What's that noise? Is something wrong?" I scanned the area for police or military units, descending on the party and scattering the children like a tossed bucket of popcorn.

"Oh, it's pin the tail on the donkey," Imogen said.

"What's a donkey?" Mousie asked.

"I dunno. It looks like a horse?"

"Wouldn't that hurt the donkey?" I wondered if the guests were torturing long-extinct animals. That would explain the shrieks, and my spiking heart rate.

"It's only a picture," Imogen said, giggling. She pointed to an oversized poster of a horse-like creature pinned to the wall with various tails plastered over it. Some on its head, others off the picture altogether. One blindfolded kid moved towards it, hands outstretched, feeling for the paper on the wall.

I had a flashback to wearing a rancid hood, terrified, just as blind as the kid reaching for the paper. Only my memory surfaced from somewhere much scarier—the Elditch Research Facility, where I was held with the other snatched kids, enduring experiments from Dr Figg. Flashing recollections: an antiseptic smell, the painful tests, and the knowledge of what she'd done to my sister.

The sister Figg had accidentally killed.

My eyes flitted to Demi's memorial tree, shaking off the adrenalin shooting into my trembling hands. Would I ever recover from the events at Elditch?

Ignoring the shouts and the good-natured jeers, I reminded myself to treasure the happy moment. Precious time with my sister. She might not celebrate many birthdays.

Aze made bunny ears behind Mousie's head and crammed her face full of cake.

"How's training going?" she asked around her mouthful.

"It's going well," I said, a half-truth for Imogen's benefit.

Imogen doubled over with a wheezing fit. Mousie rubbed her back. We waited for Imogen to catch her breath.

I locked eyes with Mousie and mouthed, "Thank you."

She lifted her chin. At least my friends could watch my sister while I was gone. Imogen would have someone if I didn't make it home.

The pause in conversation lingered. Imogen's chest had deteriorated, confirmed by the concern in Mousie's eyes. Aze stopped cramming cake into her mouth, waiting until the wheezing subsided.

"You'll be brave, Limpet?" I said.

Imogen nodded, regaining her breath.

"Don't go," she whispered.

I draped my arm over Imogen's shoulders and exhaled slowly. "I made a promise."

She just smiled back with a reassuring gaze. "Trix can't lie, so the Kaseath don't have the cure. There's no need for the mission. Stay here."

Her words stabbed a sharp pain into my chest. I kept my voice hopeful, not letting the cracks through. But every fracture shattered under the weight of my purpose.

"Trix hasn't spoken to the Kaseath for twenty years," I said. "They could have discovered your cure by now. I have to try."

"What if the aliens are right?" Imogen said, avoiding my gaze.

"What do you mean?" I asked.

"What if humanity's not worth saving?"

"Well, maybe not *all* humans." I grinned. "But *we're* worth saving, right?"

"Darn straight," Mousie rallied.

"I'll be okay without you," Imogen said, winding her arm around mine. Hers felt too angular and thin. I squeezed back.

"In that case," my mischievous grin returned, "see if you can catch this one!"

I kicked the ball high in our circle, avoiding the kids strewn across the yard. Imogen zoned in on the ball's trajectory. She was off balance, and the ball arced away. Mousie and Aze butted heads as the ball dropped. They kicked it about on the grass, trying to steal it from each other.

"I've got it," Aze said, feigning right but nudging left. Just as she gained possession, Mousie swooped in and stole the ball. "Hey!"

We focussed on Mousie keeping the ball from Aze's tackle. Then, Imogen doubled over, wheezing.

"Oh, Limpet." Fear shot up my chest. Our game was forgotten. I'd pushed her too hard.

Imogen wheezed asthmatically, one symptom of the plague. The air snagged in her windpipe like a clawing cat escaping from her lungs. She gasped and couldn't breathe normally.

At least she no longer had the telltale dark blue plague sweat pushing painfully from her pores. Her sweat was clear now, a translucent sheen on her forehead. The contagious period was long over. She wasn't a threat to others—people who recovered were immune. But Imogen's condition was permanent.

"Take it easy for a bit," I said.

But Imogen couldn't catch her breath. She didn't protest as I guided her to the cane outdoor seat on the cool patio.

"I'm alright," she protested in a small, wavering voice. She tried to smile, but her scraping breath was more solid than air-like. Her back shook as she tried to cough. But it was only breath. It shouldn't sound like that.

"You're not okay," I said. "I'll get Mum."

"Please... don't... She'll call the doctor," Imogen wheezed, her eyes downcast at the tiled patio floor.

"Maybe that's a good idea?"

Mousie and Aze crowded around, concern on their faces.

Imogen closed her eyes, waiting for the convulsions to pass. But she couldn't fool us.

"That's it. We're calling an ambulance," I said. "Will you watch her?"

My friends nodded, concerned, and gathered close to hug my sister. I headed back into the party to find my mum.

A hazel-brown tint touched Mum's greying hair, a previously unthought-of luxury. She turned her attention to the phone call. Her eyes were as piercing as a sharp knife, slicing me open and exposing all my insecurities. Her gaze flicked to Imogen as she listened to the response.

Mum hung up and smiled, not wanting to spook my sister. "An ambulance is on the way."

Imogen, too miserable to worry, let her shoulders slump. My step-dad and I exchanged a concerned glance.

"Hey, Limpet," I said, "I'll pack a bag for you."

I didn't run, which would alarm Imogen. But I power-walked into her bedroom, flinging open the wardrobe and snatching a bag from the top shelf. I stuffed clothes inside, and her favourite plush unicorn from her bed. Glancing at the horse posters on the wall, my eyes watered with the fear of losing my sister.

Not Imogen, too.

I headed to the front lawn, ignoring the guests milling around.

The smoke-tinged air was less like sweet incense and more like a plastic chemical burn. A wind gust fluttered the balloons and whipped the 'Happy Birthday' sign around like a flimsy tissue.

The kids squealed with the sudden gale, paper cups blew off the tables, and guests secured the food on their paper plates. Hats fell to the grass. I flinched as a balloon burst.

A distant siren wound closer, growing more urgent. Despite these summer temps, Mum rugged Imogen up in a sweater and jeans. I held her overnight bag. We stepped into the driveway as the ambulance pulled up. Two paramedics opened the back doors.

The straggler guests watched the paramedics settle Imogen on the wheeled bed. They placed an oxygen mask over her face. She seemed tiny and out of place. She should be back at the party, playing soccer with our friends.

The paramedics wheeled her into the ambulance. Mum crammed in beside her, perching on the narrow side seat.

Mum pushed me away as I tried to climb in.

"I'm not leaving her." My lip quivered.

"There's no time to argue, Ofelia," Mum said harshly.

My step-dad, Roland, held my shoulders. I tried to pull away and crawl into the ambulance.

The paramedic shook his head at me. "There's no room."

"But I have to stay with her!" I fought towards the doors.

"Kid, you're slowing us down. Let us take care of her."

"Come on, Ofelia." Roland steadied me with both hands.

"I'll see you soon, Imogen, I love you!"

But she didn't respond. Her eyes fluttered closed.

The paramedic hopped in and slammed the doors. The ambulance tore away, its siren screaming.

"We'll follow Imogen to the hospital." I remembered as I said that... Roland couldn't drive.

The last of the guests left discreetly. My step-dad shook his head, his eyes heavy with sadness.

"You have your mission, Ofelia."

"I'm not leaving—Imogen needs me."

"Exactly," Roland said, letting that sink in.

To my surprise, I threw my arms around his shoulders, tears stinging my eyes. I didn't want to get emotional, and losing my cool within earshot of the wailing siren seemed silly. But Roland hugged me back, rubbing my shoulder with his palm.

"I can't go," I said. "What if she gets worse?"

"The mission is too important. Think about the people you'll help."

"I don't care about anyone else, only Imogen." I pulled out of the hug.

"You don't mean that." Roland placed his rough-skinned hand on my arm. "You care deeply, and that's your burden."

"But I can't do the things they're asking."

"You are the most unique person in the history of humankind, remember?" Roland said with an ironic smile. "Go. There's no choice. This is your purpose."

"I won't pass the training." Sure, I aced fake spacewalks in a swimming pool. The rest seemed impossible.

Roland's deep brown eyes connected with my pain. He knew loss—Demi had been his daughter.

But I was just a scrappy teenage Northies rat. What could I do? Who did I think I was?

"We all love you very much. Your mum—well, she's not angry at you."

"That's *so* not true."

"She's worried she'll lose her surviving daughters. If it's just me and her—that's not much of a family."

I grunted in reply, glancing at the dot of the ambulance, its wailing lost as it rounded the corner. My anger dissipated, leaving me empty. If Mum loved me so much, why was she so hard on me?

Roland leaned in so that I caught every word.

"You must pass the training, Ofelia, and save your sister. You're her best hope."

The responsibility weighed heavily. More than a lowly Northies rat like me could handle. But Roland was right.

Imogen's fate depended on that mission, and I was the only obstacle to its success. I had to try.

The familiar black government sedan approached and parked in the driveway, its grating engine idling.

It was there to take me to Space Camp.

CHAPTER 2

I SWALLOWED hard and concentrated on the pulsing alert lights on the panel overhead. The mission was doomed—I was definitely failing this procedure. And on top of that, I was about to lose my lunch.

"This is the most complicated part of the mission, besides launch and re-entry," the commander said through my helmet's CommLink. "We've made it this far. It's up to you, recruit."

"Just perfect," I replied under my breath, checking the screen mid-way inside the space shuttle. Why did the commander call me 'recruit' in her procedural way? As if 'Ofelia' was beneath me. Most likely, it was to remind me of my place.

Weightlessness was not fun. I swallowed an acidic burp, my head slipping with the vertigo of our rotation. Which way was up? My inner ear found equilibrium.

A bead of sweat floated towards my nose. My guts constricted like a squeezed wet towel. The heart monitor on my CommLink beeped, adding to the warnings on the panels.

All I could think about was puke clogging my helmet in zero-g.

Our shuttle spun like a fairground ride, matching the alignment of the alien ship's orbit. 'Cause there's, like, no standing still in space. The alien ship was smooth, gunmetal grey, like a massive mercury globule lurking outside the cockpit, hanging in the blackness of space. We headed towards the faint outline of its docking bay.

"Just breathe, recruit," the commander said from the cockpit.

"I mean, that's obvious," I said to myself. "We all need to breathe. Breathing is the easy part."

The commander glared at me, returning her attention to the cockpit controls.

I closed my eyes, and an image flashed—my little sister lying in a hospital bed as black-blue plague sweat oozed out of her pores...

My reason for being here.

Get it together, Ofelia.

I slowed my breathing, concentrating on the joystick-controlled robotic arm. I trembled when I should be ice-calm. This procedure required exacting precision, and I was no space ace.

From the cockpit, the commander eased the controls, bringing us closer, inch by inch. I gripped the joystick tighter.

"Fifteen metres..." she said. "Extend the docking arm halfway."

I nudged the joystick, and the arm extended, pulling the round cover, then the chute.

"Five metres," the commander said. "Extend to full length."

I tapped the controls. The arm groaned as it extended.

Then the nausea hit—we made another rotation. My head pulled to one side as I fought the sensation, swallowing hard. My hands trembled, the joystick slipping.

The chute extended to full length.

The commander continued, "Thirty centimetres... twenty... ten... aligned. Initiate lock."

I mashed a button on the touch screen, sending the docking arm's claw-like grip to the indentation in the other vessel.

The cabin shuddered as the docking arm scraped the hatch on the other ship. Our shuttle's warning sounded.

BEEP, BEEP, BEEP. Docking alignment failure.

Yeah, okay, I got that, brainiac.

"Try again, recruit," the commander said. "Moving us back to 30 centimetres..."

I nudged the joystick to retract the arm, waiting for the commander to put us in position.

"Aligned, initiate lock," she repeated, making light adjustments, venting air, and keeping us in line with the other ship.

I pressed the button again, nudging the joystick.

"Are we attached, recruit?"

"I think so..."

"*You think* isn't enough. Precision, okay? Are we attached?"

"Nope. I mean, maybe?" My hands trembled with the pressure.

Breath escaped my lips, fogging my visor. I nudged the joystick with my forefinger, waiting for the flashing green indicator. The cabin's lights strobed red as I engaged the lock.

"There's a problem," Lopez said, fingers flying over the touch screens in front of her.

"Problem?" I couldn't even pretend to keep the alarm out of my voice.

"Debris at twelve o'clock—evasive manoeuvres."

"What?" I swallowed hard, tasting bile.

"Retract the arm, now!"

I grabbed the joystick, retracting the pressurised latch, and the arm flapped, then ground still.

The commander's voice returned. "Mechanical failure. What do you do?"

"Whatever you tell me! How do I fix this?"

"It's up to you, recruit. I've gotta fly this bird."

"Ahh... um..."

I checked the blinking control panel above me. Panicking, I scanned the whole panel, but the options were overwhelming. I jabbed the 'override' button.

The commander pulled us to starboard, missing the alignment with the other ship.

She jammed the engines on full.

We angled away, my stomach dropping at the sudden thrust. I grabbed the joystick and yanked.

The retracting arm lacerated the side of the alien ship.

"Status?" she said, and I choked up. I was failing this mission.

"I can't retract. The arm is stuck."

The docking arm severed the other ship's hatch.

A sickening crunch.

Shrapnel broke free of the alien ship. The entire docking hatch spun in zero gravity, forming a saucer of doom. The hatch swivelled towards us like a wheeling firecracker.

"Watch out for debris!" I shouted.

Too late—the hatch smashed into our shuttle.

The interior lights blinked, and the ship lurched to the side. The impact cracked the outer porthole.

Lights flashed, and warning sounds pierced the cockpit as air sucked away, bleeding into space.

The whirlwind of the vacuum was terrifying. We resisted

the pull into deep space, strapped into our seats, the shuttle disintegrating.

An internal panel shot past me. Then, the bucket chair next to the commander jettisoned into space. Debris flew everywhere, chunks in a tornado.

This was it. This was the end, and my racing mind panicked.

A flash of fire.

The thrusters overloaded.

I closed my eyes against the flash of light through the cabin, cringing at the rush of heat and pain.

Then, all sensations stopped as our ship exploded.

Lucky for me, this was just a hyper-realistic simulation.

I removed my helmet as the residual pain in my sim suit subsided. Sure, I knew that what I had just experienced wasn't real. But try telling my pain receptors that.

"Mission aborted," Commander Lopez confirmed, shaking her head and removing her helmet and sim goggles. "You need to pass at least one practical, Ofelia. I'm not joking, or they won't allow you on the mission, even as a tourist."

"I'm no astronaut," I said.

"That's for certain."

The simulator recalibrated. We stopped spinning, and my nausea subsided.

My eyes glazed over, the intensity overwhelming. I turned away from the commander. This couldn't be happening again.

I'd never make it out of this simulation alive. This was my twentieth failed mission. Nobody *physically* died. It was just a sim. But I was sick of all the virtual deaths I'd racked up since coming to Space Camp. I wanted to ace the training. Would I ever pass the tests?

"I'm sorry, Commander Lopez," I said.

"I know." Disappointment wavered in her grey-flecked eyes. She was in her forties but fit from intense physical drills.

"She's mission-critical, Lopez," a voice said through the comms. "So make it work."

"We'll try again tomorrow," Lopez said, unzipping her gloves.

Our cockpit was a replica of the actual shuttle, complete with working panels, touch screens to control the ship, and the seats and modules where we would live for the mission's duration.

Someone outside of the simulator removed the hatch from our cockpit.

I crawled into the brightness streaming through the skylights above us in the massive training terminal, happy to breathe clean air after the stuffiness of my helmet.

Large mechanical simulation machines were spaced around the hangar. At the far end, a swimming pool glittered, where we trained for zero gravity. Platforms and machines straddled the pool to access the submerged replica space shuttle.

I yearned for the pool, the only simulation I could stomach. It was the reason they were persevering with the rest. But what good was walking in space? I couldn't handle the launch. My motion sickness could prevent me from going on this mission. I had to be there for my sister.

Our mission was to obtain the cure from the alien Kaseath, and I could bridge the communication divide. Being the only alien-human hybrid in existence was a real drag.

Not only that, but Earth was past its use-by date. It would be unliveable in less than a decade, so I'd secured my friends and family a spot on the Interplanetary Voyager Ark. Between war, climate change, and the global plague, we'd exhausted our planet's capacity to support human life—and, importantly, most animal and plant life, which was disastrous for the planet.

But the problem? The Kaseath didn't want us to leave Earth. And we needed their permission, according to my alien friend Trix.

I eased a shaky leg onto the stairs outside the simulator, miserably sucking in fresh air. A technician offered their hand, which I took to steady myself.

I plodded down the stairs to the smooth concrete of the facility flooring. The technicians helped me remove various parts of my space suit, starting with the gloves, then the arms and torso, and then my boots and legs. I peeled off my simulation suit, revealing the figure-hugging undersuit, and I sat on a bench, sweat sticking my frizzed brown hair to my forehead.

The rash of alien scales on my stomach itched, and I rubbed them. The scales responded to heat and disliked the sim suit. I scratched the scales on my upper arm, hardly feeling part Kaseath, but very aware of my human limitations.

Lately, I couldn't even control my alien powers.

I was just a kid. I'd turn sixteen in a few months. The Aces, the first-choice crew, and the Betas, our backups, had been training for decades. Their whole lives had led to this moment. The mission seemed impossible. I wouldn't pass the training.

Commander Lopez removed her suit, joining me on the bench. She hadn't broken a sweat. Her black helmet hair was matted down, fuzzy around her middle part. She rubbed her face with both hands, wiping disappointment from her grave brown eyes. But she glanced at me with compassion, just inching out her annoyance.

She played with the dog tags she wore around her neck.

They made a grinding metallic sound as she massaged them between her fingers.

"Look, kid. We're running out of time." She kept the exasperation from her tone. "Our launch window is in one week. Tomorrow is your final grading, and you must pass."

"No pressure, then," I replied.

"This mission will be nothing *but* pressure. You need to harness it."

She was trying to help, but my confidence oozed out of me like a squeezed bottle of barbecue sauce, leaving only the dregs at the bottom. And everyone knew those dregs remained in the bottle, discarded with the trash...

Lopez softened her expression. "Diplomacy requires talking to the Kaseath. There's no mission without you. Can you try harder?"

"Is there any news about my sister?" I asked, eyes on the glassy, polished concrete floor.

"She's still in hospital. There's been no change," Lopez said.

"I want to speak to her."

"Maybe tomorrow, after your final practical grading. We need you focussed on the mission."

Lopez used contact with my family to keep me motivated. I was sick of the secrecy and drip-fed information. It was the prime minister's style, and Lopez was probably following his orders.

Lopez patted me on the back of my sweat-soaked undershirt, and I forced a smile. She joined the technicians, readying our next simulation.

The mission would find the plague cure.

A chance to save my sister and humanity.

So, yeah. No pressure at all.

I left the training hangar, navigating back towards the Camp Kiddies barracks on the hill above the Space Camp complex. I was training with the fast-tracked kids, those whose future was inevitable in the space program. My real crew would be experienced adults. None of the other kids were going on the actual assignment except for me. Yep—being mission-critical caused some jealousy amongst Camp K.

I'd study my butt off with Maya, my super-smart neighbour from Cookham East. We'd been through so much together after escaping the Elditch Research Facility. She'd just turned fifteen, the same age as me. She was my emotional support person in the program, someone familiar to train with.

I had to pass the next practical grading. My other results were mediocre, but all I needed was a C+. I had half a chance in the pool. Then I'd get the heck on that mission to save my sister.

A pathway followed the grassy area behind the massive hangar. The night air was uncomfortably humid. The wind caught my hair in my face, and I batted it out of my eyes. Smoke wafted about—something was always burning in London. It was probably from the hearths of the Northies shacks beyond the launch pad.

On the far side of Space Camp, single-storey bungalow houses, painted orange with white trim, dotted the rise of the hill. Camp K didn't get as many luxuries as the Aces and Betas. I turned towards a ramshackle two-storey building.

A kid shouted, followed by the crash of something heavy dropping to the floor.

I hoped it wasn't a body.

Storming into the barracks, I prepared for a fight. Wasn't there always a fight?

Our Camp K weirdo, Phoebe Griffin, leaned over my friend Maya, who backed into the bunks.

Griffin's default mode was aggression.

She was average height for a sixteen-year-old, but her biceps and calves were out of whack. She looked like a lopsided balloon animal or a bodybuilder who focussed on limited muscle groups. I wondered how she kept her balance. She was rumoured to be a super soldier, and I never mocked her. I hadn't seen her full potential, which was fine with me.

No reason to give *her* a reason.

Tears formed gleaming tracks on Maya's cheeks. I recognised her expression. She was just as terrified as when I had first met her at Elditch.

Another time, another bully.

"Hey, cut that out!" I said.

"Or what?" Griffin raised both eyebrows in a challenge.

"Come and fight someone who can fight back." I squared my shoulders, planting both feet on the smooth concrete floor.

"There's no Commander Lopez to save you now." Griffin swivelled to face me.

"I'm used to worse than you," I said.

Which was true. At least she didn't have...

... Griffin pulled a handgun from the pocket of her uniform.

Great. It was back to dodging bullets.

But instead of pointing the gun at me, Griffin waved it at Maya.

"Hey, stop, you lopsided freak!" I said.

Griffin turned, her face screwed up in unflattering rage. She pointed the gun at my chest.

"Do it," I said, facing the potential super soldier with a deadly weapon.

Then I noticed the gun's tip. A red plastic ring surrounded the muzzle. Wait a minute...

Griffin concentrated, taking her shot.

The dart blew from the gun. It sped towards me.

Before the missile hit, I threw up my force field, the unique power that stopped time for everyone in front of me.

My shield was as thin as a sheet of clingfilm. It was translucent, without its former green solid state. Lately, my shield failed when the others were around. Yeah, my powers were less than impressive these days.

I scrunched up my face, willing all of my concentration into the shield.

But the flashes took over.

Flashes of Maya cowering on the bare cell floor. Muscled hands clamped over my arms. Fighting for air around the rancid hood. Flashes of Imogen, with greyish, sunken eyes, black-blue plague sweat needling out of her pores...

... I could barely keep the flimsy shield open for a half second before it glitched.

The edges sparked like a welder cutting metal, and a firecracker force hit me in the arm.

"Ouch!" My shield disappeared, and I couldn't catch the dart before it hit. My powers vanished like the effervescent fizz on a newly poured soda.

I flinched from the burn on my forearm.

The rubber bullet kept going, clonking on my chest before falling to the floor.

It looked to Griffin that I hadn't stopped time at all.

She shook her head, grinning at her practical joke. Her weapon was nothing but a kid's toy, a plastic dart gun.

She smirked and sauntered towards me. I flinched, expecting her to shoulder-charge me on the way through. Instead, she bent to pick up the spent dart at my feet, whistling and leaving the barracks.

"That was so uncool!" I rushed from the bottom bunk to hug Maya.

Maya shook like she'd had a flashback. Her straight black hair was messed up, and her usual smooth, brown complexion was blotchy from crying. She buried her face in her hands, letting the tears flow.

"Maya, you're safe." I rubbed the singe mark on my wrist from my glitching shield.

I sat for a moment, then roused my friend. "We're done with those bullies. Help me study like a Mathlete so I can launch into space."

CHAPTER 3

MAYA MET me at the pool, the training sim I had somewhat mastered. I hadn't learned how to swim—there was nowhere to practise in Northies, where I grew up. We barely had enough drinking water and even less to bathe in. Northies residents would pilfer that pristine pool water for weeks without rain.

Northies rats made the best of what we had.

My moon-booted toes dipped in, and the indulgent situation hit home. My feet refracted and wavered, less like they were connected to me. As the platform lowered into the pool, my body became light, my mass mimicking the weightlessness of space.

Maya stood beside me on the platform, suited, leaning into the water as if she couldn't reach the submerged shuttle quickly enough.

I told her, "The timid suburbs mouse from Elditch is totally acing Space Camp."

"I'm not acing it..." She half smiled, acknowledging the truth.

Our helmets submerged into the water, the light above wavering like flags.

"Yeah, right," I said. "You're younger than me but a few thousand kilometres ahead."

"We're the same age, dummy." She turned on her helmet lights.

"Not for long. But seriously, I wish you were going instead of me."

"Maybe I will, someday."

"There's no 'maybe' about it." We stepped off the platform, 'swimming' towards the submerged replica shuttle, our heavy suits pulling us under.

Maya motioned to her helmet lights, miming that I should turn mine on, too.

"See, I'd forget my way without you," I said.

Maya had the aptitude and smarts for Space Camp. Me? Not so much.

"Concentrate on what you're doing." Maya's voice cut through my helmet.

The indoor lighting above the pool rippled around us. The deeper we went, the farther we travelled from the hangar's overhead lights. Our forms took on a weightless feeling, submerged in the murky water.

I enjoyed the swimming sensations, my suit lightening, my movements becoming more graceful. It was impossible to go too fast. Each motion had a delayed consequence as the softer gravity caught up.

It was like being in a slow-motion movie.

Dean was already near the bottom of the pool. His form seemed like a distorted, white-suited stingray grappling with the replica shuttle resting on the bottom. He'd been training to be a pilot for two years and was the official leader-slash-bully of the kiddies' training group, Camp K. He would grade my final lesson today.

I had to pass this test, or they wouldn't let me fly. And, as everyone kept reminding me, there was no mission without me, no chance to save my sister.

"Ofelia, Maya, tether to Valentina One," Dean said, not bothering to say hello.

"Nice to see you too, *Dean*," I replied, sarcasm seething.

He hated it when I didn't use his surname or 'Squad Leader', which was more in line with Space Camp etiquette.

To heck with etiquette. 'Dean' was an insult, which was fine by me.

I nodded to Ruby Hellcat, who leaned casually against her tether on the nose of the ship like a rock climber taking a breather near the summit.

Hellcat stared at Maya and me, ignoring Dean.

"Shouldn't she be in the flight sims?" Maya hooked her tether onto the narrow railing running the shuttle's length.

I glanced at Hellcat, who turned away. She was a year younger than Dean but a better, less arrogant pilot. But she was super strange. She'd earned her renegade name, so I was relieved she wouldn't fly on my mission.

Kiku Speckle pulled on the handholds to 'walk' herself over the spine of the shuttle, past one of the round gun bays. Kiku's distant ancestors were from Japan, but her family had been in London for generations. Like every other country in the northern hemisphere, all borders had become amalgamated.

We were lucky, on the winning side. But the war was too close now.

Kiku Speckle waved and lifted the gold visor, which would protect us from space radiation. We were to keep them down while the sun was in our direct line of vision. But the light was sparse at this depth.

Kiku rolled her eyes in Dean's direction. I couldn't help giggling. Apart from Maya, Kiku was my favourite Camp K training buddy.

"What's so funny, Ofelia?" Dean faced the Camp K contingent.

"Nothing, Dean." I turned to hide my smirk.

But Phoebe Griffin wiped it off as she came into view.

Honestly, I was surprised they made space suits big enough to accommodate her asymmetrical muscles. Something was off in her gene splice, beyond her physique.

Dean noticed Griffin swimming behind him, her jet packs venting air, shifting her about the ship. Even in simulated weightlessness, she moved awkwardly.

Maya, Kiku, and I let Dean sweat, then joined him at the ship's underside for today's grading.

"Right, we're all here then." Dean stared pointedly at Hellcat, who hung off the shuttle's nose.

Hellcat turned to look at Dean. Her expression didn't change as she returned to the shuttle's windshield, checking out her suited reflection in the tempered glass. She waved a gloved hand at her reflection.

"Anytime you'd like to join your squad leader would be fine." Griffin's voice hardened, as usual, like she was giving commands to a poorly trained lab rat.

Lab rat. Northies rat. Scavenger scum.

That was me.

Dean scowled, seeking Griffin's support. But Griffin's tether snagged on her oversized biceps, and she tried to escape before we noticed.

"How are things going down there, Squad Leader?" Our technician's voice filtered through our helmets.

"We're about to begin the grading," Dean said, glaring at me.

Challenge accepted.

Maya noticed my combative expression and nudged me in the arm. I hardly felt the bump, protected by the bulky suit.

"C+, remember," she said.

I wasn't about to let Dean fail me. I wouldn't leave Space Camp if I didn't pass today's lesson with at least a C+ grade. Failing this test was not an option—it was time to stop antagonising Dean.

"Who wants to go first?" Dean asked.

Maya shot her hand in the air so fast she created a whirlwind of water, unsettling us all from our tethers to the ship.

I glared at Maya—not angry but, if I'm honest, feeling slightly betrayed.

Maya noticed my reaction.

"What? I need the practice." She shrugged as much as was possible, dressed in a full space suit.

"Ofelia, you first." Dean pointed to a panel on the shuttle.

"Aren't you going to show us how to do it?" I asked.

Maya raised her eyebrows at me in a 'you've got this' way.

I totally didn't have this.

Spacewalks in the pool—yes. Manual maintenance tasks and not dropping the all-important drill or the even-more-essential screws—not so much.

Dean pulled his face closer to mine, and I was glad for the buffer of our helmets.

"You're the one going to space," he said. "We'll follow you."

"Can't argue with that." I pasted a sunny smile onto my face and held up the drill attached to my utility belt.

"Hmm," Maya whispered. "Backwards."

"Oops." I turned the drill around, noticing the pointy end. "Well, that makes more sense..."

Dean scowled in his self-satisfied way. He checked for validation from Griffin, but she was busy pitting her finger guns against the missile bays on the ship's side.

At least her finger guns were proportional to the rest of her body.

Dean held out his CommLink, his finger poised over the timer. "You have five minutes. Ready?" he asked.

The moisture seemed to wick out of my mouth faster than a desert sucking up drizzling rain. My hands shook. The drill seemed to weigh as much as a car. My mind returned to the flimsy 'happy birthday' sign whipped about in the wind. Imogen's flushed face as the ambulance took her away.

"You've got this," Maya said, her voice clear through my helmet, and I met her supportive gaze.

Kiku gave me a thumbs-up. I ignored the others.

I sucked in a lungful of air, lifted the drill—pointy side up this time—and waited for Dean's countdown.

"Three... two... one... start procedure."

I eased the drill bit into the first screw head and jiggled it until the contact was seamless. The drill felt connected, so I held it steady and pressed the trigger button. The drill vibrated with a muted whine, and the screw loosened. I grabbed it before it floated away. So far, so good.

"Nice one, Ofelia," Kiku Speckle said.

I held my breath as I clipped the drill to my utility belt and tucked the first screw into the pouch, zipping it shut.

Remembering to breathe this time, I positioned the drill over the second screw. I repeated the sequence until all the screws were tucked in the pouch, then removed the panel, revealing the wires beneath.

"C+, C+..." I muttered to myself before realising the others could hear me.

My face reddened. *Nice going, idiot.*

"You're almost there," Maya said.

"Time check, Squad Leader?" I asked.

"Two minutes, thirty seconds remaining," Dean counted off his CommLink.

The wires beneath the panel were a jumble of colours and out of order.

What the—

They had all been in order when we'd practised before. Why did they look like a bag of tangled, multi-coloured wool now?

"Someone's messed with this panel," I said.

I glanced at Dean, but he studied the timer on his CommLink.

Griffin's eyes narrowed with a self-satisfied smirk.

"Two minutes, sixteen seconds. Fifteen, fourteen..." Dean said.

"Got it, thank you." I settled beside the panel.

Did I replace the green wire... or maybe the red wire hidden behind? I doubted myself, blinking away the glassiness around my eyes. On top of everything else, I was about to blubber like a kid.

Dean wouldn't ruin my chance of going on the mission.

The replacement wire was in my utility pouch. I unzipped it, pulling out a green one—see, I knew what I was doing. I stowed the faulty green wire from the panel in my pouch, then twisted the replacement wire into the sockets.

"Thirty seconds," Dean said.

I placed the panel back into its grooves, bringing out the first screw.

"Twenty, nineteen, eighteen..." Dean said.

I let the drill rip on the first screw, not hesitating to settle the second one into its thread.

"Fifteen, fourteen, thirteen..."

The second screw was in place. I pulled the third free of the pouch and sent it home. The last screw was in place.

"Five seconds, four, three, two..."

I shoved the drill back onto my utility belt, lifting my hands.

"One... stop work," Dean said.

I grinned at Maya and Kiku Speckle, who rushed forward in the swirling water to high-five me. 'Cause it was impossible to hug in these suits.

I'd done it! Holy heck on a stick. Dean had to pass me. The training was over.

I had a chance to heal Imogen...

Dean vented air in his pack to float closer. He punched things into his CommLink and filled out the rating form. Inspecting the panel, he ran his scanner over the ship.

He shook his head, a smirk forming.

"I'm sorry, Ofelia," he said.

"What do you mean? I aced it!"

"It was shoddy work at best..."

"There wasn't one slip-up."

"You didn't complete the procedure in time..."

"Like heck she didn't," Maya said.

"And you replaced the wrong wire," he continued.

"She absolutely did not..." Kiku Speckle fired up, too.

"But you finished the procedure," Dean said, reading off his CommLink. "Your grade is a C-."

"But I need a C+..."

"Sorry, I guess you're not going on the mission."

"You can't do that—" I said, swishing myself closer.

"I can, actually." He hit a button on his CommLink. "We're finished here, returning to base."

I resisted the urge to punch Dean straight in his helmet. But it would take more than my gloved fist to crack it. I wanted to send him to the bottom of the pool. For him to drown. Just like my sister, who would one day succumb to flooded lungs.

Maya grabbed my shoulder, and Kiku Speckle shook her head.

"He's not worth it," Kiku said.

"What if I can't go?"

"We'll talk to the commander," Maya said.

"Yes, run to your commander friend," Dean said.

Except that the commander was no friend, and she knew all my screw-ups.

But I had to try.

I took charge, helping Maya and Kiku back onto the platform and winching us out of the pool. We rose from the water, leaving the submerged shuttle like a white dragon unfurling from an age-long sleep, about to send a fireball our way.

Kiku, Maya, and I helped each other out of our dripping suits.

I pulled on my daywear. This wouldn't be my last time wearing the baby blue uniform. Dean wouldn't beat me. My body thrummed with purpose.

"I'm going to fix this." I approached the nearest technician. "Have Commander Lopez meet me in the barracks."

Maya and Kiku wanted to come with me, but I shook my head.

I strode to the barracks, barely noticing my surroundings until I entered the chilly building.

The deep bunk bed rows settled like guards. My steel-capped boots echoed on the polished concrete floor. I shivered in the cool of the barracks, the gloomy light filtering through narrow windows. The musty air reeked of the cheap detergent of the freshly-washed blankets on each bunk. Outside, the thumping blades of a chopper echoed as it took off from a nearby flight pad, arcing up over our building.

The Aces' and the Betas' fancy white sedans drove past the barracks windows.

Their houses were farther away than the barracks. The cars wound up the rise, like termites settling into wood. The crew exited the vehicles, nailing the astronaut vibe in their pale blue suits. They smacked each other on the back—the elite of the elite, like the top zero-point-zero-one per cent. And they knew it.

They entered one of the orange-painted houses with the white trim. At least my crew would know what they were doing.

I sat on the nearest bottom bunk bed. Had I let my sister down? Would Lopez kick me out of the program?

Lopez made me simmer for too long, and I distracted myself from spiralling thoughts. I found a tennis ball underneath my bunk, ran my fingers over the fluffy threads covering it, and felt less freaked out. I bounced it against the nearest wall and caught it in my force field before it hit. Practising my powers helped calm my mind, but my shield weakened whenever I couldn't focus.

Since I'd left for Space Camp, I had trouble enacting my shield when other people were around. I'd lost confidence or something. My powers were paper thin.

The entire purpose of my shield was to protect other people. It was no use if I couldn't even protect myself.

Just as the ball hit my shield, I noticed Commander Lopez in the doorway. She froze, mid-step, in front of the shield.

My powers glitched instantly, then fell. A rebounding spark hit my cheek, and I flinched. The tennis ball scooted away under the opposite bunk.

Lopez sat next to me. She was uncomfortably close, and a hint of her floral deodorant wafted my way.

"You wanted to see me?"

"I passed the grading today—" I began in a rush of adrenalin-fuelled fury.

"Well—" Lopez began.

"I won't let the Squad Leader ruin my chances of going on the mission."

Lopez opened her mouth.

Before she could talk over me, I continued, "I replaced the correct wire within the allocated timeframe, and Dean sabotaged the test."

Lopez shut her mouth and waited for me to finish.

"Nothing will stop me from finding the cure for my sister. I deserve a pass. I'm mission-critical."

A second later, Lopez asked, "Are you finished?"

"Yep. I think so." My face felt heated, like a radiator.

A smile flickered at the edges of Lopez's mouth. "I agree with you. You completed the procedure to the letter. The squad leader was too harsh in his grading."

"So what's my grade?" I asked in a small voice. Could Lopez be on my side?

"You only need a pass." Lopez handed me a yellow envelope.

I tore it open, the grade floating at the top of the page. I couldn't believe it. Tension eased out of my clenched jaw.

"Final grading is a B-." I sighed with genuine relief. Then I asked, "What does that mean?"

"You're cleared for the mission," Lopez said, trying to hide her relief.

She held out a hand for me to shake. I would be petulant to ignore the gesture, so I accepted her firm grip against my sweaty and unpractised handshake.

"Dismissed," Lopez said. Then she softened. "Congratulations, recruit. You're going to space."

And, before I had time to process anything...

The first bomb dropped.

The ground shook so hard that I fell off my bunk.

CHAPTER 4

THE FORCE THREW Commander Lopez and me to the floor of the Camp K barracks. I whacked my head on the bunk bed's steel frame, and it throbbed like I'd squeezed my consciousness into an alternate dimension. Debris littered the floor. For a moment, I wondered why the concrete below me felt so hard. There was something odd about the tennis ball under the bunk.

The ball was on fire.

The fire spread to the blankets of the bunk above. I batted the flames until the blanket simmered, the ball like blackened corn on the cob.

Dust particles swished as if an indoor hurricane had just visited. Its aftermath was deadened sound and an almost-solid air, making breathing impossible.

I helped Lopez to her feet. Her panicked eyes searched mine.

What had just happened? The shocked aftermath made the moment surreal.

Would the barracks hold?

Lopez stumbled. I grabbed under her armpits, dragging her to standing. My legs wobbled, and I leaned against the nearest bunk. It didn't feel steady—or was I the unsteady one?

Lopez shouted at me as a trickle of blood snaked down her temple, running towards her eye socket. That blood trail transfixed me. I dragged Lopez away from the bunks where my friends had slept. The thought of my friends shocked me out of my hazy state.

My ears weren't working.

Were my friends okay?

My feet wobbled, but I kept a grip on Lopez. We exited the barracks. Smoke covered the rise of the hill, where the orange houses with white trim had been.

The entire rise was a burning crater, and the force of the explosion had tossed splinters of the houses like broken matchsticks, littering the ground. Spot fires burned the remaining housing estate. The charred remains of the fancy white sedans sat in front of the houses. The cars' tyres burned, and the cabins turned to black, beetle-like shells.

"No!" Lopez screamed.

We watched as a figure consumed by fire ran from the decimated house and then dropped to their knees.

Nobody inside the houses could have survived the blast.

The space camp building had been spared the actual bomb, but the lower level's exterior was charred, the windows stained with soot. Figures ran from the building in shock, surveying the damage. Then they noticed the Aces and Betas camp. They didn't know how to help.

Two fighter jets slammed overhead, engines tiny in my shocked sound. I instinctively ducked. But they were our aircraft, deployed for the counterattack.

I tugged Lopez's arm. She shouted at me. Sound was like an underwater dream, and my ears throbbed. I led Lopez towards the Space Camp building. Was Space Camp safer than the barracks?

Ground staff and technicians followed as I helped Lopez.

The first sound I discerned was a siren piercing the air. It sounded like an echo, winding up and down like a distressed accordion.

A second bomb dropped, this time slamming into the Camp K barracks.

The impact threw Lopez and me into the air. I landed in the dirt a few metres from the Space Camp building.

The barracks caught fire. Black, billowing smoke obscured the building.

Lopez and I found our feet. I wound my arm in an exaggerated circle and pointed to the Space Camp building. We retreated to the larger one. People pushed past, heading to the same place.

We entered the ground level, and I dragged Lopez to the emergency stairwell to the basement. I pushed the door ajar, and a new alarm sounded. I led the growing crowd down the stairs. Everyone rushed in a panicked state. Bodies around me jostled, and I almost tripped down the steps.

The lights failed, and people screamed, a muted echo in the tight space. Red emergency lights took over, washing us with bloody pink hues. We clattered down. The sound echoed like a single, high-pitched scream.

We reached the bottom of the stairs and poured through the fire doors into the basement holding room. Everyone milled around, unsure of what to do. Lopez assessed me and asked me things I couldn't hear. I let her tend to a superficial cut on my face, relieved that I was alive.

Someone limped over, blood oozing from their leg, the bottom of their pants blown off. Another held out an arm that was bent at an unnatural angle. The wounded were too shocked.

My ears were ringing.

Were my friends okay?

Lopez and I huddled in the basement. More dust-covered personnel flowed into the ample space. I sat on the floor, watching the panicked people. Lopez directed everyone to sit down.

I leaned against the cold concrete wall, feeling like my body was someone else's. I searched for my friends as people filtered through the basement doors. My ears rang, the sound like training underwater in the pool.

As more people crammed into the basement, I hoped I'd see Trix, Maya, or Kiku. I'd even take Dean or Griffin. Heck—even Hellcat would be a welcome sight.

At first, I didn't recognise the person with Lopez. Then, the sensation of a red-hot knife dug itself into my guts as I decoded her latest disguise.

She was a chameleon, slithering her way into any situation, using people to her advantage. She'd been a jeans-and-baseball-cap-wearing child snatcher, a lab-coated virologist, and a camera-ready polished aide to the prime minister. Now she was playing astronaut.

Dr Figg stood in the pale blue uniform—just another camouflage.

She created my nightmares. Revealing my true identity, the coward, hiding from Figg and her Snatchers under my hessian sack. I had let Figg take my sister—Demi—and then Figg had killed her.

Maybe I'd never get over Demi's death. My memory grew stale, glossed over. Time was like waves against glass, rendering her face smooth and featureless.

I shook with a new fury at seeing Figg. Lopez, knowing our history, had kept her training with the Aces.

Figg's eyes darted around the room, squinting through the dusty air. She seemed relieved to see me and waved.

I ignored her so I could stand sharing space with her. Intense emotion overcame me, and I closed my eyes.

The familiar sensation took over.

Please, not this again.

The floor spun beneath my sit bones, and I grabbed the wall to steady myself. My chest constricted. I sucked in air, but it seemed too solid to breathe. It was as if I were sinking through the floor, being consumed. My body was too heavy, like gravity was crushing my chest. Every particle squeezed into the moment. I had to feel it. There was no other option.

Then the flashes started...

... I crammed into a metal drum in the junkyard, cradling the bony frame of my sister, Imogen, crushed beside me, hiding from the Snatchers. We weren't supposed to be here. What if we were discovered? We held our breath as the gravel crunched underneath the Snatcher's boots. He searched closer. Surely he could hear my hammering heart? Or Imogen's snuffly breath, catching in panicked waves. The searing metal drum burned my forehead, the stench of rotting sludge on Trash Mountain nearby. I held my sister, willing Figg and her Snatchers to pass.

I cowered in the chilly basement cells of the Elditch Research Facility. Desperate sobs of the snatched kids echoed in my cell, the light stark, revealing scratched-over paint plastering the walls. Figg locked the cell door as she squatted to observe me. The antiseptic stench of the steel toilet in the corner, the slam of an orderly's nightstick on the doorjamb as he made his rounds. The nightstick chased the tortured screams of another kid as the lights strobed red.

I hid in the war bunker's storage room, the metal door peppered with bullet holes like Swiss cheese. The door neared collapse. My family huddled around me, knowing there was no way out. Figg's smashed fake cures oozed from the splintered crates, pooling beneath our feet. I clawed at the yellow liquid, saving some for my sister. The shattered test tube glass cut through my fingertips. The door flew inwards, revealing the military might. Figg's eyes were ablaze, firing the bullet at my little sister...

I fought my senses, breathing deeply, warding off the flashes and returning to the present moment—to the basement at Space Camp.

But not away from Figg. It was always Figg, sparking my nightmares. I slowed my breathing, fighting the panic attack echoes. I had to think of my friends.

Figg touched my arm, and I flinched. Maybe she recognised my panic attack. I felt exposed. Could she see my flashes, probe my mind for nightmares?

Figg's smile was genuine, because her eyelids crinkled. "I'm so glad you're alright, Ofelia."

She laid a hand on my shoulder.

Pushing her away, I approached the entrance to find my friends.

What waited on the surface? Had they blown the shuttle into pieces? It didn't matter. Now, we had to survive. Maybe we wouldn't escape the basement.

Dr Figg tended to the wounded. It was incredible, but nobody in the basement had been badly injured. A dislocated shoulder, superficial cuts and burns.

Something compelled me to help, so I moved towards a skinny technician, still wearing his headset, maybe on shift at mission control. He bled from a deep cut in his arm. I reached out, and at first, his expression was panicked, like a trapped wild possum. But I nodded, reassuring him.

I closed my fingers around his wounded arm, as his blood dripped to the floor. Closing my eyes, I imagined his cut repairing, regrowing the skin. I weakened, transferring my energy to his. When I opened my eyes, his panic vanished. His cut stopped bleeding.

He thanked me. I approached the next casualty, who had burn marks on her cheek. The skin was angry and already blistering. She had seen me heal the technician and didn't flinch as I touched her cheek. A few seconds later, pinkish skin remained beneath. The blisters healed.

I tended to the injured. Figg followed, applying makeshift bandages and pulling a dislocated shoulder into place. My healing skills were popular. A moment passed between us as I tended to a technician with a singed eyebrow. We worked in tandem, but Figg followed my lead, waiting for my healing powers before assessing the residual injuries.

Someone called my name. I turned, confused, to see Kiku, her forehead furrowed, pushing through the crowd. Maya followed.

They were alive!

At first, I couldn't fathom why Maya was crying or Kiku's forehead was wrinkled with concern. They must have seen the Camp K barracks.

"We thought you were..." Kiku stopped before the inevitable end of that sentence.

Maya flung her arms around me in a hug so tight I struggled to breathe.

"We weren't inside when the bomb dropped..." I said. "Are you hurt?"

"Not badly," Maya said.

The three of us hugged, my eyes misting. We were all in shock.

"Where's Trix?" I asked as we released from the hug.

Trix ducked underneath the doorway, parting the crowd. Most hadn't been near my alien friend. Trix stood with her seven-foot magnificence in the middle of the basement.

She had brownish-orange hexagonal scales. The curled loop on the top of her Brazil-nut-shaped head drooped when she was out of energy. Her eyes shone luminescent and orange, with deep black pits piercing with intensity. Three elongated fingers on both hands ended in pointed nails like brittle twigs. Her slug-like feet left a slimy trail in the thick dust.

She joined us. I hugged her middle, since I was short for my age and she was seven feet tall. My tummy fizzled in an electrical jolt, like liquid sparking a power outlet. It focussed my mind and eased my body aches.

"I am unharmed, Ofelia," Trix said inside my head. Nobody else could hear her. I could only do so due to my shared Kaseath DNA. Trix was the mission's key and the whole reason I was vital.

Thank you for looking after them, I replied.

Oh yeah, Trix could hear my thoughts, which was convenient for us but excluded my fully human friends.

I checked Maya's and Kiku's injuries.

Kiku had a minor head bump, and Maya's long-sleeved shirt was bloodied near the wrist from a grazed burn. I laid hands on their superficial injuries. Then Kiku, Maya, and I hugged again, relieved.

Dean and Griffin pushed through the crowd uninjured, which sparked my anger. Why was life easy for them? Hellcat arrived a few minutes later, looking dazed, but that was normal.

Dean's bravado disappeared, and he morphed into a frightened kid rather than our bossy group leader. He gripped his iScreen like it was the last can of beans at a derelict store. Griffin punched one fist into the other, excited by the violence. Hellcat sat apart, preferring her thoughts.

I nodded to the other three Camp K members. We weren't friends, but I wasn't a monster. They nodded back. Whatever our differences, we were glad we were all accounted for.

We were all alive, unlike the Aces and Betas. What would we see outside the basement?

The prime minister spoke over the loudspeaker.

"It's safe to return to the second floor for briefing. We still have to launch the mission."

This elicited confusion from the crowd. We'd just survived a bombing with multiple casualties. Were we considering going ahead with the mission?

But I had to save my sister. The mission had to continue.

As the rest of the crowd hesitated, I moved towards the stairwell, Camp K following. I peeked up the stairs. The air was pinkish-red, with thick dust particles dancing around. White light glinted farther up the stairs.

"Is it safe?" Dean asked, forgetting his usual bossy tone.

"If the PM says so." Griffin punched one fist into another.

Hellcat shrugged, hiding behind her hair.

Kiku, Maya, and I gathered closer, with Trix in earshot over my shoulder.

"I'd rather stay down here for a bit," Maya said, on edge.

I recognised the fear in her eyes—the fear of captivity in the research facility. Maya also had unsettling flashbacks.

"It's safer here," Kiku said. "There could be more bombs."

Something occurred to me. "Have they bombed the suburbs, too?"

Maya and I both thought—were our families safe?

That thought galvanised us.

I led Camp K up the stairwell, and the staff followed.

On the ground floor, black-suited security personnel guided us to the second floor of the Space Camp building.

This area housed training simulators and mission control. We milled in front of the stage, which had blue skirting and a speaker's podium. The crew's briefing table sat behind it, ready for media questions before the mission.

Except there was no media. And the crew had been obliterated. How could the mission go ahead? What did Prime Minister Pollins have in his scheming, slippery mind?

The ground staff and technicians milled about while our Camp K crew hung back. Dean's eyes darted, as he seemed prepared to abandon, rather than lead, his Camp K buddies. Lopez stood behind us to stop us from leaving. Were we any safer in the building? Space Camp was a glowing target for our enemies.

Trix loitered in the connecting doorway. Everyone at Space Camp knew of her presence—she'd been an integral part of the training—but she had no part in our war. She just wanted to return home.

Floor-to-ceiling glass walls overlooked the launch pad behind the stage. The shuttle seemed intact, but detecting damage from this distance was impossible.

Black smoke billowed in the opposite direction, dispersed by the wind, and the taint of floating ash gave me a headache. A backdrop of sirens set the room on edge.

The PM stood at the podium, pale, with permanently flushed cheeks, dressed in a royal blue military uniform adorned with multiple stripes and patches, like a macrame project. I guess to reassure the public of his military prowess, although it was more likely that he'd be watching from the sidelines.

He held up his hand and paused until he had our attention.

"We've taken some damage from enemy fighters amassing on our doorstep. I can assure you that our response was swift; the rebellion was quelled. We will eviscerate all rebels against the NAC."

For now, I thought, while Pollins continued.

"We have, unfortunately, lost people today. The first responders confirmed there were no survivors from the main blast area. This news will shock you; our thoughts are with their family and friends. And to their colleagues—all of you. You have each suffered deep personal losses today."

The prime minister held back while that sank in. Sniffles peppered the air, the first grief surfacing. But he hadn't finished yet.

"However, we are at war, meaning we must continue. The mission is too critical to abandon. Our engineers have reported minimal damage to the operational areas and almost no damage to the shuttle. This means tomorrow's launch is still a go."

That set the room abuzz with conversation. Amazement gave way to shocked exchanges.

"We've had only one survivor from the original Aces crew and none from the Betas. Thankfully, we've had a backup crew training for this mission. Will the following seven crew members join me on the stage?"

My friends and I shot worried glances at each other.

"His timing is terrible," Maya said.

"How does Pollins have a secret backup crew?" Kiku asked.

I also wondered who could have been training this whole time. Who would join the mission with Trix and me?

Pollins continued, "Dr Melina Figg is the sole survivor of the original Aces crew. She is our foremost expert on the plague cure and will take point on the scientific and medical operations."

Figg plastered on a patriotic face, strolling to the front to muted clapping. Events moved too rapidly for us to comprehend.

We hadn't buried the dead yet.

Figg climbed the stage's stairs and shook hands with the prime minister. Then, beaming, she seated herself at the conference table behind the PM. Typically, she hadn't read the room.

Pollins continued.

"Every mission needs a commander, and none is more skilled than Commander Luz Lopez, who has spearheaded our training over many decades at Space Camp. I have every faith in her abilities."

All eyes swivelled to Lopez's surprised expression. She nervously massaged the dog tags hanging around her neck. Then she took a breath and strode to the briefing table, to hearty clapping. This over-the-hill instructor had her chance, but how would she perform outside the simulators?

The first two crew members weren't my favourite people. Who would they dig out next—or dig up? I wouldn't put it past Pollins.

"Our best pilot in the program has outperformed them-selves in every sim we've given them and logged thousands of flight hours. It is my pleasure to present Genevieve Rumbottom."

We scanned the room for this secret ace pilot.

Hellcat tapped the person in front on the shoulder.

"Excuse me," she said to the confused technician. Hellcat pushed forward through the crowd.

"What are you doing, idiot?" Dean yell-whispered. "Get back here!"

Hellcat shrugged and moved forward, shaking the PM's hand and slinking onto the chair beside Lopez. Hellcat's hair flopped over her eyes, protecting her from the room's scrutiny.

"Her name is Genevieve Rumbottom?" Maya asked.

"No wonder she goes by Hellcat." A smile took over, but worry nudged my mirth aside. She would be my pilot. She was just a kid—and a kid I didn't like. How had she earned her rene-gade name?

"It should have been me," Dean said, shooting a potent stare through Hellcat's fringe.

Well, okay—Hellcat was better than Dean. That was something, right?

My nerves kicked in. Spending time inside a cramped shuttle would be tricky, even with people I liked. I couldn't have asked for a worse crew.

But the PM wasn't finished.

"Next, we have our security detail, who will assess and neutralise potential threats en route. Please welcome Phoebe Griffin."

Oh, like crap in my pants. Not that lopsided super soldier, Griffin. I wished they didn't need me on this mission. It was me and my worst enemies.

Dean huffed out of the hall, banging my elbow as he nudged through the crowd. I'd pay for Dean's damaged pride.

"And, finally, our chief engineer and mission specialist, with a perfect score on the practical exam and prowess in the simulators, is Maya Chodankar."

Oh no. I glanced at Maya, whose complexion turned a little grey. She hadn't expected to go. She wasn't prepared.

Neither was I. I told her, "You don't have to go..."

Maya bit down on her trembling lower lip. She pushed through the crowd.

Maya would be with me. My support human was joining me in actual freakin' space.

But her life was in peril on this dodgy mission. I had expected it to fail, but now that looked certain. Not one of us had flown an actual mission.

Maya, blushing like a ruby stone, sat next to the rest of the crew on stage. Kiku stood beside me. Only two positions remained in our crew of seven—me and Trix. This meant that Kiku wasn't going.

"I wish they picked you instead of Griffin," I whispered to

Kiku, whose eyes glistened with happiness. No, with intense disappointment.

But Kiku was supportive. "You'll do great."

"And last, our two mission-critical members, Ofelia Stykes and our alien emissary, Trix."

I preferred not answering media questions, my heart pounded as I approached the stage.

I sat beside Maya. We shared a worried look, ignoring the unfriendly crew. Trix parted the crowd, who drew away as if she were dangerous. She stopped beside the stage because of her sluggy feet, which couldn't negotiate the stairs.

Trix, Maya, and me, against Dr Figg, Commander Lopez, Hellcat, and Griffin.

Three allies to four foes. Those were not favourable odds.

The PM ended his round of applause. Then he turned his attention to the crowd.

"So, give it up for our crew." The PM acted like we were in a celebrity TV show rather than a war zone.

"They'll be heading out to Valentina One tomorrow. So, game faces, people. We're at war; no war waits until we're good and ready. There's just one more thing..."

What now? I thought as I twisted in my chair, grabbing Maya's hand to stop her from crying. Or to stop breaking down myself.

"There is a complete media blackout. The recent bombing has shown our internal security weakness. You are to hand the security personnel your iScreens and cell phones. We will prosecute anyone who initiates communication. Am. I. Clear."

The only sound was the emergency sirens outside, the ambulances ferrying the sick to the base's hospital and the fire engines rushing to smother the blaze.

We'd been shellshocked in here, too.

I squeezed Maya's hand, and she squeezed back.

Maya hadn't asked to go. Would we return to our families?

CHAPTER 5

Prime Minister Pollins stepped away from the podium and sat in the middle of our briefing table. Lopez looked uncomfortable, but Figg beamed as if starstruck by the PM's celebrity.

Trust her to be eternally camera-ready.

Hellcat buried her face behind her hair, her foot tapping. Although she had experienced flying aeroplanes, she hadn't flown a shuttle outside the sims. Dean scowled from the back, and Griffin lifted an unevenly biceped arm to wave at him.

I squeezed Maya's hand, which was moist with sweat. "Maya, you don't have to go..."

But I desperately wanted her to go. I needed a friend up there, and Trix couldn't communicate with the crew, so she couldn't support me in an argument.

Maya tried to form words, then shook her head.

The lights dimmed, and a massive screen descended beside the stage. I swivelled my chair to watch.

The shuttle's launch pad was superimposed with the Remaining Countries' flag. Smoke whispered from the rocket's engines, ready for launch.

The footage cut to the suited Aces crew holding helmets, including Dr Figg, the last in line. They beamed at the crowd as they passed, picking out their friends and family and waving the Remaining Countries' flags.

I was confused—was this a tribute prepared to play at their funerals? How did they get the footage? And why was their family smiling rather than in mourning?

Then I realised this was the deep-fake video Pollins would show the world. He wouldn't air the actual renegade, scrappy crew that wouldn't make it into the upper atmosphere, let alone the QyronNexa. He said the shuttle hadn't sustained 'much' damage, but any damage was dangerous.

Pollins stared at me, and for once, he wore a hangdog expression. He knew. Not even the PM could play his own propaganda game.

He believed we wouldn't come home.

Holy heck on a stick.

The Aces in the footage climbed into their fancy white sedans, which were now blackened shells. They wound down the windows to wave at the crowd, their expressions elated and relaxed.

The propaganda music swelled to a rousing crescendo. As the Aces climbed the last steps of the tower, the flag was super-imposed over their figures. The camera followed them to the shuttle's egress point. They boarded and settled into their snug seats. The Aces Commander waved as the technicians yanked the heavy shuttle door, locking the handles into place.

As the video faded to black, the music trailed off, a rousing final note.

Pollins paused before standing up. Apart from muted sniffles, the room was silent. We were in shock, still processing.

If the training pool was like a slow-motion movie, the recent events swirled in my mind like fast-forwarded sections of all the television ads ever made. An overload of thoughts collided, smashing into me in chunks—the sensation of blowing up in the sim, the scorching heat, the pain. Imogen being chased by Snatchers on Trash Mountain. Muscly orderlies in white, holding me down...

Then, thoughts coiled to the beginning of the jumbled loop —out of order. I couldn't grasp one thought before it was snatched away.

I struggled to concentrate on Pollins's words.

"The world can follow along with tomorrow's launch. Hand in your devices, and let's get to work."

He lifted one hand to the crew on stage, and we stood. He gestured for our crew to wave. Maya looked super confused and quite shy. Hellcat lifted her hand briefly, then hid behind her hair. But Griffin lifted Figg's hand like a referee announcing the winner at a boxing match. Griffin could pass for a boxer, with muscles punched free of her lopsided arms.

Security men dressed in black and sporting brawny physiques penned the crowd. A moment of panic swelled as the crowd followed orders. This had ceased to be a regulation launch and was more like a military coup.

The security personnel led the crowd to the back, where more guards patted everyone down and placed their devices into large crates.

How would I contact Imogen to check on her?

Would Maya and I ever make it back to Earth alive?

Lopez, still embarrassed by the recent events, nodded to me. I led the crew from the briefing stage and into the confused rabble below.

My real crew—not the deep-fake Aces—nudged through the crowd, flanked by security guards making a path. The technicians and ground staff jostled, heading to mission control for a briefing or wherever the non-astronauts went.

I clung to Maya's hand, crushed by the confused crowd. Griffin and Hellcat followed. Lopez's downcast eyes apologised for some cosmic mistake. She had never expected to go.

What good was an over-the-hill commander with no practical experience leading a mission? Or a renegade, loner pilot? Or a trigger-happy security grunt? Putting up with the child-snatching Dr Figg was already unbearable.

At least I had Maya, but guilt pinged. She was in harm's way. She had as much reason as me to hate Figg.

Would we survive the mission?

Trix lumbered through the crowd, falling behind. I checked on her.

"Do not worry about me," she said.

The Camp K barracks were visible through the front glass doors. Firefighters trained their hoses on the smouldering support beams and fallen walls like an elaborate water show.

I'd hidden out in shells of buildings, sheltering from the Snatchers, with Imogen. Cowering in the dark...

My heart raced, and I fought off the pull to the ground, my compacting chest. Warding off the flashes.

Please, not now.

Prime Minister Pollins appeared, and the security detail rushed to protect him. The crush separated me from Maya, leaving me alone.

Ahead, the security detail blocked the basement entrance. The guards stood aside to let Pollins pass. This mosh pit could pulverise me before I reached the basement's safety.

Kiku dithered outside the guards' containment line. The crowd shuffled me in her direction.

"Kiku!" I waved frantically.

The crowd pushed me towards the front entrance, jostling her in another direction. She noticed my distress.

"Don't worry, Ofelia. You'll do great for your sister," she said.

"You should come with us..."

"Someday. We'll talk when you return, okay?"

The crowd swallowed her in their ranks, taking me with them.

Lopez beckoned from the stairwell door. But my attention flicked to the corner beside the exit. Someone stood behind a pillar, and a familiar, white-ish glow emanated. Like a weak torch...

A scuffle broke out as the crowd morphed into panic mode. People screamed as there was another loud crash outside. More bombs?

No, just the skeleton of the Camp K barracks collapsing.

The security detail lost control, and the crowd panicked. They shoved each other, taking me to the Space Camp exit.

I led the surge from behind to avoid being crushed. Someone slipped near the basement entrance, and the security guards made a human shield, holding hands around the fallen comrade like crowd control at a concert.

I slithered behind the pole, next to the figure. Dean was plugged into his headphones, his face backlit by his iScreen, watching a clip of aerial acrobatics.

Really? He thought that was most important right now?

"Can I borrow that?" I asked, snatching the iScreen before he could react.

Dean ripped the earphones free.

"Why, so you can boast to your friends?" he shot back.

I yanked the device out of his reach.

"Look around, idiot," I said.

Dean noticed the semi-wild crowd and the surrounding chaos. His eyes darted, taking in the scene.

The out-of-control mob triggered his fight-or-flight response. Dean stood.

Before he could react, I scooted towards a small lectern by the wall. It was hollow, and I folded my body underneath, with my back turned to the outside. Dean followed, shouting bloody murder at me, his words lost amongst the crowd. He scooted behind me, away from the mob. He pummelled my back with punches, trying to get his iScreen back.

OOF... OOF.

The pain barely registered.

I signed into my iScreen account and started the call.

Mum answered, her haggard face too close to the screen. She wore a casual t-shirt rather than her usual work attire, and her mascara had run. Her eyes were glassy, as if she'd been crying.

"Hi, honey—where are you? Are you okay? What's happening?"

"I don't have much time," I said, which worried her more. Dean's fist pummelling wasn't helping.

"Is someone attacking you?" Mum said.

"That's. My. iScreen!" Dean said, thumping me extra hard, so the breath knocked out of me.

I sat forward in the box, preparing myself. "What's happened? How is Imogen?"

Behind Mum, Imogen lay curled up in a hospital bed. A drip fed into her arm, her thin body tucked underneath the white blanket. She seemed so fragile.

Her face turned to one side, her eyes closed.

"Imogen!" I said.

The falling sensation was back. The ground seemed to tip onto its side.

"Is she... is it too late?" I asked, not wanting to hear the answer.

"She's just sleeping," Mum said with a brave smile. But her watering eyes gave up her worry.

"Can I talk to her?"

"They scheduled her surgery for tomorrow, the same time as your launch," Mum said. "Don't worry—she will be fine. It's a common procedure."

But I could tell from Mum's expression that wasn't true.

"Common for someone who's already sick?" I steadied my voice.

"You just concentrate on that launch tomorrow. We might get a link through once you're in space."

"I doubt they'll allow that now."

An ambulance screamed past, the siren ablaze with urgency.

"What's happening?" Mum asked, noticing the panicked surge behind me.

"Don't believe what you see. We're going to space," I said.

"Yes, I know..." Mum said, confusion narrowing her eyebrows.

Imogen stirred in her bed and opened her eyes. Then shut them.

"Limpet," I said. "Bring me closer, Mum. Limpet, it's me."

What if she didn't answer?

"Ofelia, hey," Imogen said, her eyelids fluttering.

"I'm sorry, sis, I'm not there with you." Conflicting emotions collided, but guilt and fear topped the list. I barely kept it together.

"Where are you?" Imogen said, her forehead scrunching with concentration.

"I'm at Space Camp."

"Why aren't you here?" Imogen said, her eyelids closing.

A pang of guilt cut through me, with more impact than any

bomb blast. My ribcage felt like that collapsing Camp K building. I couldn't breathe.

My sister needed me, and I wasn't there. This could be the last time we spoke.

"I'm going to get your cure!" I yelled over the rising chatter of the crowd and more passing sirens.

"What?" Imogen asked, searching the hospital room.

"I'm GOING TO GET YOUR—"

"What did you say?" Imogen said, her eyelids shuddering. "I'm scared."

"It's okay..." I said. "Imogen, you'll be fine."

Had she heard me before she closed her eyes?

My sister was terrified, and I might never see her again.

As tears pricked my eyes, I turned away from the iScreen. My shoulders convulsed as I held back sobs. The panicked mob bumped into the lectern, which crashed beside me. I scrambled back inside as a security man headed my way. I gripped the iScreen like a lifeline.

"Mum, tell Imogen—"

A burly security man, busting out of his black t-shirt, grabbed me under my arms and yanked me upright. He snatched the iScreen and turned it off.

"Hey!" Dean said. "That's mine..."

The security man shoved me towards the basement stairs. He kept his burly arm on my neck, pushed me into the dark stairwell, and slammed the door.

The emergency lights' sinister glow was like my recurring nightmares, and I was about to be devoured by a wily monster.

Tears misted my vision. My lip quivered, and I threatened to break down. How could I go when Imogen needed me? I wouldn't be there when she woke up.

Please let her wake up.

I clattered down the stairs, winding through the basement

56

containment area, and wiping tears as I pushed into the classroom.

Maya shot up from her desk and squeezed me in a relieved hug.

"Where were you?" she asked, checking for injuries.

I just shook my head and sat beside her in the classroom's front row. There was no time for tears. My face was splotchy red, but I forced my attention to the PM standing before us.

I had to go—this mission had to succeed. There was nothing else to be said.

Lopez's words from the training sim resonated: *"This mission will be nothing but pressure."*

And I sure as heck had to harness it.

Pollins waited for our attention. The front touch screen displayed the International Space Station video feed screensaver, the gunmetal-grey alien ship lurking in the backdrop.

Hellcat, Griffin, Dr Figg, Commander Lopez, and Trix were also in the classroom.

"The facility is locked down," Pollins began. "Do not leave this classroom. No excuses."

He challenged the petulant teenagers, then turned his attention to Trix. But she could out-stare a mountain forming over a couple of million years. You know, no eyelids and everything.

Pollins was the first to look away. "Thankfully, we have one survivor from the original Aces crew. Dr Figg will begin the briefing."

Figg cued a presentation on the touch screen.

"Thank you, Prime Minister," Figg said, appearing calm and knowledgeable. I almost missed her briefing while I subdued my outburst of rage. How would our crew coexist in close quarters? Apart from Trix and Maya, they weren't my first-choice companions.

None of them had chosen to go.

What if something happened to Maya? Was it wrong to want one friend aboard the shuttle? I'd resigned myself to working with Figg. But Maya had suffered at Figg's hand at Elditch. She also had flashbacks.

Simmer your hatred, I told myself. *Don't get sucked into Figg's vortex. Think about Imogen.*

Figg continued, "The primary mission of our shuttle, Valentina One, is to rendezvous with the QyronNexa, which is orbiting Earth. Our diplomatic objective is to meet with the Kaseath and obtain the cure to the plague. We know the Kaseath must have the cure because of our testing on Trix. The plague contains alien DNA. Which means the plague is of Kaseath origin. They must have the cure, as the Kaseath are not sick. Trix confirms this from her time aboard the QyronNexa."

She took a breath and continued.

"The main mission: retrieve the cure. Our secondary mission is to ask the Kaseath to leave. We've evacuated select groups to the Interplanetary Voyager Ark to find our next habitable planet. Earth has reached a tipping point from the triple threat of war, climate change, and the plague. Life on our planet is no longer sustainable, so we must abandon life here— however, Trix claims the Kaseath won't permit us to leave Earth. We must seek a diplomatic solution first, but if a military response is required, we rendezvous back at Space Camp to launch our assault. We are prepared to use force to ensure humanity's survival. Are there questions so far?"

Griffin put up her hand super politely.

"So we fly to the alien ship, get the cure, ask them to leave, then hotfoot it back to Earth," she said. "Seems pretty simple."

She smacked bright blue gum, but her uncomfortable glare was laser-focussed on me.

"Hopefully, yes, it will be simple," Figg said. "However, we'll be in their territory, so we must prepare for any scenario."

"We're prepared." Griffin lifted her head. "We've loaded the shuttle with weapons. We're ready for ship-to-ship defences."

Did I imagine it, or did a glance pass between Griffin and Figg? As if sowing the seeds for later thought. Trigger-happy Griffin itched for a fistfight, well-suited to war conditions.

"Right, that's caught you up. I'll hand over to Commander Lopez, who will lead the mission," Figg said.

Figg returned to her seat, smiling at the Prime Minister. The PM beamed back.

The PM sought Griffin's attention and she inclined her head.

So Griffin had a pass from the PM himself. This didn't look good.

Imogen lay in her hospital bed, surrounded by machines pinging death. A drip fed into her arm, with clear liquid dropping into a saline bag.

A doctor approached, white lab coat swishing. She held a syringe of yellow liquid in her hand, reaching for the saline bag. She stabbed the needle into the bag and plunged the yellow liquid inside.

It swirled like dye dropped into water. Tendrils reached closer to the base of the bag until the entire liquid spun and was stained a dirty, jaundiced hue.

"Hey," I said. "What are you doing?"

The doctor turned. It was Figg.

She held the false cure in the syringe. The one that didn't work.

I swiped the syringe from her claw-like grip.

"Get away from my sister!" I screamed as loud as I could.

My whisper echoed. It was as if I couldn't speak.

Imogen's heart rate beat in the display's corner. Slowing, then slowing some more. The distance between the beeps grew until the heart rate flashed dangerously low. Forty... thirty... ten...

Flatline. A hot tone of breath silenced, a heart no longer beating.

I threw myself on Imogen's bed, holding her head, brushing sweaty hair from her eyes.

"No, no, NO!" I cradled her face, her eyes closed. One final black-blue bead of plague sweat squeezed from her pores.

Figg had killed my sister because I wasn't there to protect her.

"Imogen, I'm sorry!" I silenced myself in the nightmare's aftershock.

I woke up in the basement classroom with a start. The low glow of the red emergency lights illuminated the surrounding room.

"Ofelia, are you okay?" Maya asked, unfurling from sleep.

The ragged crew lay on mattresses dragged from the gym, and my neck was stiff from sleeping without a pillow.

Adrenalin coursed through my legs, so tense that they ached, and my breath came in shallow pants. I remained as still as possible as if predators lurked. It was ridiculous, but I preferred returning to sleep, reliving the nightmare, rather than checking for intruders in the creepy, red-lit room.

How could I leave Imogen now when she needed me the most?

"I have nightmares, too," Maya said. "But they're not real."

"They seem more real than when I'm awake." I blinked away the tears.

"Me too." She squeezed me around the shoulders as the room stirred.

Commander Lopez flicked the fluorescent lights on, returning the room to a fake yellow-white glare. The crew wiped the sleep from their eyes. None of us was well-rested.

Commander Lopez approached, now that I was having nightmares and crying out in my sleep like a scared kid.

"Are you good, recruit?" Lopez asked.

Couldn't she stop calling me that? I had a name, but my scowl did nothing for Lopez's worry. I nodded and slowed my breathing.

Dr Figg approached, casually studying the space posters on the wall above my head. Lopez moved away.

Figg settled on my mattress. She pulled something from the pocket of her astronaut's uniform—a yellow envelope that bulged in the middle.

"Not more test results." My mood deflated.

"Your friends brought this." She handed me the envelope.

Maya scooted beside me, squeezing my arm.

The envelope's seal was broken—they'd screened for contraband or threats. I pulled out a postcard with a childish, hand-drawn cartoon of a beach—a child's round writing on the back.

Wish you were here ~ love, your little Limpet.

Tears brimmed as I read the card from my sister. My limpet, because she'd never let me go. We would always be connected. I remembered a similar postcard she'd found while scavenging in Northies.

Next was the photo of my family at the hospital—a ridiculous selfie Roland had taken. I ran my fingertips over our smiling faces, and the hospital backdrop focussed my motivation.

Then, I pulled out a photo of my friends, Mousie and Aze, posing with push bikes in our cul-de-sac in Cookham East. Their relaxed expressions beamed back from their new neighbourhood. I held up the photo so Maya could see.

"So they can launch with us." Maya's eyes misted.

I pulled another item from the envelope—a small turquoise rubber ball. I bounced it on the floor and caught it. My fingertips closed on the familiar talisman, knowing its weight and velocity.

Imogen and I had won the ball at Trash Mountain, playing the mech car games for a chance of a better life. We had scavenged together, roaming free with the other Northies rats. Before we'd left that desperate place, that ball tethered me to my family while I fought to return. The ball reminded me of the stakes.

"Ofelia?" Figg said softly. "None of us are made from concrete. We're all human. I hope this helps you on the mission to come."

I forgot about my dislike of Figg, Griffin, and Hellcat. Even Lopez was being friendly. I held onto my love for my family and friends.

Figg moved away, leaving me shoulder-to-shoulder with Maya.

"How can we go with this lot?" I asked, waving at the crew.

"We'll manage," Maya said.

"It's too dangerous, Maya," I whispered. "What if we don't return?"

Maya fixed me with an earnest stare, bucking herself up.

"If you haven't noticed, the world is already a pretty

dangerous place. Just yesterday, they bombed Space Camp. I'd rather risk the mission than stay here to die."

She was right. We were bigger than that. We could swallow our distaste for our travelling companions and concentrate on the future—everyone's future, not just the elite.

My eyes were bright with resolve as I grabbed her hand.

I said, "We'll do this together."

But I searched the faces of my new crew. We were absolutely terrified.

CHAPTER 6

I SAT in the space shuttle with the last-chance crew as the launch sequence began its countdown. There were no sims this time, no simulation suits, and zero options for failure.

The stakes were higher than ever as I strapped myself into the shuttle, bound to tanks with enough fuel to blow London into rice-sized particles. The pre-burn shook the ship, and I dreaded what would follow. I'd only been able to maintain consciousness for one sim. But it didn't matter if I blacked out. There was no aborting this mission.

Trix sat beside me, wearing her space suit and an oversized oval helmet. Since she didn't breathe, she wasn't attached to an oxygen tank. She was more fit for space than her human crew, able to use space radiation as fuel.

Maya and Griffin sat in the middle row ahead, with Commander Lopez and our pilot, Hellcat, upfront. They checked the controls and pressed the touch screens, responding to instructions from mission control.

Dr Figg strapped into the seat behind me. I didn't have to see her during takeoff and could pretend she wasn't aboard. Our helmets impeded our peripheral vision, which meant I couldn't twist in my seat to give her a parting, greasy look, even if I'd wanted to.

I had no room to hate when fear overrode all other emotions.

Mission control checked in via our helmets' headsets.

"Comms check, Ofelia," crackled a voice.

"Comms check confirmed, I hear you," I replied.

"This is Dr Wood. I'll be your comms buddy throughout the launch. Stick with me, and you'll be fine."

I felt secure with someone talking me through this launch stage. But I knew that voice...

"Hang on—is your first name Sebastian?" I asked.

"One and the same. I requested to be your comms buddy," Sebastian said, as my heart felt like it had toppled off the rocket's nose. Sebastian and I had a... complicated relationship.

He had worked with Dr Figg in the research facility. And he was technically my father—at least biologically. Anger spiked in my reply.

"If I die today, tell my family I love them. You know, my *real* family members who raised me."

Sebastian ignored my hostility. "We'll move to engine checks."

"Copy." I winced at the increased vibrations in the shuttle. Fear overrode my anger. Sebastian was one more person to endure.

"You'll be fine, Ofelia. You've done this before."

Around me, the crew was doing their thing—enacting system checks and confirming instructions from mission control. I clenched my muscles, ready for what was to come.

"What if I black out?" I gritted my teeth as the engines ramped up.

"I won't tell anyone," Sebastian said in his clinical way, shooting more tension through my body.

"Do not panic, Ofelia," Trix said inside my skull. At least I could hear her over the engines because her voice was directly inside my head and didn't rely on my eardrums picking up her frequency.

I hope so, I thought.

"We're ready for countdown, Ofelia," Sebastian said. "Start the Anti-G Straining Manoeuvre as you practised. Remember the breathwork."

I stopped my petulance towards my test-tube father and followed his instructions.

"Tense the muscles in your lower legs. Good. Tensing in the abdomen. Now breathe. Remember to hold your breath on launch."

"Got it." I felt brave for a split second.

"We're ready," Trix said.

Sebastian's comms went dead, and mission control took over.

"Valentina One, 'go' for launch."

"Confirm mission control. We are 'go' for launch." How did Lopez sound so calm? I peeked at the screens before Lopez through the gap between the seats. The crew's vitals were on a secondary screen. Lopez's heartbeat pulsed in the green zone. She hadn't raised her resting rate a single beat. I distracted myself from my situation by marvelling at how Lopez kept calm.

"We are T-minus ten seconds. Nine... eight... seven... six..."

I gulped air and swallowed, readying myself for the g-force.

"Three... two... one... lift off."

I couldn't think, breathe, or exist on any plane except now. The cabin shook as the engines roared. I squeezed my eyes shut as the pressure crushed my chest.

I held my breath and tensed, willing oxygen into my brain.

The ship trembled like a leaf stuck in the mudflap of a speeding car. Body-jarring pressure shook my bones.

As we rose higher, holding my breath was no longer practical. I panted in and out, around the intense pressure compressing my lungs. The seconds elongated. I yearned for this ride to finish.

We ascended in a fireball visible outside our window.

My head was light, and a dark veil crossed my eyelids, blocking the heat.

My vision drifted, and I lost consciousness.

There was a hot flash, and my view changed from the space shuttle. I was no longer strapped into my seat, launching from Earth.

Another vision appeared.

From space, two objects approached in the inky vacuum. They moved too rapidly to be ships. One was shaped like a cigar; orange flaming rockets propelled it forward. The other was a scorching flash of deep, sparkling blues—a glowing fireball. It glided through space using its energy. I feared the objects as the two forces approached.

They headed straight for each other. They were going to collide!

Could that cigar-shaped object be a warhead?

The Interplanetary Space Ark floated between the two objects. Right in the path of the approaching missiles.

My little sister waved from the Ark's window, her face full of wonder at the light show outside.

"Get away from the window!" As if that could prevent a nuclear blast.

The objects smashed into the Ark, and the most intense explosion followed. The white-hot ferocity consumed everything.

Including my sister, who disintegrated with the impact.

We blasted into billions of atoms—a light shock and my sister's searing flesh. Painfully ending all life.

I realised I wasn't dead, regaining consciousness in the shuttle. What did the vision mean? I had sensed the future before. Would my premonition come true?

We may nuke ourselves before we escaped Earth.

My arms floated in the shuttle's zero gravity.

The intense vibration disappeared, the launch a success. Now, the shuttle's movement had a dream-like quality, elegant in the zero gravity of the upper atmosphere. Out the porthole window, Earth's curve was a pale blue gradient against the black of space.

"Comms check, Ofelia. This is Sebastian. Repeat, comms check."

"Confirm comms, Sebastian." I forgot my petulance.

"You're alive!" Sebastian wound back his enthusiasm. "I believed you'd succeed."

"Don't tell Lopez I blacked out."

"We've checked your vitals. Can you regulate your breathing?"

"Okay," I said as our rocket detached and fell back to Earth to be reused for another launch. It glided back into the thin atmosphere.

The vibrations stopped altogether, and the ride smoothed. Now, this was fun!

Lopez and the crew checked instruments and screens and

responded to orders from mission control. Hellcat fabulously piloted the ship, with Lopez assisting. Maya and Griffin checked the status of the ship's components displayed on the screens. Figg's buckle snapped as she unfastened it and floated past me in the cabin with a wondrous expression. She gave me a jubilant thumbs-up as she passed.

Earth solidified as we moved farther away from its thin atmosphere. The aura formed a skin of sorts. I felt tiny, viewing the borderless continents beneath me and the daylight curve over the northern hemisphere.

Something wasn't right about the scene. I couldn't pinpoint it at first. Darkness enveloped the outline of the southern hemisphere. But pinpricks of... weak lights dotted the land contours.

Pollins claimed nobody had survived the war in the southern hemisphere. But civilisation hung on there. A faded version, but not extinguished altogether.

Wonder overwhelmed me, as did the familiar motion sickness as we drifted farther into space.

"What's wrong, Ofelia?" Sebastian was back in my earpiece.

"Just a touch of nausea," I replied.

More than a touch. That thought worsened the sensation.

"Remember those exercises. Breathe deeply; fix your attention on Earth."

I did as instructed and ignored the panic rising through my veins. My head felt hot, and I gulped back the throaty taste of bile.

But nothing stopped the reflux, and I spat up in my helmet. The smell was rancid, and my body convulsed with more vomiting.

"Ofelia, unstrap and go to the bathroom," Sebastian said.

"Oh crap." I struggled with the straps holding me in. My

gloved fingers couldn't negotiate the buckles. I unzipped my gloves and pulled them off, jabbing frantically at the clasp.

"Calm yourself, Ofelia," Trix said, reaching to help.

She released the buckle, but I felt worse as I floated a foot above the ground. I couldn't orient myself. The shuttle seemed inverted, a bizarre sensation. There was no anchor point in space. I couldn't see through the sick floating around in my helmet.

"Whatever you do, don't remove your helmet," Sebastian said, but he'd put the idea in my head. I'd feel better escaping the smell.

I unlatched the helmet as I swam to the bathroom. The helmet spun in the air, droplets detaching and flinging into the cabin. I squeezed into the tiny bathroom cubicle. There wasn't much room around my suit, so I grabbed the suction cone and retched. The suction grabbed the liquid, and my panic receded.

I remained in the bathroom for a few minutes. I could lose my guts, and nobody would know.

Raised voices argued in the main cabin as I returned.

"This is so not cool, Lopez," Griffin said, wiping the front of her space suit.

"How did she pass for the mission?" Hellcat said while concentrating on piloting the ship.

"She's a liability." Griffin shifted her head to avoid being smacked in the face by a globule of floating vomit.

"I'm so sorry." I grabbed my helmet, stopping its trajectory offloading droplets into the cabin.

"Clean up your mess, please, Ofelia." Lopez passed me a handheld vacuum.

I moved about the cabin, sucking my sick back from its zero-gravity dance. The exercise did nothing for my queasiness, which was barely under control. I burped and tasted stomach acid.

After I'd retrieved the airborne droplets, I wiped my helmet clean and placed it in my locker. Then I returned to my seat.

Figg approached and checked my vitals. First, she assessed my life support readings on the shuttle's panel.

"G-loc is no laughing matter." She shone lights into my pupils, grilling me about my family. She seemed satisfied with my responses.

One rogue globule of vomit oscillated beside me. The liquid spun, and at the last moment, before it hit my face, I enacted my shield. Time stood still as my powers sparked. The shuttle and its occupants froze in time and space.

We'd wondered if zero gravity would affect my powers, but my shield successfully repelled 'missiles'. The liquid sphere kissed the barricade.

But my powers shorted. Glitched in a spectacular fizzle of energy. I couldn't control the liquid 'missile'.

As my shield crackled and dropped, I recoiled from the electric shock that burnt into my thumb's connection point.

"Ouch!" I snatched away my thumb in response to the pain.

The sphere globule flung into a control panel, which sparked and shorted.

"What was that?" Lopez asked.

"We have a malfunctioning electronic panel." Maya unclipped her harness and floated towards it. She deciphered the glitching code on her iScreen. "Panel C-45A."

"Copy, Maya," Lopez said. "Mission control, we have a malfunctioning panel C-45A."

"Copy that, Valentina One. Confirm source of issue."

"Ofelia threw up, and it hit the panel," Figg said.

"An electrical shorting situation," Lopez added.

"Copy, Valentina One. Stand by."

Maya jabbed at the console and wiped my sick with her gloved hand. The cabin lights flickered.

"That can't be good," Griffin said, eyeing the overhead lights.

"Maya, please report," Lopez said.

"Confirm malfunctioning panel C-45A because of airborne liquid contamination. Starting panel replacement."

"Confirmed, replacement panel in container Alpha-Romeo-Charlie-900."

"Copy, mission control."

Maya removed her gloves, letting them waft in the zero gravity. She pried the panel away with a tiny metal prong. The panel sparked and popped loose, and she disconnected the wires. She then moved to the ship's rear, opened a container, and pulled out a replacement part.

The ship jolted to the side. A warning beep began.

"Woah!" Hellcat said. "Sorry, folks. Ah, Maya? Get that panel replaced pronto, please. It's messing with our position."

"On it, Hellcat." Maya floated towards the loose wires.

"Does this mean we can't fly straight?" Alarm tinged my voice.

"Don't worry about it, recruit," Lopez said.

"How will we reach the Kaseath ship, let alone dock?"

"Let the pilot do her job."

Hellcat grunted, wrestling with the ship's controls.

Griffin detached from her seat, removed her gloves, and assisted Maya.

Maya and Griffin worked as the ship shuddered. The vessel listed by about a metre, and Maya bumped her elbow on the roof.

"Darn." She held her arm.

"Are you hurt?" Griffin asked.

Maya shook her head and shoved the panel back into position. The ship righted itself, correcting course. The beeping stopped. Crisis over.

"Excellent work, crew," Lopez said, as if surprised by our cooperation. "If you feel sick again, get to the bathroom pronto. Okay, recruit?"

"Yes, Commander." Red shame climbed my neck and cheeks.

I'd jeopardised the mission in my first ten minutes in space.

CHAPTER 7

AFTER I OVERCAME the embarrassment of losing my breakfast only minutes into the launch, I concentrated on reducing my nausea. I couldn't orient myself while the ship rotated and the view of Earth changed. There was no anchor, no constant position.

This wasn't somersaults in the training pool.

I hung out in the bathroom until the queasiness subsided. The crew didn't miss me; they were busy flying the ship and enacting protocols. Maya faced the unfriendly crew alone, the air crackling with unspoken tension, a palpable unease.

Trix floated outside the bathroom, monitoring me. Being unable to communicate with humans had its advantages. Lopez hadn't given her any tasks except communicating once we reached the QyronNexa.

I hit my head on the tiny cubicle's roof as I floated. Remembering the toehold on the bathroom floor, I hooked my foot underneath. Zero gravity would be awesome fun if I could stomach the sensation.

The cubicle mirror reflected my crinkly brown hair, the ponytail's ends splayed like the mane of a lion. My orange-flecked eyes appeared dull, and my face was pale and sickly.

"You will feel better if you exit the bathroom," Trix said inside my head.

I'm gonna live here for the rest of the mission, I thought.

"We need you."

None of them need me. They're all competent. I'm a liability.

"Not true. Make yourself useful, and they will respect you."

But how can I be useful?

"We must establish communications with my ship."

Oh yeah, right.

I stowed the suction chute and opened the small concertina door. Trix hovered outside, bending her head to fit under the cabin's roof. This cramped shuttle wasn't meant for her kind.

I hesitated outside the bathroom.

I'm going to be sick again...

Trix reached for the arm of my suit. But nothing happened —the usual electrical jolt was missing. The suit was too thick.

Trix projected her touch as she projected her thoughts. With an electrical fizzle, she breached the many layers of my suit. The jolt travelled through my arm, shoulder, chest, and stomach before passing into my legs. I felt charged and... no longer nauseous.

"Thanks, Trix," I said, clear-headed and not queasy. I reached to give her a high-five, the movement angling me towards the ship's ceiling. Or was it the floor?

"Except I have to get used to this..." I giggled, pushing off the roof to float in the ship's middle.

"Isn't it wonderful?" Figg said, 'swimming' towards me, avoiding the walls and ceiling with the gentlest, most coordinated movements, as if she constantly swam in zero gravity. She marvelled, "This is a dream come true!"

I scowled as she handed me a translucent pouch filled with liquid.

"You'll need to stay hydrated, especially if you've just been sick," Figg said.

A hot flash of anger jumped into my mind.

But Trix was there, too. "She is just helping."

I took the pouch and mumbled thanks. Realising my thirst, I was keen to remove the residual acrid taste. I sucked the water up the straw, each sip revitalising.

My inner ear adjusted to zero gravity, and my head pounded less. But it still felt like I was riding a giant roller-coaster in the dark, with unexpected twists and dips.

Figg floated away to the porthole at the rear, taking the iScreen from around her neck and snapping pictures. She shoved off the wall, performing a perfect somersault and propelling herself to the ship's front.

"Show off," I said under my breath.

"Be nice," Trix said. "We need everyone's coop-eration."

"I don't need her for anything."

"You all have to work together." Trix moved the corners of her mouth slit upwards, approximating a smile, and I couldn't help reciprocating. If Trix could play nice after suffering at Figg's hand, I had no excuses.

Lopez and Hellcat strapped into their seats, with Figg up the front, peering with awe through a side porthole. Griffin hung by the ship's rear, performing systems checks. She gave me a dirty look, chewing her blue gum with a fake blueberry scent made in a lab.

I was made in a lab, too—a human-alien hybrid of Figg's making.

Maya took a break from whatever task she excelled at to join me.

"How amazing is this!" she said, her eyes wide with wonder.

"Pretty cool," I said. "I wish everyone could see this view. Then maybe they'd stop fighting each other."

My eyes travelled to the four gun bays on our shuttle, their round windows pointing into space. I hoped we wouldn't have to use them. They seemed underwhelming compared to the size of the Kaseath ship.

Wasn't there always a fight?

"How are things with Jumpy-Trigger?" I asked.

Maya rolled her eyes. "Griffin's kept things profesh, but I'd rather work with you. Will you come help me?"

"Great, everyone's making friends except for me."

Figg swished past, grinning at me and Maya. We gave her an icy stare in return.

"How can you tolerate her, Maya?" I asked.

"Why do you think I studied so hard at Space Camp?"

"Because you're a brainiac?"

"Because facts don't change. They are true or not, and concentrating on facts helps me forget."

Maya touched my shoulder and floated to the rear to assist Griffin.

We all had our unique ways of coping.

I retrieved my one personal item—the turquoise rubber ball from Imogen—and placed it in the cabin. It stayed put, rotating. Or did *we* rotate around the ball?

I swished the air, and the force moved it around. Then I threw Trix the ball. My body arced back with the motion. Trix enacted her shield before the ball hit, but I didn't see since she caught me within her time-stop. The frozen moment resumed in the shield's slipstream, not in front. The ball ricocheted back to me when she dropped her shield.

"Nice," I said, catching the ball. "Now I'll try."

I 'rolled' the ball to Trix. She caught it before it became a missile. She bent her arm and flung it as hard as possible. The ball sluiced through the air, and I enacted my shield. Up front, Trix, Hellcat, Lopez, and Figg were all suspended in time. Maya and Griffin were safe behind the rear of my shield, still checking comms.

"Wait, we lost them again," Griffin said.

"It's just me." I waved from mid-ship, pleased that my powers hadn't suffered their usual stage fright.

"Spectacular!" Maya said, waving back.

Griffin scowled.

This was the longest I had enacted my shield recently.

But then the flashes returned.

Imogen, in the hospital bed. Her heartbeat slowing... slowing... then the flatline...

I'd been so engrossed in the launch and in not losing my lunch that I'd forgotten my whole reason for being here. The shield sparked instantly as a blade of panic stabbed into my ribcage. The electrical power arced back at me with a kick to the stomach.

I recoiled from the force, the breath knocked out of me.

"Are you all right?" Trix asked.

"What's happening?" Lopez asked.

"Sorry, we're testing our powers in zero-g," I wheezed.

Trix approached, glancing out the porthole at her ship.

"You are more than you realise, Ofelia," Trix said.

"I don't believe you," I said out loud as Maya and Griffin floated closer towards the mid-ship.

"I thought Trix couldn't lie?" Maya said.

"Unlike humans," Griffin said, flipping a switch and joining our conversation. "I'm lying right now when I say I trust these aliens. What if something goes against their best interests?"

"Doesn't matter," I said. "It's impossible for the Kaseath to lie. Trix said all things are known to everyone. It's part of why they are so evolved—knowledge is shared."

Griffin scowled. "I bet Trix has learned from humans over the last twenty years about keeping secrets."

"Has it been that long?" I asked Trix as she floated closer.

"Honestly, I do not know," Trix said to me. "I had not counted in Earth years when I arrived. But it has been a long while."

I relayed Trix's thoughts.

"She also said she's never been to her home planet," I said. "She was born on her ship and then arrived on Earth. Isn't that weird?"

"How did the Kaseath get here?" Maya tapped notes into her CommLink.

"Trix said over many generations."

"And what is their family status?"

"All Kaseath are related."

"And they're all female, right? Just like our crew..." Hellcat said from the cockpit, stating a fact rather than an anomaly.

"You got it." There was no prospect of a private conversation aboard the cramped shuttle. But wait, how had Hellcat formed actual words in an actual discussion unrelated to flying the shuttle?

"You're chatty, Hellcat," I said.

She shrugged, attention fixed out the front window. "Flying relaxes me."

"Woah, look at this!" Lopez said, breaking our conversation.

At first, I worried something else might be wrong, but then I followed her pointed finger out the front windows.

After Trix's touch, I no longer felt the motion sickness. I joined the rest of our crew.

"Do you see that?" Figg asked, pointing to Earth below us.

Lopez dimmed the interior shuttle lights.

We gathered beside the cockpit, watching in awe from a vantage point that few humans had witnessed.

I squeezed beside Griffin, who gave me a dirty look before we turned our attention out of the front windshield.

The sun dipped behind Earth, plunging the shuttle into black space. Then, the northern lights—the aurora borealis—settled over the planet's tip.

Tendrils of greens and aquas broke from Earth's dark skin and wafted in colourful waves. Swimming on the edge of our atmosphere, they turned and dissipated like dolphins frolicking. Then, they broke apart from the atmosphere and dispersed into space, to be replaced by more colours below.

The crew was mesmerised. It was the most beautiful thing I had witnessed. Nature was incredible, and I felt an affinity with the phenomenon. It seemed to keep everyone safe, like a magical incarnation of some god. The feeling transcended the everyday, and my fears calmed.

I was lucky to experience this with my crew. The moment brought us closer. How had a Northies rat made it into space? I wished I could share this intense feeling with my friends and family. My perspective seemed to shift, and I focussed less on my immediate bodily sensations—my nausea—and more on the wonder.

"Would you look at that," Maya said.

I grinned at Maya while Figg popped in and out of the cockpit, taking videos and photos. This was an unexpected team bonding exercise.

Better than lukewarm hotdogs and mini-golf.

The rest of our crew enjoyed the scene. A crackle over the comms broke our paused moment.

"Rec time is over, folks," Lopez said.

"Systems checks, Commander?" Hellcat asked, strapping

back into the pilot's seat and flicking the cabin lights on. The radio crackled with static.

"Comms are spotty," Lopez replied, returning us to the mission. "We're having trouble raising mission control."

"But Maya can fix it, right?" I asked.

It was dangerous without comms. Mission control relayed instructions and expected to guide us, since the trip was short—just reaching the QyronNexa.

"Don't sweat it, Ofelia." Hellcat minutely shifted a gear stick with her finger.

"Any chance you could ask for news about my sister's operation?" I almost wished they hadn't heard me.

"Sorry, Ofelia," Lopez said. "We have to prioritise the mission-critical channel."

My stomach dropped, but I kept the panic at the edge of my mind, concentrating on my surroundings. Imogen might still be under anaesthesia. Which meant it was too early for news. And anyway, I still had to find her cure.

I forced my head back into the mission. "What about comms with the Kaseath?"

"Probably busted, too," Lopez confirmed.

"But we have to tell them we're coming."

"I can speak to them from this shuttle," Trix said. "But we have to be closer."

"Won't they be suspicious if we don't warn them of the mission?" I said to Trix. "We can't get too close, right?"

Griffin punched one fist into the other. "If they don't know we're coming, we'll have to hope they don't blow us out of orbit first."

A beeping panel caught her attention, and she jabbed buttons.

"Right, Maya, Griffin, Doctor, get the comms working again," Lopez said. "Hellcat, hang back until we sort this out."

They all replied, "Affirmative, Commander," and saw to their tasks.

Maya did not enjoy being paired with Figg.

Maya's arm accidentally brushed Figg's, and she pulled back as if the touch caused her physical pain.

"Are you okay?" I asked Maya.

Her expression changed from scared to determined. She gave a terse nod in reply.

Figg didn't notice Maya's reaction, and she beamed as if I'd been asking her. As if I'd forgiven all the past hurts.

"Yes, thanks, Ofelia."

Yeah, right, like I was going to forgive Figg for locking me and Maya up, experimenting on us, and *killing my other sister...*

"We're good over here," Maya said calmly, returning to her task.

"Your anger is not useful, Ofelia," Trix said.

I let my irritation subside, relaxing my breathing like Trix had taught me. My mood flattened out.

Peering at Earth, I'd give everything up—the excitement of being in space, my mission-critical position—for one more moment with Imogen.

But we had to complete the expedition, so I peered through the side windows at the sleek gunmetal-grey alien ship. More liquid than solid, it hung menacingly in outer orbit, waiting for our approach.

Their ship lacked windows, a propulsion system, or anything else denoting a human-like ship. Trix had mentioned their advanced technology. They didn't need liquid fuel engines. Their craft ran on a superior energy source. The Kaseath were well-evolved, possibly beyond what humans could ever become.

I'd joked that they'd just had a head start, that their life-forms had appeared before ours. But Trix believed the Kaseath were superior. How would she act when she reunited with her kind, her family?

Will Lopez's plan work? I thought.

"It depends," Trix said. "The Kaseath do not trust us. Convincing them to talk will be difficult. Especially if that one shows off her weapons."

Trix waved an elongated finger at Griffin, who posed with both handguns cocked in the shuttle's reflection.

Griffin 'shot' them at the window. "Pew, pew."

Do we need someone so enthusiastic in security detail? I thought with a smile.

"We have a challenging time ahead," Trix said.

What do you mean?

"They have not seen a Kaseath-human hybrid before."

That's because I'm one of a kind.

"They might accept you, or they may fear you. It depends on how the mission goes."

Why would they be afraid?

"Even the Kaseath have limits. Caution is sometimes the best course of action."

I checked on our crew. Lopez and Hellcat yelled into the comms units, which crackled static in reply. Figg held a laminated ring binder out to Maya, who avoided all eye contact. She mashed buttons and unscrewed a panel, revealing a mess of coloured wires. Griffin re-holstered her laser guns, hidden in the pockets of her space suit as if she expected the Kaseath to materialise inside the ship at the drop of a pin.

Except pins didn't drop in here—they floated.

Another object appeared out of our right-hand windows, reflecting the sun's light against its enormous white frame. It was in a loose orbit next to the International Space Station—the Ark that Pollins was building—our evacuation vessel to start again on a new planet.

The Interplanetary Voyager Ark, or IVA, was mostly finished. A welding flash confirmed someone on construction duty against the pot-bellied structure. The tiny astronauts assembled the almost completed IVA. Large robotic arms—minuscule from here, but about the size of a mature redwood tree—assisted the astronauts. The Ark would become an inelegant, chunkier version of the Kaseath's ship.

But our mission was useless if we couldn't raise comms with the Kaseath. They didn't want us to leave Earth. And I had to find Imogen's cure.

I drifted up to Lopez and hung onto a toe hold near the cockpit. Her heart rate monitor had jumped to yellow, but she forced a brave expression.

What if I could use my healing powers?

I removed my glove and rested my hand on Lopez's shoulder. Maintaining my gaze, I projected my touch through the multiple layers of her suit until her heart monitor pulsed green again.

"Good job, Ofelia," Trix said.

Maybe I was helpful after all?

Once comms were restored, I hovered behind Lopez while she went through more protocol checks.

"Are you going to float there all day?" Lopez finally asked me.

"Please, I have to check on my sister." I put on my best 'holding back tears' face. Being a kid when it suited me worked. Lopez relented.

"We have a break in checks. Be quick."

"Thank you, Commander." Relief flushed my cheeks. I resisted snatching the headset from her.

Lopez smiled, knowing what this meant to me. She vacated her seat next to Hellcat, who kept us steady.

Hellcat dialled into the operations centre, inside mission

control. Then she donned her headset, blaring the jarring sound of death metal guitars and giving me privacy, which was touching. Hellcat had a sensitive side, too. Maybe she enjoyed being a team player.

As I waited for the link to establish, my heartbeat became noticeable in my chest. Mousie's friendly face appeared on the video CommLink, and her squeal came through the headset.

"This is sooooo cool! You're actually in space!"

"Hey, Mousie," I said, embarrassed at her enthusiasm in front of my crew. I wanted them to think I was at least partially cool.

Mousie clapped her hands and jumped like she was Imogen's age.

"Um, I don't think I have much time," I said, my expression serious.

"Imogen and your parents are still at the hospital," Mousie said. "It's taking longer than expected. But don't stress. It's too early to worry."

"When will we know?" I asked.

"Maybe in another hour? I don't know. They're not telling me much." Mousie's expression filled with wonder at the peek into our shuttle.

"Tell me as soon as she's out," I said.

"I'm getting the wind-up signal. Earth-to-space Comm-Links charge by the millisecond."

"Tell Imogen we'll get her cure," I said.

"This is mission control. Comms are needed for a systems check," a voice interrupted.

"Better go," Mousie said with a wave.

"Tell her I promise—" But the screen blanked, and I returned the headset to Hellcat.

Disappointed, I moved away from the cockpit, peering back at Earth. Suddenly, I felt adrift, like I was apart from the world, from my friends and family. A thought stabbed—would I return to our planet? Or was this a last goodbye?

"Let's resume the mission." Lopez strapped into the seat next to Hellcat, who switched off the death-metal jangle.

Maya and Griffin were busy with their tasks. Figg took pictures of the alien ship from the porthole and made notes on her wrist CommLink.

I ignored Figg, avoiding a confrontation in front of the crew.

Mission control provided instructions and coordinates and kept the crew busy. We tested and re-tested the comms ahead of the most important part of the mission yet. We were to communicate with the Kaseath.

My guts made a beeline outside my body at the thought.

It would be up to me.

This could go well or poorly. Failure meant no plague cure and no diplomacy with the aliens. There was nothing to stop them blowing our ship—and the Ark—into smithereens. And without the IVA, my family, friends, and human civilisation were burnt toast in a kitchen's inferno.

Trix was inside my head again. "Do not think of those options. We have to stay positive. You must overcome your fears, or the Kaseath will know, and they will not respect you."

I told you, private thoughts are private thoughts.

"Get used to no privacy. The Kaseath do not play by your rules."

"Approaching the QyronNexa," Lopez reported into her headset.

"Copy, Valentina One," mission control said. "You should be in comms range now."

"Switching to comms with the Kaseath."

"Good luck, Commander."

Trix and I floated to the front set of seats, closest to the comms unit, and buckled in. Lopez and Hellcat hovered behind, with Maya and Griffin staffing the control panels at the back in case of more malfunctions. Figg joined Lopez and Hellcat, which didn't help my nerves. But I focussed on the connection as we dialled in.

Trix took over the comms controls and checked a few buttons. She donned a headset, as did I. Trix reached out, grabbed my hand in a fizzled touch, and held tight. She nodded, and I grinned defiantly. My fingers found the outline of the rubber ball in my pocket, and I massaged the item from home. It was a comfort, reminding me of my promise to my sister.

I was ready to speak to the aliens.

CHAPTER 8

I RUBBED the sweat on my clammy hands as Trix and I strained to hear the Kaseath through our headsets. The alert crew appeared calm, but nervous tension thrummed through the shuttle. This had to go well.

We guessed Trix had been on Earth for twenty years. She hadn't spoken to the Kaseath for those two decades. What would they think of our crew? We ignored their instructions to stay on Earth, heading to the QyronNexa for a grand ole boarding party.

Trix nodded, and I flashed a thumbs-up—I had to concentrate to ensure an accurate translation.

Words were tricky.

'Words gone wrong' started wars.

Trix said something incomprehensible. Unsurprisingly, the Kaseath didn't speak English.

She lifted her long thumb from the radio button and waited for a reply. I didn't sense a response, and she repeated her greeting.

"What's happening?" Lopez whispered.

"She's still making contact." I locked on the settings.

Trix explained, "I have said we are a peaceful human

envoy, returning to the QyronNexa. The purpose of our mission is diplomatic; they have no quarrel with the Kaseath."

The high-pitched underlying static was the only reply. We waited, hoping. I swallowed around my dry mouth. How were my hands clammy and my mouth so void of moisture?

Then I felt it—not the words themselves, which were incomprehensible. But I heard the reply and the sound bouncing its frequency through Trix's mind.

I felt her understanding, and then she replied for my benefit, "Copy, QyronNexa. It is Trix who left decades ago, in Earth's terms. They are returning me as a goodwill gesture."

"She's made contact," I said aloud to the crew, whose expressions relaxed. They must have taken from my tone—and my interpretation of Trix's tone—that we were over the first hurdle.

We no longer yelled into the void. The Kaseath had spoken back.

I couldn't hear the Kaseath themselves, but I relayed Trix's communication to our crew.

Trix said, "Confirm exact coordinates for docking."

I translated the technical instructions as best I could. Maya tapped notes in her CommLink for the exact telemetry and thrust needed for alignment. She input the figures into a panel to cross-check with mission control.

Trix spoke with the Kaseath, the words flowing over my mind like discordant music.

What are they saying? I thought to Trix.

"I am catching up," Trix said. "They thought I was dead."

Were they thrilled to hear from you?

"Not as much as I hoped."

Trix concentrated on the alien conversation. The sound buzzed, unlike actual language.

"What is Trix saying now?" Lopez asked.

I said, "I can't understand the Kaseath. Just Trix."

"Maybe you'll understand once we arrive," Maya said, noting my disappointment.

In my fantasies of this moment, I joked with the Kaseath to break the ice before we boarded their ship as unwanted space guests, returning with a cure Trix maintained they didn't have.

"It was worth a try," Lopez said with a rousing consolation smile.

"The Kaseath have demands," Trix said, and I translated for the crew. "They will not allow weapons aboard."

Griffin grinned, patting the ankle guns strapped to her trousers.

Trix continued, "And they want us to follow Kaseath protocols once aboard the ship."

I nudged Trix, eager to hear my mission's purpose.

"I mentioned the trade," Trix said. "Swapping me for the plague cure, but I was correct. They do not have the cure."

When I relayed that to the crew, they didn't believe me. Figg's eyes flashed in a surge of anger.

"The plague has alien origins," she said. "They have the cure. Otherwise, the Kaseath would have died out."

"The Kaseath can't lie," I said, feeling the weight of what that meant. That fact doomed my sister to more suffering.

"And you believe Trix?" Figg asked.

"Trix has never lied to me," I said. "And I'd be able to tell. It's impossible to keep secrets when you can hear their thoughts and feel their emotions."

But of course, Figg couldn't understand that. Griffin also looked suspicious.

"Even if Trix can't lie," Griffin began, "Ofelia can. Is she translating correctly?"

"Of course I am!" I said, incensed at Griffin's accusation. "What happened to working together?"

"Take it back a notch," Lopez said. "We have to trust our crew."

"If we can't trust each other, this mission won't succeed," Figg said, staring at Griffin. Figg noticed me noticing. She averted her gaze, almost in embarrassment. What was she up to?

Maya said, "Could the Kaseath not recognise the cure?"

"That would make sense," Lopez said, dissipating the rising animosity.

"Could that be true?" I asked Trix, reluctant to sign my sister's death notice just yet.

"Maya could be right," Trix said. "The Kaseath may not identify a human cure."

"That's got to be it," I said, relieved. But my tummy jittered like a vibrating radio speaker.

"So, we'll need Dr Figg aboard to identify the cure, if there is one," Griffin said, blowing and popping a blue gum bubble.

Figg didn't acknowledge Griffin, and I couldn't figure out why—Griffin was saying precisely what Figg wanted. Figg wished to board the QyronNexa.

And now, I wanted her aboard, too. Conflicting thoughts swam in my mind, sluggish with emotion.

I had to admit a brutal truth. As it broached my mind, I felt like a traitor to my family and humankind.

I was relieved that Figg would accompany us. She might be able to identify the cure and be my hope for saving Imogen.

"We'll talk with the Kaseath on the QyronNexa," Lopez said.

The Kaseath signed off, and I felt their vibrations retreat across the space between our ships.

Trix said, "You and I have shared DNA, Ofelia. Remember, Dr Figg created you from parts of my DNA. That is why we are connected."

Will I ever communicate with the Kaseath?

"You may, with practice. This is new for me, too."

"I'm one of a kind," I said out loud, and then was intensely embarrassed. It sounded like I was big-noting myself.

Maya's eyes crinkled with amusement, and she broke the tension by saying, "Yes, Ofelia. Yes, you are."

Lopez gave orders to keep us busy so we wouldn't worry about our diplomatic encounter. The crew performed multiple tasks. Every action required exact instructions from mission control—the crew re-checked settings, coordinates, and readouts. Valentina One moved closer to the QyronNexa.

I hadn't appreciated how large the alien ship was from our initial orbit. As we approached, the vessel expanded. It dwarfed the International Space Station, which we left behind, along with the Ark.

From this angle, the Kaseath ship appeared as large as our moon. That wasn't possible. Or was it? They must have powerful fuel to move something that massive.

I checked out a bank of computer screens on the shuttle's wall, away from the cockpit. I swivelled, revealing a slice of Earth, luminous against the blackness of space.

Figg stood beside me, jamming her foot under a toe hold to keep upright. I also hooked my toes underneath the toe hold to free my hands.

She worked on her calculations while I read the PM-approved script for our arrival with the Kaseath. Lopez would do all the talking, and I would relay the responses, but I had to familiarise myself with the script.

Déjà vu tinged the moment. Figg stood beside me in her space suit, without the helmet. She turned to face me, smiled, and then pointed to something on my display.

"That should be interesting," she said, joking colleague-to-colleague as if I was her equal. Why did this moment feel so bizarre?

I'd had a premonition in the research facility on Earth when Figg held me captive. Figg ran experiments, believing my unique human-alien DNA was the key to the plague cure. I'd seen this exact moment in the shuttle, cowering in my cell at Elditch. When the idea of launching into space had seemed laughable.

When I first had the vision, I couldn't understand why I would be working with Figg. I despised her. But she was part of my crew, and I'd been at least civil for the mission's success to help my sister. We would never be friends, but I'd tolerate her like a wayward, snappy dog. She had used me, but I used her too.

Thinking back, I felt compassion for my former self, the scared kid in her cell. Another lab rat, waiting for the final test, the one nobody survived.

Except I had survived, and now I was instrumental to the mission's success, perhaps even more critical than Figg. There was no mission without me.

I smiled to myself, not giving Figg the satisfaction of a shared moment, and moved away. She tried hard to ingratiate herself, but she wasn't my mother. That was all she wanted to be. It was kind of sad.

But my vision had come true.

I tried to recall the rest of the vision—a missile trailing fire as it hurtled towards the Kaseath's ship. Then, a massive explosion ripped the fabric of space apart.

In the present, there was no missile. Did that mean it didn't come true, that we didn't nuke the Kaseath?

But the first part *had* happened. The timing may be out. Would we all die in a blue-orange fiery explosion?

Was our mission already doomed?

I moved to Trix to share the unnerving information with her.

"I am unsure of your vision's mechanics," Trix said. "In some ways, your visions are more certain than mine. All Kaseath can see our most likely future."

The visions don't always come true?

"We can change our destiny. But you keep seeing the same vision. That makes it more probable."

Yes—the explosion. Will that happen?

"Search for clues. Some things will remain the same. Look for the details that differ. It might help."

Help how? Are changes bad?

"Changes are good. They mean the vision is less stable, more open to interpretation."

"There's always an explosion," I said out loud.

Maya floated closer, having overheard.

"Another vision?" she said.

"I can't stop it," I said, the residual flashes overwhelming.

"Not on your own."

"You don't get it," I huffed. "The past, the future—it all haunts me. It's too much."

"I get it, Ofelia." Maya turned her head away.

Her response surprised me. She held back a flood of hurt, her eyes glassy.

"It's easier for you," she said.

"How is it easier?" My irritation spiked. I hadn't expected to disagree with my only human ally.

Maya stared into my eyes, hers full of sadness. "Because you don't have to work hard. You're the special one."

"Are you kidding me?" I replied, shocked at Maya's response. "I'd regenerate all the extinct mountain goats in Tanzania to be normal. To not be a freak."

"Yeah, the freak who can save us all."

"Maya, come on," I said, my voice cracking. "I need you..."

"You don't," Maya said, a tear trembling on her eyelash. "You never have."

It was awful having flashbacks to a traumatic past and visions of a cataclysmic future. Now, my present was intolerable. My best friend on Earth and beyond was... jealous of my powers.

Maya was mistaken. I needed her most of all. I couldn't do this alone.

"So tell her," Trix said.

I lifted my eyes to Maya's back. She huddled over a compartment, pulling packets out and huffing. Then she stopped, and her back shuddered as she cried silently.

I wanted to make things right. Maya suffered flashbacks, too. She'd endured Figg's tests—and the memories—but I'd assumed she coped. I hadn't considered how difficult her situation was.

Figg tapped me on the shoulder, oblivious to the exchange, and pointed to the screen blinking for my attention. Pushing away the hurt, I concentrated on not losing it like Maya. Our mission had to succeed to avoid the nukes. I shook off my déjà vu and fake-smiled back at Figg. Her hopeful face softened as if we were finally friends.

I averted my eyes in case I laughed hysterically in her face. She was no friend of mine.

Lopez noticed me studying Maya and ignoring Figg. Griffin sized up Hellcat, whose hair flopped over her eyes like she was tapping out. Trix jabbed the garbage chute, which suctioned her sluggish foot into the evac tube. Lopez checked one glitching panel, then another.

We were seconds shy of anarchy.

"We're making history today," Lopez announced, jolting us

out of our funk. "I know conditions aren't ideal, and you'd prefer to be with your loved ones right now."

She massaged her calves as if they ached. Spending the night before launch on a gym mattress hadn't helped.

"Our crew is thirsty." Lopez nodded to Maya, who slashed a tissue around her eyes, catching her beaded tears. She sent a pained expression my way.

"Yes, Commander," Maya said, her voice croaky.

She pulled caffeinated soda pouches from the rear storage cupboards.

"Thank you, Maya." Lopez twisted the lid and raised her pouch. "Let's toast our team."

The humans lifted our pouches, preparing for Lopez's toast. Trix hesitated, realising that was the extent of the gesture. She raised her pouch. But her arm was too rigid, the angle of her elbow too stiff.

I smiled at her attempt at bonding with her human crew. I checked Maya's reaction to our shared inside joke. But she studied the small print on the soda pouch rather than making eye contact.

Lopez said, "This mission must succeed. Heck—we're eradicating the plague and ensuring humanity survives on another planet. It doesn't get bigger than this. But we can do it. Together."

"Together," we chimed in, clinking pouches before sipping. Well, we all sipped except for Trix, who didn't consume nutrients like humans. All she needed was radiation; she had plenty of that aboard the shuttle. She put her pouch down.

"You humans are strange," she said.

"What's the crucial element of our mission?" Lopez said.

"I don't know." I was genuinely curious.

"It's not the mechanical elements, the protocol, or the

calculations. There's one crucial component. And if we have it, we're guaranteed success."

I leaned in, concentrating on Lopez's grave expression.

"The most important part of a mission is its crew," she said. "Cooperating, working as one unit, moving towards our common goal. So, today, we're the first humans—ever—to board an extraterrestrial vessel. Are you ready?"

"Heck no," I said, which drew a smile from Lopez.

But I was serious. If the key to a mission's success was a harmonious crew, we were royally screwed.

Yep—this could be a superb start to a doomed operation.

CHAPTER 9

THE CREW QUIETENED as we approached the QyronNexa. The air seemed tense enough to carve like a roast dinner. Our vitals blinked on the screens around the ship, not quite in the green zone.

This might not go down as intended.

"So what's our angle, then?" Lopez flipped a switch on the console above her.

"We discussed this in the briefing." Figg frowned.

Lopez hooked her foot under the bar to steady herself. "I was hoping for more access to the conversation. But Ofelia can't hear them."

"Yet," Figg said.

"So you could in the future?" Maya asked, forgetting to be upset with me.

Did that mean we had a truce?

"I don't know," I replied. "Even Trix doesn't know how it works. I'm not Kaseath, but I'm not all human. We're figuring this out as we go along."

Lopez fiddled with the dog tags around her neck. "We can't rely on Trix's translation."

"I trust Trix completely," I said.

"Me too, of course." Maya averted her gaze.

Okay, not a truce. But at least she supported me.

"But based on what?" Griffin stretched her neck like she had just started a strenuous workout.

"My experiences so far." I lifted my shoulders back, matching Griffin's challenge. "Trix has always been my ally. She had no reason to help without knowing we'd return her to the QyronNexa. Not when we were in Elditch. There seemed no way out back then."

"What about the visions? She could have seen her future," Maya said.

"I saw my possible future," Trix told me.

"What did you see?" I arched my eyebrows, studying Trix's poker face.

"I saw our escape from the facility, but the violence interfered with the vision. We did not survive."

"Like my visions? You saw the missile, too?"

"What missile?" Griffin asked, and I wondered whether to share my premonition with the team.

"We might not make it." I watched their concerned expressions blossom.

"Care to elaborate on that, recruit?" Lopez's question was more of a command.

Before I responded, a warning siren flashed in the cockpit.

"What now?" Lopez fumed and propelled herself towards the front. "Maya, Hellcat, up here, please."

Maya and Hellcat followed their commander to the chatter on the comms.

"Valentina One, collision course alert with space debris. Confirm your coordinates?"

Technical instructions followed. Hellcat regained the controls. Lopez and Maya strapped into their seats, punching information into their iScreens. Hellcat took back the manual controls, and the shuttle shuddered.

"What's happening?" I grabbed the handhold beside me as the ship jittered like a skipping record player.

The crew ignored me, following evasive manoeuvre protocols.

"Strap yourselves in." Lopez maintained an in-control demeanour. But despite her composure, she wiped sweat from her brow.

I helped Trix back to her seat, and we strapped in behind Maya and Griffin. Figg also returned to her seat. Warning flashes in my peripheral vision distracted me.

"This is just procedure, folks," Lopez said. "An actual collision is unlikely."

Just as the words left Lopez's mouth, the shuttle banked downwards. Hellcat propelled the ship away from our current course.

"Sorry about that!" Hellcat gritted her teeth.

Lopez grabbed the comms. "Mission control, there are smaller objects. Please confirm you're seeing them?"

"Negative, Commander. We cannot see what you see."

"Hellcat, do your best. Mission Control, we need a moment."

I peered into space beyond the front windows. Tiny, spinning, metallic objects caught the sun's rays. Almost undetectable, but all space junk was dangerous. Enacting evasive manoeuvres was a worrying sign.

The bottom dropped out of my stomach as the ship dived. Hellcat wrenched the controls to align us with the Kaseath's ship.

Was Hellcat as sharp a pilot as Lopez assumed?

The blinking lights remained, as did the shrill warnings.

Lopez peered out of the cockpit. "Is that it?"

Hellcat scanned, too, and Maya checked her iScreen.

"Negative," Maya said. "I see more shrapnel by our starboard side, just above the wing."

"I see it—" Hellcat wrenched her controls. A gleaming fist-sized shard spun towards our cockpit. "Hold on!"

I pulled my seat restraints tighter and clutched the armrest.

The shrapnel ricocheted against the side panel's heat shield, and a hairline fracture appeared at the point of impact. The shrapnel skidded past the window, and the shuttle lurched to the side.

I jerked in my seat. The restraints held everyone in place, but Maya's iScreen flew out of her grip.

The iScreen smacked her in the face, knocking her unconscious.

Her head lolled to the side, her eyes closed.

"Maya!" I reached out, but she was unconscious.

The iScreen gained kinetic energy and smashed against a side console. Shattered glass ricocheted about the cabin, and the iScreen itself smashed into another console. It hurtled back towards the cockpit.

"I am on it." Trix caught the iScreen before it could do more damage. But the shards of the screen flew about. We held up our arms to protect our faces from the razor-sharp glass.

Just before the shards hit me, I enacted my shield.

I squinted at the shrapnel, willing my shield to stay open, fighting with every morsel of concentration.

But my shield sparked again, glitching out. The shrapnel sped towards the front seats. Then, it ricocheted off at odd angles.

Glass shards broke up and shot in every direction, speeding with the lack of gravity. Before I could stop myself, my next shield shot up—a hindrance rather than protection. I couldn't control it.

My shield caught the next wave of glass shards headed my way—a thimble-sized cluster on my right flank. My shield's energy exploded, kicking back into my chest. I jolted in my seat, senses dazed. The glass flew towards Figg, who sat behind me.

The glass ripped the upper arm of Figg's suit. A smaller shard lacerated her cheek.

I had to get the shrapnel out of action, or I'd bat it around the whole shuttle and slice and dice the crew.

I detached from my seat, holding on as we banked hard to starboard. The vacuum cleaner hung on the opposite wall, and I propelled myself towards it, keeping my arm in front of my face to protect against rogue shards.

It was impossible to move while the ship zigzagged all over space.

"Trix? A little help?"

Trix projected her stronger shield. It covered me as I inched to the opposite wall, gritting my teeth in concentration. I grabbed the vacuum and hoovered the glittering shards nearby.

The shards had penetrated every crevice of the ship, and Trix's shield threatened to fail. Sweat formed on my forehead.

I gritted my teeth, vacuuming every visible particle.

I returned to the ship's front. Trix restarted time.

Droplets of blood from Figg's shallow cheek cut hung suspended in the air like little red cranberries. Blood dripped off Maya's head wound near her temple. The globules detached and floated in the air, forming elegant bubbles of red liquid.

Maya's butt hovered just above her seat. The straps tethered her, but her arms and legs floated in the air. She was out colder than a bag of frozen peas.

"Hang tight." Hellcat wrenched the controls.

I jabbed both booted toes underneath the nearest foothold

and grabbed the bar above my head with one hand, the other gripping the vacuum cleaner. Holding steady.

Hellcat stabilised the shuttle, pulling the controls hard to correct our deep dive. We had deviated from our course to the alien ship. This detour had cost us some time.

"Status checks." Lopez unbuckled and headed towards Maya.

"We've lost telemetry systems." Hellcat punched buttons and steadied the controls.

"That sounds bad," I said.

Lopez tilted her head. "Doctor, you're up."

Figg unstrapped herself, dabbing at the tiny droplets of blood from her cheek. She made it to Maya and put a hand over her wrist.

"I have a pulse. She's having palpitations. Maya, can you hear me?" Figg put a hand to Maya's head and tilted it back. "The gash needs stitching, and she'll have a concussion."

"Will she be alright?" I asked.

"If she doesn't remain unconscious for an extended period."

Conflicting emotions welled up—distaste for Figg and gratitude that she was helping Maya. She was a competent doctor, and I trusted her medical expertise.

"Wake up, Maya." I shook her arm gently.

Lopez said, "Ofelia, grab the vacuum."

"Yes, Commander."

I kicked off from my toe hold and hoovered the tiny blood spheres out of the air. The blood continued to detach from the globular mess, sliding around Maya's forehead, forming spherical patterns like flowing, red liquid mercury. I didn't want a repeat of the panel-shorting incident. Blood represented a biohazard, too.

"I'll get my medical kit." Figg went to the rear compartment and pulled a powder-blue bag from inside. She returned and gave Maya a shot of medicine in the arm. I hoovered the blood as it broke free from Maya's head.

Maya's eyelids fluttered open. "Huh? What happened?"

"You hit your head during evasive manoeuvres," Lopez said. "How do you feel?"

"I'm okay..." Maya scowled at Figg, who was hovering close.

"Follow my finger." Figg moved her finger up and around Maya's peripheral vision.

"Which one?" Maya said.

"You're seeing more than one?"

"And my head hurts. Am I... bleeding?"

"I'm going to give you a local and stitch you up," Figg said. "Ofelia, a little help?"

I drifted closer, sucking the blood into the vacuum cleaner with one hand.

"Just a little prick." Figg administered the needle.

Figg had said that to me during those deadly tests in the Elditch Research Facility. Like the 'little prick' was pleasantly rewarding.

Figg had said that to Maya, too. I shook off my distaste for Figg while Maya needed her help.

"Ouch," Maya said.

Figg removed the needle. "The local injection is more painful than the actual stitches. We'll wait for the anaesthetic to work."

After a moment, Maya seemed more alert. Figg appeared competent, stitching her up. She clipped the end of the stitches and stuck a bandage over the area, then ran a medical scanner over Maya's forehead, punching data into her CommLink and checking the shuttle's life support information. Satisfied, Figg packed her equipment into a plastic bag.

"All done here, Commander." She stowed her medical bag.

Lopez turned to Hellcat. "Can you correct our course to the QyronNexa?"

"We need fresh coordinates."

"Maya? Are you with us?"

"Yes, Commander," Maya said.

Griffin handed Maya an undamaged iScreen, but Maya just peered at it as if the data were as foreign a language as the Kaseath's.

"Sorry, Commander. I'm having trouble reading the screen." Maya held her head. "And my head's pounding."

Lopez shot a worried look Maya's way, then addressed Figg. "How long before she's better?"

"Head injuries are tricky—it could be hours or days. Worst-case, a week or more."

"I'm so sorry." Frustrated tears pooled in Maya's unfocussed eyes.

She winced with pain, and it wasn't the stitches that caused her distress. She wanted to help ensure the mission succeeded. One of her tears sprang free and floated in the middle of the cabin. I sucked it up with the vacuum before anyone else noticed.

"Are you okay?" I asked discreetly.

Maya nodded, her tears brimming over, not meeting my concerned gaze.

"Who'll do the docking procedure now?" Griffin peered at Maya. "She's the only one with decent hours behind her."

"Ofelia trained, too," Lopez said.

"Only in the simulators," I said. "And I messed up almost every time."

"Except for the times you succeeded."

"We're chancing the mission on that?" Griffin shot back. "On her not crashing a few times?"

"It's all we have." Lopez gave me a rousing grin.

"I can do it." Griffin lifted her chin in a challenge.

"We need you on comms with mission control. Ofelia can't do the calculations but she can wrangle a joystick."

"What about you, Commander?"

"I'll assist Hellcat with the telemetry projections."

"What about Dr Figg?" Griffin asked. "Literally, anyone else but Ofelia!"

"Gee, thanks." But not-so-secretly, I agreed with Griffin. Was I up to performing the docking procedure for real?

"Dr Figg hasn't trained for the docking procedure," Lopez said.

"Maya might be better by then, anyway," Figg said.

"Hellcat, assuming we get the coordinates soon—how far are we from the QyronNexa?"

"At a guess, I'd say thirty minutes?"

Lopez nodded, scratching her chin. "Trix, we'll need those new coordinates. And Ofelia, you're up."

A layer of dread settled over me as I floated in the middle of the cabin, still holding onto the ridiculous vacuum cleaner.

I could play maid, sucking up biohazards and projectiles and assisting Figg's surgical procedures. But could I enact a docking procedure requiring precision? The sims were tricky enough, and my success rate was below a pass mark.

Trix was in my head again. Maybe she had a motivational speech that would improve my confidence. Then maybe I could do this.

"You had thirty-three attempts, with a 51.54% success rate," Trix said.

This is a helluva time for statistics that do not help.

Maya had to recover for the docking protocol. Otherwise, our boarding party might not make it off our shuttle.

CHAPTER 10

I STRAPPED into my sleeping cocoon in my quarters, a compartment about the size of an old-fashioned phone booth. I had ten minutes to take a breather and psych myself up, but it was difficult to concentrate when painful thoughts jumbled like clothes in a tumble dryer.

My best friend was injured.

My powers were glitching.

There was a massive probability of blowing the shuttle into a million chunks in a failed docking procedure.

Commander Lopez's words returned to me: this was the most dangerous part of the mission, after launch and re-entry. And it was up to me.

The timer on my CommLink sounded its alarm, mimicking a bird's call—a hardy bird that survived, sitting in the branches of the sapling in our backyard in Cookham East. Demi's memorial tree that Imogen and I planted.

Pain stabbed into my breastbone at the memory.

Was I flying towards Demi, who was already gone? Or closer to Imogen, the sister I could still save?

My fingers found the smooth reassurance of the turquoise ball in my space suit pocket.

Before I sealed the mission's fate, I had to call home.

I switched on my iScreen and patched into the shuttle's comms with Earth. Bypassing Mission Control wasn't protocol. But then, this mission hadn't gone as planned.

I dialled in, and the screen froze. The connection wheel turned, froze, and nudged again. Mum appeared, her face pixelated like Lego blocks. The sound echoed, the reverb cutting through.

"Are... hel... who... are..."

"Mum?" I shouted.

"Of... eeee... lia?" The static severed her face in two.

"Mum, is Imogen okay?"

"Ofelia?" The choppy video lag caught up, morphing from each one-second slice to the next.

"Yes, it's me, Mum. Is Imogen out of surgery?"

"She's out," Mum replied.

I took a steadying breath, my mind jagging on that fact. "How is she?"

"She hasn't woken up," Mum said.

"Is that bad?" I asked, still hearing audio feedback.

Mum held the screen out to Imogen, and I caught a split-second image of my sister in the hospital bed. Eyes closed.

"We won't know—" The feed broke off.

"Mum? What does that mean?"

The image was grainy now, lopsided solid blocks of colour.

"Mum!"

The audio lurched into a glitching, distorted whine.

"Sssssshhhhhheee's..."

"What, Mum? I can't hear you!"

"Doooooo... iiiing..."

The connection severed. The iScreen's screensaver returned as the video feed disconnected.

Imogen hadn't woken up. But the operation was over. Had it gone well—or poorly?

Would my sister survive?

I shook off the lump in the back of my throat. I tried to reconstruct the image of her in the hospital bed. Had she looked peaceful, about to leave this realm?

I dug my nails into my palms, easing my thumping heart, which seemed to enlarge beneath my ribs. I returned to a calmer state.

Maya poked her head around the stiff curtain into my sleep station.

"Are you ready?" she said flatly, not making eye contact.

"I wish *you* were." I raised an ironic eyebrow.

Maya still couldn't look at me, so she didn't notice the ironic eyebrow. She moved away.

"Maya... I'm sorry..." By the time I'd unstrapped myself from the sleeping cocoon in my quarters, Maya stared back at Earth through the starboard window.

She was adrift, and I didn't know how to help. I needed her support. My being seemed to break apart. Imogen was stuck in a hospital bed. It may be hours until I could talk to her, assuming I didn't implode our shuttle first.

My shoulders felt heavy, like someone had piled on the Camp K gym weights. The barbells threatened to bury me. I had to climb free.

I'd do this without Maya. For Imogen.

I composed myself, wiping my eyes with a tissue, taking deep breaths, and repeating the only mantra that could keep me sane.

Imogen is alive. I'll make her healthy and find her cure.

Shaking off my dread, I floated into the mid-ship.

Hellcat kept us steady, although she struggled with the controls. Lopez read coordinates from the screen as Hellcat made adjustments. Our position from the QyronNexa shifted out of the porthole window.

Griffin scanned data from the screen beside the docking bay, jotting down notes on her CommLink.

Figg donned a spare, undamaged space suit and bandaged the minor cut on her cheek.

"What's your assessment, Doctor?" Lopez asked.

Maya looked at me and burst out crying.

"Ah, what's going on?" Lopez's voice softened.

Figg pulled out a handheld scanner from her medical kit and ran it over Maya's forehead, checking her CommLink and the shuttle's life support screens.

"A concussion causes an inability to regulate emotions," Figg said.

"Regulate my—you've got to be kidding." Maya's eyes flared at the doctor.

"Outbursts of sudden anger—yep, I don't think she'll be mission-ready in time."

"Maya, are you okay?" I rested my hand on her shoulder. This wasn't like her.

Maya's glare cut through Figg as she shrugged off my consoling touch.

"So Maya won't be docking?" Griffin turned from working at a screen.

"Ofelia will do an excellent job." Lopez's oversized grin barely hid her lack of conviction.

"Excellent for getting us killed," Griffin said under her breath.

"We need to stay positive. We also need to work together. So—we act as if everyone is competent."

Griffin reached down to touch her ankle gun. It was like her tic or something. Trigger-happy and combative, as usual.

Figg packed away the handheld scanner in her medical bag.

Maya felt the bandage on her head. The beginning of rage tears glistened as her eyes flashed.

Lopez continued. "Hellcat will remain with the ship since our auto calibration isn't working. Maya isn't cleared medically. So everyone, except Hellcat and Maya, will board the Qyron-Nexa. We'll keep an open feed to the shuttle to relay orders from Mission Control."

How did Maya feel about staying behind with Hellcat? They weren't strictly friends. Maya and I weren't exactly friends right now, either.

"Put these on." Lopez handed out round earbuds about the size of my thumbnail. She handed a pair to Trix, who looked at her with amusement and pointed out her lack of protruding ears. "Sorry, Trix, you'll have to stick with Ofelia."

Trix nodded, her oversized head grazing the shuttle's ceiling.

Lopez continued, "We could encounter hostility in their camp—only vetted communication aboard the QyronNexa. Griffin, advise us of any changes to the threat levels. Understood?"

"Yes, Commander," Griffin said.

"Good. Dr Figg? You'll take point on obtaining the cure. Either the Kaseath don't recognise the components, or they might not share them. Can you run tests aboard the ship?"

Figg took her scanner from the medical kit and slipped it into a suit pocket. "All I need is a sample."

"Copy that. Ofelia, you're in charge of comms with the Kaseath. You did a sterling job before. Once the docking is complete, we must stay sharp—anything can happen."

"Yes, Commander." A knot formed in my guts, as if my stomach had closed over spoiled food.

What awaited us on the QyronNexa? I'd been preoccupied

with the launch and the impending docking procedure. Was the worst ahead?

"Commander?" Hellcat called from the cockpit. "We are twenty seconds from the docking point."

"Copy, Hellcat. Ofelia, start your initial docking arm tests. Maya can be on hand for questions, and Griffin will assist you."

Maya and I both said, "Yes, Commander."

I turned to Maya. "Snap!"

But she didn't respond. I hoped it was just the concussion and that she'd come around.

Griffin scowled at me until she noticed Lopez's frown.

"Let's go." Lopez roused our ragtag team. "Remember your training, and let's create history!"

Maya joined me at the docking station. It was a set of controls positioned by a window with a direct line of sight to the outer docking hatch. Between the outer hatch and our ship was an inner room, which would pressurise to match the QyronNexa before opening the outer hatch.

A mechanical arm extended on pistons, with a joint in the middle, capable of rotating 360 degrees and extending or retracting.

Just like the docking sim at Space Camp.

I settled before the controls while Maya relayed mission-critical instructions. I had to make things right with Maya, just in case I exploded us into the vacuum of space. If there was an afterlife, I didn't want to spend eternity bickering with my best friend.

"Wish me luck?" Hope tinged my voice.

When I turned for Maya's reaction, she was staring into space. Like, the actual vacuum of black, inky nothingness of space.

"Docking's easy. You've got this," Maya said.

Griffin attempted to stuff another laser gun into her space suit pockets. Thankfully, it didn't fit.

"Easy for you, Maya," I joked.

Her mouth twitched. It was something.

The QyronNexa dominated the porthole view—a minuscule section of the massive ship. As we inched closer, the grooves of a gunmetal-grey round hatch appeared.

I caught a whiff of Griffin's fake blueberry gum as she slipped into the spot next to me, ready to assist. Anticipating Lopez's instructions, I wiped sweaty hands on my space suit. But the suit repelled liquids rather than soaking up the clammy moisture on my skin.

I moved the arm with the set of controls inside the shuttle, checking the progress from the large porthole window. Above, a screen displayed the correct coordinates and our distance from the QyronNexa. But to me, it was a hieroglyph of numbers and mathematical formulas. I concentrated on the joystick, with no need for complicated maths.

"Thirty metres, Ofelia," Lopez said. "Twenty... fifteen..."

"Extend the arm to the first quarter," Griffin said, and I moved the joystick, mimicking our ship's approach.

"Steady," Lopez ordered, and Hellcat eased our approach. "Five metres, Ofelia. Hellcat, hold us there."

"Extend the docking arm to full length," Griffin said.

I pushed the joystick a little too hard, and the arm jolted. Then it stuck in place.

"Something's wrong." I tapped the joystick. But the arm wouldn't budge in either direction.

I jabbed at the joystick. The mechanism groaned, and a metallic crunch sounded.

"Brilliant..." Griffin hovered closer. "What can I do?"

"Listen for a moment. Everyone quiet." Maya held a finger in the air.

The seconds ticked as Maya cocked her ear. She listened over the dull breath of air sucking in and out of the oxygenation pumps. Above the creak of the arm itself, the gears inside the spaceship's panel stuck in place with the groan of something mechanical.

"The piston's jammed," Maya said.

"Jammed with what?" Griffin asked.

"The mechanism sometimes seizes up. Hellcat, get us clear until we can fix the problem."

"This bird is retreating." Hellcat's voice ground with the effort of pulling us free.

The shuttle banked hard, the docking arm dangerously close to the other ship. I braced myself against the wall and held tight as the shuttle accelerated.

The partially extended arm grazed the Kaseath's ship. It glanced off the finish, scratching the exterior.

One grabber tooth broke off the end of our mechanism's arm.

"We have external damage to the docking arm," I confirmed.

"How did that happen?" Lopez kept her voice steady.

"We scraped the side of their ship." Griffin stared daggers at me.

"That wasn't my fault," I huffed.

"What will it take to fix it?" Lopez asked.

Maya answered, "We should be fine without one grabber. But we'll need to repair the docking piston."

"Does that require a spacewalk?"

"Affirmative, Commander."

"Hellcat, how are we looking?"

"We've burned fuel on our detour earlier," Hellcat said. "But we have enough for one more docking pass. Otherwise, we might not make it home."

"Can you hold us steady until then?" Lopez said.

"How long do you need?" Hellcat stretched and then grabbed the controls.

"As long as it takes," Lopez said. "Griffin, suit up."

Griffin donned her full space suit, with Figg's help, while I observed the broken docking arm. The teeth flapped in the zero gravity. The piston didn't budge.

I envied Griffin's spacewalk. It was the one thing I had nailed back at Space Camp.

Space Camp's *pool*, I reminded myself. Actual space was more daunting. Griffin couldn't tap out of this if things went south, north, or... whichever direction we pointed.

She realised the dangers while she suited up, giving me an uncharacteristic, friendly wave. With Maya out of action, Griffin needed me on her team.

At the docking hatch, I handed her a tube of grease, the sponge, and the tether.

Griffin clipped the tube and sponge onto her belt's carabiner. Figg gave last-minute encouragement before I heaved on the door lock.

Griffin entered the inner docking chamber, which depressurised to match the vacuum of space. She opened the outer hatch and attached the tether to a railing alongside the ship.

She eased out of the hatch into the deep nothing of space.

Watching her move into the void was exciting. My heart tap danced as she cleared the hatch. The flimsy tether connected her to our ship, her life support.

I glimpsed just how tiny humans were in the vast universe. We must seem miniscule to the Kaseath.

"The view ain't bad out here." Griffin allowed only a tinge of excitement into her voice.

"You're on the clock, Griffin," Lopez said.

"Affirmative, Commander."

Griffin sealed the door behind her, and I moved back to the window beside the docking arm.

We plugged into the comms as I settled into position. I relayed instructions from Mission Control. At least I excelled at something—translating for others. But my mouth still felt dry as I concentrated on the comms.

"Tether to the next rung," I said. "Then move to the middle of the docking arm."

"Copy."

"Slow down, Griffin," Lopez said. "Life support has your heartbeat a little high."

"It could be a glitch." Figg watched proceedings from my peripheral vision.

Griffin's white space suit appeared out of the docking window. It glowed like a bright bulb, backlit by the inky space, tiny against the much larger docking arm.

"Aim for the middle piston," I read from the written feed.

"I see the piston," Griffin said.

"Good, apply the grease," I said.

"Copy that, Ofelia." Griffin hooked her tether into the hand-hold and unclipped the tube, then the sponge. She squeezed paste onto the sponge, then reattached the tube to her carabiner.

Griffin dabbed the lubricant all over.

"Don't be shy," Lopez said. "Use the whole bottle if you have to."

"We'll test the arm," I said.

"Wait until I'm clear." Griffin clipped her tether closer to the hatch.

Every movement seemed taxing, and although spacewalks were exciting, I was glad to be inside the shuttle. I would have enough pressure after Griffin returned.

Assuming she could fix the docking arm.

"Time checks?" Lopez said.

"We've got five minutes, Commander," Hellcat said.

"Get a wriggle on, Griffin."

"Copy, I'm clear." Griffin disappeared from the docking window view.

"Testing retraction." I held my breath as I nudged the joystick.

The docking arm groaned, catching the oily piston section. It slid forward and back, responding to the joystick. I rotated the arm 360 degrees.

"Confirm docking arm is operational." My tension partly subsided.

Griffin gave a thumbs-up. She reattached the sponge to her carabiner, but the tube floated away from her grasp.

"Damn it." Griffin reached for the escaped tube, drifting away from the ship.

"What happened?" Lopez asked.

"I dropped the tube." Griffin swam out after it, leaving the ship's safety, her tether extending like a writhing snake.

"We can't have that floating around the ship," Lopez said.

Griffin grabbed the middle of the tether and used it as a slingshot, propelling her faster towards the tube. She deftly caught the tube in her glove.

Figg sighed in relief. I stopped holding my breath.

Griffin pulled on the tether to return to the ship. She wedged her toes into a foothold, clipped the tube to her belt, and ensured the sponge was snug.

"Nice work." More sweat pooled on my brow.

"Two minutes to get inside," Hellcat said. "Then I'll fire her up again."

"Returning now." Griffin moved more urgently. This time, Lopez didn't scold her about life support. Griffin's heartbeat was faster than mine, and I felt jittery.

"Meet Griffin at the airlock, Doctor." Lopez hung by Hellcat, helping with fresh readings from Mission Control.

"She's through," Figg said.

"I'll restart our approach," Hellcat said.

Figg helped Griffin back into the shuttle.

"Good job, Griffin." Lopez turned in her seat. "Ofelia, we've got one pass at this."

"Yes, Commander." I smiled at Griffin.

Griffin didn't return the smile but dipped her head.

That was enough for me.

We'd finally acted as a team. And I'd helped, not hindered, our mission. My welling pride could be premature. I still had to enact the docking procedure.

The joystick appeared too tiny for my clumsy hands. Several buttons blinked, and the arm outside the window flapped in zero gravity. The missing docking grabber reminded me of Imogen's gap-toothed smile. But I couldn't think about my sister now. My video call couldn't be the last time I saw her. Time for positivity.

Griffin didn't bother taking off her suit before returning to assist me with the readouts from Mission Control. My mood elevated as if I'd enacted the successful spacewalk myself. But I wasn't ready to move Griffin from the 'foe' box to 'friend'.

So, where did that leave Maya?

There was no time—Hellcat approached hot. My hand hovered over the joystick, ready for my part.

I concentrated on the controls and the QyronNexa as if I wore blinkers. Everything else dimmed.

"Fifteen metres," Lopez said.

"Extend the arm to the first quarter," Griffin instructed.

"Five metres, Ofelia. Work your magic," Hellcat said.

"Extend to full length," Griffin said.

"Copy." I nudged the joystick, waiting until the pistons moved and our alignment matched. This was precise work.

"Arm extended, initiating lock." I extended the round hatch through to the end of the docking arm. I grunted, keeping the joystick in place. Any unnecessary movements would misalign the docking hatch.

The teeth clamped down—then flipped up.

"I don't have it!" An exasperated sigh escaped my body.

"One minute, Ofelia, before this mission is aborted," Hellcat said.

"Way to give a girl confidence," I shot back.

"Concentrate, Ofelia," Trix said inside my head.

I can't do this, I thought.

"Yes, you can. I have seen our potential future. We board the ship," Trix replied.

I closed my eyes for a half-second, visualising the ball in my pocket, my love for my sister flowing through my fingertips. Then, I concentrated on the docking latches.

"Trying a final approach." I moved the joystick as if nudging crumbs to a mouse. *Gently, don't spook the tiny rodent. Just concentrate.*

I lowered the teeth and waited. Had they caught?

A beep sounded. Was that a positive beep? Then, a robotic voice from the ship said, "Docking arm attached."

"I did it!" I hugged Griffin, her asymmetrical biceps jagged as stone. Her scowl jolted me back to the task.

"You're not finished, Ofelia," Lopez said over the comms. "Extend the connecting walkway."

That was the straightforward part. I shifted the tube, and

the tunnel's hoops formed a cocoon, sticking both ships together.

"Align air pressure," Griffin said, and I concentrated on the read-outs, aligning with the other craft.

"Do we have air pressure?" Lopez asked.

"Affirmative, Commander."

Elation filled me like a swelling belly after a delicious meal. I'd made it happen.

Well, with the help of my crew.

I couldn't leave my only human friend with our friction unresolved.

"Hey, Maya, we did it!" Excitement overrode my annoyance.

Had she forgiven me?

But when I searched for her, she was in her quarters, the stiff curtain ajar.

Her shoulders shook, and her head was in her hands.

She was sobbing.

CHAPTER 11

I LURKED outside Maya's quarters, not knowing whether to interrupt. Her timing was terrible—I had worries, too, but it didn't seem the place to share them.

Would Imogen recover? She had to live. *Right—think about someone else.*

"What's wrong, Maya?" I asked.

"I can't stop it..." Maya's voice broke.

"What can't you stop?"

"The flashbacks, the terror."

"The panic attacks—I get them, too."

"I know!"

My lip quivered, feeling her pain like an unsettled sickness. I paused, searching for the right advice. "It helps to talk about it..."

"I definitely *don't* want to talk."

"But giving it a form, releasing the memory, helps destroy its power."

"That doesn't work for me, Ofelia. We have different ways of dealing with things..."

Except those *things*—the flashbacks—were exceedingly

real. They overtook the daylight and hijacked all thoughts. They became a new reality all on their own.

I resisted my flashes of Imogen in the hospital bed, pixelated and grainy...

"You have to face it." My voice wobbled. "Or it will take over..."

"I can't push it away. Usually, I distract myself, learn something, or immerse myself in a problem. But with this concussion, my vision's blurry. I can't read. I can't distract. And so I'm thinking and I can't stop the awful... painful..."

"It's okay, Maya, you're safe." I moved to the door of her quarters.

"This feeling is not safe at all."

"It's true. There's no danger here." I placed my hands over her hair, cradling her head. Maya's whole body shook, her tears hot, her expression pained. "Just breathe."

"Breathing's the easy part," Maya shot back.

"That's what I said to Commander Lopez." I grinned at the memory. "But it works. Come on, breathe with me, slow everything down."

"I can't..."

"You're already doing it."

We huffed in and out, our breathing laboured. We exaggerated the inhale and blew the exhale extra hard until Maya relaxed and breathed normally. I realised I was too.

Maya opened her eyes and looked into mine. I sent my healing powers through her hair, into her scalp, and then deep into her mind, easing the shooting chemicals.

I said, "We each have our ways of coping. I didn't realise yours would be different. We don't have to talk if you don't want to."

Maya sighed an extra-long, release-of-tension sigh. She turned her eyes to the QyronNexa attached to our shuttle.

"Make sure we come back." I grinned. "I'm counting on you, okay?"

Maya nodded, grabbed a tissue, and blew her nose.

Lopez approached, and I realised the entire ship had paused for Maya and me to pull it together.

Well, Maya had pulled it together. Now it was my turn for tummy jitters.

"Okay, recruits?" Lopez asked us.

"Yes, Commander," Maya and I said simultaneously.

"Snap." I smiled.

Maya raised her eyebrows, conceding the joke.

"Are we good, Maya?" I asked.

"We're good." She smiled weakly, still struggling, but she'd progressed from her full-blown panic attack.

Lopez shot a worried look my way, and I just shrugged. What did you say when your best friend was hurting? But at least I hadn't exploded the ship into a billion atoms with a failed docking procedure.

I joined the boarding party, who were suiting up. Trix declined to wear a space suit or helmet. Unlike her human counterparts, she didn't breathe oxygen.

Figg approached to help me into my suit. I flinched, unnerved by her proximity. But I needed her now—for support on the QyronNexa.

Figg's worried expression passed as she helped me slip on the thick legs, heave on the torso section, and hook into the arms. The others suited up like practised deep-sea divers. I felt clumsy in front of my crewmates. I couldn't grip the tags of my zippers, and a wardrobe malfunction would be deadly. Figg noticed I was stressing out.

"These zippers are confounding, right?" She placed a reassuring hand over mine.

I stopped struggling with my suit. She helped me zip everything together, airlock-ready.

"This is so exciting." Figg patted down my last Velcro pocket. "The Kaseath will welcome you and share the cure for your sister. They will help us."

I shoved my anger far into the toes of my space suit. Trying something new—called 'don't antagonise the only person who could recognise Imogen's cure'.

"I hope so, too."

Trix's worry became apparent. Unease washed over the group as I wondered if we shouldn't just turn around now and save our skins.

What did you see in our future, boarding this ship?

"I hope it does not happen."

Why? What did you see?

"It's go-time, people." Lopez interrupted our private conversation. "Last suit checks. Trix has confirmed there is no breathable air aboard the QyronNexa. So, do not compromise the integrity of your suits. Agreed?"

We all replied in the affirmative. I sympathised with Maya, who was on the verge of sobbing.

Hellcat clipped a small round camera to the front of my suit.

"So we can see, too." Hellcat's hair parted, revealing her sincere blue eyes. "Maya and I will monitor the comms. Tell us everything when you return, okay?"

"Just don't leave without us."

"Go find that cure so we can save our families."

So, Hellcat also had family on Earth. We all had something to lose.

Griffin slipped an ankle laser gun into her space suit pocket, patting down the Velcro and concealing the weapon around her oversized calf muscles. She positioned herself first inside the docking tunnel and blew an underwhelming blue gum bubble, snapping it back into her mouth. The regular chewing motion must keep her alert. I would worry about swallowing the gum.

Lopez lined up behind Griffin, concentrating on the hatch. Figg followed, with Trix and me in the vulnerable last position. I preferred not to be a rear-guard casualty but secure in the middle of my team.

The enormity of what we were doing settled on my chest like a heavy lead apron, reminding me of an X-ray machine in Figg's tests. Except now, we would enter the Kaseath's turf. They hadn't been too happy to hear from us.

Our trials so far could be dwarfed by the mission ahead.

"Let's go, team." Lopez nodded to Griffin.

Griffin crawled headfirst, on all fours, through the docking tunnel, followed by Lopez, Figg, Trix, and finally me. There was wiggle room for the human crew and the taller, broader alien. We followed each other head-to-toe like a link of sausages. Griffin made it to the QyronNexa's hatch. We stopped in formation.

Griffin's voice filtered through the comms in our helmets.

"Valentina One, confirming we have reached the docking station. We will board the QyronNexa. Do you copy?"

"The Kaseath are ready," Trix said to me.

"Copy and confirm we're clear to board," I translated.

"Good luck." Hellcat's voice crackled through our comms.

The hatch inched open with a metallic groan.

A whoosh of atmosphere joined us from the ship into the tunnel. We landed on the floor as artificial gravity enacted. It wasn't as strong as Earth's gravity, but we still found ourselves like fish on the deck of a boat, flapping about.

The corners of Trix's mouth turned up. "I should have warned you about that."

Yeah, you think?

"No, I know."

I smiled back at our shared joke, releasing the tension in my jaw.

We crawled forward on our hands and knees to the end of the tunnel, where Griffin and Lopez worked together to open the hatch fully. A blinding white light, yellowing at the edges, greeted us.

"Visors down, people," Lopez said.

"Trix says it's not dangerous."

"Doesn't Trix feed on radiation?" Griffin flipped her visor down.

"Let's err on the side of caution," Lopez replied.

Figg and Lopez also lowered their solar visors while Trix shrugged.

"It is best to follow my instructions," she said.

I felt conflicted. I trusted Trix. But also, that light looked hotter than our shuttle's engines.

I flipped my visor, feeling disloyal to Trix but questioning her instructions. She might not recognise dangers to humans within her familiar ship.

"Let's go." Griffin edged forward.

My body registered the heat of the light as we inched forward on our hands and knees through the tunnel towards the QyronNexa. We made awkward progress, as if we'd forgotten how to walk in gravity after the shuttle's weightlessness. The connecting tunnel was narrow, and my suit's oxygen tank grazed the ceiling. Trix charged up, her shoulders straightening, her forward movement springy. That light emitted radiation, just like our sun.

"Keep your visors on until we assess the conditions," Griffin said.

"Agreed," Lopez said. "Dr Figg, what's your take?"

Figg nudged forward in the tunnel, handing her medical scanner to Lopez. The commander waved it towards the QyronNexa and then returned the scanner to Figg to assess the readouts.

"The radiation is high but not fatal. We should limit our exposure aboard the ship."

"Copy that," Lopez said.

Griffin passed through the hatch and into the room beyond, alert to danger. "We're clear here."

"Stay chatty on the comms," Hellcat said.

We filtered into the ship one by one, clumsy as sailors disembarking after a long cruise. Once we were through, Lopez and Griffin closed and armed the hatch.

We stood in a decontamination chamber about the size of our entire shuttle. A door-shaped depression formed in the far wall, the edges rounded, meeting a yellow floor made of a sticky, porous substance. Trix moved freely, but the rest of us bounded off the gravity. We moved with excessive springiness.

Circular coils descended, flowing out of the rounded ceiling material. The coils brightened from shiny obsidian black to glowing red.

"Uh, what's happening?" Griffin aimed her laser gun at the coils.

"It's just decontaminating the crew," Trix said.

"Will it harm us?" I asked Trix for the benefit of the others.

"The process will not kill you," Trix said, deadpan.

I shifted towards the room's edge, seeking an exit. Griffin, already on high alert, pushed against the opposite wall. But it lacked panels or controls that would open a door.

The coils heated, glowing a luminescent shade of red, and I was glad of our visors. Trix spread her arms, turning her face to the ceiling coils. I shielded my helmet with my hands, feeling the searing blast. The rest of my crew also panicked and crouched against the heat. The disadvantage of having our gold visors down was that we couldn't see each other's expressions, just our reflection on the metallic surface.

Griffin's finger gripped the laser gun trigger, ready to fire. The coils clicked off like a light switch. They dimmed, morphed into the black obsidian, and retracted into the ceiling. The room glowed white, and Figg pulled out her medical scanner. She checked us all out. We were uncooked, with rapid heart rates and a sunburnt sensation.

"What was that?" Griffin placed her laser gun back in her pocket.

An eight-foot door materialised and slid open. It revealed a white, glowing corridor into the QyronNexa.

"Stay alert." Lopez gestured to the door.

Our crew left the decontamination room. We were the first humans in history to board an alien vessel. The sticky floor felt strange beneath my boots. We stood in the corridor of the alien ship, marvelling at the structure.

The walls were eggshell white, with rounded corners that met the yellower flooring. I traced a damp line on the wall with my gloved hand. My finger ended in a droplet—not water, as there was no oxygen aboard, but yellow liquid covered every surface. The air hazed with intense humidity.

Multiple corridors stretched hundreds of metres in either direction. The ship seemed as expansive as an entire city. This QyronNexa was like our Ark—built for long journeys over generations. The Kaseath's home, not a temporary mission.

The walkway was a yellow-white glowing mass without detail. I couldn't see practical storage bins on the walls, control panels, or video screens. A purple light blinked at the corner of each intersection. Strange writing in metallic logos sat underneath each light. Marking the way?

The flooring underfoot squelched. Yellow liquid oozed

after each moon-booted footfall, like indents of sand near the water's edge at a beach. Pools of liquid formed and were sucked into the flooring.

Solids were less stable here, and liquefaction was normal. Was the flooring a waste-gathering system that recycled the Kaseath sludge?

Several corridors split off from the main arterial one. I peered closer at the symbols on the discreet panels demarcating each section.

"Here's our welcome party." Griffin widened her stance and planted both boots on the porous floor.

Four large aliens stepped forward and flanked us shoulder-to-shoulder. They seemed taller than Trix's seven-foot bulk and had imposing expressions. Gleaming purple collars draped around their broad, scaly shoulders. They were identical to Trix but more orange, less brown, and silent.

Shock and awe.

Trix conversed with the escorting aliens, but I couldn't understand. They carried handheld laser guns like the one Griffin had stowed in her suit.

"They are like your military." Trix flicked her eyes at Griffin. "The weapons will harm, not sedate."

Griffin shrugged when I translated, flexing her arms like she was preparing for a casual jog. I hoped we didn't need her particular skills.

Trix transitioned into an alien language I couldn't understand. It flowed like a soft shower, not unpleasant but unintelligible. Someone else controlled the language taps.

"Hello there," Lopez said to the nearest alien.

"They don't understand," I said.

"I'm sure they get my meaning." Lopez stuck out a hand for the closest Kaseath to shake.

The alien faltered, as if the gesture were aggressive.

"Just let Trix talk," I said.

Lopez stood as if giving a speech at the training academy.

Trix spoke to our escorts, and the language grated like a choked staccato. I couldn't wait any longer.

Ask them where the cure is.

Trix raised her non-existent eyebrows.

All things are known to everyone. That means the guards know, too.

Trix took her time replying.

"They say they know nothing of a cure."

A hot flash of anger warmed my face, bright as the decontamination chamber coils.

Maybe Griffin was right. Could Trix lie now amongst her kind? Perhaps the Kaseath weren't always truthful, or they could keep secrets. I felt disloyal, but I doubted my earlier trust.

I would do anything to help my family—including double-crossing the aliens aboard the QyronNexa.

Thankfully, Trix didn't hear my thoughts, or at least she didn't react. Her attention remained on the guards.

"Go with them," she said.

Our escorts pushed forward from behind our pack, urging us on.

"I guess we're following them." Griffin touched the pocket with her weapon.

Figg noticed and shook her head at Griffin, who straightened. Figg had herself a new minion.

"This way." Trix's feet rippled on the sandy-coloured floor, with no remnants of the sludge I was so used to seeing on Earth. The other aliens' feet also undulated.

I felt clumsy and clod-footed in the weak gravity. My feet pinged off the ground with each moon-booted step. We bounced along in this not-quite-gravity with the awkward leap of a newborn deer.

130

In my excitement at being inside the alien ship, I forgot my anger at Trix. The elusive cure remained, and I had to guard my thoughts from intrusion.

The scale of the ship was unprecedented. The walls seemed to throb with latent power—an electric sizzle shot through my arm as I waved it closer to the wall.

I turned my body towards the blinking light and markings on the corner of the corridor—the Kaseath's version of writing.

"Are you getting this, Maya?"

But only static replied.

"Hellcat? Are you still with us?" Lopez registered the lack of comms as well.

Silence.

Lopez tried again. Then Griffin and Figg checked their comms—a last-ditch effort. We couldn't raise either Hellcat or Maya.

"We are too far inside the QyronNexa," Trix said.

"So we don't have access to the shuttle or Mission Control?" Figg asked.

"Correct," I translated.

But Figg's reaction was unusual. Instead of worrying, she smiled—the expression not reaching her eyes. She wasn't being truthful. She glanced at Griffin, who smirked subtly. What were they up to?

I recognised Figg's devious expression. Nothing good would follow.

CHAPTER 12

THE FOUR ALIEN military escorts led our crew into a nearby corridor. I hesitated to follow until our escorts herded us with their massive seven-foot bulk. Trix was intimidating enough, but four military grunts with no sense of humour increased the rate of my beating heart. Their invasive stares drove us forward.

Beaded condensation ran down the inside of my helmet. The QyronNexa was humid, like a tropical destination. I peered about the ship, marvelling at the corridor's expanse. The lead military host noticed my curiosity and waved us towards a passageway.

I took the lead, ignoring my pounding heart. Who could I have been if I had a heftier splice of alien DNA?

We approached a recreation area, with the Kaseath seated at tables, shining lights from handheld torches into each other's eyes.

"Cool," I said. "Are those radiation lights?"

"Don't get too close," Figg said.

"It's just the Kaseath's version of a bar," I translated for Trix.

The bar's lighting was softer, with strobing flashes from rotating lights on the ceiling. Strange music, like dissonance rather than melody, sang below the Kaseath's collective conversation.

Windows led into the area. The Kaseath language washed over me, an unintelligible jumble—there were many threads to catch. I concentrated, but my head throbbed with the effort. I let the sound tumble, appreciating the tones and mild curiosity. The Kaseath at the tables closest to us turned, and I waved.

Not a single one waved back.

Way to leave a girl hanging, I thought.

"Why are you hanging? It makes no sense..." Trix said.

At Trix's words, the Kaseath at the closest table stood, alert to our exchange.

Their thought-chatter rose, like greeting guests at a party. We were being acknowledged. But was it a joyous welcome or a threat to leave? A dozen Kaseath crowded at the window, peering at our party.

"Is this feeding time at the zoo?" Griffin ceased her nervous chewing, reaching for her concealed gun.

Figg shook her head, and Griffin straightened.

One alien pushed closer to the window. She turned her head and assessed our party.

Trix spoke to the alien, but it was in their rapid Kaseath language.

"Slow down," I said.

"I am catching up. We will continue the tour now," Trix said.

Trix nodded at the closest alien, who mimicked the gesture and fluttered away. The Kaseath returned to their seats, their thought chatter more animated than before.

Who was that?

"My mother."

Was she glad to see you?

"Not as much as I hoped. We must be careful, Ofelia."

"Why?" I said out loud.

"We are safe only while you are a novelty."

A projected image covered the walls and ceiling in the next room, a shifting light show. The lights scattered patterned colours and geometric shapes. An adult Kaseath stood at the front of the room, more expressive than the Kaseath at the bar. Smaller versions of the adult Kaseath sat in rows on beanbag-like seating. The shorter aliens lacked the curl at the top of their heads. Their skulls were shaped like a more rounded Brazil nut. Light orange scales covered their bodies without the brown timbre. The beings' bright orange veins pulsed with vigour around their smaller hexagonal scales.

"Is this a school?" Lopez asked.

Trix nodded.

One schoolchild turned from observing the patterned wall and noticed our crew. Her eyes widened, locking onto Trix. The alien girl stood, and the rest of the Kaseath youth turned away from the patterned lesson to watch.

"Lileau," Trix said.

The small alien pressed her palm against the scanner and rushed into the corridor. She stopped short of hugging Trix, who held her palm outwards.

Lileau did the same. They almost touched each other. It was like a practice kick in a karate lesson. Connected by thought and the space between them.

They stood for a while, and then the chatter began.

The schoolchildren stood from their beanbags, and the teacher dropped the light show. The students turned to watch us, and one pointed.

So their young started with body language. Was it conditioned out of them?

Lileau and Trix spoke, and I sensed their pleasant conversation. Trix's connection with the young alien slipped into my consciousness. Similar to the Kaseath at the bar.

Trix and Lileau touched palms, and a sparking sizzle pulsed. Light travelled up and down their bodies, and their expressions entwined. Thought and touch connected them.

I projected my thoughts to the alien girl, Lileau.

Hello.

Lileau locked her eyes on mine. The black depths of her irises tinged with orange at the edges.

Just like the orange flecks in mine.

Hello, Lileau.

Her attention fixed on me, and she responded with thought, the language just audible.

"He... louw."

I smiled, and the child tilted her head, observing my expression. She tried to smile back.

My name is Ofelia. I touched my chest. *Oh-fee-lia.*

"Is this your daughter?" Figg asked, waving.

The girl recoiled as if threatened. Even the alien kids could sense that Figg meant danger. Trust Figg to ruin the moment I first met an alien kid.

Trix nodded for Figg's benefit, and Lileau's veins pulsed in an orange flash—a surge of emotion.

I thought the Kaseath didn't have emotion or attachments. Wasn't it beneath them?

"How old is she?" I asked.

"She is fifteen in Earth years, same as you," Trix said.

Then, the adult teacher stepped into the corridor, and Lileau turned. Trix addressed the teacher, and there was a three-way conversation. Lileau's contrite expression fell, and she returned to the classroom. Her classmates crowded around, questioning her in their alien tongue. The teacher waved our crew onwards.

The next room had a yellow, sulphuric smell like pungent food turned sour. Adult Kaseath worked in protective clothing. Did they cultivate something—plant life? But the scent seemed more volcanic.

Ahead was a series of rooms with blacked-out windows. We couldn't see through.

What's in there? I asked.

"It is not for your human eyes." Trix refused to answer more questions.

A small blue light flashed behind the corner window, where the blackened substance had worn thin. The blue light was like a tiny crackle of lightning-like energy.

Is this where our powers come from?

"It is not your concern."

What do you mean? It's part of who I am...

The lead military alien moved close to Trix, and then the escorts ushered us into more connecting corridors, herding us into a medical bay.

"I don't like this," Griffin said.

"Just stay alert." Lopez eyed the military escorts, who held back near the door.

Our wary crew shuffled inside.

The small room contained four raised, moulded beds, a slick trolley with medical-looking devices, and five aliens in white aprons. Our military escort waited until we were inside the room, flanking the outer door as it slid shut behind them.

"They are doctors," Trix said.

"More tests?" I asked, looking at Dr Figg. She averted her eyes at my challenge. Figg loved a test or two—the kind that killed children, like my sister, Demi.

But I needed Figg onside. The stakes were too high.

I took a steadying breath, its echo muffling in my helmet. I translated Trix's reply.

"They just want to check us out."

"I'm ready." Griffin grinned, patting her suit pocket with the concealed weapon.

The closest alien doctor seemed in charge, observing our crew. Of course, I could have projected my trepidation. Like the other adult aliens, she lacked body language, so I couldn't connect to her energy, thoughts, or feelings.

"This is our head doctor," Trix said. "You can call her Assuth."

"Hey there, Assuth, nice to meet you." I waved nervously.

She didn't react. She was shorter than her other aliens—maybe she had stunted growth? Her eyes were black, emotionless pits. A white apron hung around her thick, scaly neck, tied across her waist. Faint symbols were embedded into the shoulder of her white doctor's apron, like several shooting asteroids.

She looked like an ancient surgeon, from the days when operations were more like butchery and patients rarely survived.

Would she carve us into chunks and feed us to the Kaseath? But then I remembered the Kaseath didn't eat like we did.

"Trix says we are to lift our outer visors so they can see us."

"So they can *fry* us," Griffin mumbled.

But our crew complied.

Figg seemed intimidated by her proximity to the Kaseath. She took everything in with a nervous but professional eye. She may learn something from her well-advanced peers. Lopez held her body rigid, on high alert. Griffin blew a bubble and smacked the gum back into her mouth, daring a fight.

Assuth flinched at the smacking bubble gum and stared at Griffin, who glared, then avoided the challenge—intimidating our war-ready security detail.

Medical instruments sat on the smooth, liquid-like metal

trolley. The handheld scanner was like Figg's but more sophisticated. Long needles filled with liquid lay beside smaller devices of unknown use.

Thinking back to my treatment at Elditch, I was pleased not to see a scalpel. Thoughts returned to my doctor-test-tube-father's incision, lifting one of my scales away for it to disintegrate into ash...

"Concentrate on where you are," Trix said.

The other four aliens paused, waiting for Assuth's instructions. She waved a hand towards a bed, one for each of our human crew. This was the doctors' first body language. Did this mean they were familiar with humans?

"They have seen humans before," Trix confirmed.

How can that be?

"They experimented on humans for years. Your response to my arrival on Earth is similar."

That's ironic.

"I expected to be treated differently," Trix continued. "We are superior, and I thought humans would understand this."

The Kaseath experimented on humans before Trix travelled to Earth. Why hadn't they rescued her? The Kaseath could extract humans from Earth, which meant they could get to my family.

My mind froze at that possibility, and a jolt of fear shot through the base of my neck, giving me tingly jitters.

They could take my family.

To ward off more panic attacks, I visualised a victory lap through Cookham East, clutching Imogen's cure and saving humanity. I had to play this highest-of-stakes game.

"They will take scans," Trix said. "They won't hurt you."

Our crew complied with the instructions to lie on the beds. Griffin unclasped her ankle pocket, which contained her weapon. She glanced at Figg, who shook her head. Griffin closed her pocket and lay back.

Lopez hadn't noticed the exchange. Figg and Griffin had buddied up. Would Lopez do the right thing? I was like a service animal to her—necessary but inferior.

Assuth waited as we settled on the beds.

"Remember," Figg said, "we can't waste time aboard their ship. Just comply, and let's leave quickly."

The other alien doctors waited for Assuth to examine me. She moved forward, her feet rippling as she swished closer. Her gaze felt intense, not hostile—but not welcoming.

"She is pleased to meet you," Trix said. "She hasn't seen someone like you before."

Please tell her not to hurt us.

As she approached, I sensed her body's electrical energy. My cells reached out, my DNA connected to the Kaseath. But Assuth's scrutiny made me nervous. Would I pass her test?

She was shorter than the other Kaseath but towered over my bed, running scanners from head to toe. The light didn't hurt. She checked the read-outs and pointed to the slight bulge in my pocket.

I removed the turquoise ball, my talisman from home. She held it in her three long, twig-like fingers. She ran her scanner over the ball, then returned it to me. I tucked the sentimental object in my pocket.

Assuth peered, being-to-being. It was intensely intimate, even through a thick helmet.

She opened her mouth and nodded, and I supposed she wanted me to follow suit. I complied. She shone lights into my open mouth and studied my orange-flecked eyes. Her deep black pits revealed nothing. She was slower than her companions, her movements efficient but laboured. Was it from age or reduced capacity? Could we use that to our advantage?

She stepped back and stared at her scanner. I felt her concentration, even in the absence of words. Trix confirmed the doctors directed their thoughts into the scanner. Why did the Kaseath need records if they shared knowledge telepathically?

"Even we have our limits," Trix replied to my thought question. "It is tiring, knowing all things since the beginning of our species. To not burden our people, we compartmentalise information."

They might have compartmentalised details of the cure! I thought.

"I wish that were true," Trix said.

My heart hammered, and I caught my breath at this fresh development. Hope sparked in my chest. A frisson of possibility! Why hadn't Trix told me this sooner? It wasn't an outright lie, but she had withheld critical information. What else hadn't she told me?

I focussed on the present while Assuth analysed the results in her scanner. Her gaze lingered on an image on the screen, outlining the rash of scales on my upper arm and stomach beneath my space suit. The experience was preferable to the more invasive scans Figg had ordered in the research facility.

Assuth pointed to me.

"She wants you to confirm where your scales are," Trix said.

I patted my upper arms and stomach to signal the rash of scales underneath my suit. I would cooperate with my alien friends. Wasn't I part Kaseath, after all? We were so close to Imogen's cure!

Assuth held her three-fingered hand above my suit, her long, twig-like fingernails hovering above my abdomen.

She pressed her hand into the outside of my suit, above my scales.

As her finger projected contact, I felt the usual electric shock.

My powers worked on other aliens, too. She wasn't prepared for the sensation. Shying back, she alerted her fellow doctors, who crowded around my bed. Alien language flowed over me.

Assuth made eye contact with another doctor, who slipped by the door. She was ready to hail her military friends.

As I sat there, nothing further happened. The head doctor grilled Trix. Trix must have confirmed the jolt's safety as Assuth moved back around my bed, no longer on high alert. The other doctor returned, and I endured more scans as Assuth resumed her examination.

Afterwards, the other doctors touched my suited arm above the scales, each receiving an electric shock. I was the latest curiosity at the human-alien freak show, and the doctors silently interrogated Trix.

The doctors turned their attention to the rest of my human crew. I propped myself on my elbow, watching the proceedings and observing the crew enduring their tests.

The junior doctor waited by my bed, closest to the door, and watched me while Assuth scanned Figg, working down her neck and chest. The scanner beeped at Figg's breast pocket, and the Assuth pulled back. Her team was alert, and the alien guarding me tensed.

Figg immobilised her body until Assuth relaxed. Then, Figg motioned to her breast pocket and retrieved her handheld medical device connected to her CommLink. It was inferior to the Kaseath scanners, a simplified child's toy. Assuth examined it then handed the device back. Figg stowed her medical device, irritated, but remained still for the body scan. She didn't enjoy playing patient.

Once they finished with Figg, Assuth scanned Lopez in the

same way. Lopez followed instructions, preferring our testing to end quickly.

They moved to Griffin last, and she had a defiant expression. Assuth scanned Griffin's head, moving down to her torso, then approaching her upper legs.

The scanner beeped at her ankle pocket; this time, the tone continued, a shrill warning. Assuth jumped back. She had found Griffin's concealed weapon.

"The game is up," Griffin said, and Trix appealed to the doctors.

The laser gun's tip peeked out of the pocket, and Griffin reached inside.

Griffin eased the weapon out of her ankle pocket, trying not to spook our captors.

The closest alien sprang forward, holding Griffin down.

Griffin wrestled with the doctor. The others restrained her, but the Kaseath was stronger.

"Let them take it!" I shouted.

Griffin's finger jammed on the trigger, unable to stop what happened next.

She fought with superhuman effort, but the gun angled towards Assuth, caught between Griffin and the alien restraining her.

"Wait—don't!" Griffin struggled. "Here, take the gun!"

She immobilised her finger, but the aliens were too strong. Before the doctors wrenched the gun away, Griffin accidentally pulled the trigger.

Assuth enacted her shield, stopping time. Since we weren't behind her time-stop, the red laser deflected, slicing through the wheeled medical trolley.

The trolley banked to one side and fell over. Medical objects slid off, and the needles fell onto the spongy floor.

The laser deflected from the trolley.

Angled straight at me!

Repelling the laser required a millisecond-fast reaction time. These weren't controlled conditions at the practice range. And my powers had been glitching.

This was life or slice.

I forced my eyes wider to observe the laser beam. I enacted my shield, catching Trix and me behind it. Concentrating, I held the shield—and time—open for a second.

I'd caught the laser on the other side. Its impact made a circular dent in my green-tinged shield. But my weak powers shuddered...

The energy flowed into me and my force field, giving me the confidence to open my powers for a few more seconds. I fought the glitch that teased at my mind as my shield fissioned at the edges. Painful slivers of green-tinged sparks burned my skin. I resisted the pain.

The aliens were suspended in time, like everyone else. One alien was mid-struggle with Griffin.

Do they know about my powers?

"Not entirely," Trix replied.

Pretend this shield is yours, so the Kaseath don't learn about my powers. It might help us later.

"All things are known to my kind, but I will attempt this for you."

We'll see. Ready?

"Yes."

I dropped the shield. The red laser deflected to the side, embedded into the spongy floor, and left a black burnt residue.

The aliens were preoccupied with wrestling Griffin and hadn't noticed my shield.

One doctor confiscated the laser gun. Assuth approached with a needle as the remaining doctors restrained Griffin.

She swore, struggling against the doctor's attempts to stick her with the needle.

"What are you giving her?" Figg demanded.

"Hey, now, that's enough." I slid off the bed and tried to pull the alien doctor off Griffin.

The junior alien trained Griffin's gun on me, and I stood back with my hands in the air.

Griffin's expression grew darker than gathering thunderclouds, a pulsing vein throbbing in her cheek. Assuth hovered the needle above her helmet and shone a light into Griffin's eyes. Griffin fought for consciousness, the aliens restraining her until her body went limp.

"Is she alive? Griffin, can you hear me?" Lopez asked.

"Trix says she's just sedated."

"That was so stupid!" Figg said. "Why provoke the Kaseath?"

"Trix says that their leader, Hulgrod, will be disappointed," I said.

"Not as disappointed as I am." Lopez gained control of her anger and turned to Trix. "Tell them we're sorry. Tell them we mean the Kaseath no harm."

Trix spoke to the doctors, but I couldn't understand their response. They continued to assess the data in their scanners as if nothing unusual had happened, and their conversation was rapid-fire as they worked.

All things are known to everyone.

Hulgrod would know, too.

The junior doctor herded us like wayward goats, waving a sedating needle as motivation. I led the crew to the back. A door materialised from the wall.

"What about Griffin? We're not leaving her." I pointed to her prone body on the table.

The junior alien doctor grabbed Griffin. Griffin was short

but compact, but the alien carried her easily with one arm. The junior doctor ushered the rest of us—including Trix—into the much smaller room, then deposited Griffin on the floor. We were back to the soft red light.

The Kaseath locked us in.

I tried the panel by the door. My touch emitted a jarring bass sound, and the door didn't budge. Trix tried next but with the same result.

"Is Griffin okay?" I said.

Figg knelt beside Griffin and checked her medical scanner. "She's sedated, like Trix said."

"So what now?" Lopez asked Trix.

I replied, "Now we explain ourselves to Hulgrod."

CHAPTER 13

TRIX STOOD by the door beside the medical bay, waiting for her military friends to return. Lopez and I rested on seats embedded in the walls, observing Griffin, who lay on the floor. Figg checked her CommLink for Griffin's life support readouts.

Griffin came to, propping herself on her elbow.

"Where are we?" She looked at Trix. "And what the hell is *that?*"

"Where do you think you are?" Figg ran her medical scanner over Griffin.

"I don't know, but this is one hell of a sim."

"What's wrong with her?" Lopez asked Trix in a low voice.

I translated, "The doctors made her more compliant."

"That's a first," Lopez said, then checked herself. "Can you restore her faculties, Doctor Figg?"

Figg helped Griffin sit on the floor, propped against the wall. Griffin opened the Velcro pocket on her space suit and batted it closed. She opened and closed the pocket flap, her delight apparent when the Velcro ripped free.

Lopez frowned at Griffin's repetitive gesture.

Griffin stopped the playful habit. "Seriously, where are we?"

She pushed woozily to her feet. Figg held the heavier, asymmetrically muscly teen steady.

"We're on the QyronNexa, extracting the cure from the Kaseath. You're our security detail. Do you remember?"

Griffin grinned like a kindergartener on the first day of school. She didn't know who her friends were.

"I remember fighting with someone like that." Griffin pointed at Trix.

Figg checked her CommLink. "Sedatives can affect the memory."

Figg scanned every inch of Griffin and gave her a shot from her medical device. Griffin appeared as alert as if she'd just had her morning coffee. But she struggled to follow our conversation. Lopez approached to assess Griffin.

"Are you good, Phoebe?"

Griffin said agreeably, "We shouldn't annoy the aliens. Let's follow their instructions."

This did not bode well. We needed our security support alert and suspicious, not compliant and pleasant. Griffin smiled, wincing as the unfamiliar expression exerted underused muscles.

"You remember the mission?" Lopez asked.

"The Kaseath won't share the cure with an inferior species," Griffin said.

"Now they think we're dangerous, thanks to you," I grumbled.

"It was an accident." Griffin's eyes flashed with the excitement of shooting something.

At least it wasn't shooting *someone*. And unless the medical trolley had sentience, nobody had been hurt.

The door slid open, and our crew jumped to their feet. Our purple-collared military escorts returned, their stance less friendly. Or did I imagine that?

Adrenalin coursed through my veins, and my hands trembled. How much could I take? As I forced breath into my lungs, I fogged up my helmet. My CommLink beeped at me to slow my breathing. Figg raised an eyebrow. I shrugged. Our purposes were aligned. We both wanted that cure.

Around my fear was disappointment that I didn't feel kindred with the Kaseath.

Maybe I was more human than alien.

A vision appeared—I was a prisoner again. The whiff of antiseptic from the medical bay flashed me back to my cell at Elditch...

I fought the vertigo that pulled me out of reality.

Not now. Stay in the present moment.

"We are to follow them," Trix said.

Our crew exited the holding room, passing through the medical bay and into the corridor. The soft yellow light held humid condensation. My suit warmed, the atmosphere unlike the cold shuttle. Trix enjoyed the heat, and the round question-mark curl on her head was perky as ever.

At least one of us was healthier on the QyronNexa.

"Our escorts have requested no talking," I translated.

You and I can talk, though, right, Trix? I thought.

"It is best if you stay silent. They can tell when I am talking to you."

How is that possible?

"It is the same for you—they hear language but cannot understand the meaning. It is very impolite to talk in another language around the Kaseath."

Proving the point, the front guard stared with deep, unfriendly eyes. I shut the heck up.

Trix asked the guards more questions in their language, but they didn't respond. Our escort seemed unconcerned that Trix was part of our cavalcade. They treated her no differently than their human visitors. Why weren't they happy to see her?

We approached a new corridor, and Trix mimed putting down our visors. Our crew, except Griffin, secured our gold helmet visors.

I helped Griffin, who had forgotten protocol and stared out the window in awe.

"Here, let me help," I said.

"Are we friends?" Griffin asked without irony.

I slapped her visor into place before she suffered a solar-sized sunburn. "Just keep quiet. You're embarrassing us."

I imagined Griffin's grin beneath my impenetrable reflection. Her state of mind wasn't helping the nerves that shimmied around my tummy, putting pressure on my innards. Who would protect our crew?

We entered the massive six-storey atrium. A window-fronted area, like a grand casino lobby, overlooked black space. The shimmering, glass-like material improved our view of Earth, the moon, and the distant Ark. Inside the atrium, grand, carved white columns reached the ceiling high above the scattered seating. Layers curved like a rice paddy gradient up a mountain.

From this view, Earth appeared tiny. That precarious sphere contained my whole life.

Kaseath swished about, lounged in seats, or silently conversed in groups.

Seeing the gathering was unnerving. Their silent words rippled through the atrium, chattering in my mind like a crowd's roar at a football game, overwhelming my senses.

The Kaseath noticed us, and all language ceased.

At least a hundred aliens fixed their voiceless, emotionless stare at us.

Even Griffin stepped back, taken out of her pleasant haze.

Trix, however, spread her arms wide to catch the glorious space radiation. She put her arms back down at the guard's stare.

"This is our recreation area, where we relax and recharge."

Our alien escort turned, and Trix kept quiet.

The waterfall of alien language flowed into my mind via Trix. She connected with her kind, and the alien chatter grew animated. It was impossible to interpret their reaction to our crew without body language or facial expressions, but the flowing babble seemed curious.

Curious or harmful—we were in their home, scrutinised by at least a hundred Kaseath.

The aliens turned their attention to me.

My face heated beneath my helmet, and I was glad for the privacy of the gold visor. The Kaseath observed us moving towards the opulent columns.

Our escort led us to a spacious elevator, large enough for our crew, Trix, and escorts. Once inside, we rode to the sixth floor.

The lift arrived, and we exited, passing more Kaseath on the circular walkway, flanking the uppermost floor. Aliens crowded closer in the much narrower space. The Kaseath stared at us as we passed.

Another alien read a handheld device and almost collided with Trix. The other alien's concentration broke, and she noticed us approaching. The perky, scaled, soft-serve droop at the tip of her head was a little misshapen. Compared to Trix, and the other Kaseath, it bent like a broken radio antenna, pointing to the side instead of ending in a neat, question-mark fold.

Her face was passive, but she maintained eye contact with Trix. They spoke briefly—what they said was unintelligible—and then moved on.

Who was that? I thought to Trix.

"You might call her my sister."

That's amazing! I bet she was relieved to see you, I thought, glad to take my mind off the aliens' piercing stares.

"Yes, she was."

Will you catch up with your family later?

"That is up to Hulgrod. I may never be accepted as a true Kaseath again."

What do you mean?

Our escort turned around, blocking our progress. They stared at Trix. "We must stop conversing now, Ofelia."

Sure. I mean, sorry, I did it again—shutting up.

I considered Trix's predicament. She'd learned humans' ways and was rusty amongst her kind. But there must be others like her daughter, sister, and mother. People who could vouch for her.

Did Trix know everything, as she claimed? Could the Kaseath have discovered the cure years ago and compartmentalised the facts? They couldn't hold every piece of information from all time. Trix had confirmed this.

An ancient cure could be possible—we just had to extract it from the history of their knowledge.

Griffin tripped in front of me, and I collided with her.

"What's wrong?" I asked her.

Griffin frowned at the sticky flooring and stood stock still. She lifted her boot and watched the sludge flow back into the floor.

"Don't you think it's weird?"

I rolled my eyes. "Keep going, doofus."

Instead of outright hostility, Griffin replied breezily, "Copy that."

Still a soldier, even after a shot of make-me-compliant-and-forget-everything.

The aliens led us to a holding room. It faced a smaller atrium overflowing with white carvings and scattered seats where the Kaseath conversed. We were more like guests here than experimental fodder, and my hopes climbed. Was the medical room incident forgiven?

"We are to wait here," Trix said.

Our military guards stood outside the room, preventing us from leaving.

Okay, less like guests and more like rotisserie chickens for the Kaseath's feeding pleasure. However, the Kaseath only ate space radiation.

We perched on the seats, ready to spring into action. My heart pounded at a running pace. I checked that my camera was still recording. I thought about Maya aboard Valentina One and fought to return my attention to the moment. The Kaseath knew little about humans, right? So how could they understand what made us sick—or cured us?

"Trix says we can lift our visors."

We lifted them, glad not to stare at our warped reflections in the gold sheen. Now, I could study people's expressions.

"Let's align with the plan." Lopez hushed her tone as we huddled in the holding room. "We still need the cure. Doctor, are you ready for your diagnostics?"

Figg replied, "I can analyse the cure with my scanner."

"Good. Ask Trix if Hulgrod will have the cure nearby."

I translated, "Trix confirms there's no cure. But the Kaseath compartmentalise information. The details might be lost."

Trix observed me, raising the places where her eyebrows should have been. I shrugged in reply.

"Or the Kaseath might not believe they have it," Griffin said, pleased with herself for remembering, glancing at Figg.

Figg weighed her words. "I have seen the object of our mission."

My heart jolted, and I scrutinised Figg to see if she was lying. Lopez and Griffin also stared at Figg.

"It can't be possible," Lopez said.

"It's true," Figg continued, appearing contrite. "We found something amongst the wreckage of Trix's ship. But the object was badly damaged."

"Doctor Figg is lying," Trix said.

"Why are you lying?" I asked Figg.

"Trust me, Trix doesn't know everything, or she's hiding information." Figg's curious smile challenged Trix.

Lopez glanced at our guards. "After seeing the Kaseath reaction, it's possible. Trix might withhold sensitive details."

The tipping sensation returned, the floor less steady beneath me. Conflicting feelings swirled around—distrust of Trix and massive pangs of disloyalty. Didn't I owe her my life? But when Lopez and Figg agreed, it felt real—this could be confirmation that Imogen's cure was obtainable. What would Trix do to return to her kind? In her situation, I'd do almost anything.

"Ofelia said the Kaseath can't lie." Lopez scrutinised me.

Figg stepped forward. "The Kaseath didn't have body language either until Trix was stranded on Earth and had to communicate. Beings evolve. Maybe they *can* lie. I bet Trix has learned that by now."

"Learned from a deceitful human like you," I scoffed, my reaction automatic.

"I would never lie to you, Ofelia." Figg's eyes crinkled with sincerity.

Was she telling the truth?

"Tell us what you found, Doctor." Lopez peered at the guards.

"It's a purple crystal about the length of my palm. The

Kaseath will hold it close. It's small enough for a person to carry. Hulgrod may have it with her."

"Why not mention it until now?"

"I hoped not to divulge too much before we reached the Kaseath."

My head spun as I assessed Figg. She believed her words. Was this the TV-facing public relations figure working for the PM, spinning a half-truth? This was our best lead.

"So, where's the crystal?" Lopez stood, moving towards Trix.

Lopez set her feet on the floor, bringing her body close—a challenge of authority.

"The crystal is not the cure," I translated, frowning at Trix.

Now, I was furious with my alien friend. Instead of feeling powerless, I felt solidarity with my crew. Some of my hope returned.

"We demand that you cooperate." Lopez stepped closer to Trix. Lopez was no match for Trix's height, but her intentions were clear. Trix was under Lopez's command.

"This crystal is more dangerous than any cure." Trix stood taller at Lopez's challenge. "It could destroy the QyronNexa, the Ark, and even your planet."

"How could the cure do that?" I asked.

"What did she say?" Lopez said.

"She said it's too dangerous."

"Yes, too dangerous for us not to pursue it." Figg stood shoulder-to-shoulder with Lopez.

It was all too much for Griffin, who returned to batting her Velcro pockets with a weird-ass grin.

It grated against every atom of every cell in my entire being, but I agreed with Figg.

"We've got to get that cure, whatever it takes." I ran my

fingertips over the rubber ball in my pocket. "I made a promise."

Our crew studied each other, our loyalties splintering. Griffin viewed Trix curiously rather than sizing her up as a threat. Lopez stepped back, monitoring her whole crew. Figg studied readouts on her scanner, and I listened to Trix's thoughts. But she spoke in her language, which I didn't understand. She tapped into a communal conversation, and I realised what she meant about 'all things are known to everyone'. The thoughts rose and ebbed like a symphony—the Kaseath spoke as one.

Maybe I would understand their language someday—but we were out of time. We had to obtain the cure and return to Earth.

Our alien military escort stepped into the holding room. Trix put a finger to her lips.

Lopez nodded to Griffin. "Stay alert."

Griffin popped a blue gum bubble and casually resumed chewing. Our crew filed out of the holding room.

We travelled through the centre of the atrium, which was abuzz with Kaseath conversations that my human crew couldn't hear. As we passed, they turned to watch. We were a curiosity, like travelling circus performers.

But we were prisoners, a number rather than a person. My mind flashed back to the cold cell of the research facility. I sent a death glare to Figg, but she was busy taking everything in, her hand in her pocket, holding her precious scanner. Lopez's face was unreadable, and Griffin's expression held wonder at the sights. I couldn't face Trix because I didn't want to reveal my feelings. I no longer trusted her, but that was just self-preservation, clinging to hope, however minuscule. It wasn't a betrayal. Or was it?

We approached two massive doors set into the wall. The guards halted.

This was the moment we'd trained for. Everything hung on this meeting.

Our crew milled at the door, like long-extinct cows waiting for milking—or, perhaps, the slaughterhouse. My heart felt ready to pound right out of my chest, and I ignored my Comm-Link flashing for me to keep my cool. Well, flashing my rapid heart rate, at least.

The military escort stood to attention.

The doors opened onto a cavernous throne room about the length of a football field. A squishy purple pathway led to a massive throne.

And sitting on the throne, at the opposite end, was Hulgrod herself.

CHAPTER 14

TWENTY GUARDS STOOD to attention as we entered, flanking the pathway. They carried handheld laser guns and were on high alert. Each guard wore the same purple neck collars as our military escort.

If the Kaseath wanted to intimidate, they had succeeded. My stomach felt squished by diabolical clamps. My crew seemed just as nervous—except for our space cadet, Griffin. She grinned as if we had entered a fairground and she'd joined the roller coaster queue.

The room was eerily silent, but I felt Trix talking to Hulgrod, and then our military escort marched us forward.

The oversized throne sat on a platform accessed by a decorative ramp. The structure was the same gunmetal grey material as the ship's exterior. Purple flooring led to the throne. White columns rose; intricate designs, like ripples of flowing water, were carved into them. The pillars' height was lost in the murky ceiling, but the throne itself was smooth and commanding.

Our escort marched us to the ramp's base. Hulgrod sat on the raised throne, her direct gaze unnerving. She remained silent and imposing.

Our military escorts stood to the side. I nudged closer to my crew for safety. We were like cats huddling under cover to avoid the rain, waiting for a thunderstorm of authority.

The Kaseath were in charge. We were a mere annoyance.

"Greetings, Hulgrod." Lopez kept her voice calm and even. How could she find confidence now?

Trix relayed our message, and I repeated Hulgrod's reply via Trix.

"Hulgrod wishes it were under friendlier circumstances."

"We apologise for the medical bay incident," Lopez said.

"We expected your aggression," Hulgrod replied via Trix, then via me.

Lopez raised her eyebrow at Griffin, who grinned, entranced by the entertaining show.

Griffin frowned as if remembering and said, "It was an accident. You guys are awesome! Why would I shoot you?"

"I will concede this time," I translated for Hulgrod, "but future transgressions will have dire consequences for your species."

Griffin nodded, her expression contrite.

"We hope to strike a deal," Lopez said.

"The Kaseath have been watching your Earth for decades now, in your years," Hulgrod replied. "We have watched you mismanage your environment and destroy each other. The Kaseath will prevent you from leaving Earth and contaminating the worlds beyond. Your existence threatens the balance of the universe. We must maintain this balance, whatever the cost."

Lopez glanced at me as I translated, then responded.

"I am sorry you feel that way, Hulgrod. Our leaders have made mistakes. But surely, self-preservation is a universal truth for all beings?"

"Self-preservation is not a universal truth. The Kaseath

would sacrifice our species for the balance of the universe. It is why we are babysitting you."

Lopez shifted her gaze to the floor. "The Kaseath brought a plague to Earth. Our doctor has seen the cure, and we respectfully ask that you share it. In exchange, we will return Trix. This shows our peaceful intentions."

"We do not have this cure you seek." Hulgrod turned her head.

"Doctor Figg says she has seen the cure. You are to share it." Lopez averted her gaze, as if embarrassed.

"Where has your doctor seen the cure?"

"Our team found a crystal aboard Trix's crashed ship." Figg's voice cracked with uncertainty. Even she was intimidated by the alien leader. Hulgrod paused, and the wave of language passing over me ceased.

She waved her hand over the throne's armrest, and a small container rose as if on an invisible string. A gleaming purple crystal necklace levitated out of the container. The crystal within was about the size of my palm, hanging like a pendant. It rose into mid-air, hovering above the armrest.

So, it did exist!

"Is this the crystal your doctor speaks of?" Hulgrod said.

"Yes, that's the same crystal!" Figg said, her eyes entranced by the small object. We all were.

Relief overwhelmed my senses, and I could only stare at the cure for my little sister. I grinned as the crystal's light reflected in my eyes. Darker, purple liquid swished inside the crystal. Orbs of light broke free and swirled, captivating our crew.

I was confused, wondering why Trix had said there was no cure. Here was the answer to our fears—the saviour of all humanity. We just had to persuade Hulgrod to share it.

"This is not the cure you seek," Trix relayed.

Mesmerised by the crystal, I forgot to translate, realising the language flowing in my mind still raced on. Lopez nudged me.

"What is Hulgrod saying?"

"She says that our doctor is lying, that this is confirmation that humans are not fit to exist. We are forbidden to have this crystal."

"We thought the Kaseath couldn't lie," Lopez said.

"Everything is known to all beings. Ask your doctor for the truth," I translated.

The crystal's purple light reflected in Figg's eyes, which were gleaming with tears—of happiness? The fulfilment of her life's work, saving humanity from extinction.

Emotion overtook me—elation at finding the cure and anger at Trix's betrayal. I blinked away tears, locking my attention on the crystal. It was the most elegant, perfect thing I had ever seen. The falling sensation was gone. I could finally help my sister.

Who was being truthful—Hulgrod or Figg? Was Trix translating faithfully? Or were we embarking on a merry caper of fabrications and distrust?

As much as I hated to admit it, I trusted Figg. How else would she have described the cure?

"So you won't share the crystal?" Lopez asked.

"Correct," Hulgrod said. "It represents a danger to everyone on this ship. It could destroy all beings and burn a hole in time and space. We will not share this with you."

"Then you have doomed humanity," Lopez said.

"We will accept Trix aboard this ship, and you are welcome to return to yours. You will remain on Earth. There will be no further expeditions beyond your world. This is not negotiable."

"We will only trade Trix for the cure." Lopez stepped forward.

Forty alien military escorts also stepped forward, drawing their weapons and pointing them at our backs.

"Your novelty has expired," Hulgrod said. "I will keep Ofelia for further testing because of her shared DNA. We may learn from her. Afterwards, you are free to return to your shuttle. We will use force if you cannot comply."

I relayed this to the crew, then added, "Trix says that Hulgrod won't budge."

"Your response disappoints us," Lopez said. "We don't want war with the Kaseath."

"Likewise. Go in peace, human. You would be wise to heed our commands. Trix will remain with your party to facilitate communication before reporting to my quarters."

Hulgrod leaned back on her oversized throne and stared as our military escorts flanked our party, indicating the end of the conversation.

What now, Trix? I asked, my prior elation dissipating. We had been so close!

"Is that the end?" Figg's disappointment was apparent.

I hated that Figg and I shared this feeling.

Trix turned to me. "Do as Hulgrod says. We will not win a confrontation with the Kaseath."

The crew fell into line between the escorts.

I was the eternal lab rat—a dangerous curiosity. What tests would they run? I flashed back to the research facility, the cell door clanging open to reveal Dr Figg, menacing as ever. Except this time, the doctor was a Kaseath, wielding a pain-inflicting medical device.

I followed the rest of our crew as the military escort marched us from the throne room. Our mission seemed as doomed as ever.

What would I tell Imogen now?

The escort returned us to our cell behind the medical bay. The door slid shut, locking us in. Trix couldn't open the door—it was locked from the outside. The room lacked windows, vents, or any other exit. Lopez addressed our crew.

"Our mission's gone sideways. I guess we return to our ship now."

"The prime minister won't be pleased." Figg paced the small room. "We don't have the cure or the Kaseath's permission for the Ark mission. Plus, we're losing our only bargaining chip—they're taking Trix."

"We're not giving Ofelia over for testing," Lopez said.

"I'm used to tests." I stared at Figg, who, to her credit, withered under my challenge.

"Maybe the tests are harmless," Griffin said, still cheery.

"Of course, that's the condition of allowing them," Figg said.

"Thanks for backing me up," I said under my breath.

Once again, Figg was ready to throw me under the hover bus whenever it suited.

"We can't sanction the testing if the Kaseath won't cooperate," Lopez said.

"We must return to the shuttle and restore communication." Figg glanced at Griffin, who sobered under her glare.

What were those two up to?

"We don't have another choice," Lopez said. "Trix, is there a way out?"

Trix's words washed over me, but I didn't want to believe them.

"She says if we escape, there will be dire consequences for more than just our crew. The Kaseath will wipe humans off our planet."

My voice cracked as a flash took over—Hulgrod, bashing the door of our home in Cookham East, as the imposing military Kaseath swarmed, grabbing my frail sister...

"So we let them experiment on Ofelia and return empty-handed?" Figg asked. Of our crew, she was the only one without a family on Earth. I was her only family, an experiment, her Frankenstein creation.

"Trix tells me there would be no permanent damage and minimal pain," I said. "And the alternative means the end of human civilisation."

"Mass extinction," Lopez said.

"They can try." Griffin reached for her missing laser gun.

"I can't jeopardise one of my crew," Lopez said. "My job is to keep you safe and return to Earth."

Figg said, "We must take the crystal."

That stopped everyone faster than a brick wall appearing on a four-lane highway. It was ballsy, even for Figg. Lopez didn't like it.

"You heard Hulgrod. Our mission has failed. We're returning without the cure. The alternative means human extinction. Everyone we've known and loved..."

"I must insist." Figg held her shoulders straighter in confrontation.

Lopez matched Figg's body language, squaring her shoulders. "I am in command of this mission, and the best course of action is to return to the shuttle and determine our next steps from Mission Control."

"But you can't contact Mission Control without comms with our ship," Figg said.

"Correct," Lopez replied warily. "What are your intentions?"

"That means, technically, I outrank you."

"What do you mean? You're a civilian."

"Prime Minister Pollins saw to that before we left." Figg held her head higher. "I have Admiral status—honorary until now—but I can pull rank anytime."

"Why would you pull rank? We can't confirm your status without comms. Why didn't you mention this sooner?"

"Our mission is to obtain the crystal, whatever the cost."

"And how will we do that?" Lopez asked. "It's well-guarded and difficult to access. And we're conspicuous. We can't roam onboard the ship."

"Even if we could access the throne room, Hulgrod won't let us keep the cure," I said.

Griffin said, "Couldn't we enter when Hulgrod's not there? Nobody would know we took the crystal."

Griffin made sense. Her space-cadet grin morphed into a sly smile, and she returned to her usual combative self.

"Does Hulgrod leave the throne room?" Figg asked, warming to Griffin's plan.

"Yes, she is only there for official occasions," I translated. "She spends most of her time in the command centre."

"And the guards?"

"The guards follow Hulgrod for her safety."

"But won't Hulgrod take the crystal with her?" Lopez asked.

"When not used, the crystal is stored in the throne."

"And they're about to let Ofelia free-range in the medical bay," Figg continued. "We've seen Ofelia's powers. She could escape from the alien doctors and unlock our cell door, and then Trix could act as our Kaseath escort back to the throne room. We break in and out before anyone notices, grabbing the crystal. Hotfoot it back to the shuttle and return to Earth."

"Easy as, humanity saved!" Griffin grinned, then winced. The sedation was wearing off.

"This would start a war with the Kaseath." I wrestled with

my terrifying vision—the one where we nuked the Kaseath's ship, destroying everything around it.

"There's no alternative." Figg's eyes moistened with tears. Was she sincere?

"I'm ready for battle," Griffin said, way too cheerfully. She was only ever upbeat about a fight. Yep, she was getting back to normal.

"We won't win a war with the Kaseath," Lopez said. "Hulgrod was right—they have superior technology, which gives them an advantage. I'm not sure it's worth it."

"You're saying it's not worth saving my sister?" I said, incensed. "You're saying it's okay for her to die?"

"That's not what I meant..."

"But it is," I said. "It's *exactly* what you meant."

Lopez was ganging up on me. Fear sifted back into my being, a familiar panic brewing. Would she back out because the situation was difficult?

They didn't know suffering. I did—it was melted into my DNA at birth, from a singed hearth in our shack in Northies. I wouldn't fail Imogen.

Figg said, "Commander, we proceed as I suggested. And that's an order."

Lopez's jaw clenched, but she kept her expression neutral. She didn't enjoy this challenge to her command, but she followed the rules. There was no way to disprove Figg's ranking status without comms to our ship.

The tension was incredible. Lopez curled her fist as if punching Figg would stop her insubordination. Lopez wasn't impressed with me, either.

As Figg and Lopez faced off, the door sluiced open. Two armed guards stood beside three alien doctors dressed in white aprons.

I searched for Lopez's reaction. But instead of lashing out, Lopez looked away.

I touched her shoulder. "Even though I agree with Figg, I'm not taking her orders. You're my commander."

"Then it's my order," Lopez said evenly. A rage vein pulsed beside her temple, but we could not see an alternative. As unlikely as Figg was as an ally, I believed her. This was the way to save Imogen.

The moment held. Figg had always had the power, outplaying me. I had one option—to do as she wished, even though my heart blackened.

I would start an unwinnable war to save my sister.

The guards by the door shuffled, and one doctor waved me into the medical bay.

I stepped into the medical room. The door snapped shut behind me, locking my crew inside the cell.

CHAPTER 15

THE HEAD DOCTOR, Assuth, waved to a bed in the medical bay. I recognised her shorter stature and the shooting asteroid symbol on her white apron.

Even in the room's humidity, nervous sweat cooled beneath my space suit, and I shivered, eyeing the two medical doctors assisting Assuth. Two military grunts stood by the door inside the medical bay. They observed as I approached the raised bed.

Five aliens to subdue—three medical doctors and two military personnel. And then a ship's worth of Kaseath once we escaped the medical bay.

The mission ahead seemed treacherous without my crew, without backup—it was left to me.

Maya's friendly face would be welcome. The one person I'd thought would never lie—Trix—might have another agenda.

Assuth motioned for me to remove my helmet, but I wouldn't let them kill me that easily. I mimed choking on the lack of breathable air. A junior doctor offered a breathing tube plugged into the wall. The tube hissed softly, so I guessed it provided oxygen. If they'd taken humans before, those they'd abducted wouldn't have been dressed in full space suits. But did they keep their human experiments alive?

"Yes, they do," Trix said.

At least I could communicate with Trix, even though she was locked in the cell. Our thoughts bridged the space between us.

You'd better be right.

"You have been through worse before."

I doubted Trix's words as I eyed the medical doctors, who wore surgeons' coats and had icier bedside manners than Dr Figg.

I unclasped the airlock on my helmet, took a deep breath of the remaining air, and lifted it over my head.

A junior doctor took the helmet and placed it on a spare bed. Another handed me the breathing tube. First, I let out a lungful of air, anticipating sweet oxygen. I sucked in a mouthful—the air was stale, but it would keep me alive. My heart slowed as I considered my next move.

I sat on the bed, alert to what would follow. Assuth stepped forward. She pointed to my suit. De-suiting took a few minutes, leaving me in my snug grey undershirt and track pants.

The room was warm, like a humid summer's day back home, culminating in an afternoon tropical storm. My body shivered; I felt much colder than the room. I rubbed my arms.

The junior doctor laid my suit on the bed. She discovered the rubber ball in my breast pocket and held it up for Assuth to see, then placed it on the bed beside me.

Assuth encouraged me to lie down. I ensured the tube didn't twist from its position on the wall, conscious of needing oxygen. I lay down, breathing the stale air with a tinge of cleaning products, like an alien version of lemon-fresh dish-washing liquid. My tongue felt soapy, like I'd licked a plate straight from the sudsy sink.

But at least I could breathe.

Assuth ran her scanner up and down my body. A slight

pinching sensation followed the scanned area. The scanners hadn't hurt before, so I assumed they took a deeper image. Assuth paid particular attention to the scanner's light affecting my irises.

The junior doctors assisted Assuth in taking pictures of my body. One motioned for me to lift my shirt, revealing the rash of scales across my belly. She lingered over an external examination, taking more pictures, and then withdrew blood with the aid of a medical device that was more painful than the needles Figg used. Assuth motioned for me to take a deep breath, then moved the cup to one side while I opened my mouth. She took a swab of saliva. I resumed breathing air from the tube.

Assuth positioned a sizeable medical device above my head. A metallic contraption—wait, was that an electric drill? Were they about to perform a dental procedure? Was my novelty over, and now I'd be chopped into pieces—a diced human-alien hybrid, preserved for an age of experiments?

The tests were more invasive than I had hoped.

I felt the alien language—it was almost familiar now. While I didn't understand their words, they felt hostile, as if they were arguing.

The junior doctors left. Assuth remained, with the two military escorts flanking the door.

The military grunts stared ahead, clearly rating my threat levels as low, which played into my plans.

Assuth turned towards the samples she'd taken, transferring them to clean containers.

This was it—my chance to escape.

I eased my feet to the floor, lunging for the ball on the next bed. The breathing tube limited my progress, but my fingertips closed over the smooth rubber ball.

I threw it at the wall. It bounced back, creating a 'missile', activating my shield.

My shield stopped time. I'd caught myself cleanly, the dry heat of the force field cutting through the ship's humidity. Assuth was dropping my blood samples into a container. Now, I had the stealth advantage. They didn't know about my powers.

I ignored the glitching corner, the spark that peeled off and hit my arm. My powers threatened to fail, and Trix wasn't around to amp me with her jolt. I breathed deeply, avoiding a panic attack.

Just thinking of a panic attack made my bowels constrict.

To distract myself, I checked my space suit. I had to escape the medical bay, which meant holding my shield open while I suited up. There wasn't another option; I couldn't reach the door to my crew. The breathing tube didn't stretch that far.

I grabbed my suit, maintaining the frozen time, bringing the shield with me.

The air hung heavy and damp as I forced my legs into the constricting suit. The soapy taste was acidic now. A bead of sweat traced a path down my temple, the rough zipper catching on my skin as I pulled it closed. I secured the airlock on my boots and gloves.

I checked for my helmet—which sat on the other bed. Farther than the breathing tube reached.

My shield flickered at the edges—another sign that my time-stop approached its limit. More sparks shot off, striking my cheek.

The shield failed, restarting time.

The rubber ball clinked against the floor.

Two military grunts turned at the sound.

The first guard lurched forward, noticing me out of bed. The other guard flinched, as did Assuth.

Sucking in one last breath from the breathing tube, I leaped towards my helmet, shoving it on—no time to enact the seal to deliver oxygen. I held my breath as the first alien guard aimed their laser gun at me.

Lopez's words from training came back to me: "*You've got one breath, recruit. What do you do?*"

The laser fired. I enacted my shield.

The ray crackled close to my body, charring the outer layer of my suit. I risked swivelling the airlock on my helmet with a satisfying click. The wheeze of oxygen was the best sound. My panic dipped as I sucked the sweeter air back into my lungs. I concentrated on the shield where the laser stung, singeing my suit.

My concentration failed, and I let the shield go and dropped to the floor, rolling out of the laser's way.

There was no time to panic. I grabbed the rubber ball and commando-rolled into the first military escort, my body weight aimed at their slug-like feet. The alien tripped over me and fell, not expecting my assault. The other grunt approached. I pushed from the spongy floor around the splayed first guard.

The second guard shot off her laser gun. This time, my defence was better. My shield stopped time, the three aliens caught in front again. I felt less exposed now that I was back in my suit. Hoping beyond hope that my powers would last. My wrist comm already blinked its heart rate warnings. Could I deflect the laser back onto the guards?

I shifted my shield, assessing the angle. Then I slanted the force forward as I dropped my shield. The laser complied, shooting back at the alien, a burn glancing off her hand. She hadn't expected the rebounded attack, so she hadn't enacted her shield. She dropped the gun, grabbing her hand. Her pain flashed as a distorted crackle in my mind. The first guard went to the injured guard, abandoning me altogether.

I jabbed the panel to open the cell door. Assuth threw a scalpel at me, blade first. I swivelled just in time to repel it before it hit. With my shield open, I unlocked the cell door, keeping time stopped.

"Gotta go!" I shouted to my crew. They huddled behind my shield, so time travelled forward for them.

My crew, including Trix, stepped in the wake of my shield. Trix projected her touch through my suit, and my power surged with new electrical energy. My shield solidified, forming vital greens, and the crackling sparks dimmed.

Once my crew were crowded behind my shield, I inched closer to the medical bay door, struggling to keep the force field open. Griffin relieved the guards of their laser guns, cocking them at the ready.

"Just stay behind me," I said.

"Copy that." Griffin armed her new weapons.

Figg plucked the scalpel from mid-air, where it grazed my shield.

Trix assessed the scene in the medical bay.

"I will help you if I can," she said. "But I cannot hurt my kind."

I understand.

We had one opportunity to escape.

I checked out the two alien escorts—one on the ground, holding her twiggy-fingered hand in pain, the other bending to help her, and then Assuth, in the aftermath of throwing her scalpel.

Trix slapped the panel to open the medical bay doors, taking us into the corridor. We inched past the alien guards and doctor, frozen in their response. I gritted my teeth, concentrating on the fresh pain near my chest where the laser had glanced off.

My shield flickered.

I concentrated on the shield instead of my pain receptors.

Our crew piled into the corridor. The alien doctor and two

escorts remained behind us. I couldn't wait for the door to close again before dropping my shield.

Two additional guards flanked the outer door beside us.

Griffin reacted first, shoulder-charging one guard into the other. They lost their footing and sprawled on the ground. One guard dropped her weapon, and I grabbed it. I aimed at the guards' heads, and the other surrendered, handing her gun to Trix.

Now our crew was armed, at large, and freakin' dangerous!

Trix clipped the guard's purple collar around her neck. She completed her disguise with the laser gun, making her indistinguishable from the military aliens.

I pointed the muzzle of my weapon at the guards and motioned them through the door into the medical bay we'd just left. The door shut behind them, and Trix keyed in a code. The door armed, a red light blinking on the panel.

Trix said, "The emergency lockdown code. They cannot open the door until it is deactivated from the outside."

"Right, gather around, people," Griffin said. "If you're happy with me taking the reins, Commander?"

"This is your domain, Griffin," Lopez replied.

I hoped Griffin was back to her usual trigger-happy self. That hope was a surprising development.

"We'll act like prisoners. Put your weapons in your pockets. Do not engage unless someone fires on us first. Agreed?"

"My suit is losing integrity," I said, pointing to the charred area.

"Then we'd better make this quick," Griffin said.

"Are you injured?" Lopez asked, concerned.

"I'll be okay." I sounded braver than I felt.

Trix straightened the military collar that she'd swiped from the guard.

"Won't they punish you for helping us?" I asked Trix out loud.

"I will help you, but I won't harm another Kaseath. If I do, they will never allow me to return."

"What did she say?" Lopez said.

"She's sticking with us for now."

We shoved our guns in the pockets of our space suits, and Trix fell behind, aiming a laser at our backs. I placed a gloved hand over the charring on my suit, trying not to look suspicious.

Well, more suspicious than our crew currently appeared.

"Straight to the lift," Trix said, and I led the group towards the throne room.

"Won't the doctors make the mind meld with the rest of the Kaseath?"

"They are not used to projecting their thoughts as we can," Trix replied. "They need to be in closer proximity."

"Like a physical link to each other?"

"Yes."

The corridors were empty until we hit the atrium, and I thanked all the gods who existed. Unless Trix clued them in, the Kaseath there wouldn't know anything was amiss.

Our human crew put down our gold visors.

There were fewer Kaseath than before, lounging in seats or huddled around benches. As I attuned to their words, the language felt familiar.

The Kaseath glanced our way in what I hoped was a curious, rather than suspicious, manner. We continued towards the lift in the large atrium.

Trix concentrated, resisting the mind-meld with the rest of her kind. The Kaseath knew all things, including Trix's thoughts. Her conflicted nature resisted the one thing that bound her to her people.

Will it help to talk? I thought to Trix.

"That would not help. They will know that you are the human-alien hybrid. I must concentrate."

I understand. We're almost at the lift.

If I was sweating buckets, the rest of our crew was nervous, too. They stared straight ahead, as inconspicuous as a group of four humans and a fake Kaseath military escort could be.

We arrived at the lift, and I reached to press the button—but Trix shoved her body in front and pushed it for me.

"You are under my command, remember?" Trix glanced at the other aliens.

Sorry.

The wait for the lift was excruciating. The Kaseath hadn't registered our group's danger, and our mirrored visors concealed how worried my crew was.

The lift arrived, and we stepped in and ascended.

We arrived in the corridor with the holding room. We scooted past the Kaseath, who were lumbering down the halls with their rolling, sludgy feet. This time, they weren't curious—more mildly alarmed. Or was that just my interpretation of their language? It came in bursts, and each Kaseath assessed us as we moved into the inner atrium towards the ornate, carved white doors.

Our crew approached the entrance to the throne room. We lifted the gold visors, silently checking on each other. Griffin nodded at Trix.

Trix swiped at the control panel and opened the door.

Our crew stepped into the cavernous throne room.

CHAPTER 16

THE ENORMOUS THRONE room was darker than before, shrouding the purple path before us. At the other end, the throne sat on its platform above the flat area below.

The guards were gone, which felt eerie, like an imprint of unseen beings watched us. The silence beat in my ears as if sound was the blood vessels pulsing through my skull.

As we crept forward, I imagined the Kaseath morphing from the shadows, aiming lasers at my head. My rapid heart-beat induced queasiness, like I was in the zero-g of the shuttle. I was also as jittery as if I'd just drunk a whole jug of the nasty powdered coffee on board Valentina One. I couldn't wait to get out of this room, preferably alive.

And with the cure.

Griffin led the charge to the throne at the other end. The ground was semi-soft, and the slight squelching of our boots echoed around the enormous space. We followed Griffin, focusing on the throne holding the crystal.

We hesitated at the base of the ramp, and Lopez asked Trix, "What now?"

"Only a Kaseath can open the chamber," I translated.

Trix moved towards the platform, but she hesitated.

"Trix asks if we're sure," I said. "Once she opens the chamber, there is no return."

Figg exchanged a look with Griffin. Lopez appealed to each of us, and I averted my gaze from her scrutiny. Siding with Figg felt like a betrayal. This wasn't what Lopez, our commander, wanted. But it was the only way.

"Alright then," Lopez said. "For humanity."

Trix approached the platform and climbed the tall ramp. She settled on the throne and stretched her three-fingered hands over the armrest.

A laser shot out of the throne's base, angled towards the room.

Shooting directly at our crew!

I threw up my shield without thinking, just reacting.

The laser's power exceeded the handheld guns the Kaseath used. I ground my teeth and immobilised the massive ray.

My crewmates huddled behind the shield, watching the laser spark and fission on the other side. It danced like a shooting comet, fizzing, trying to penetrate my defences.

Trix's forward time had stopped. Would additional lasers fire from the throne?

"Are you okay, Ofelia?" Figg asked, and I glanced back at my worried crew's faces.

"I've got this." I hardly believed myself. My concentration was strung like beads on a too-tight wire.

I let the shield drop, absorbing the laser's power. Trix noticed my scarlet face, hot from the laser's heat.

"Are you alright?" she asked.

"The throne is booby-trapped," I replied.

"It is booby-what?"

"There are traps to protect the crystal."

"Shall we stop?"

"No, keep going, just—slowly."

Trix nodded. She laid her hand back over the throne's arm, which opened at her touch.

Three lasers flew at our party, glancing off in each direction: centre, right, then left.

I threw up my shield again, but this time it was weaker. The laser glanced off the shield and almost hit Lopez. She dove behind my flank just in time.

Figg and Griffin were already safe behind me. I raised my eyebrows at Lopez as she lay on the spongy floor.

"Careful," I said. "Stay behind me."

She took a breath. "No need to repeat."

She pushed up from the ground, brushing off her suit, wet from the squidgy flooring. The liquid left a yellowish residue on her suit. Figg helped Lopez while I struggled to keep the shield open. She ran her medical scanner over Lopez's suit in case the sludge was toxic.

"It's just the Kaseath's waste product." Figg twitched her eyebrow. "It's harmless."

"Gross," Griffin said.

I dropped my shield, and Trix remained stock-still, waiting for us to be ready.

Trix held her position.

I regained my breath. "Right. Do it!"

Trix held her hand over the open container on the arm of the throne. The steps of the throne parted beneath her. I braced for what was to come. Could I do this? I imagined my family at home. Doubt forced itself into my thoughts like a tiny splinter. Just enough pain to distract my concentration. Maybe I wouldn't see them again? Did our mission fail? Did that explosion happen in the end?

The container opened at Trix's touch.

A fireball.

As tall as me.

Flying towards us!

We felt the heat before I enacted my shield. This was a colossal force, searingly terrible. The flames licked around my shield, and Lopez, Griffin, and Figg pressed behind me, crouching to avoid the tentacles of scorching heat.

One blazing finger reached out from the right flank of my shield. It licked the side of my helmet, its power seeping through. I ducked, but the flash singed my cheek. My concentration slipped as the pain registered.

My shield flickered. I heaved a breath to distract myself from the pain.

Crouching low, I fought the force on the other side.

My shield grew smaller, absorbing the energy. Every muscle tensed, every particle of me focussed. The fireball swirled and massed on the other side of my force field. Would my shield disappear with the fireball? Would the fire consume us?

"Aaargh!!" I deflected the blast back towards the throne, dropping it so Trix would have time to react.

The fireball rebounded into itself, swirling back to Trix.

I stepped forward, my boots squelching.

Trix and I enacted our shields together as the fireball retreated and advanced. We stopped time on both sides of the throne.

We struggled to hold our duelling force fields up, and Trix held her fingers over the container.

The crystal floated upwards as if pulled by an invisible string. Trix waited until the entire pendant pulled free, then grabbed the chain.

"Ready to neutralise this sucker?" I asked.

"What is sucking?" Trix replied, confused.

"Ingest the fireball. On three. One, two... three!"

Trix and I drew the energy back into our shields. The fireball imploded, absorbed by the force fields. We threw the energy into the ceiling of the cavernous space, and the flames dissipated.

A scattering of fiery embers floated down like ignited orange rain. They landed on the ground, and the wet surface ingested the embers, leaving a grey, ashen trace.

Our crew checked each other for injuries. Lopez rubbed her shoulder where she'd dived away from the lasers. Figg blinked at the orbs of light from the fireball but seemed unhurt. Griffin might be injured but would never admit it. My right cheek had a slight burn from the fireball's tentacle. It was tender as I moved my cheeks, testing the pain levels.

Lopez slapped my shoulder, releasing the tension. We'd done it! We had the cure.

But we weren't safe.

As Trix climbed down from the throne, a piercing alarm sounded in the throne room, echoing around the enormous space like a squealing pig retreating from a meat cleaver.

Hulgrod knew where we were.

Trix joined the crew and handed the crystal to Figg, who ran her scanner over it. Her mouth was a surprised round shape at the results. She shared a look with Griffin, then turned her back on the crew, taking in the device's readouts.

"Is it the cure?" I shouted around the alarm.

"This will change everything." Figg shoved her device back in her pocket, her face in awe of the crystal's power.

She handed the crystal to Lopez, who tucked it into her breast pocket. My eyes followed like it was the last food tray in Northies.

We'd done it! I could save Imogen and the world. My sister could board the Ark.

But first, we had to escape the QyronNexa.

We sprinted down the purple path, which seemed to elongate. Trix swiped her hand to open the door. It took an enormous amount of time to open. We couldn't be caught in here.

Stepping through, we left the throne room behind us. Back to the smaller atrium, with the Kaseath on high alert as the alarm pierced the entire ship.

Our crew took advantage of the aliens' distraction. Nobody saw us leave the throne room, and Trix straightened her purple collar, digging her laser into my back.

None of the Kaseath stopped as we approached the lift that would take us into the large atrium. You know, the one filled with hundreds of Kaseath. Out of the frying pan and into our mission's most dangerous fireball yet.

We crowded into the lift, and Figg pushed the button to take us down.

My heart beat so fast that my CommLink blinked.

I ignored it. My pulse joined the red zone in the throbbing, heart-shaped graphic.

The lift opened into the atrium, which contained the Kaseath and the massive window to space. We slapped our visors back down.

The Kaseath chatter seemed concerned, if they could feel that emotion. They were disoriented, searching for the alarm's cause.

A dozen turned as we exited the lift. At least the ship's alarm drowned out the noise of my CommLink alerts. We were about as inconspicuous as buffaloes walking between a pride of lions drinking at the waterhole. The Kaseath outnumbered us, and their powers outstripped my own.

Trix nudged Lopez's back with the pointy end of her laser gun, and we moved towards the corridor that would take us back to our ship.

Trix hesitated.

"What's wrong?" Lopez whispered.

"She's resisting the mind meld," I said. "It's impossible with the Kaseath nearby."

"So let's jet," Griffin said.

Trix fell behind us. The aliens projected their chatter, their conversation like a physical thing reaching out, thought arms with an icy grip.

"All things are known to everyone," Trix said. "We must hurry."

The nearest Kaseath broke their silent conversation, staring at our crew. More Kaseath focussed their attention until the whole atrium monitored our every move.

Then, video screens on the atrium walls flickered to life, showing our escape from the throne room. The last frame ended with Lopez tucking the crystal into her suit pocket.

The Kaseath's silent chatter was outraged. Hulgrod appeared on the screen.

"Um, folks?" I stage-whispered to the crew a few steps ahead of me. "The cat has officially clawed out of the bag..."

"Run!" Griffin said.

We took off, with Trix sloping after us as rapidly as her slug-feet allowed.

The Kaseath sprang into activity. Several pursued us, while most fled out of the atrium.

A jumble of alien conversations confused my thoughts. I had a hard time hearing Trix.

"Keep going," she said.

Our crew had a marginal head start. The Kaseath moved slower than the humans but as fast as Trix. Figg, Griffin, Lopez, and I sprinted ahead, with Griffin pulling two laser guns from her pockets. She handed one to Lopez. I hoped we didn't have to use them. I didn't want to hurt anyone.

A dozen Kaseath pursued us from the atrium as we headed to the corridor leading to our ship. I snuck a glance behind—

none of them were armed. They were civilians, not guards, but their combined bulk was intimidating. Their stares fixed on me as they moved into the corridor. They blocked the way behind us like large, scaly-skinned vehicles barrelling in.

They gained ground on Trix.

The human crew sprinted along the doughy flooring, our moon boots leaving obvious impressions on the ground. We were easy to track. Trix fell behind.

I had to help Trix. I grabbed her hand and fused my energy with hers. She perked up and stepped more easily.

More thought-language overcame my consciousness, and the Kaseath parted, revealing two guards with purple collars.

My pupils widened, and Trix noticed.

One guard fired a laser gun at me.

Trix turned just in time. She enacted her shield. The laser glanced off its right flank, hovering in time at the edge, burning Trix's arm.

She grunted. I felt her pain shudder as she snatched her arm away from the laser. She almost dropped her shield with the loss of concentration.

Our crew, caught in the time-stop, noticed us trailing behind.

"Are you hurt?" I reached out to heal Trix's burn. She swiped her hand at the nearest door.

It slid open, leading into a dark space.

"Hide, Ofelia," Trix said.

"Hey, over here!" I beckoned to our crew.

They backtracked and joined us.

Trix grimaced and held her open wound, her bright orange veins pulsing. The brown-orange scales were already closing over, healing themselves. It was a small gash, but healing took energy. I placed my hand over hers, gifting another electric jolt.

Trix nodded through the door.

Griffin entered first, laser gun drawn. Figg followed, and Lopez was next.

They moved cautiously, and I wondered why until I followed.

The cavernous space seemed endless. It was cold in here, unlike the humidity of the rest of the ship, as my sweat cooled beneath my suit.

The vast room stretched before us, engulfed in gloom from floor to ceiling. The dim glow of our helmet's lights illuminated our narrow walkway. Others crisscrossed above and below, forming a network, like giant fingers reaching across the darkness. Vertigo took over as I realised a fall would be fatal.

The sizzle of Trix's shield folded in on itself as she followed us in and locked the door behind her.

Trix's powers weakened, far from radiation in the cold room. "They will not follow into this place."

Trix stood stock still, watching our crew shuffle into the cavernous arena.

"You're not coming with us?" I asked out loud.

"What's happening?" Lopez noticed Trix standing by the door.

"I can't betray my kind," Trix replied. "My place is on this ship."

I understand. The reality hit me.

Conflicting emotions surfaced. Had she betrayed us by keeping the cure from us? She knew the crystal existed. Despite that, we couldn't leave her behind. Could we?

The pain of a guilt-sharpened knife severed my innards, one careless slice at a time. She'd saved my life on many occasions. She understood me like no human could. We were connected, our DNA fused, like sisters. We had shared many adventures.

·"I cannot resist the mind meld with the other Kaseath," she said. "I will give your position away."

"But I don't want you to leave." Then I remembered Trix had denied the cure was real, even though it was in Lopez's pocket.

I'd do anything for a family reunion. I had to allow Trix the same choice. Leaving her behind was painful, but there would be unimaginable pain if we didn't make it safely home.

"This was always the plan," Trix said. "Me, for the cure. I hope Dr Figg can find this cure for you. I still believe you can save your sister."

But you don't believe the crystal is the cure.

"That is true."

Then you're lying.

"You know that to be an impossibility."

I'm sorry to end things this way, Trix. My loyalty is to my family. It has to be.

"Understood, Ofelia, and while it is a futile quest, good luck. I hope you succeed in your mission."

How could I leave Trix? But time was scarce.

"How are we doing, recruit?" Lopez asked.

"Trix is leaving us."

"Let's get the heck outta here!" Griffin said.

Trix handed me a tiny disc resembling their ship's metallic, solid liquid. "This will show you the way forward, wherever you are."

I shoved it into my breast pocket and smoothed over the Velcro.

Thanks, Trix.

"This will be considered treason, but I believe the Kaseath will forgive me. Do not tell me your plans, or they will be known to Hulgrod. Wait until after I am gone. Whatever happens, do not open the crystal."

A profound sadness filled me, and I threw my arms around Trix's middle—she was, after all, a seven-foot alien, and I was just a runty almost-sixteen-year-old. Our touch fizzed for the last time.

"I will be okay," Trix said, deep into my inner ear.

I lifted a hand in one last wave, and Trix returned the gesture.

She undid the clasp on her purple military collar, allowing it to fall to the floor of the slick walkway. The collar slipped over the edge and fluttered into the gloomy space below.

Trix disappeared through the same door we'd entered, leaving our crew hiding in this creepy, murky place.

I rejoined my crew, careful not to trip and fall into the cavernous depths.

Sadness descended at the intense loss of my friend. Lopez enveloped me in a rough bear hug.

"You did well, Ofelia," she said. "Trix did us proud."

"Trix will be fine. She's home now." My chest tightened as if Lopez's embrace were vice-like. "And we have to go home, too."

CHAPTER 17

THE NARROW WALKWAY trembled under our feet as we traversed the cavernous space, a dizzying drop below. Dark air plunged us into frosty gloom, unlike the brightly lit corridor. Our elevated position spun vertigo around my head like a ball in a pinball machine.

The room's vastness neutralised sound itself. There was no trace of the ship's alarm here, but my CommLink bleeped, my heart rate spiking in the red zone.

The burn mark on my singed cheek throbbed. But I couldn't allow the pain to dominate my concentration. We had to push forward.

The surface of the treacherous walkway was slippery, providing no traction against the soles of my clumsy boots. I edged forward, mindful of the yawning abyss on either side.

There was another abyss, too. My chest felt caved in by emotion—Trix was gone.

I couldn't process that, so I pushed my feelings way down. I would mourn her later. Not that she was dead, like Demi. But she was lost to me, and we were a family of sorts.

Also, Trix strengthened my powers. How could I face the

Kaseath now? We were far from the docking hatch. I was the only defence for our crew, fending off the Kaseath's laser fire.

"Where do we go now?" Lopez asked.

"This will guide us." I pulled the liquid-metallic disc from my pocket.

The disc snuggled in my palm. Its warm surface was the same liquid-metal substance as the outer QyronNexa. How could it tell us the way?

A small purple light glowed on the disc as I faced the door. I turned back to the cavernous room, and the light disappeared.

"The fastest route is where we entered," I said.

"Straight into the Kaseath's military forces," Griffin growled.

Figg said, "We'll find another route."

I glanced at Lopez, who seemed resigned to following Figg's orders now. She shrugged.

"Doctor Figg outranks me." Lopez's voice hardened with sarcasm. Our crew was losing its cohesiveness.

I remembered Lopez's training and the most critical part of the mission. We had to get along.

"Commander Lopez, you're still in charge," I said.

Lopez turned to me. "What do you think, Ofelia?"

I thought momentarily, pleased that Lopez was consulting me on decisions and ignoring Figg.

Trix had returned via the quickest route to the docking bay. She didn't know our plans beyond that. Maybe she had led the Kaseath in another direction to confuse them.

"I say we go forward, not back." It sounded more decisive than I felt.

"So we go forward." Griffin inched past Lopez on the thin walkway. "I'll take point."

"Careful of your footing," Figg said.

Griffin led, followed by Lopez, then Figg in front of me,

and I brought up the rear. Once again, I was the last in our sausage-links along the walkway. Our rear deflection for the Kaseath lasers.

"Can I turn this off?" I jabbed at the alarms on my CommLink.

"There's no override for life support systems," Figg said. "Are you okay?"

My heart hammered, and I couldn't quiet its thumps. "Let's make this quick."

We moved farther into the cavity aboard the ship, and a soft wind began. It was like a breathing lung, sucking in and out. According to Trix, there was no oxygen aboard the ship. Who knew what type of invisible gas surrounded us?

Figg waved her medical scanner. "The gas is residual vapour, and there's no radiation."

"That's why the Kaseath didn't follow us," Lopez said.

"Let's see where this walkway leads." Griffin cocked her laser gun at the ready.

I checked the disc, and the light had gone. As my concentration moved towards the disc, my footing faltered. My booted toes dipped over the edge, and I flapped my arms to regain my balance.

"Careful." Figg grabbed my arm until I steadied.

I almost pulled us both over the edge. A surge of adrenalin focussed my concentration as I regained my footing.

It would be easy to push Figg to her death...

The thought was a brief glimmer, but I reminded myself I wasn't like her. I valued the lives of others.

Figg was now my ally. She knew the stakes, and I believed she valued saving humanity. And she would administer Imogen's cure.

Shoving the disc back into my pocket, I concentrated on the walkway.

We inched forward, placing our clumsy boots as if walking a tightrope. We approached the middle, with an equal journey to either wall. Griffin paused while we caught our breath. I rechecked the disc, which remained unlit.

"Everyone okay?" Lopez's forehead creased.

"I'll be happier when we're on our shuttle." Griffin adjusted her grip on the laser gun.

"Let's keep going," I said.

We approached the walkway's end, grouping by the door.

"It might be best if I take the disc," Figg said. "Griffin can cover us with laser fire ahead, and Ofelia can protect us with shields."

"Agreed," Lopez said. "We need Ofelia's powers, not to act as our GPS."

I handed the disc to Figg, but it faded to dull grey. The metallic finish lost its sheen, like an unremarkable, weatherworn pebble on a beach.

"Looks like it needs the Kaseath's DNA." Figg handed it back to me. The disc morphed into its metallic, bright-sheened former self.

"Just great. It's all up to me," I muttered, my hopes dipping.

"Why don't you lead, Ofelia?" Lopez nodded.

Was I more nervous about bringing up the rear or leading us? Neither was a pleasant option.

I inched past the rest of my crew, positioned in front of the slight depression outlining a door.

"It's go-time," I said, slamming my fist on the glowing control panel, the hum vibrating through my bones. The door hissed open.

Blinding light greeted our crew, searing my retinas. We shielded our faces with our hands.

"Visors down, people!" Lopez shouted over the ship's alarm, piercing after the silent darkness of the abyss.

We slapped down our gold visors, squinting ahead. The ship's alarm was relentless.

Figg faced us. "There's extreme radiation here. We have to move!"

We were in a small containment area. Stark corridors branched off from the main room. The disc wasn't purple-lit, so we headed the long way. But it didn't matter. We had to escape this toxic environment.

Our crew ran along more spongy flooring, bounding with each step in the lower gravity. Figg's scanner slowed its warning beats as we progressed down the corridor. We rounded a corner and pushed through another door, and the scanner ceased flashing altogether.

We paused, regaining our breath. I leaned against the wall, feeling nauseous. My face burned like molten slag.

Figg made a show of scanning us all. The shrill alarm was less intense, but we had a galactic-sized sunburn.

"We can expect radiation sickness from that exposure," Figg said.

"What does that mean?" Lopez reached for her dog tags, remembering they were underneath her suit.

"We must get off this ship via the absolute quickest route."

I could barely hear their conversation over my beeping CommLink and the warnings inside my helmet's intercom.

"So less talk. Let's move." Griffin aimed her laser gun and peered down its sights.

"Come on, recruit," Lopez said, grabbing me under my arm and dragging me along.

I frowned as Lopez half-carried me. But as we progressed, an intense energy drain descended as my body fought off the radiation exposure.

We reached another door. Glancing at the disc, I didn't discern the purple light showing the way.

Griffin swiped at the door panel, but nothing happened. She tried again.

"It must be a biometric scanner," Lopez said.

"Huh?" Griffin said.

"It needs Kaseath DNA," Figg said. "Like the disc."

I swiped the door panel, and it slid open.

Our crew filtered into an expansive atrium with lower light.

Metallic liquid flowed in the atrium around the narrow path. The light was softer, the porous flooring suspended above the metallic flow on each side. The rushing liquid emanated from vents in the ceiling, which met the walls. It oozed and squelched.

Figg hovered her scanner just shy of the metallic waterfall, but the diagnostics were inconclusive. At least she didn't yell at us to run.

We flipped up our visors to check for injuries.

Our faces were redder than a skinned rabbit at the Northies' butcher. The whites of our eyes were bloodshot, and I blinked orbs of light. Our teeth glowed whiter against our cracked red lips. Blisters formed around Griffin's eyebrows.

I checked my CommLink, which had slowed its beeping.

Figg put her scanner away. I checked out the disc again. Was that a purple light, or just an orb halo from the radiation exposure?

Several Kaseath teenagers, their lizard scales more orange than brown, moved beyond the waterfall. They peered from a walkway, shielding their bodies behind the silvery liquid as if observing dangerous animals at the zoo. We both delighted and terrified them.

One Kaseath teenager maintained eye contact with me. It was Lileau, Trix's daughter! She lifted one corner of her mouth with her twiggy finger. A smile. Her language reached out to me, awkward and unpractised.

"He-louw!" Her thought language came to me.

Nice to see you again, I thought.

"Nice to see," Lileau said in her alien language.

Wait—I could understand her! My ear attuned.

Which way to our shuttle?

She pointed to our left. She understood me, too!

There was no time to second-guess my new alien friend.

I swiped at the door panel leading to another winding corridor. Our crew took off, leaving the teenagers behind.

Lopez's grip weakened below my shoulder. Now, I felt like I was carrying her, that we propped each other up. Our energy waned, and I knew the way ahead may be treacherous.

Our crew limped forward, our laboured breathing audible in our helmets.

We rounded the bend...

...straight into an alien military patrol, their weapons drawn.

Five guards faced us, ready for battle. They aimed laser guns at our heads, daring us to make a move.

The alien thought language was in high chatter, and I fancied they'd raised the alarm.

The aliens' weapons locked on us, their lasers deadly. Even if Trix were still with us, we couldn't repel five laser guns fired from different angles.

How could I protect the crew by myself?

"Don't lower your weapons," I said.

Griffin and Lopez trained their laser guns on the patrol. Figg pulled out her scalpel and slashed her tiny sword.

I tossed the disc in front of my chest, which caught the aliens off-guard.

One shot a laser at the disc out of reflex.

I enacted my shield as the laser hit.

But I mistimed the force field.

A purple, crackling laser ray poked through my shield.

The heat was unbearable, even though my suit could repel the intense radiation from space. Fabric charred in a clear circle of greying outer material. A thread of smoke rose from the front of my suit.

There was a sharp, burning pain as the laser burned the skin on my chest.

A tiny vent of oxygen escaped from the front of my suit. Thankfully, we weren't in the vacuum of space, or I would have imploded. Would I run out of oxygen before returning to our shuttle? The hole from the concentrated laser point was tiny, but my suit was like an air-filled balloon. It would eventually deflate, and then I'd suffocate.

"There's a hole in my suit," I said, placing my thumb over the hole to slow the escaping oxygen.

"Make this quick then." Lopez's eyes furrowed with concern.

The searing pain throbbed, matching my heartbeat as my veins pumped blood to the area to heal it.

I beckoned my crew to crowd closer.

"Stay behind me." I gritted my teeth.

My chest ached, and my face smarted. I tasted metallic blood from my cracked lips as I held the shield steady, focusing my powers.

I moved the force field, matching each step of my crew.

We filtered past the five aliens in a single file. I was careful not to restart time by capturing the Kaseath behind.

My shield's heat crackled against the closest alien's face. Her skin glowed brighter, illuminating her orange network of molten lava-coloured veins between her brown hexagonal scales.

We passed into the corridor.

I couldn't hold concentration any longer and dropped the shield. We'd encounter tougher tests ahead. I had to conserve my energy.

I plucked the disc from the floor where it dropped.

The ship's alarm was shrill in my ears. My CommLink still bleated, but the shrill warnings abated.

I turned the disc over, and the light returned! We were headed in the right direction. This corridor must wind around the ship's outside, like interlocking arms. We should pop out near the docking bay.

My breathing quickened with excitement. My Commlink flashed red warnings again.

"I have five minutes of oxygen left!" I shouted.

Griffin twisted her helmet, unlocking the seal. She took a deep breath of remaining oxygen and lifted her helmet over her head.

"What are you doing?" Lopez asked.

Griffin took the blue bubble gum from her mouth and held it out to me.

"Ah, no thanks," I said, recoiling.

Griffin said, around her held breath, "for your suit hole."

"Oh, thanks," I said, taking the gum.

Griffin placed her helmet back over her head, reenacted the seal, and breathed in, hardly breaking a sweat.

I stuck the blue gum around the venting hole. It would buy me some time.

Griffin nodded as she pushed past, taking the lead. We rounded a bend in the corridor.

Directly ahead, a group of Kaseath amassed around the corner.

It was an ambush.

The dozen-strong Kaseath stood between us and the decontamination room's door while the five military guards advanced from the rear, no longer in our time-stop. Griffin led the way in front, her laser gun drawn, while I could protect us from behind. Lopez shifted closer to Griffin, cocking a gun of her own. We were two guns too few. How could we survive?

The subtle outline of the door to the decontamination room beckoned, linking the docking bay with Valentina One.

Just as I thought it couldn't get worse, two aliens joined them, one with a military collar, one without. The one without had a slight suntan mark where her purple collar had been.

And they dragged another Kaseath with them, one on each arm.

Their hostage, Trix.

CHAPTER 18

My heart fell a few storeys to the bottom of the enormous QyronNexa. Yes, we had to escape, but not if they hurt Trix.

Sorry about this, I thought. *You're in trouble now.*

"Do not worry about me, Ofelia."

They deposited Trix by the decontamination room's door while one of her military friends shoved a laser at her back. The laser was too close for her to enact her shield.

The time for diplomacy was over. If they hurt Trix, I would never forgive Hulgrod. Or myself.

The alarm was shrill as ever, piercing my skull and grinding a colossal headache. I rechecked my oxygen levels—five minutes remained. The blue bubble gum held the vent in place but wasn't a perfect seal, so it didn't prevent the seeping oxygen.

There was no escape. The guards hemmed our crew in on both sides, and we had to reach the docking hatch through the decontamination chamber.

I felt lightheaded as my oxygen levels ran low. The pain in my chest throbbed, strobing in waves of sensation.

"I can deal with sunburn," I said. "But if I can't breathe, you're on your own."

"That won't happen." Lopez rubbed her shoulder against mine. Holding me steady.

We faced off for a few seconds, which elongated with each beeped warning of my oxygen levels. They only had to wait until I passed out.

"Trix," I said, for the benefit of my human crew. "Can you translate for me?"

"Yes, of course," Trix replied.

"Can you ask them what it will take for them to release us?"

Trix spoke to those closest to her, and I felt the rest of the Kaseath listening.

All things were known to everyone. So, that meant that the aliens concentrated on Trix's thoughts.

With the aliens distracted, I mumbled to Griffin and Lopez, "Switch places."

I inched past, standing next to Figg at the front of the crew. Griffin and Lopez fell back, facing the rear guards.

The aliens noticed our movements, and the guards waved their guns.

I held up my hands, grinning. "It's all good, friends."

The front dozen guards moved in closer.

Griffin and Lopez pressed their backs into mine, facing the rear guards, while Figg and I assessed the front contingent.

I swivelled and fired a warning shot into the wall. But the Kaseath advanced, led by their military escorts. I checked in front and behind. Now, they were two dozen strong in front and five behind.

"We attack together," I said.

"Yes, recruit," Lopez said.

"Ready?" I said. "Fire!"

Behind me, I heard Griffin and Lopez fire their laser guns.

The military grunts closest to Lopez and Griffin must have

activated their shields, because the laser glanced off and embedded into the floor beside me.

"Wait for it..." I counted a second in my mind. "Duck!"

I hit the porous flooring with the black residue burn marks. As I rolled on the floor, the laser glanced off my shield. It caught the aliens in front, frozen in my time-stop.

Hopefully, the rear aliens thought the shield was the Kaseath's origin, not mine. They wouldn't expect the attack to follow.

I concentrated on the shield's power, the laser's pinpoint, and the front attack frozen in my time-stop.

Lasers fired behind me, hitting two of the Kaseath. I felt the guards' pain receptors, like jarring metal on metal.

I snuck a glance behind me—the two injured aliens fell behind as the remaining three advanced. Griffin and Lopez held them off, firing their lasers. This time, the rear guards deflected with shields of their own.

I turned back towards the connecting room to the docking bay, advancing, keeping my forward time-stop open. If only the shuttle were closer. We had a hundred metres to go.

The ping of Griffin and Lopez's cover fire allowed Figg to fall back and join them.

Taking a breath, I heaved forward, listening to the scuffle at the rear. My mind fused into my shield, keeping it open. I had to freeze the front guards in time, allowing my crew to fight the rear guards. Otherwise, we were outnumbered and out-classed.

I pushed the shield with all my strength, reaching the forward contingent. The shield's edges became less green and more translucent. It cracked, the green fading to a more translucent, thinner force field.

Lasers burned into the floor, singeing little smoke spires as my crew and the Kaseath swapped shots.

I shoved my shield into the aliens in front, between us

and the decontamination bay. Their bodies were heavy. My shield didn't shift them. And I couldn't hold the shield any longer.

My hands trembled with effort. My laser burn throbbed, and my head jarred with the shrieking alarm. I was almost out of oxygen.

I twisted to see Griffin, Lopez, and Figg facing the two remaining guards behind. The rear aliens retreated, nursing laser injuries.

My crew shuffled to join me, facing off with the two dozen strong aliens standing between us and the docking bay. Two military aliens gripped Trix underneath her shoulders, locked like a police blockade.

I dropped the shield, re-starting time for the dozen-strong forward guards. Their confused chatter was like a musical crescendo. Then they realised the shield was mine.

Lopez raised her hands in what we hoped they knew was the universal body language of surrender.

But Trix had other plans. She twisted free and launched herself at the military grunts holding her captive.

Neither one expected her attack, and they dove to the side. A laser gun fell free, rolling on the floor. Trix grabbed it, aiming it point-blank at the nearest Kaseath.

Our party jostled shoulders, moving closer to the front. Now, we fought the guards ahead. But there were too many!

Griffin roared, shoving the nearest alien off Trix. The surprised alien misfired into an overhead vent, and a massive steam jet spurted.

Griffin rolled away from the steam's heat.

The gas parted the Kaseath, trapping them behind.

The whooping alarm in the corridors made talking tricky for our crew. My CommLink blinked like a malfunctioning video game, and my head felt light.

I had run out of fresh oxygen. Now, I gulped the air in my venting suit.

Trix wrestled with the two aliens upon her, and our crew moved to help. I fired lasers into the aliens' arms, not wanting to kill anyone, just to disable them. The two aliens rolled in agony on the floor, holding their superficial injuries.

Three more aliens stepped through the steam, baulking at the steam burns that lit their orange veins with strobing flashes —the last Kaseath between us and the hatch. Trix stood beside me this one last time.

"Move towards the chamber," she said.

The three remaining aliens fired at Trix and me, facing the front, the steam dividing the Kaseath attack.

Trix and I flung up our shields to match the laser fire. Our crew inched closer to the shuttle's connecting room, approaching the panel and the faint outline of the door.

Nearly there!

We're coming home, Limpet, I thought.

As my concentration failed, I mistimed my next shield. A laser slipped by, punching a hole straight through my space suit and searing pain into my shoulder. The already low air from my suit hissed on its escape. The pain was unbearable, and I cried out.

I grabbed my shoulder, stopping the escaping air.

Four more aliens stepped through the steam, joining the fight. One alien tackled Trix around the torso.

Griffin shoved me behind her and let her lasers fly at the aliens, creating cover for us. The aliens reacted with their shields, ready for us this time.

Lopez, Figg, and I reached the door.

Lopez swiped the locked panel, which didn't respond. "Can Trix open this?"

"Trix is a little busy." I squinted around my searing

shoulder pain. I couldn't concentrate on creating the shields, and Trix lost the skirmish with her fellow Kaseath.

Griffin glanced at Lopez, struggling with the door panel, and Trix, restrained by four remaining military guards.

Griffin's eyes mirrored my terror as we realised we were outnumbered and overpowered.

Let my friend go, I thought in the alien tongue.

I pulled the dormant language from an under-used part of my mind, realising I'd known it all along. I had shared knowledge because I was part Kaseath.

The guards faltered, surprised they could understand me. It was all the distraction we needed.

Griffin launched herself at the military guards holding Trix, bashing their heads together and firing point-blank into their suction feet.

The guards let go, recoiling with pain, and Trix broke free. She hurried to the panel and punched in the override key. The door sucked open. Gravity surged from the Kaseath ship into the connecting decontamination bay.

"Griffin, come on!" Lopez shouted.

Figg dove into the room connecting the Kaseath's ship with our shuttle. Lopez shot off laser fire as cover. Griffin turned to sprint back to us. An alien grabbed her in a tackle, and she fell hard, her helmet imprinting on the spongy floor.

"What's happening, Commander?" Hellcat's voice crackled over our helmet comms.

We had comms with our shuttle!

"Prime us for a speedy escape!" Lopez dove into the tunnel.

"Copy that, Commander. Maya, get the door."

I followed Lopez to the hatch. We had disabled the rear guards, but the front guards regrouped.

I shot off a laser to protect Griffin as Trix surrendered to the advancing front guards. She stepped back.

"It is up to you now, Ofelia." Trix disappeared behind the aliens' bulk.

My throat constricted, and my head seemed to float outside my helmet. The scene became otherworldly.

I was half in, half out of the connecting room, shooting cover fire to protect Griffin.

But reinforcement aliens arrived, rushing from the rear, threatening to join both alien forces—forming one massive attacking force of seven-foot strength. I shimmied farther into the room, feet-first, so I could help Griffin. I held out my hand.

Griffin glanced at our crew—inside the decontamination chamber—then at the aliens. A moment passed between Griffin and me. I was closest to the corridor.

"Come on!" I stretched my reach.

"It's been a heck of a ride, Ofelia." Griffin nodded respectfully. Then she pivoted, diving away. She was lost in the scrum of aliens, who relieved her of her weapons. Griffin went limp, letting them take her.

"Let her go!" I screamed.

"Keep going," she said. "Get that cure home safe. Save the world."

"Griffin, no!" Lopez yelled through the comms in my helmet.

The aliens held Griffin down while one of them aimed their laser at her head. They had her hostage. She had no fight left.

"It will be okay," she said.

"Don't leave us!" Conflicted feelings emerged. I wanted to follow, but we had to escape. If we didn't close the connecting door, the shuttle wouldn't detach, and we were dead.

"Come on, Ofelia." Lopez grabbed my suit and pulled me farther into the room. Griffin watched us leave her behind.

Trix stood behind Griffin, also no longer fighting back. She raised her hand in a last wave.

"Don't trust Doctor Figg, Ofelia," Trix said. "You will know what I mean. Do not open the crystal."

My mind flashed to my sister Demi, being dragged away by Figg's snatchers. Hopelessness crushed my chest like a physical weight. Tears welled in my eyes, my throat a jangly ache. How many people could I lose?

Lopez pulled me farther into the connecting room. Two aliens leaped towards the door, and Lopez and I fought them off. The Kaseath struggled to pry the door open.

Lopez and I pulled with everything we had. The door inched closed. I swiped the panel to lock it. A hiss sounded as I armed the room. The obsidian lights descended, then glowed red.

The decontamination door wouldn't open during the cleanse.

My shoulder whooped in agony as I helped Lopez open the connecting hatch to our shuttle. We crawled through into the connecting tunnel.

Lopez and I wrenched the lock mechanism into place. I gasped for breath.

The artificial gravity sucked away with the connection, and we floated in the tunnel. I wasn't prepared, and a wave of nausea washed over the back of my throat. I grabbed the edge of the tube with my uninjured arm and propelled myself towards the inner shuttle hatch.

My CommLink blinked like a light show, and my head felt light with the low oxygen in my helmet. I took shallow breaths, fighting to stay conscious and holding back the tears.

Lopez must have grabbed my feet and pulled me through the tunnel. The ridges of the cocoon passed overhead. It felt like jettisoning into space, floating like trash.

At least I was no longer Northies trash.

"Retract docking hatch," Lopez said.

"Copy, Commander," Maya said.

Was Maya still mad at me?

I was about to pass out, panting in shallow breaths, my sight dimming at the edges, my head floating above the ship, heading to another galaxy.

My crew's voices floated across my consciousness, like slipping into a dream.

"Are we all accounted for, Commander?" Hellcat asked.

"We had to leave Griffin behind." Lopez's voice caught.

"We have to go back!" Maya said.

"They're gone," I said.

Lopez's voice sounded distant. "We have to enact our mission. They would have wanted that."

Alarms all around me. The ship's controls at the front were shrill, and my wrist comm was flashing like I was already dead.

Imogen lay in a hospital bed, the curtains open. She was attached to machines that bleeped and pinged. Those alarms meant trouble. Nurses and doctors rushed to her bedside, shouting frantic commands. One nurse lowered the bed, and another shot medicine into Imogen's arm. A nurse placed a breathing bag over her nose and mouth and squeezed it. Pushing air into her lungs, willing Imogen to breathe again, as I watched her tiny body. Willing her back to life. And then the alarm sounded a single tone—the tone of death.

I'd doomed my sister. She would die now.

I shook off the vision, realising the tone was in my helmet. My head lolled in the zero-g.

"Remove your helmet!" Figg shouted.

I grabbed the clasps sealing my helmet in place, but my thick, gloved fingers were clumsy. Figg's voice drifted away, and I felt as if I was joining Imogen. As if I moved towards her hospital bed, yearning for that reunion.

Joining her flatline.

Just before I blacked out, hands removed my helmet.

"Breathe, Ofelia," Figg said.

I wanted the opposite—I yearned to join my sister.

But instinct kicked in, and I gasped at the air in the shuttle. I choked, feeling the air like a solid thing, panting until my head cleared. As I opened my eyes, a tear slid free into the cabin; the globule of liquid solidified my pain.

I hovered in the zero-g's, breathing in fresh oxygen and realising I would survive. But guilt surfaced—Griffin wouldn't.

Now that I was breathing, my concentration moved to the laser injury in my shoulder. The pain dialled up. I held still until the nausea wave passed. The physical pain was welcome after losing Trix and Griffin. I had an excuse to cry. I couldn't help blubbering, and Lopez grabbed me in a brief, rough hug.

"It's okay, recruit," she said. "You did great."

Lopez pulled the crystal from her breast pocket, ensuring it was intact. The crystal's purple glow reflected in Lopez's irises. The outer crystal seemed solid, with a cap at the top. Mesmerising, darker liquid surged inside.

We'd done it! We'd obtained the cure—now we just had to return home.

"Hellcat," Lopez said. "Let's get the heck out of here."

CHAPTER 19

THE EJECTED DOCKING tunnel rotated in the vacuum of space, the alien ship still dominating the porthole view. We were far from out of trouble. We still had to return home.

Griffin was gone, and I felt guilty that I hadn't been nicer to her. She had sacrificed herself to save her crew and humanity.

She wasn't my friend, but that lopsided, trigger-happy, sarcastic puppy was still a freakin' hero.

Losing Trix was more painful, even though it was planned. She belonged with her kind, right? Just like I belonged with my family. Eventually, the Kaseath community would welcome her. She was home.

I had to trust that Trix would be okay.

Time to concentrate on the mission.

"Hellcat, Maya, stay up front," Figg said. "We've been exposed to radiation aboard the QyronNexa."

"I'll alert Mission Control." Maya didn't meet my gaze. Had she forgiven me? Our bickering didn't matter compared to our current predicament.

Figg, Lopez, and I moved towards the back of the ship. Figg pulled a curtain across that divided the back third of the shuttle.

"To keep Hellcat and Maya safe while we de-robe," Figg said, then raised her voice so the cockpit could hear. "Hellcat, Maya, please get into your suits so we don't contaminate you. That includes your helmets."

"Copy that, Doctor," Hellcat said.

The flimsy curtain wouldn't prevent the spreading radiation. It wasn't just the physical body that needed protection; we also had to protect our morale.

Figg turned her attention to me. My shoulder felt like I'd seared it in a hot pan on the stove, and my face throbbed. Figg helped me de-robe. Every time she tugged at the suit, it felt like she tore a new nerve receptor loose. I cried out with each jerk.

"I'm sorry, Ofelia. I'm being as gentle as I can." She averted her eyes.

Did she feel guilty about my pain?

She checked my shoulder; there was a large burn near my arm socket. The laser had cauterised the wound. She grabbed her medical kit and wiped the wound with antiseptic cream.

"Sorry," she said as I flinched.

White, scarred tissue surrounded the wound, stabbing with excruciating pain. Two teardrops escaped my ducts and floated beside my head.

Figg spoke with compassion. "I'll give you a shot for the pain."

There was no medicine for the genuine hurt—the people we had lost. And Figg had caused me that hurt in the past. No amount of patching me up would help. But she was also the key to my sister's survival. Without her, we wouldn't have the cure.

Figg injected medicine into my skin.

"See, just a little prick." Her eyes searched mine. We were rarely this close to each other; her minty breath reminded me of home. "We'll have to isolate our clothes."

Figg, Lopez, and I stripped down to our underwear and bra,

and Lopez took our contaminated suits and clothing, sealing them in the docking area.

When Lopez returned, Figg scanned us with her medical device. It hummed a low tone without the alarms.

"There's still background radiation," she explained. "But it shouldn't be fatal."

I felt exposed enough in my undergarments and crossed my arms over my chest. My head pounded, and my face felt like it was seared with flames. Nausea also returned.

"Time for your first space bath." Figg grabbed a bottle and soft gauze from her medical bag. She handed gauze to Lopez and me and took some for herself. We squeezed the bottle onto the gauze, ensuring the liquid wouldn't escape into the zero-gs of the ship, then wiped ourselves from neck to toe.

The gauze-type fabric rubbed my inflamed skin where the helmet hadn't protected me, where the gold visor had been. I caught my reflection in the shuttle's window. I looked like a raccoon, the searing red around my cheeks, lips, nose, and eyes. Pain rippled as I washed, and I re-opened my lips' bleeding cracks. I tasted blood and the artificial, stinging antiseptic gauze.

The pain from swabbing wasn't as bad as my jarring shoulder.

"I'm going to be sick." I moved towards the bathroom cubicle. But Figg passed me a plastic vomit bag.

"I'll give you a shot for that, too. It might take twenty minutes to take effect."

I took the bag and dry-retched. It didn't stop the queasy feeling. "I have the mother of all headaches."

Figg passed me and Lopez drinking water pouches.

"Stay hydrated. And take this paracetamol."

I swallowed the tablets, which poked my airways on the way down.

Then I rested my back against the wall, hooking my big toes underneath the bar.

At least my toes didn't hurt.

Lopez opened her palm, revealing the crystal cure. Figg and I froze, gazing at its power.

The chain dangled through her forefingers, splayed out in the zero gravity. The crystal was luminescent, no less bright than the sun.

I peered closer at the liquid inside the crystal, the light source. The liquid was a darker purple, like the crystal's beating heart. It surged, and I felt its energy beckon to me. The crystal had a cap at the top—to access the liquid within. I remembered Trix's warning: *Don't open the crystal.*

Could I trust her? She had no reason to lie after betraying her kind.

What would happen if we opened the cap?

This crystal had power. It drew us in, like moths to the light of our hearths back in Northies. Would we dance too close to the flame?

Lopez snapped out of the trance and tucked the glowing cure into an overhead panel. She was careful in her movements, ensuring the panel was closed with the lock initiated.

Lopez stood tall, her brown eyes sending an apology to me. Without her helmet or suit, her red raccoon face looked bloody, unlike her regular complexion.

I felt vulnerable next to the two grown women. Lopez spent more time at the gym than the training sims.

We wiped our bodies down. Then, we ran wet gauze over our faces, which needed more hydration. Our skin dried out in the cold, low humidity of the shuttle. We climbed into fresh suits to avoid contaminating Hellcat or Maya. At least Figg hadn't made us put our helmets back on.

We joined Hellcat and Maya in the cockpit.

We were a long way from Earth.

I hated being in my suit inside the shuttle. My fingers were clumsy in their gloves, and my body stiffened in the suit. It reminded me of being aboard the QyronNexa, with my oxygen depleted, the bleeping alarms, the searing pain...

It reminded me of Griffin and Trix.

Milling about the cockpit, we assessed our strategy. Hellcat kept us moving at a cracking pace towards Earth. But Figg, Lopez, and I struggled to stay focussed. We were in pain.

A thought occurred to me. I placed my hands on my face, around my cheeks and nose, and held them there. I closed my eyes, picturing my energy flowing through my fingertips. After a tiny spark, I felt better. My head cleared, and my face stopped throbbing.

I had healed myself. It was a pity I couldn't heal my sister from the plague. And not for lack of trying—for whatever reason, my powers didn't work on the Kaseath's plague.

But now we had the cure!

Lopez observed me, and I smiled back.

"Here, let me help you." I approached the commander.

Lopez let me rest my hands on her face, and her red-raw skin returned to regular tanned brown, a colour befitting a health nut. We needed Lopez to be hearty and capable.

Figg observed, as if she had invented my powers. I resented her scrutiny. But I needed Figg once we returned to Earth. She would have to help manufacture the cure. Would there be enough for everyone?

"Imogen is the first to receive the cure, okay?" I said to Figg, and held my hands steady.

Figg nodded and closed her eyes, which was a little creepy. But I rested my palms on her face and sent my energy through her. Her face lightened from red to pink.

We wouldn't die just yet.

I turned my attention to the shuttle.

Maya had restored comms to Mission Control. Figg's colossal head blocked my view of the comms screen. I floated upside down on the ceiling to see it.

The video glitched, and then a uniformed man wearing a headset appeared.

"We hear you, Valentina One," the man said. "Status report, please."

"We have it!" I shouted. "Tell my sister we have the cure, and we're getting it home, whatever it takes."

The mission control engineer adjusted his headset. "Repeat that, Ofelia?"

"We have the cure. We're coming home." I allowed the weight of that statement into my consciousness.

We'd done it. I'd saved Imogen.

Lopez said, "Starting return sequence."

Our crew celebrated, a first for our mission, allowing ourselves a minute's levity. It had been a big couple of days.

Maya hugged me, which smarted, but I hugged her back anyway.

"I'm so sorry." Maya's eyes pricked with tears.

"Me too. Let's never fight again..."

"Tell me all about the QyronNexa! What was it like? How did you convince Hulgrod to give us the cure?"

"Ah, well, we kinda didn't *ask* so much as *take—*"

Maya's mouth rounded in a surprised 'o' shape.

I glanced away, noticing Figg standing apart from our crew.

She floated to the side, her face averted, gazing at our little ball of Earth. Her expression was sombre, as if she had renounced her Hippocratic oath and was no longer saving humanity. It hurt to admit we had succeeded because of Figg.

She had helped me discover the truth about my DNA. She'd brought me to Trix, allowed our communication, and volunteered me for this mission. Figg had always been behind me, no matter the consequences. And she didn't have her own family. I was all she had.

She'd said there would be no mission without me, but my feelings towards her softened. There would be no mission without Figg.

I moved towards Figg and reached out a hand. My gaze was on my boots as I touched her shoulder. Figg turned, and her eyes moistened with intensity.

I twitched my mouth and turned away before I started blubbering, too. Tears welled, yet radiation wasn't the cause.

Maya observed our interaction, frowning at me.

"What the heck happened on the QyronNexa?" she whispered.

I shrugged. My moment with Figg was brief. I needed her to save my sister; I had to keep her close—enemy or friend.

"Please send instructions for re-entry," Lopez said to Mission Control.

"Ah, Commander? There's a complication." Hellcat pointed out the window at four small fighters ejecting from the main alien ship.

We'd stirred up a counterattack by the Kaseath.

The ships came into view—four sleek metallic shapes with smooth wings and a purple glow at the backs of their engines. The glow was the same colour as our crystal.

"We have to get the crystal back to Earth, Commander," Figg said.

"It had better be worth it. We just started an interspecies war."

I agreed with Figg. "We have to get the cure home, whatever it takes."

Lopez returned to her seat next to Hellcat, and I fought my way to the video comms.

"Fighter ships," Hellcat said. "We have a proximity alert."

To prove her point, alarms flashed on the displays.

"Maya, Doctor Figg, to the gun bays," Lopez said. "Ofelia, raise comms with Hulgrod and talk her down."

"So you speak Kaseath now!" Maya said, happy for me.

"I could speak to the teenagers we saw aboard the ship... and the military grunts understood me at the end."

I moved to the comms. Maya and Figg floated by us, settling into the gun bays, strapping into the spherical moveable rigs and taking aim. The rigs moved with them, and they had a near 360-degree rotation. Maya moved expertly, but Figg struggled, moving about jerkily.

My laser burn still smarted, so I placed a gloved hand on my shoulder, the energy flowing into my wound. My cells healed at my touch. The medicine was fast-acting, and the pain dissipated, although I felt foggy-headed. It wasn't ideal—I had to focus on the Kaseath conversation.

"No shooting until I give the order, team." Lopez nodded to me.

I picked up the comms and moved towards the video screen. As I adjusted the controls, the screen remained full of static.

"That's a wickedly close proximity alert, Commander," Hellcat said.

The sleek gunmetal-grey fighter ships circled our shuttle, which shook with the roar of a passing engine as it disappeared over our wing. The vibrations passed through our bodies.

"Maintain our course out of here," Lopez said.

One fighter fired its laser gun beside our ship—a warning

shot. The shuttle shuddered, a terrible sign. A direct hit would be deadly.

Despite the gun bays, our shuttle wasn't intended for battle with an advanced alien species. And we were missing Griffin, our battle-ready crew member.

The fighter ships circled beside us, and our sensors bleeped on every screen. The ships blocked our movement back to Earth, circling in tight formations that forced us to drift.

Lopez moved beside me to a second comms screen and found the audio feed. "Mission Control. We have a red-alert situation here."

"Roger that, Commander," the crackling returned over the comms. "State your safety level."

"I'd say it's about a zero," Hellcat replied.

"We have enemy ships firing warning shots," Lopez said.

"What do they want?" Mission Control said.

"They want us to return the crystal cure we appropriated from their ship."

"Stand by, Valentina One."

"Get a wriggle on," Hellcat said. "We're running out of fuel."

"Ofelia, how are the comms?" Lopez said.

"Still raising Hulgrod." I stared at the grainy image.

The ships tightened their formation. Hellcat's sensors bleeped like the whistles at a New Year's Eve party—this one had turned sour. The engines' crescendo was disconcerting.

One fighter fired a shot that glanced across the nose of our shuttle, frying the heat shields and leaving a black groove in the external panel.

"We've taken a hit," Hellcat said.

"Damage report?" Lopez said.

"Heat shield compromised."

"Will that affect our re-entry to Earth?"

"Most likely."

A voice whined through the comms unit.

"You have permission to engage the target," Mission Control said.

"Copy that." Lopez propelled herself to a third gun bay. "Let's disintegrate those fighter ships."

"Copy, Commander," Maya said.

"I'd advise against engaging the main alien ship," Figg said.

"Agreed." Lopez nodded. "Ofelia, keep trying the comms with Hulgrod. She can still stand down."

Hellcat kept the ship still as the fighter ships shot past the front window and twirled through space to circle again. Figg, Maya, and Lopez moved in their rigs, aiming laser cannons.

Lopez shot off a quick test, which dissipated into space.

"Don't waste ammunition, Commander," Hellcat warned.

"Copy. Are you ready for this?" Lopez asked as their rigs moved to match the pace of the ships.

But the fighter ships were in tight proximity to our shuttle.

"I can't get a lock on them..." Figg said.

The Kaseath flew in deft formations.

"They're too fast," Lopez said.

"And too close!" Maya said.

Lopez fired another shot, and the fighter twisted in a spiral to evade it. Figg and Maya fired together at the other ship. It easily evaded the lasers. The fighter ships enclosed us in their loops. One shot glanced off our landing gear.

"Landing guidance damaged," Hellcat reported.

"Hurry, Ofelia!" Maya said. "Or we're frizzled space pirates."

A grainy image of Hulgrod appeared. She didn't seem angry, but she didn't reveal emotion.

Closing my eyes, I blocked out the chatter with Mission Control and the wild shaking of the shuttle. I barred my fear and hope—both were dangerous now. I reached my mind beyond our shuttle, concentrating only on the being I wished to speak to—the being who held Earth's future in her twiggy hands.

Hey, Hulgrod, I began. *We apologise for the disturbance aboard your ship.*

I opened my eyes to the wavering video of Hulgrod's imposing figure.

"I am sorry as well, human." Hulgrod's voice resonated much deeper than expected.

Hulgrod's words came to me like a fizzle of soda foam breaking the surface.

I could understand her! My ear had attuned to the alien language, reaching out across the physical space between us. Projecting, as I could do with Trix.

"Our DNA is imprinted with our language." Hulgrod's voice vibrated in my ear. "Our children are born speaking it."

So I am part of you, I thought, keeping my tone even.

"You can speak like us, but you are not one of us," Hulgrod replied. "You have betrayed your kind and broken galactic law. It is fitting that you will end your life on the human ship."

We only want to survive.

"Survival is not a worthy goal. You have not evolved beyond your primitive instincts."

But we can learn.

Another laser glanced off our shuttle. The lights dimmed, then brightened.

"This is where we differ." Hulgrod's words were like wings fluttering over my mind. "Humans are not capable of evolving. The galactic council agrees."

Yet another misfire shook the ship, glancing off.

So let us try. I concentrated on bridging the gap between Kaseath and humanity.

The conversation paused, and I wondered if we had lost comms. But when I looked at Hulgrod's image, she was unmoved. I continued.

I share your DNA, which means I can learn your knowledge. And erase misunderstandings between Kaseath and humans.

Hulgrod stood, and the screen showed her full, imposing height.

"There is no misunderstanding. You are infinitely too dangerous to keep alive. How can we allow Kaseath powers to be wielded by an un-evolved human? You could destroy us all! You will perish along with your shuttle."

What about our crew member, Griffin?

"She will not be harmed."

"Hulgrod said Griffin's okay," I shouted so all the crew could hear.

"You can hear Hulgrod?" Lopez almost blasted our shuttle's wing in her distraction.

"You must return, Ofelia," Hulgrod said, "and give us back the stolen technology. We promise not to harm the one you call Griffin."

You can't destroy our ship while I am aboard, I thought.

There was a pause as Hulgrod stared at me. "Speak, Ofelia."

Another shot exploded, close enough to start a cacophony of even more warning signals.

"Commander?" Hellcat said. "We're getting skewered, battered, and deep-fried."

"And their ships are too fast for our lasers," Figg said.

I returned my thoughts to Hulgrod.

You can't destroy me. You can't kill one of your own. That's why Trix didn't mortally harm any Kaseath in the battle. Let us return to Earth and give our species the chance to live.

There was another pause as I felt Hulgrod process this new information.

If you destroy our ship, you will also wipe out humans. Your mandate is not to defeat humans. Your mandate is to stop humans from leaving Earth.

"You are correct," Hulgrod said.

Please, Hulgrod, let us prove we deserve your mercy and compassion.

An understanding formed between me and Hulgrod, although her reply was prickly.

"I will not call off our attack," Hulgrod said. "You may not have this technology, and you are an abomination. You cannot live."

I translated for the crew's benefit.

Lopez laid down more cover fire. "Then they can go to hell! Diplomacy is officially over."

The heat in Lopez's voice surprised me. But we faced a life-or-death skirmish—enough to rattle the stoic commander.

Hulgrod's image disappeared from the screen.

The ship jolted, and I was thrown against the wall. Then Hellcat's voice shouted above the fray.

"We've taken a direct hit!"

CHAPTER 20

Steam hissed from the shuttle's internal panels as Lopez and Figg laid cover fire to stop the approaching ships. But we were in trouble.

"What's our status, Hellcat?" Lopez steadied her aim.

"Maya, assess the damage back there," Hellcat said.

Maya unlatched from the gun bay rig. She approached the steam vent, which was ejecting into our shuttle's interior, creating a haze. She caught a handhold and punched diagnostics into the overhead screens.

"Ofelia, take Maya's place," Lopez said.

"No, Commander," I said. "I won't kill the Kaseath."

"So don't kill anyone," Figg said.

I cocked an eyebrow at the least ironic thing she'd said on this mission.

Maya said, "I can patch us up, but it might take time."

"There's no time, Commander," Hellcat said. "We just lost partial life support."

"Getting rid of these fighter ships is a priority," Figg said.

"Can you hold us steady until then, Hellcat?" Lopez asked.

"I can try my darnedest."

"Good. Let's go, people!"

My head grazed the top of the hollowed-out unit as I slipped into the gun bay Maya had vacated. I pulled my harness straps tighter. The gun bay rotated as I shifted the controls to match the fighters' trajectory. I had trained in the simulator, and taking potshots at the fake moving targets had been fun. But these were real beings—part of me. I couldn't kill those pilots, even if it meant that our crew perished.

My movements became fluid against the bay's jerkiness. I sensed the fighter ships' sweeps before they occurred.

Our shuttle shook as another laser skimmed off the window.

One fighter arced into view. I aimed and fired a shot that missed the ship but forced it to evade the laser. Figg aimed and hit home.

Figg's laser bolt cut through the enemy wing, and it spiralled out of the way, losing control of its trajectory.

The pilot righted their ship, overcompensating for the missing wing. It attempted to return fire, but the laser blast missed us by several hundred metres. The force of the shot nudged it farther off course.

The disabled fighter limped towards the QyronNexa, sparking from the open gash where the wing had been.

"One down!" Figg yelled.

Three remaining ships circled, evading my cover fire. These were more expertly piloted. My concentration deepened.

The three ships took turns circling the gun bays, drawing fire from Lopez, Figg, and me.

"We're wasting ammunition," I said.

"They're too speedy," Figg said.

"There's another fighter!" Maya pointed out the side window at a fast-moving fighter ship joining the battle.

The three ships closest to us looped and circled, keeping us in check. They stopped circling and faced our shuttle. One fired—just as Lopez fired back. The lasers met and dissipated, their energy cancelling each other out.

"That was too close," Figg said.

"Hellcat, show us your acrobatic skills. Aren't you supposed to be an ace pilot?" I fired more shots.

Hellcat flew an evasive manoeuvre, and I grabbed my harness, releasing the laser trigger.

The fourth ship approached hot and joined the others. The Kaseath ceased firing, allowing the fourth ship to join their formation.

I felt the alien language. The three original ships listened to a superior.

Three original fighters banked but didn't fire. They looped over the ship, disappearing above us. When they next appeared, their purple engine fire receded towards the QyronNexa.

"What just happened?" Hellcat asked. "The other ships are leaving."

"Yeah, but there's one more," Lopez said, her eyes trained on the lead ship. It hung there like a circular target in a firing range.

It didn't attack; it just hovered.

The fighter approached casually until I could see the lights inside, reflecting off the orange-veined, brown-scaled Kaseath pilot.

The pilot smiled.

And then she waved.

"That cheeky..." Lopez flipped the guard over the laser cannon button.

"Don't fire!" I yelled.

Lopez ignored me and laid down cover fire. The ship swerved out of the way.

"Don't—" I said as Figg fired herself. "I said stop!"

My crew fixated on the ship and didn't hear me.

"Listen—" I yelled.

"Take the shot, Commander," Figg said.

"Incinerate that sucker," Hellcat added.

"DO. NOT. FIRE," I said.

Lopez swivelled in her seat. "Why the heck not?"

"Because it's Trix." I waved to my alien friend.

The crew sprang into action, fixing the damaged ship. We might not make it, even though the attacking fighter ships had retreated. Which flashing alarm would we address first?

"What can I do?" I asked Maya, who wrestled a whole spaghetti pot's worth of wires from one panel.

She shrugged and detangled them.

Figg held a fallen oxygenator tube in place, patching the hole with medical tape.

I mean, I could help Figg, but I really didn't feel like it.

Lopez and Hellcat had their worries in the cockpit as the shuttle listed to one side. Lopez yelled commands at Hellcat, read charts, and relayed orders to Mission Control through broken comms. Mission Control might hear us, even if we couldn't hear them.

"Permission to let Trix aboard?" I asked nobody in particular. Nobody responded. "Sure, thanks, don't all greet her at once. She just saved our lives, no biggie."

I floated back to the docking bay, where Trix had attached her fighter ship to the hatch. Her fighter was small enough for a direct lock.

She passed through the docking bay on the bottom of her

ship, connecting to ours. Her language flicked back to her fighter, and the lights dimmed.

Now you're just showing off, I thought. *Seriously?*

Maya noticed me and asked, "Why are you grinning?"

"It's a mind-controlled ship," I said, but more beeping distracted Maya. "I said, it's a mind... don't worry. Sure, I see that every day, too."

Trix gave me a thumbs-up. I nodded and unclasped the inner hatch, and Trix floated into the shuttle. She armed the inner hatch behind her.

I threw my arms around her middle, intense waves of emotion overcoming me. I felt ready to blubber again, but Trix placed her rough, three-fingered hand on my cheek. The electrical fizzle was like an unending feast in the middle of Northies. I released my fear for the first time since our escape from the QyronNexa.

"I have missed you, too," Trix said.

How did you convince those fighters to leave?

"I told the fighter pilots they were not to destroy the humans."

Trix! Isn't that a lie?

"Destroying you is not the Kaseath's mission." Trix released me from the hug.

Lopez nodded to Trix and reached into the overhead panel to retrieve the crystal. It was still intact. Its purple liquid mesmerised me as Lopez tucked it into her breast pocket. She smoothed over the Velcro, a snug fit for the crystal.

Lopez strapped back into the shuttle controls next to Hellcat. "Maya, talk to me."

"We're venting oxygen," Maya said, tapping the touch screen to eliminate the blinking warnings.

As if on cue, the ship's warning signal started its shrill tone.

Hull breach. Hull breach.

"In your helmets, people!" Lopez shouted. "You've got one breath. Make it count!"

I didn't need a second invitation. Maya and I helped each other with our suits' zips and helmet seals.

I breathed sweet oxygen before realising Trix was missing. Although she didn't breathe air, she still needed to be protected from imploding in space, didn't she?

"Where's Trix?" I ignored the rest of my crew, who were suited.

"I'm here." Trix's perky curl drooped, a bedraggled, melting version.

"What's wrong?" I asked.

"Nothing. I let you suit up first and ensured you had sufficient oxygen."

"That was exceedingly polite." I helped her into her suit.

"Could we fit in your fighter, Trix?" Lopez snapped her helmet's airlock and breathed deeply.

"Not without ripping out the interior and cargo," I translated.

The shuttle's cabin lights strobed; an ominous omen.

"Maya, show me the hull breach," Lopez said.

Maya's screen revealed a tube across the ship's outer surface.

"I have eyes on the vent." I pointed out the porthole window at the gas escaping near our right wing.

"Does that require a spacewalk to fix?" Lopez asked Maya.

"Yes, Commander."

"So we have two problems," Lopez said. "One is a hull breach, which will be fatal on re-entry. We'd break up when we entered the drag of Earth's atmosphere. The other is the oxygenator, which means we'll run out of air before we return to Earth."

Hellcat switched on the automatic pilot and joined us midship.

"What do we fix first?" Hellcat asked.

"Without the hull breach fixed, we'll keep venting air," Figg said.

"But if we fix the hull breach first, we'll run out of air before Maya can repair the external damage."

The Commander said, "The hull breach is partial. Maya, run projections using our current venting rate. We could run oxygen through faster than we lose it."

"On it, Commander." Maya moved towards the panels.

"Figg, work with Maya." Lopez observed the flashing tube on the monitor. "Cross-check each other's work, then bring it to me. I'll sign off on the final calculations."

Maya wiped at her sweaty brow, then realised she had her helmet on. Her gloves left a partial smudge on her helmet's visor. She avoided eye contact with Figg. I didn't blame her.

We'd spend our last moments on the shuttle, trying not to snap at each other.

"Do not think such thoughts," Trix said.

Didn't you already see our likely future?

"Yes, Ofelia."

That's right. We don't make it in the end.

My elation at reuniting with Trix faded.

Maya and Figg were deep in their calculations while Lopez checked their work. Hellcat sat in the cockpit, ready for their final figures.

It didn't take a brainiac to see we wouldn't make it. Even if we fixed the oxygen tanks, we still had a hull breach. With

Maya's engineering skills, she might pull this off. But the ship had taken considerable damage.

Once we hit Earth's jarring atmosphere, it would only take one scratched panel to explode the shuttle into fireworks. And the Kaseath fighters had scored several panels.

What if we didn't make it? Mission Control believed we had the cure. I couldn't face disappointing my family.

I snuck back to my tiny quarters to call home.

Mission Control was out, but I could try the direct patch from my iScreen that had worked before. If we didn't make it, I had to leave a message for Imogen. I wasn't ready to say goodbye, but I could tell her I loved her, no matter what happened next.

Squeezing into the cramped cubicle, I fished my iScreen from the netting on the wall.

And dialled in.

But I couldn't even get a tone, let alone a signal. The tiny connection wheel on the touch screen turned, then froze, stuck like I'd stopped time again. But I had to speak to my sister one last time.

I was used to this hopeless feeling, like I had been transported back to the Northies shack. The tin walls closed around me. The smoke from the hearth reeked of burning plastic, bringing the shooting pain of a chemical headache. I tasted the bland, malnourished black potato soup that left me just as famished as before I'd eaten. Hunger sat in my stomach, twisting and feeding the panic attack. Deafening rain soaked me through the mislaid tin-sheeted roof. I shivered, numbness overtaking my arms and legs until I was without feeling, my whole body rigid with fear.

And then Imogen stood beside me in the shack. I tried to assure her we were safe. But her eyes were wide with fear as the walls twisted her body under their weight, as if the jaws of a massive machine ate us. Crushing her chest, silencing her beating heart.

I tasted chemicals and my sister's plague breath. My teasing thought threads unravelled, jumbling together as usual.

I fought the panic attack.

There was a high possibility of my sister—and everyone else I'd ever known—dying.

What made it worse was that I'd made a promise I couldn't keep. I'd told her I was bringing home her cure, but instead, I ensured everyone's annihilation.

Maya floated past my cubicle, jolting me back to the mission. She beckoned with her gloved hand.

She hadn't given up hope—she was busy saving us.

Could I help, after all? I could provide an answer they hadn't thought of. No more playing tourist. Time to make myself useful.

The video link failed, so I closed my iScreen. I floated to join Maya and Hellcat, catching glimpses of calculations on the primary screen between glitches.

"Will this help?" I handed Maya my iScreen.

Maya noticed my screensaver—the photo of my family in the hospital. Imogen grinned while my family fought worry. Maya's expression was sombre, but then she mouthed 'thank you' and took the iScreen from me.

She fired up the calculator and punched in projections. Hellcat and Maya checked and cross-checked the figures. They had it.

"Ready for sign-off." Maya handed Lopez the iScreen.

"It checks out. What about the spacewalk?"

"I can repair the vent and the damaged panels," Maya said. "But there's shrapnel out there. Dr Figg damaged the fighter's wing. It's all over the place."

I glanced out the porthole, where the fighter's wing particles spread like glittering confetti chunks beyond our ship.

"Hellcat, what does your course look like? Can Maya take a spacewalk?"

"Negative, Commander. Maya's right. That space junk will shred right through her suit. And we're floating farther off course."

"Solutions? Any ideas?"

Hellcat flipped switches on the console. "We'll have to do this without Mission Control."

"Fix the oxygen generator." Lopez tapped a blinking monitor. "Then we deal with the hull breach."

"On it." Maya grabbed tools from a compartment and opened a panel, revealing tubing and large connecting tanks.

"Hellcat, are you okay here so I can assist Maya?" Lopez asked.

"Most definitely," Hellcat replied. "We're drifting. I'm not much use."

"Just keep trying comms with Mission Control." Lopez scooted back to help Maya.

"Roger that." Hellcat twisted the comms, hailing ground control.

"Can I help?" I asked.

"Work with Doctor Figg on recalibrating our life support sensors," Lopez said.

I had forgotten Figg was my new frenemy, and my displeasure must have registered on my face, because Figg smiled. "You're stuck with me."

"Looks like it," I said. "Let's fix it quickly."

Figg and I floated to the ship's port side, opposite Maya and Lopez, who worked on the oxygenator. Figg flicked readouts onto the larger screens.

Seven profile pictures appeared. They pixelated, cutting in and out, and Griffin's vitals flatlined with grey.

"Does that mean Griffin's... um...?" I swallowed the inevitable end of that sentence.

"Hopefully just out of range," Figg replied.

Below each profile, our heart rates were off the charts, pumping in a red gradient. The stress indicator's mountain-like icons hit the peaks of the graphics. But the one thing that caught our attention was our oxygen levels. They were in the yellow zone, and anything below the green zone was a worry.

"We're at risk of hypoxia," Figg said.

She handed me her screen, and I ignored my pounding head. I followed along as best I could.

Lopez said, "Status report?"

"Life support back online," I said as Figg tapped the screen of the last recalibrated being—me—and it stopped glitching.

"The oxygenator works again." Maya shut the panel, and the subtle hiss of oxygen filled the cabin. We turned off the oxygen in our suits and removed our helmets.

Figg noticed me frowning in pain.

"Headache is a symptom of low oxygen in the blood," Figg said. "Stay hydrated. The oxygen in the water will help."

"On it." I returned the iScreen to Figg, glad for an excuse to leave her. I pulled pouches from a side panel and filled them with water from the inbuilt tank.

We stopped for a minute to drink the pouches of water.

"We have a limited window on that spacewalk." Hellcat pointed to the shrapnel that drifted closer and almost touched our ship.

Maya observed the mess floating towards us. "There's no time."

"And we're out of options," Lopez said.

CHAPTER 21

WE DEBATED who would go with Maya on the spacewalk suicide mission. Maya was the best at fixing the charred panels, but we also had to repair the hull breach.

"It will take more than one person to fix the damage." Maya's brow creased. She avoided eye contact, as if it would doom the mission. Her jitters shot nervous energy into my limbs.

"What about me and Trix?" I said.

I immediately regretted volunteering. You know, on the suicide mission.

"Their unique abilities could be useful," Figg said. "They can deflect missiles. Could we use that somehow?"

Lopez swivelled towards me, her pupils wide with concern. "Can you deflect debris like that?"

"Our powers work in the zero-g inside the shuttle," I said. "But Trix hasn't tried outside of their spacecraft."

"It's worth a try," Figg said.

I raised my eyebrows at Trix, searching for her thoughts.

She replied, "I sense from your facial expression that you would like my opinion."

"Yes, Trix. Are you up for it?" I asked out loud.

"Affirmative, Ofelia. We must work together to deflect the debris. But I dislike, as you say, 'spacewalks'."

"We're in, Commander." I grinned.

I was definitely not grinning on the inside, though. Why was I volunteering? It felt like facing the global media at Space Camp, tasked with manually calculating flight paths with ten seconds on the clock. And the world's fate was determined by me getting every figure precisely correct.

Did I mention Maya was the brainiac, not me?

Maybe I also wanted to prove to Maya that a spacewalk surrounded by razor-sharp shrapnel wasn't dangerous. At least I'd be close to my friends when our suits imploded.

Our training had drilled into us that spacewalks were a last resort, exposing us to the cosmic void. And with the floating junk so close, it could cut right through our suits. This was a tough decision for Lopez.

"Trix, Ofelia, and Maya, recheck your suits for damage," she said.

"Yes, Commander." Maya flicked an awkward glance my way.

Time to suit up.

This might be the moment—the end of everything. Our extinction event, as badass as the comet that killed the dinosaurs. But our 'comet' was glittering space junk beyond the port-side window.

We hadn't nicked our suits, at least not visibly. I almost wished the suits were torn. I checked on Maya. She focussed on the inner hatch, but her gloved hands trembled.

We both grabbed our helmets, accidentally bumping gloves, and I gave her a little 'you got this' smile. She nodded as we waited by the inner hatch.

Figg handed Maya a fancy-looking drill and a welding tool. Maya grabbed a wide roll of sticking plaster and a replacement panel the size of a dinner plate. She clipped the items to her utility belt.

Figg assessed our vitals with the help of her CommLink. Maya avoided eye contact with Figg. I sent a challenging stare at the doctor, willing her not to pass our detour outside the shuttle.

Yep, where we might, like, *die*.

Why didn't I mind if Maya went? I told myself it was because Maya wouldn't fail. She hadn't failed at anything in her fifteen years on Earth or beyond.

Did that make me a terrible person?

"They're ready," Figg said.

I was anything *but* ready.

But this had to work. Imogen needed me, as did Maya and my crew. Mousie and Aze depended on me back in Cookham East. Mum and Dad. Everyone I had known and cared for or would never meet—the generations to come.

I needed to protect my loved ones. It was the only way to keep my panic attacks at bay.

I had to save my sister. And in saving my sister, I might save the world.

Trix said, "Remember your training. We will have to concentrate."

"Okay, I can do this," I said, reddening under the doctor's gaze. She observed me clinically, taking my thoughts back to the research facility. Yet another 'Figg Special' test? Was I a lab rat again?

"Hellcat, how are we looking?" Lopez asked.

"Going speedily, exactly nowhere, Commander. Maintaining our distant orbit with Earth."

"Good, keep us steady. The rest of you, to the hatch."

Maya, Trix, and I propelled ourselves to the rear of the ship and the now-tunnel-less docking hatch. In its place was Trix's fighter ship.

We halted outside the inner chamber, and Lopez shook each of our hands.

"Good luck," she said, cold and formal. Lopez had already distanced herself from her crew members in peril.

Maya, Trix, and I moved into the docking chamber in single-file. Lopez armed the door behind us. Oxygen dissipated, matching the void of space. Then Trix opened the outer hatch, revealing the interior of her ship.

The sleek, minimalist console was like the control panels in the QyronNexa. Purple light surrounded it, covered with their strange symbols.

Trix went first, shimmying into the fighter ship's cockpit. She touched the panel at the top of the cockpit canopy, and it opened, revealing the dark chasm of space.

Trix clipped her harness to the fighter ship's bar. She pointed her feet first and manoeuvred out, seeming to take forever, making slight adjustments. Then, she disappeared from my view.

Once Trix was out, Maya followed. She was dextrous and had a much slighter build than Trix. But her pupils were wide, taking everything in, keeping her movements as small as possible to avoid jettisoning off the fighter altogether.

Maya left the safety of Trix's ship.

I was left alone in the cockpit, poking my head out of the fighter ship.

Space had become inky since the sun had 'set' in our current orbit. It was like a hole in the universe, swallowing me instantly, erasing my existence.

Stepping into the black void, I gripped the handhold beside the hatch as vertigo took over.

I inched towards the nothingness of space, noticing the faint outline of Earth, upside down from this perspective.

This was a terrible time for my panic attacks to return.

I warded off the panic, hoisting myself out of the fighter's canopy and vice-gripping the tether.

And then it hit me.

Space felt freezing, unforgiving, and downright terrifying.

My mind split.

The stench of smoke, the echo of tin shack doors banging. A blaring sun's UV rays cut into my pores. Gulls circled overhead, squawking as they swooped to peck my face.

I stood on the tallest spire of Trash Mountain. The blustering wind flapped my body on the precipice, nudging my back. My toes poked over the lip of the platform beneath me. I teetered there amongst the whiff of London fires. Except the stacks were thirty storeys tall, and the ground was jagged, rusting trash, skewering kids when they fell to their deaths.

The next gust blew me off.

I fell.

My stomach dropped.

It was the worst nightmare. I wouldn't wake up this time.

My body free-fell thirty storeys in a moment.

Pure terror as the jagged ground rushed up to meet me.

I hoped I wouldn't hit anyone below. Wishing for an instant impact and anticipating the extreme pain before I died.

My body smashed into the trash below.

I squeezed my eyes shut, but nothing happened.

Because I wasn't in a past nightmare on Trash Mountain; I was in the middle of space, in the present.

It was impossible to fall out here, in this weightless state, without the pull of gravity. Only the crackle of the comms in my helmet broke the silence. I panted like I'd sprinted across the shuttle a thousand times.

This is the present moment. I'm toast. I'm actually, for real, dead...

"Incorrect, you are alive," Trix confirmed.

My breath fogged up the lower half of my helmet. Soon, my vision would blur.

Had I passed through a portal, moving from life to nightmare to death? Sound disappeared altogether, sucked away before it became an echo. My flimsy tether seemed inadequate, as if I were adrift in deep space. I held out my hand for Maya, just like I'd tried to reach Griffin. Maya could save me from falling from the trash spires.

My hand bumped unexpectedly against the shuttle's side, causing panic. A shiver fluttered at the base of my neck.

I froze.

What the actual heck was I doing out here? Could I do this?

I can't do this.

"Are you okay, Ofelia?" Maya said. I struggled to hear her over my panicked breathing.

"Not really," I said.

The understatement of my entire lifetime.

I concentrated on the sensation of the tether, the slight pressure against my gloves. They were the thinnest part of the suit, with the most feeling. Outside was glacial since the sun hadn't risen yet. It felt like my face was pressed against dry ice.

I clung to the shuttle's side to prevent being sucked away.

"Calm yourself," Trix said.

I fought the sensation of tumbling head-over-heels down a never-ending incline. The shuttle's angle against the looming crescent of Earth caused more vertigo. Was I the right way up?

Or was Earth upside down? What about our ship? And where should I tether next?

Were we spinning, or was it my panic attack?

"I can't move," I said, fear overtaking my body, my muscles shutting down, my hands clamped against the bar. My breathing was so laboured that the fog in my helmet crept closer to my eyeline. The condensation would blind me.

I closed my eyes and scrunched my hands around the holds.

Maya scooted back and grabbed my hand. "It's just like the pool at Space Camp."

"This is so *not* like the pool," I replied.

"Ofelia, be calm, or your powers will fail," Trix said.

"Not helping," I replied, then realised Maya must have thought I was speaking to her. "Trix, I mean."

"We'll wait," Maya said. "Try opening your eyes."

"She's got her eyes closed?" Lopez said through the comms.

"We'll wait until she's ready." Maya pressed her gloves into my arm.

It wasn't authentic touch through the bulky suit, but Maya's presence steadied my mind. Maybe I wouldn't jettison into space like discarded trash.

"I hate to contradict you," Hellcat said, "but that space junk will collide with us in ten minutes."

"Definitely *not* helping!" I gasped.

"Count down from ten. See, I've got you," Maya said.

Ten seconds to continue this mission so we didn't all *die*.

I squinted open one eye, peering at the handrail. If I stared at my hands, I could forget that my powers only worked if I could see the missiles.

"Good," Maya said. "Now move sideways, okay? It's not far."

A white lie—the hull breach was on the shuttle's opposite

side. But I trusted Maya's advice. She needed me, so I had to perform my duties.

I gripped the handrail traversing the shuttle, squeezing both hands. The solid bar tethered me to reality. That bar became my focus; there was nothing else.

The outer panel's ridges moved beneath my line of vision as I kept pace. It might take ten minutes to reach the next section of the shuttle.

Maya said, "Keep doing that until I tell you to stop."

I took a deep breath, my confidence a smidgen higher. Maya let go of my arm and scooted ahead. I had to reach the hull breach. Worrying about what came next could wait.

To prevent a panic attack, I remembered Lopez's breathing exercises. I settled into my body, my chest contracting and filling with each breath. Concentrating on sensations: the rough ridges beneath my handholds, the metallic scratch of my tether clipping along the thread, and the cold seeping into my core from the absent sun.

Now that I wasn't a ball of scrunched-up terror, the frigidity of space wrapped around me. Goosebumps ran up my whole body, and I shivered in my suit. But my breathing didn't sound as laboured, and my visor cleared.

I snuck a peek ahead—space was overwhelming. Nothing else I'd ever experienced was as massive, not even the Qyron-Nexa. It dwarfed our entire planet, which hung like a distant ball over my right shoulder.

"Move to sector Gamma-18. Copy?" Lopez said over the comms.

Maya replied, "On our way."

The sun rose around Earth, lending more light outside my direct headlamp. Heat blasted the side facing the sun, and my other side was freezing. I focussed on the details of the shuttle.

It looked unending. How would I reach the end in ten minutes? I couldn't keep up this pace.

"Speed up, Ofelia," Maya said. "You're doing great!"

Did I detect worry in Maya's tone? Or resignation that I wouldn't make it?

Trix was halfway there, with Maya catching up. We had to get a wriggle on.

"I'm okay, Maya," I said, swallowing hard. "Stay with Trix."

"Copy, Ofelia." Maya threaded along at a decent clip.

"We have five minutes until impact," Hellcat said.

The comms chatter was a mismatched radio transmission stuck between channels. I couldn't comprehend the instructions until Maya's voice cut through the noise.

"Approaching Gamma-10."

"Ofelia, report your position," Lopez said.

I searched for the code above the panel and freaked out at the laser scar, which partially obscured the writing.

"It looks like Gamma-1," I confirmed.

"Ofelia, breathe," Figg said over the comms.

"Easy for you to say," I shot back, my composure unwinding. "You're safe inside..."

"Lopez here. Ofelia, take deep breaths. Hang out where you are. Trix can provide enough protection for Maya."

That sounded like a fabulous idea. Trix could do this.

But I couldn't leave it up to Trix. I had to protect Maya. Failing everyone, being a tourist on this mission, was not an option. Not while my sister needed me. And countless others on that wondrous planet over my right shoulder.

My world out here expanded.

I gulped at the hissing oxygen in my helmet and searched the handholds ahead.

"I'm on my way, Commander," I said, a hopeful tone to my voice. Safety in numbers, right?

"We are two minutes to impact," Hellcat said.

My tether caught at the last notch in the rail, and I reattached it to the following thread.

"See?" Trix said. "You have got this, as humans would say."

"Damn right, I've got this," I replied out loud, not even embarrassed my crew could hear me.

I was hand-over-hand, swimming towards Trix, who waited by the hull breach's venting gas, and Maya, who worked nearby.

"One minute, people," Hellcat said.

I propelled myself onwards, gaining confidence. But I scooted too fast and had to stop by the hull breach. The panel beneath read Gamma-17—one more sector to go.

"In position, Commander," Maya said.

I approached in an uncontrolled slide.

Maya noticed me barrelling towards her.

She braced for the impact—I couldn't stop my inertia.

"Help!" I yelped, and Trix noticed me.

"Slow down, Ofelia!" Maya said, bracing between the railings, hugging the ship.

I grappled with the handholds, but my body had massive momentum. Trix lodged one elbow under the bar and reached for me with her other hand.

"Thirty seconds," Hellcat said. "Twenty-nine, twenty-eight, twenty-seven..."

With one last ounce of desperation, I grabbed the shuttle's surface, my fingers burning at the slide. My body connected with Maya's, throwing us both off-centre.

Trix grabbed us with her long arms.

Maya and I wafted away from the shuttle, out into space.

Maya's tether caught, and then mine. Then Trix's tether caught, boomeranging us back to the shuttle.

"Ten, nine, eight..."

Our bodies slammed into the shuttle. Maya and I grabbed for the handholds.

And missed.

Trix grabbed hers, barely holding on. But she had more strength than two teenage humans. Trix looped her arms around Maya's middle and mine, holding us tight.

Then, the space debris hit.

CHAPTER 22

TRIX WOUND one arm around Maya and me, the other clinging to the shuttle handholds of sector Gamma-18.

She enacted her shield as the first shard of space junk hit—the solid fragment was the size of a bottle cap, as menacing as a focussed speeding laser.

Shrapnel of that size was serious. It could cause damage to the shuttle and injure the three of us, preventing us from fixing the hull breach so we could return home.

Please let us make it home.

Trix's shield heated my face, crackling in yellows and greens. The sparks left the shield and sucked into the surrounding vacuum. Solid green hues wavered like the ocean —like the aurora borealis. Keeping us safe.

Inside the stopped time, we assessed the approaching, glittering silver shrapnel confetti. Trix grunted and shifted her position, allowing Maya to float towards the panel. Then she let go of me. I grabbed a toe hold, facing deep space, towards the shards that could end us all.

"So I guess our shields work in space." My voice squeaked.

"Thankfully," Maya replied.

But the current shard was nothing compared to the scattered space junk, random and mistimed.

This wasn't like averting laser fire—more like deflecting a bag of sugar crystals flung at high speed.

Our situation required serious skill. I had made the right decision. Trix couldn't do this alone.

"In position, Commander," Maya said. But there was no reply. Trix had frozen space and time, with Maya and me in her shield's slipstream.

"You'll have to repair the hull breach without Lopez's help," I said.

"Are you both ready?" Maya asked.

"Yes."

"I'll concentrate on the repairs."

"Let Trix and I keep us safe while you work." I projected a confidence I didn't feel.

Maya grinned at me to find confidence of her own. She examined the venting gas at the hull breach.

Trix hung onto the handhold next to Maya's right flank, closest to the sun rising behind Earth's crescent. I was closest to the ship's rear, waiting for the sunrise. I gripped the handhold and nodded to Trix. We were close enough that we'd be able to capture each other behind the curved sides of our shields.

One last wave of hesitation shot over me. Could we make it home? Even more importantly, would I be too late to save my sister?

But then Trix dropped her shield.

The bottle-capped shrapnel flew away, spinning as it went, a line of shrapnel dissipating in its wake.

Slivers of wing debris shot towards us, and I enacted my shield.

Barely in time.

I caught Maya and Trix on each side, throwing my powers

wide. I grunted at the split-second vertigo, not allowing it to affect my concentration.

My shield held—although not as thick or green as Trix's. Mine was translucent, and sparks fissioned on the surface, but it held the space junk at bay.

I dropped the force field, already exhausted. Trix enacted hers.

We alternated our powers. Trix's shield. My shield. Slivers almost pierced the millisecond gap. I forgot about everything else, about what was at stake.

Concentrate on each particle of space dust. Not a single one can get through.

Maya attended to the panel. While Trix held her next shield, I checked Maya's progress. She removed three of the venting panel's screws and was drilling the fourth free.

"How are you tracking?" I gritted my teeth and swivelled to enact my next shield.

"Just keep doing whatever you're doing," Maya replied.

"Copy, Maya." I felt like a real astronaut, mastering a spacewalk and saving a crew member's life. No other human was up for the task.

We weren't out of the looming threat. A new crop of space junk hurtled towards us, broader and faster than the first wave. This would take extreme skill.

"Do you see that?" I asked Trix during our next stop.

"Yes. We can repel it, but we will have to concentrate."

I said, "Maya, hurry, it's like deflecting a shattered windscreen out here."

"Copy that, Ofelia."

I gripped the handhold, now accustomed to the floating sensation. My right side heated as the sun illuminated the shuttle. Sweat pooled in my undersuit. My sweaty undershirt would freeze with the sunset.

I faced the new shrapnel arcing towards the ship. The slivers turned to solid objects centred around a middle cluster.

Fist-sized, it would be deadly if it impacted the shuttle or any of us.

"Time this one together," Trix said.

"Agreed. Ready? Now!"

We both enacted our shields, melding them into one super shield. The middle cluster hit just above Maya's torso, about a metre out.

I charged the shield, thinking of nothing else, concentrating on the simmering heat, tracing my free hand over the surface to strengthen it. Trix focussed on the shield, too. If we applied backward pressure, we might have a chance.

Trix and I threw the shield back with everything we had.

We repelled the fist-sized cluster. It shot back from the shuttle, taking a good-sized portion of the space junk with it.

This is for you, Imogen, I thought.

"Look out!" Trix shouted inside my skull.

I saw it too late.

A globule of space junk had ricocheted off the larger cluster and shot towards us at speed.

Trix let her shield fly but was too slow. I threw mine into the mix, capturing the shrapnel. But a wand-like sliver broke through, smashing into the panel beside Maya.

The shrapnel tore a gash the length of my pinkie fingernail in the panel before sliding off the shuttle's surface. Trix and I flung the shrapnel backwards, creating a curtain that swished into space, repelling the particles headed towards us. We'd cleared the path for now.

"Holy mother of ET." Maya lost hold of the unscrewed panel. Trix grabbed it with her lengthy arms before it floated into space.

"It's okay," I said. "The shrapnel missed you."

"Yeah, but it just created something else to fix," Maya replied. "Commander, we have surface damage to the adjacent panel at Gamma-19."

"Confirm damage status?" Lopez said.

"It's just a light score, but we have a few now. I'm worried about the shuttle's integrity for re-entry."

"Continue repairs of the hull breach. Patch as many panels as possible."

"Copy, Commander."

Maya took the welder from her utility belt, soldering the venting pipe. Her competent movements were assured. As she continued welding, the gas ceased venting.

Maya took the replacement panel from her belt. She screwed it into place with the drill, a film of sweat on her forehead. She was stressed out, too.

"Hellcat, how's that space junk looking?" Lopez asked.

"All clear for now. We have another impact in twenty minutes."

I relaxed at the idea of a twenty-minute break before the next onslaught, but as the sun rose behind Earth, space heated. The sensation reminded me of the intense sunshine atop Trash Mountain back in Northies.

At the thought of my former home, I felt for the rubber ball Imogen and I had won. We'd been the unexpected winners of the first round of the mech car championship. But the small bulk was missing from my suit pockets.

Had I lost it?

Panic returned. That object represented more than just a ball; it was my pull to home. My link to sanity, just as precious as the tether linking me to this shuttle, preventing me from jettisoning into space.

My mind wandered to Trash Mountain. I couldn't resist

the pull from the present moment, tumbling me into the depths of another waking dream.

My view was the seagull's, picking over Trash Mountain, squawking and squabbling for rotting morsels of food. Imogen's body lay on the plastic bags and broken electronic devices amongst the sludge and decay. She didn't have to say it was my fault. She embedded the thought within my deepest cells. Her glazed, fierce eyes stared, shooting physical pain into my being. The unrelenting eyes of my dead sister, Demi, morphing into Imogen's decomposing face. Imogen crumpled into cosmic dust, her body dissipating, floating away.

The same dust that Trix and I were deflecting.

I pushed her fragments away with my shield. Her atoms were propelled into space, flung away. Shooting into the galaxy and scattering. She would never re-form.

And it was all my fault.

"You are thinking about your sisters," Trix said.

Her words brought me back to reality, where I could trust my senses. My body ached, my mind as disorganised as that mountain of tossed-aside junk.

Terror clung to me like a rotten thing, and for a moment, I couldn't catch my breath. The image of my two sisters haunted me. Was this how it all ended, with Imogen's death, despite my efforts up here? Would it be too late?

My hands clamped the handrail, my knuckles aching.

"It is just a panic attack," Trix said. "The danger has passed, and you succeeded. You protected the ship."

"Yeah, but it's coming back," I said.

Lopez's words from the docking sim played in my mind— *"You've got one breath, recruit. What do you do?"*

She was right. There wasn't breath to waste.

Concentrate on where you are. Don't let panic consume you.

A slice of sun formed a fierce halo against the blue skin of

Earth's upper atmosphere, just forming. The sphere transitioned from darkness to light. Soon, the sun would set, repeating the process. That thought was calming.

From here, Earth looked fragile, as precarious as our shuttle. I had to save the people on our planet so we could leave.

With a thumbs-up, I moved back into position next to Maya and prepared for the next wave to hit. I was finally ready.

Maya patched the panel scoring, laid the tape, then pulled it free. She left behind a solution that instantly solidified, creating a smooth surface beneath.

I concentrated on Earth, mesmerised by its greens and massive blue oceans beneath swirling white clouds. The portion of brown land beneath me seemed distorted. The continents' masses didn't have visible borders, but I could see the lines of mountain ridges and open areas of desert.

A massive swirl of puffed white obscured the ocean, the islands beneath dwarfed by cyclonic clouds dumping sheets of rainwater below. Ground level would be dark, with gusting winds tearing debris around. It was the ultimate force of destructive power, but from this vantage point, the clouds were elegant against the stark black space.

A cyclonic feature of an ever-changing Earth. The clouds would be smaller when we made our next pass and, after another couple of rotations, would move on altogether.

At least the northern hemisphere countries weren't covered in clouds. London was safe, where my family watched our mission. I had to return, which meant helping Maya, even if I still felt like I was about to lose my lunch, breakfast, and dessert.

"Sector Indigo-10," Maya said. "I'm out of solution. I'll need the second patch kit from inside."

"Copy, Maya. You're clear to return for the patch kit."

"I'll do it," I said before my mind caught up.

"Repeat, please, Ofelia?" Lopez said.

"Returning for the patch kit. Maya can stay out here with Trix to assess the remaining panels."

"Are you up for that, Ofelia?" Maya swivelled to see me.

I saw my reflection in Maya's gold visor, surrounded by a burst of light from the rising sun. My reflection was one hundred per cent astronaut. I raised my fingers in a peace sign, grinning at my reflection. Maya returned to work.

Lopez said, "Doctor Figg, would you meet Ofelia at the hatch?"

The route back to the fighter's cockpit involved tethering to four sectors. I didn't feel nauseous if I watched my hands as I slid them along, heading back to the hatch. The physicality of the spacewalk kept me focussed. My fingers cramped, but the pain kept me in my body. My breathing and comms were the only sounds I concentrated on. I forgot about the instructions for Maya. I had one thing in mind—reaching the hatch.

This time, I tethered confidently beside the fighter's canopy. The shuttle's movement wafted me in and out like ocean waves on the pebbled shore.

The hatch groaned as it pushed free. Figg wriggled into the fighter ship and poked her head out of the canopy.

She peered into the blackness, space untouched by the sun. The lights in her helmet illuminated her expression—she was both scared and fascinated. She extended her arm, reaching into the void, catching at nothing. Mesmerised, like a moth batting against a glowing fluorescent bulb.

She gazed into my eyes, and I felt her obsession with me. I looked away, embarrassed. I grabbed the bag.

"Ofelia has the patch kit." Figg regarded me.

"Approaching final panel," Maya said.

Trix dropped her shield.

Something massive came into view.

An object so large that it cast a shadow over the shuttle. What could be that immense? Had the Kaseath returned? Then I realised what it was.

It was the severed fighter's wing from the battle.

And it was headed straight for us!

We had concentrated on the space junk ahead and forgotten to check our periphery.

The wing approached—a jagged triangle. Electronics shorted in bursts of light. It loomed over the rear of our ship, ready to collide with Trix's fighter, attached to our docking hatch.

If it impacted, the shuttle would implode.

"Hellcat, do you see this?" I squeaked.

"Crew, return to Valentina One, like, now!" Hellcat said. "I'll have to perform an evasive burn. You need to be inside when that happens!"

"Time until impact?" Lopez asked.

"One minute, Commander," Hellcat replied.

"What about the final panels?" Maya said.

"Leave it. Get inside as quick as you can!" Lopez's voice wobbled.

Maya clipped her tools to her carabiner, and Trix and Maya pulled on their tethers, threading back to the hatch.

They were too far away.

They wouldn't return in time, and the looming wing was about to crash.

CHAPTER 23

TRIX SCOOTED BEHIND MAYA, who was the closest tether on the handrail. Maya threaded hand-over-fist as rapidly as possible, not worrying about stopping. Trix's tether pinged as it caught the next rung.

The approaching severed wing dwarfed the shuttle, jagged where the laser had cut through. It sparked with latent energy.

My heart rate spiked, and I fought all-out panic. I couldn't succumb to the terror. My panting breath echoed in my ears, the chatter on comms panicked and urgent, shouting over each other.

Stopping might be the challenging part for Maya and Trix.

Maya threaded her way to me. Trix had fallen behind.

Hurry, I thought.

"You must enact the shield," Trix said.

The wing angled towards the cockpit of Trix's fighter.

Its shadow crossed my face, plunging me into the cold void.

We'll do it together, I thought.

"There is no time. You must do this alone, Ofelia."

"Twenty seconds until impact. Status report?" Hellcat said.

"We won't make it." Maya glanced at Trix.

"Ofelia, protect the ship," Trix said.

"Okay, brace yourselves." I clipped onto Trix's fighter ship at the hatch.

Figg remained at Trix's fighter canopy, ready to help us inside. She reached from the cockpit to guide me inside. But I turned away from her.

I wedged my space boot beneath a bar beside Trix's fighter ship. Winding both arms behind me, through the handholds, I faced outwards into dark space.

The wing was the length of a semi-trailer truck, with a narrow edge, fattening towards the part once attached to the ship. It spun on its trajectory towards us.

"Five seconds," Hellcat said.

My wide eyes took in the view. My heartbeat was faster than a collapsing avalanche of junk on Trash Mountain.

I took the deepest breath I'd yet taken on the mission. The wing hit. I enacted the shield.

The first corner of the wing kissed my green shield—my strongest so far—and I froze time.

The wing was a massive object to repel. It would take all my strength. The structure loomed overhead, solid and menacing.

Trix and Maya were outside of my shield's flank. They were suspended in the moment; Maya was threading along from a metre out, and Trix beyond her.

They wouldn't make it back to the shuttle before impact.

I was the best defence. It was all up to me.

Oh heck.

I grunted with concentration, reaching out with immense effort. Tensing, I wiped the shield's surface, painting solid crackling greens and sparking yellows until my reflection wavered in the shield's light.

Figg's helmet poked out of the fighter's cockpit, caught in the forward-moving slipstream of my shield.

"You can do this, Ofelia," she said.

I'd have to push the wing back away from the shuttle. We couldn't enact the evasive burn without jettisoning Maya, Trix, and me into space. Figg was at the open hatch—the shuttle would lose its integrity.

No more time.

I concentrated. Closed my eyes. Opened them again.

Figg reached out to me. At first, I flinched, not expecting her to be so close. Her voice crackled in my helmet.

"You must save us. We can't destroy the crystal; it will take us with it."

"What do you mean?" I gritted my teeth, forcing my shield to remain open.

"The crystal is not what you hoped."

"Is there something wrong with the cure?" Confusion overtook my senses. My shield sparked as I waited for Figg's reply.

"I said the crystal would save humanity. But it's not the cure."

"You specifically said it was the cure..." I said, almost forgetting to keep the shield open. "That's the whole reason we broke into the throne room and started a freakin' inter-species war!"

"I didn't lie to you, Ofelia. I've never lied to you. Maybe I let you believe something else. It brought you to this moment. For you to save humanity."

"Don't give me that 'save humanity' crap..."

"I'm sorry, Ofelia. The crystal can still save us all."

"What the hell is it, then?" I checked Figg's sincerity but only saw my gold visor reflection.

"It's an anti-matter device, a source of tremendous energy."

"So it's not the cure?" My face simmered with fresh anger.

"If we destroy the crystal, it will obliterate everyone you love, and Earth, with a power fiercer than a human-made bomb."

My shield flickered as my emotions caught up. That familiar feeling of betrayal. Figg's lies on lies. I lacked power, unable to protect what mattered most.

My family.

Would Imogen die now, and would my visions come true?

Would we nuke ourselves in the end?

Confusing thoughts tumbled. I had to concentrate on the shield. But I had to ask, "Why did you lie to us?"

"I didn't—well, fine, maybe I misled you. But we need the crystal's power," Figg said, smiling at me. "You wouldn't have come otherwise."

A shot of anger surged up my spine. I couldn't save my sister. Even the combined power of all the Kaseath couldn't save us.

Were we meant to be saved?

The shield faded at the right edge, crackles of greens sparking on the surface. Not even the shield's warmth could penetrate my freezing suit. My powers were as useless as a tiny, helpless baby fighting off the most significant earthquake of energy that any human had endured.

I had lied to my sister and told her I was bringing her cure home. Now Imogen knew not to trust people. She couldn't even trust her sister.

"This is unforgivable," I said.

If nothing else, I had to explain to Imogen why I'd given her false hope.

Figg was why.

Thoughts of home, of Imogen, sparked my defiance. Not like this. When our lives ended, it wouldn't be preventable.

While I breathed, there was hope. I could still protect my family.

Figg didn't care about anyone else, but I did. That had always been the difference between us—real, human connection, not just using people or clamouring for power.

Power was useless if everyone you loved was dead.

I might be a Northies rat, but I could save this mission. Then, I would expose Figg's lies. She wouldn't get away with her behaviour.

I will end her.

That thought focussed my energy.

Turning back to the wing, I concentrated on the triangle's tip, meeting my shield, imagining it crumpled under the impact.

I was ready.

With my face scrunched and hands clenched, I repelled the force of the wing with everything I had.

Pushed it backwards, away from the shuttle.

Let the force of the shield drop.

The wing shifted backwards. But it also spun.

The underside of the wing pinned me against the shuttle!

Gut-wrenching pain.

The wing scraped along my stomach, then it slid off. Edging away from the shuttle.

"Ofelia!" Figg grabbed my arm.

I checked my space suit, expecting my severed innards to float into space. The suit's outer layer was grazed, the wing causing an intense crushing injury. The pain was deep, stealing my breath, wringing my organs flat.

My last thought was, "At least my suit isn't ripped."

And then everything went wonky and surreal. The pain took over.

Panicked voices floated over my helmet's comms like a television show in the background. Heated voices, shouted commands, words tumbling about. Things went wrong, and hope slipped away.

My vision changed from the blackness of space to the moodily lit fighter cockpit, and then to the subdued fluorescent lighting of the connecting docking bay. Figg spoke to me, her face directly above mine, but I couldn't hear her.

Only pain consumed me. My helmet fogged as I breathed too rapidly, muting sound and sensation.

All but the sensations in my stomach.

My breath caught as hands pulled me deeper into the shuttle. They removed my helmet and ripped my suit free.

Figg cut off my undershirt. I glanced down at my middle, expecting a bloody mess.

A small incision sliced next to my belly button, beside my rash of scales, purple-bruised and swelling.

The wing had caught the mostly human part of me.

Maya's face hovered into view, concern imprinting on her forehead. I smiled at her to tell her I was okay. But was I?

Figg waved a scanner over my body. She had forgotten to remove her helmet. She took a moment to twist it free and set it in the zero gravity beside her. My gaze followed her helmet, calm in the fray as it rotated. The helmet was unconcerned, only existing.

Figg spoke, and I must have responded. She seemed to understand, and then she reached down, feeling my injury.

A searing pain throttled my breathing. My side twisted away from the pain, a reflex. Figg's worried expression confirmed I was properly hurt.

The volume turned down, and confusion settled. What had happened?

Then I made out Hellcat's command, "Evasive manoeuvres in thirty seconds."

So, I could hear speech again.

"Get strapped in, people," Lopez said.

I forgot to react, as if she'd spoken to someone else.

"Here, let me help you." Maya guided me to my seat. I still couldn't comprehend what was happening.

My body was rigid. Bending at the waist was excruciating, but I couldn't strap into the seat standing up.

"I don't need to sit," I said. Floating was just fine.

"We're about to burn. You need to be in your seat," Lopez replied.

Figg hovered over me, giving me a shot of something from a needle. I didn't even feel the sharp scratch as it went in.

My vision blackened at the edges as if I were still on the spacewalk.

Maya and Trix folded me like pita bread.

I screamed.

Excruciating pain knocked the breath out of me.

Trix held my midsection and pushed me into my seat. The electrical fizzle at her touch didn't help. The injury was too fresh.

"How are we looking, crew?" Hellcat asked.

Trix clipped my seatbelts into place, and I grimaced, straightening in my seat. I ground my teeth, concentrating on the pain, willing it to leave my body like a gentle haze. But it had a clenching fist around my innards. And it twisted and clamped like a dog shaking a toy in its mouth.

"I'm sorry, Imogen," I sobbed.

The weight of my insignificance, my vulnerability, pushed into my pain. The ache of failure was worse.

Then, the shot that Figg had given me kicked in. Reality bent and time expanded—I existed on all planes simultaneously.

So this was how it ended.

CHAPTER 24

I STOOD outside my house in Cookham East, at the bottom of the driveway winding towards the garage. The overcast sky loomed in ominous greys with flashes of sheet lightning teasing the horizon. The musty air reeked of approaching rain.

I stepped towards the front door and huddled under the porch shelter. The door was locked, so I rang the bell, but nobody answered.

"Imogen!" I called.

Was that a muted reply?

Something told me I had to get inside, that my family needed me. I rang the doorbell again, but the only sound was the electrical buzz from the meter box beside the porch.

There wasn't a single living thing in the cul-de-sac. The birds were absent, the other houses locked, their interior lights off. Parked cars were missing from the driveway. Scattering leaves rattled against the concrete gutter in growing gusts.

Panic swelled as I realised things were not okay.

As if confirming my thoughts, thunder growled, rolling overhead and dissipating in the distance. The first rain fell, enormous drops heralding a massive storm.

I had to get inside.

I shoulder-charged the door, the impact stinging, until it swung inwards.

Inside, the house was gloomy with a stale, undisturbed smell. It was familiar but foreign, like another family had moved in.

Or... we had moved out?

The rooms were bare of furniture. Where had our couch gone? And the massive TV my sister loved to watch. I burst through the door to Imogen's bedroom. Her horse posters lay like discarded relics, crumpled in the corner. Her bed was missing, as was her desk. I flung open the door to her walk-in wardrobe, where Trix had hidden a lifetime ago. The clothes were missing; only one misshapen coat hanger remained, shifting in the wind gusting through the open window.

I slammed the window shut, resisting the storm's force, and searched the other bedrooms, the lounge room, and the kitchen with rising panic.

Nobody home.

Where was everyone?

I ran to the backyard, my bare feet irritated by the brown, brittle grass. Overhead, the wild storm descended.

Demi's tree was dead.

Its branches were bare of leaves, its trunk blackened as if burned in an intense fire. One branch had cracked and met the ground like a broken leg.

I sucked in a sob, turning to search inside the house, passing from one room to another, refusing to give up hope.

"Imogen, where are you?"

The doors and windows flapped with the wind. The gusting storm blew inside like a hurricane, whipping my hair around my face and making me squint against the dust. Grit flew into my eyes.

Leaves flowed into the halls, bedrooms, and lounge room

until the floor of the entire house was buried in leaves. Then the leaves morphed into garbage, jagged and pungent. The trash filled the house, consuming all available space. It flowed out of the windows, taking me with it until the garbage created the spires of Trash Mountain, and I stood on their stacks, teetering in the wind.

Imogen lay on the trash-strewn ground with her eyes closed.

"I'm here!" I called, but she didn't respond.

A blue-black droplet of plague sweat pushed out of her pores. She writhed in agony, but didn't open her eyes.

More dark plague sweat pushed through her skin until her forehead shone. The sweat dripped down her temple, staining her grey t-shirt. More beetle-like beads became a torrent, washing over her closed eyelids and covering her face. Seeping into her eyes and nose, choking her through her open mouth.

Her eyes opened, the blacks of her irises the deepest pits, like a Kaseath. She was already dead. But then her mouth opened, spilling the oily liquid across her lips and cheeks.

She was trying to talk.

"Why did you leave me?" she asked.

Her eyes were rigid, her face expressionless.

"Imogen, I'm sorry," I said, around a flood of tears. I willed life back into her body.

"It's your fault I died."

A knife of dread slashed through my consciousness. There was nothing more I could say. She was right.

Her eyes remained open, staring but not seeing as the dark sludge filled her eyes, nose, and mouth.

Her body jerked as the blue-black plague sweat consumed her. Trash tumbled from the stacks, covering her body and pinning her beneath. Then, her face was swept over with garbage.

Burying Imogen alive.

"Imogen!" I yelled, confused.

Was I alive or dead? Did it matter anymore?

Figg hovered over me, her gaze concerned.

I was back floating in the middle of the shuttle, and the familiar crew's chatter was a discordant haze. So it had just been a dream.

My stomach ached deep inside, but the edge of the pain was less jagged. At least I could breathe. Chatter drifted over me, as if the crew were talking about someone fictional, like a child's imaginary friend.

"Status report on Ofelia," Lopez said from the cockpit.

Figg hovered above me. "I need better diagnostic equipment, but I suspect she has internal injuries, which means she needs a hospital. We can't operate on the shuttle."

"How much time does she have?" Lopez asked.

"It depends on her injuries. But she's got maybe one, two hours max?"

"And then what happens?"

"She could go into shock. Re-entry is arduous enough, even for someone healthy—the stressors might kill her."

"Just great," I groaned, pepping the pitiful doctor up.

"She's conscious." Figg placed a hand on my arm like a doctor with actual bedside manners.

"Ofelia, are you with us?" Lopez asked.

My head felt light. The pain was less intense, as if I had dissipated into another section of the ship. I was fragmenting into nothingness.

"I'm like, not all here." That was literally how I felt.

Maya was at my side, too. "I'll have what she's having."

"It's not the cure," I croaked, too softly for Maya to hear. She had to know. So did Lopez and Hellcat.

"She's a little groggy." Figg was poised to give me another shot from her needle.

"Don't." I waved Figg away.

"It's okay, Ofelia." Maya squeezed my hand.

My tears overflowed, but not from pain.

"It's not. Nothing is okay!"

"Just relax." Figg shifted to gain access to my shoulder.

"Commander, you need to hear this." I glared at Figg.

"I'm a little preoccupied," Lopez said.

Maya searched deep into my eyes, knowing even before I said it.

"The crystal isn't the cure," I said. Hating my words. Dooming my sister and humanity.

"What?" Lopez asked, lifting the crystal on its chain from beneath her undershirt.

Figg couldn't maintain a poker face.

"What do you mean?" Hellcat asked, twisting in her seat to join the conversation.

"We must return the crystal safely to Earth," Figg said.

"So there is no cure?" Lopez said, confused.

"Keep up, Commander," I said as my crew finally twigged to Figg's true collusion. "Trix told us, but you didn't want to believe her. Neither did I."

"Because Doctor Figg confirmed the cure's existence." Lopez barely controlled her temper. "You've been lying to us?"

"I didn't specifically use the word 'cure'," Figg said, eyes downcast. She knew she'd crossed a line that she couldn't reverse.

"What is it then?" Maya asked.

"It's the Kaseath's energy source," Figg said. "It's what powers their ship. And it will power our Ark."

"I don't understand," Lopez said.

"It's an anti-matter device—an unending source of energy. The Ark lacks sufficient fuel for interplanetary travel. But the crystal gives us infinite power."

Maya's eyes searched mine. She knew what this meant.

"So yeah, we're not saving all of humanity," I said. "Just those who don't need the cure."

"Your sister..." Maya didn't need to finish the sentence.

My anger focussed. I couldn't look Figg in the eye.

This meant I couldn't save my sister's life, and she would die before her time. There was no cure—not in Figg's failed human trials back on Earth, not via my hybrid DNA, not even amongst the Kaseath.

How could I have naively believed in the cure? Why had I let Figg mislead me? She was a despicable human being, the worst of us. Of course she had lied.

"Is she lying now?" Lopez asked Trix, not wanting to hear the answer.

"For once, Doctor Figg tells the truth," I translated. "The crystal cannot be damaged. Its power is greater than any bomb. It would destroy everything, including our planet."

"So that's been our mission all along?" Lopez huffed. "To steal the Kaseath's energy source?"

"Would you have come otherwise?" Figg asked.

Defeat washed over me. "What good is the most powerful energy in existence if we can't save the ones we love?"

I was stuck in this explodable shuttle, dying anyway, having lied to my sister about bringing home her cure. I was about to return empty-handed, pursued by a band of alien fighters. Having started an inter-species war, dooming humanity to fail in its quest to start over on a new planet.

Oh, and yeah. We would never see our family again

because our shuttle would combust on re-entry, taking everyone with us.

My vision was about to come true. We were about to nuke the Kaseath, our ship, and everyone we knew back on Earth. If our shuttle was destroyed, the crystal would implode.

And that meant destroying Earth.

"Everyone will be gone," Maya said, the ramifications sinking in.

I forced my mind to concentrate, the last rally before my final breath.

"There's something I have to do."

Figg moved aside, no longer focussed on knocking me out cold so I didn't reveal her secret. Now, everyone knew her true self.

I left the crew to bicker and learn the full extent of Figg's deception.

Grimacing against my pain, I found my iScreen intact in my quarters. Inevitable doom descended as I waited for the video to load. It was the same feeling I'd had during the final test at the Elditch Research Facility. When Figg had me strapped to a chair in that cold, sterile place. The fear wedged into the back of my throat like a familiar pest.

I desperately needed an exterminator.

Breathing was difficult, but my mind was clear. I clipped in the earbud headphones and watched Imogen's cheery face, wishing me well in the recorded video. Her voice was just audible above the fighting crew in the cabin.

"If anyone can succeed, it's you—my big sister. I love you so much. So this isn't goodbye, it's see you soon. We'll start over on a brand-new planet. It's so exciting! I can't wait to see what it's like."

The back of my throat congested, the video obscured by

blurring tears. I captured them with a tissue so I could keep watching.

"I wonder if we'll be able to ride our bikes on our new planet," Imogen said, her face full of wonder. "We're so lucky. And it's all because of you."

I couldn't take it anymore and stopped the video. The frame froze on Imogen's hopeful face, full of love for me. Holding her image in my mind, I traced my finger over the screen.

My remaining tears floated around like soft butterflies, and I mopped them up with a tissue. I didn't want anyone to see, so I wiped my eyes and blew my nose, depositing the tissue in a waste receptacle.

Maybe I'd meet my family in the afterlife. Perhaps they would forgive me. But could I forgive myself?

Time to say goodbye.

I pressed the 'record' button on my iScreen selfie video.

"It's probably a waste of time recording this, but I wanted to say my goodbyes. We won't make it, and that means neither will you. We get to see Demi sooner than we thought. If we survive, I will hug you with the fiercest grip I can, even if it takes every bit of energy I have. Because I love you all so much. And I miss you. We almost did it—we almost saved you, Imogen. I had to try. This was always how things ended. I just didn't want to believe it."

My throat felt hoarse, like I'd been screaming for days.

I kissed my fingertips and laid them on the iScreen.

The shuttle shuddered, and I peeked around my quarters to the midship.

My dream haunted me—Imogen's face, consumed by the plague-sweat, dying alone. But it had just been a dream, enhanced by whatever pain meds Figg had injected into me.

Now that my head had cleared, my vision returned. The

image of the nuclear warhead, fired from Earth, passing by our shuttle. The hot purple-yellow explosion before the vision cut out.

Had they already fired the warhead? Was our future set?

Trix approached, floating just outside my quarters.

"I have to detach my ship for your re-entry to Earth," she said.

"Will you come with us?"

"That is not wise."

"Please don't leave again, Trix. I can't take much more." Overwhelming sadness knifed into my being.

"I will follow if I can."

"Commander." I floated back towards the cockpit, where Hellcat and Lopez struggled to control the ship. "This is where Trix leaves us."

How much more could I endure? But if we all died anyway, what did it matter?

"It matters, Ofelia. Do not despair," Trix said.

I don't know how to escape this feeling.

"There is always hope."

"Figg, help Trix at the docking hatch," Lopez said.

"Thanks, Trix, for everything." Maya hugged Trix around her middle. They floated there for a moment.

Then Trix turned to me.

"Trust that you will survive. You have each other."

"Yeah, for the next few minutes before we vaporise everyone," I muttered.

I held Trix's hand one last time, closing my eyes and savouring the jolt. My veins fizzled with vibrance, my mind cleared, and I said out loud, "I... we... I mean..." And then I broke down entirely.

The hurt in my body had nothing to do with my injury. The ache of loss clung deep inside, an unwanted but familiar parasite. I cried, my face hot with tears, my mind a mess of welled emotion.

Maya grabbed me, sobbing with me. "We'll do this together."

Trix squeezed my hand with just enough pressure. Then she let go, and Maya and I sniffled, watching her enter the docking hatch.

Trix disappeared inside her ship. She detached her fighter, hanging outside our wing, keeping course with us. She aligned her fighter with our side windows, nodded, and then concentrated on flying.

Saying goodbye was hard. And now I wasn't just losing Imogen, Trix, or even Griffin.

We were about to obliterate everyone we had ever known.

CHAPTER 25

"How are we looking for re-entry?" Lopez strapped into her seat at the cockpit. Hellcat mashed glitching buttons and held the manual controls steady.

"We could end up landing anywhere at this point."

"How are you feeling, Ofelia?" Maya asked.

"Like I'm in space, about to float away."

The shot of medicine that Figg had given me fuzzed my head. Where was I again?

"Strap in tight," Lopez said.

"Roger, copy, a-okay." My mind travelled outside of the shuttle.

Maya helped me back into my seat. Bending still sent excruciating pain through my crushed middle, but at least I didn't pass out. She pulled the straps extra tight because these next few minutes would get us home. Then she strapped into her seat ahead of me.

The empty seat beside me, where Trix had been, seemed forlorn. Trix's fighter's purple engines reflected off the side window, keeping pace with our shuttle.

Trix held out her twiggy finger. I reached out, but couldn't touch her.

"Countdown to re-entry," Hellcat said.

"Copy, Hellcat. Hold on to your insides, folks," Lopez said.

Did the commander address me specifically? The idea wasn't completely terrible, and I cradled the searing sensation, the heat radiating through my palms. But I didn't have the energy to heal myself.

Hellcat wrestled the controls. "Three, two, one—starting deceleration."

The shuttle shook like rice grains bumping up and down in a shaken bowl. The pain in my stomach intensified, and I clutched the armrest. I scrunched my face and closed my eyes. The deceleration ended, and we dipped into Earth's atmospheric drag.

Except this time, we were in the path of the residual space junk from the destroyed fighter ship. It had found its way between us and Earth.

"Damage report," Lopez said.

Maya replied, "Mostly cosmetic. The heat shields are holding for now."

"Will we still make it home?" Hellcat asked.

"Just don't hit anything else," Maya said.

"You might want to avoid that." I wondered if it was the pain medication or if there really was a small object hurtling towards the ship.

Just before the shrapnel bumped off the windshield of our shuttle, Trix enacted her shield, covering her fighter ship and Valentina One. Her shield stretched outside the shuttle, preventing the object from pummelling our front windshield.

This time, her power reached my foggy mind.

My head cleared, and I projected my touch to her fighter. I made contact past our shuttle, into space, and then through her cockpit.

I had never projected my powers so far beyond my body.

My touch reached the arm of her suit, then probed beneath. Her power rebounded through me, into my stomach, into my fingertips. The same power I possessed.

My mind bypassed the pain. Trix and I could help each other. I could make it home.

Trix dropped her shield, and the sensors went wild for a moment.

"What was that?" Hellcat asked.

"Bit of debris," I said. "Trix had us covered."

"We might need more cover." Maya pointed to a cluster of space junk on our starboard side.

Hellcat said, "We don't have enough fuel to burn around it."

"We've got you." I grinned at Trix, my personal wingwoman.

As my mind cleared around the meds, I focussed on our shuttle and nothing else. I imagined the wings on either side of me and the sloping ceiling above. Visualising the smooth, aerodynamic underbelly and the engines propelling us for one last burn.

The ship felt whole, held in my mind. The only thing that mattered. I forgot about the passengers, about the beings we were saving. The ship became my new obsession, pinpointing my concentration into a tiny view.

The translucent veil of dust stood out in the sunlight bouncing off Earth. But it also had solid portions, the clumps woven into place. The solid particles took our focus.

Trix fired off her first shield, protecting our shuttle and her fighter. She held her shield until I was ready.

"See how I projected the shield forward?" Trix's voice rang clear in my mind. "You need faster reflexes than enacting it closer to your body. Do you understand?"

I nodded. *Let's do this.*

When Trix dropped her shield, I was ready with my next one. I projected out past my seat, past Maya, and past Griffin's seat—my mind went out to Griffin, and I decided, at that moment, that we would go back for her. We wouldn't leave any team members behind. She was our crew, and our priority was to keep each other safe—crewmates for life.

That moment of hesitation—thinking about Griffin—threw me off course. My shield extended to the front seats, where Hellcat and Lopez handled the controls. I captured them behind my shield, but it didn't make it outside the shuttle.

I swore as the shield stopped just shy of the glass cockpit windows. The cosmic dust grazed the windshield, and I worried it had cracked the glass.

"Sonova..." Hellcat said, keeping us steady.

The shuttle shook.

Trix was ready with the next shield. She maintained it, catching the crew in her time-stop.

"Can Trix do this on her own?" Lopez noticed my wince as fresh pain tore a hole in my middle. Even if I could bend to check my wounds, my waterproof suit wouldn't allow the blood to seep outside.

"She doesn't have to." I took a shallow breath, careful not to disturb my injury.

Trix, I'm ready.

Trix dropped her shield, and I projected instantly, like my reflexes enacted on supersonic speed. And this time, the shield extended past our seats, beyond the controls, out the wind-shield, to hang centimetres beyond the reinforced glass. Kissing the shield, visible in the sun's glare rounding Earth, was a thumb-sized cluster of debris.

"Argh!" I pushed the shield back with everything I had.

It was a tremendous effort, and I calmed my breathing against the searing pain in my stomach. I took smaller breaths in and out, panting, as Trix enacted her shield straight after I let mine fall.

The healing energy of her shield rebounded and focussed my thoughts.

I had to do this.

Ready? I asked Trix.

"Always." Trix turned the corners of her mouth slits up for me.

I nodded to Trix as our shuttle hurtled back towards Earth at massive rates. Trix and I worked in tandem, reacting to the speedy objects while our shuttle travelled many kilometres per second.

Our shields were like a crescendo of sound, a symphony of displaced energy. We fired them so rapidly that the crew couldn't react outside their time-capturing presence. Every other moment, Trix enacted her shield. And in the alternating milliseconds, I responded with mine. We were entwined, two beings in complete synchronous tune. A duelling of forces, and the shuttle kept advancing.

I felt like I had learned to read music, and Trix and I played a haunting duet. It was an understanding, a truce with something I'd been wrestling with. I had access to parts of me I didn't know existed. My body sang with a new frequency that only Trix and her kind shared with me.

I was Kaseath, and I was human.

We dipped into the farthest reach of Earth's atmosphere, kissing the gases swirling up there, and the shuttle reacted to the new drag on the ship. The shuttle shook, gravity enacting again in crushing g-forces. Our view dipped into the pale blues of the upper atmosphere, leaving the blackness of space behind. We'd done it—we'd cleared the orbiting debris. Now, I hoped the ship would hold together.

"How are we looking, Hellcat?" Lopez said, around the

massive forces crushing her chest. How could she talk around that pressure? It was astounding.

"This won't be textbook," Hellcat grunted. "Hang on."

So there we were, hurtling at massive speed back towards Earth, and it occurred to me we had to stop somehow. We were coming in too hot.

The view out the window shook, and I was glad for my fuzzy head. This time, I didn't black out, but everything seemed unhinged, like I was sitting in the seat beside me, watching from a distance. I fixated on Hellcat's face, reflected in a mirror above the controls. Her expression tensed with the gravity crushing the ship. She concentrated on her job, struggling to pull up the controls. But she was as calm as anyone I'd ever seen in an emergency.

I decided I'd never fly with anyone else. Hellcat had us covered.

Or did she? The shuttle slammed to one side, hitting intense atmospheric pressure. I remembered the terminology from Space Camp.

One of the heat shields outside the window appeared to be on fire. Not the best sign.

Another heat shield flew off the ship's side, burning up. Warning lights flashed, and the shuttle shuddered.

We dipped beneath the clouds, revealing the white terrain below us.

Where on Earth was there still snow? We were very far north—or south.

The shuttle approached the smooth terrain, an ice shelf. Beyond it was a swathe of ocean. The shuttle could crash-land on water, but we wouldn't survive the freezing sea temperatures.

We'd have to land on the ice shelf.

Lopez said over the comms, "Brace positions."

I crossed my arms against my chest, like we had during training. Something told me it wouldn't help when we crash-landed. Our bodies would be crushed, along with the crystal. And we'd take Earth's population into oblivion with us.

Hellcat deployed our chutes out the back of the shuttle, whipping us into our seats. The landing gear crunched out of its bays, adding to our drag. The overpowering rage of the engines blocked all other sounds.

The shuttle lowered, and I forced my head to the side, checking our landing situation. All around was snow and ice, a white canvas.

Where were we?

Hellcat grunted as she avoided landing right in the middle of a snowdrift.

As our wheels touched the ground, we skidded into the clear white space of the ice shelf, sending shards of white chunks up by our side windows. The surface was too slippery to slow us down. Our flaps were on maximum extension. The tyres blew.

The shelf in front of us dropped away into the ocean.

We needed more runway.

With one last effort, Hellcat yanked the controls, her expression determined. She fought the landing mechanism, and the shuttle lurched sideways, moving side-on to the edge of the shelf. And then Hellcat did something unexpected—she tapped into our remaining fuel and forced one last burn.

The shock of the sudden energy release shot us parallel to the ocean and the edge of the ice shelf. She yanked the controls and twisted the shuttle so that it faced away from the edge. The landing gear collapsed altogether. The shuttle's underbelly thudded into the ice below us, still skidding.

I closed my eyes.

Please, let us be okay, I thought.

"I wish for that too, Ofelia," Trix replied inside my head.

Did that mean that Trix was nearby?

The ship jarred, and the shuttle crashed into the ice, the nose pushed inwards, the walls bending like a crushed soda can. Metal-on-metal screeched like a thundering mechanical beast. The air vibrated with the jarring impact.

Would we be squashed alive before we stopped moving?

We ground to a messy, scrunchy halt.

I opened one eye. Nobody moved. Were we suspended in the holding place between life and death?

The ice crushed the shuttle's nose, embedding it against the front windshield.

I checked on our crew. Figg was fine in the seat behind me, but I could tell this ride had exceeded her worst nightmarish fantasies. Maya unbuckled in the seat in front. And Hellcat checked comms.

Lopez kept her voice steady. "Are we all accounted for?"

Maya climbed out of her seat, around the cabin debris, and hugged me, her eyes moist with relieved tears. "We made it!"

"Nice landing, Hellcat." I hardly noticed my pain.

"I've gotta look after my crew." Hellcat grinned.

Finally, we'd made Hellcat into a team player.

But Lopez hadn't moved.

CHAPTER 26

THE SHUTTLE'S crumpled frame buckled outwards in places and crushed inwards in others. Our ship had taken a beating, but also kept its crew safe. The heat shields had done their job. But this bird would never fly again.

I tasted salt on the bracing wind shooting through the cracks in the sides of the shuttle as the sea pounded against the ice shelf. It was a droning soundtrack, and we had to yell to be heard, even within the shuttle's flimsy shelter.

The interior was a mess of wires and glitching screens. Tossed-around supplies spewed from broken compartments.

I'm not going to lie. My pain intensified, and my body felt heavy, unused to Earth's gravity. Each movement was agonising.

But I was more worried about Lopez.

A rod of ice had pierced the shuttle's windshield and embedded through her shoulder. The shard pinned her against her seat. She said, "Doctor, I may need your help here."

Hellcat moved to help the commander out of her harness, but Lopez waved her away.

"We've just landed—where exactly?" she asked. "Establish comms and report our location."

Hellcat grabbed the comms unit. "This is Valentina One from the Northern Alliance of Countries. We have landed at coordinates: latitude 74 degrees, 29.4 minutes south, longitude 104 degrees, 59.4 minutes west. Requesting extraction at these coordinates. Over."

Lopez reached into the pocket of her suit around the ice shard. She pulled out the crystal—it looked intact. She sighed and placed it back in her pocket, patting down the Velcro.

Hellcat continued on the comms. "Request immediate extraction. We have injured crew members in need of medical support. Over."

Figg navigated through the mangled interior to Lopez and assessed her shoulder. The ice shard pierced through the back of Lopez's seat, pinning her in place.

"It looks like a clean entry and exit wound," Figg said. "It also missed major arteries and bone. You may have muscle damage, though."

Lopez winced as she shifted in her seat. "Get this icicle out!"

"Don't pull out the knife," Figg said to herself.

"What?" Hellcat reached for the shard to wrench it free.

"Stop what you're doing!" Figg commanded. Hellcat stopped, confused. Lopez looked relieved not to have someone yanking on her shoulder. "It's better to keep the object in place, or she'll lose too much blood. We have to find help."

"And won't the commander freeze to death before we get help?" I asked. Our earlier crew cohesiveness was falling away, tacked together with ineffective glue—melting, just like Lopez's icicle.

Lopez shifted, wincing with the pain from her skewered shoulder.

"Copy, Valentina One," a voice crackled over the comms.

We'd been found! Lopez grabbed the comms from Hellcat.

"State your location," Lopez said.

"Your name and rank?" the accented voice on the comms asked.

"I am Commander Luz Lopez, and who are you?"

The comms cut out, and a high-pitched whine lay over the top of the feed. We heard the reply.

"This is Pierre Franco. I am a geologist with the Red Star Antarctica expedition."

"Request medical extraction from our current location," Hellcat said.

"Negative. The weather's about to turn. We can't reach you in time."

"So what do we do?" Lopez asked.

"Meet us at the research base. Head southwest from your current location. It's about eight kilometres away."

"Wait—" Lopez said, but the signal cut out.

"There shouldn't be anyone down here." Maya huddled closer, away from the icy sheets of wind slicing through the gaps in the shuttle's crushed frame.

We were far from London, where humans shouldn't exist.

"Do we trust them?" Figg asked.

Maya said, "Will we make it in these conditions, with Ofelia and the commander injured?"

"We could stay and wait for rescue." I nodded pointedly to Lopez, stuck in her seat.

"We might be out of time." Hellcat pointed to the ship's rear.

Was it... glowing?

A small fire sparked at the back of the shuttle. Flames licked at the debris thrown from the storage compartments. Electrical pops produced new spot fires.

"We've gotta move." Hellcat grabbed a jagged, bent metal

rod. She snapped it free from the ceiling and sawed at the back of Lopez's ice spear to dislodge Lopez from the seat.

Maya moved closer to the fire. She grabbed one of the damaged space suits and slapped it like a fire blanket over the flames.

Figg clawed at the shuttle's sides, searching for an exit.

Gasping at the clenching pain in my middle, I pushed through to help Maya at the back of the shuttle.

We battled the spreading flames in the cargo area.

Maya fell towards the cockpit. I threw the debris aside, clearing a path. It was like scaling Trash Mountain amongst the rotting garbage. We could be buried alive in here, like my nightmares.

I slammed my fist to dislodge a cracked panel, using it as a heat shield.

"Careful," Maya said as another loose wire sparked with power.

I swiped at a wire. It sparked, and electricity flowed into my hand. My fist clenched, an automatic reflex, and I braced for the jolt. But the electricity felt around my pain, dislodging the sharp edges. I could move again, and could tolerate the tenderness.

It was like Trix's healing touch.

Had she crashed, too? Was she lying hurt somewhere, alone?

Maya and I retreated as the flames spread like a rapid rash. Each time we squashed one spot fire, another sprang to life.

Hellcat's makeshift saw squeaked on the ice as it grated through. Hellcat sped up the sawing in response to Lopez's grunts of pain. The friction must have been agony.

"Nearly through," Hellcat said.

Lopez roared in pain as the saw clunked on the chair

beneath her, and she sat forward, the spear of ice visible out the front and back of her shoulder, her suit dripping blood.

"Maya, Ofelia, get out of there!" Lopez shouted.

The flames surrounded us on three sides, licking at the shuttle's ceiling and crumpled interior.

Then I heard it—Trix's voice. "Are you safe, Ofelia?"

I banged my head on a compartment door hanging at a crazy angle. Maya reached out to help me.

"Trix made it," I replied. "Are you close?"

"Yes, I will catch up," Trix replied. "But you have to leave imminently."

Before that sank in, an explosion shook the ground beneath the shuttle.

The ship skidded, unsteady on the ice, tossing us around inside. I fell on my side, tearing fresh pain into my stomach. I landed closer to the fire consuming the back half of the shuttle.

The rest of the crew hung on as the groaning shuttle stabilised.

"That way!" Lopez pointed to a massive fissure on the shuttle's side, opening our tin can like a cracked egg. The rip widened, revealing the ice shelf beneath us and the shuttle melting into the crash site. Our rear engines turned the back area to slush, and the shuttle groaned and shifted as the fire engulfed the entire rear section.

The roaring fire popped as it consumed new tinder—food stores, medical supplies, and the sleeping bags in our quarters— melting the plastic and electrical displays.

It spread through the discarded cargo.

Holding onto the crushed ceiling for balance, I waved to the widening crack in the shuttle's side.

Figg slipped through the crack, careful not to snag on the jagged edges. Hellcat followed. Maya spotted the satellite phone resting amongst packets of freeze-dried space food.

"Hurry!" She waved at Lopez and me.

Lopez was closest to the fissure and dove through. Standing straight was agony as I manoeuvred through the gap.

I peered through the crack at Maya, who inched towards the fire, grabbing the satellite phone.

The flame licked out after her, singeing her hand, and she pulled away from the burn.

Maya ducked through the gap, landing beside me in the snow.

"Are you both okay?" I bent around my smarting middle.

Maya shoved her hand in the snow at her feet, then wrapped her beanie around the burn.

"It's not bad." She held up the satellite phone, grinning.

"We've got to keep going." Lopez hunched over, nursing her skewered shoulder. Hellcat propped her up.

Flames engulfed the shuttle, a blackened, collapsing skeleton. We moved away, avoiding the heat.

The wind was like a screeching animal against my eardrums, and the cold was a solid weight around my chest, squeezing my breath out.

The surrounding terrain revealed the path of our crash and the chunked-up ice clocking our journey. About a hundred metres away, an ice shelf marked the sheer drop into the ocean, the waves crashing against it. Roaring winds wedged into my face with a blasting sting.

A flat area lay farther inland. A mountainous mass was visible in the snow-filled distance. Thick snowdrifts covered the terrain.

"Which way?" Figg kept her composure.

Maya pointed her satellite phone into the wind, searching for a signal.

The approaching storm loomed large against the ice shelf, a

solid back swarm of clouds and thrashing snow. The menacing clouds seemed to touch the ground in their fury.

Lopez knelt where she had fallen, assessing the threat, wincing.

Maya checked the satellite phone and shouted over the wind, "I have a signal!"

She wound her arm around and then pointed forward, deeper into the terrain, over a hilly section.

We left the burning carcass of the shuttle, dented and melting into the ice.

We sank up to our knees in the thick snow. It was like running into relentlessly tall ocean waves. We were burning too much energy, but the thundering wind kept us moving.

We crested a snow mound, and the weather cleared just enough to reveal a large swathe of icy terrain in front.

Lopez pointed to the side of the mound, a pathway closer to the edge of the ice shelf. Fresh blood from her skewered shoulder spilled into the snow.

We pushed forward, each painful step bringing us closer to either rescue or freezing to death.

The snowstorm hit, slicing down from above and tossing snowflakes in the scudding wind. Deep patterns formed in the dumping snow, like the peaks on a sand dune. The black clouds closed in, shutting out the sun and creating a false nightfall.

Adrenalin kept me going. The air was too thick. I couldn't see beyond our crew in front of me.

My moon boots sank, the snow reaching my knees as we fumbled through the storm, our faces numb with cold. I followed Lopez and Hellcat, watching my feet with each painful step. Maya was by my side, holding me up.

"Hurry!" Lopez yelled.

We followed, losing sight of Lopez in the storm.

My focus fuzzed because of the extreme cold and the pain

meds. The sensation was like swimming in the training pool, not trudging through snow.

I dropped to one knee in the snowdrift, and Maya tugged at my arm, pulling me back to standing. My strength had gone.

Trix's voice was louder in my head, above the storm and my ragged, struggling breath.

She appeared like an apparition through the storm, the orange outline of her veins muted by the atmosphere.

Trix stopped beside me. "Are you okay?"

"Time to rest." I sat in the snow.

"Let me help you." Trix scooped me up into her long arms. My skin came alive, crackling with her energy as I snuggled next to her body. My head bumped against her chest with her fluid footsteps. I shivered against the cold.

Trix carried me, rallying our crew. Lopez and Hellcat struggled through the deep snow up ahead. Maya ran beside me and Trix. Figg scrambled to keep up, panicking at the flinging snow and the buffeting wind.

Mechanical engine whines wavered on the wind. Three small vehicles sped through the snowy fog towards us. The jet-black snowmobiles sliced through the terrain and sailed over the ice bumps. They were headed straight for us. The drivers wore thick, mottled grey and white jackets, helmets, and black snow goggles. They drove their vehicles expertly, like an extension of their bodies, kicking up snow in their wake.

The one in front signalled to the others in a circular motion, and the snowmobiles skidded to cut off our path. They left the engines idling, just audible over the rushing wind.

My eyes fixated on the machine guns slung over their shoulders.

There was nowhere to run.

CHAPTER 27

THE SNOWMOBILE MEN wore mottled camouflage jackets, puffing around muscular frames with wind-bitten features that had endured this frigid climate for a lifetime. They slung automatic weapons over their backs, and smaller handguns were strapped to each ankle. The rear one touched his earpiece as he listened to instructions from back at his camp.

"We didn't think you'd make it on your own." The closest man's thick accent was faint in the wind. He wound a snow-flecked scarf over his nose and mouth, warding off the elements. He was taller than the other two, with a shrewd, calculating glare. "Hop on."

The men glanced at Trix casually, not drawing attention to her. They didn't flinch, didn't let their shock register. Did they know about the Kaseath already?

Thunder cracked overhead.

"If we don't move now, we'll all freeze," another growled. His thick forehead was carved with two interlocking scars from countless brawls.

I said, "Do you work for Pierre?"

The three men smirked at each other.

"No, Pierre works for us," Scarface said. I couldn't tell if he was serious.

"Who are you?" Figg used her no-nonsense tone.

"I'm Fari," the lead man said. "And we're out of time."

Lopez sought her crew's permission over the roaring wind. Could we trust them?

Another gust flurried the snowfall, threatening to knock us off balance. We had to escape the elements.

None of our crew objected, so we climbed onto the backs of the three snowmobiles. Trix and I joined Fari. Maya and Hellcat went with Scarface, and Figg and Lopez took the final one with the man plugged into his earpiece.

Trix bent into the seat behind Fari, holding me in her lap. There was just room on the snowmobile's long seat. Trix held my middle with one arm, and the other grabbed the bar underneath her seat.

Fari swivelled to check on us. "Hang tight."

Trix managed to keep from crushing me between her chest and Fari's back.

He kicked the snowmobile into gear, turning it in a tight circle. We roared off.

The ride was bumpy as all heck, and I held onto painful consciousness. Each bump stabbed new knives into my middle. There were constant bumps.

The white mass shot by at ridiculous speeds through the gap between Trix's stomach and Fari's back. His puffer jacket trembled in the fast-moving air, which whipped into my eyes. The cold intensified. I hung on, willing the ride to end.

The engine's whine was shrill, but the growling wind was louder. It felt like we were racing the clouds to the base. Would we win or lose?

Fari zigzagged through the powdered terrain to avoid

chunks of snow. The movement sent jarring shockwaves of pain through my belly.

The front ski pinged into the ice next to my feet. Our other crew members' snowmobiles raced on either side, visible through the snow haze.

The snowmobiles raced up steep terrain between the mountains on our left and the ice shelf, dropping into the ocean on the right.

The snowmobile sailed over a large bump on the ground. We got air, and I braced for the impact as we banged back onto the surface. I was pretty sure I had torn something important, and my head fogged with pain. I gripped Fari's jacket. I had the sensation of falling off Earth into a gaping hole's cold, tumble-dry depths.

Our snowmobile caught another jagged snag in the snow. I couldn't take any more pain and was close to blacking out.

Barricades loomed in front—wooden spears in a cross shape, laid in three lines next to a path. The sharpened tips of the spears poked out from the snow—a line of deep trenches.

The way forward was through the gate.

The turrets matched our snowmobiles' movements, keeping us in their sights.

Why were we heading to a fortified compound? Where was the research station?

The heavy gate winched open. We sped towards it.

How would we stop? I closed my eyes, waiting for the impact against the gate.

Fari turned our snowmobile to the side, and we skidded through the gap in the gate.

Guards inside the compound leaped out of the way as the snowmobile drifted to a rocky stop, just shy of hitting the two-storey buildings inside the gate.

Hellcat and Maya followed, hanging on. Lopez and Figg's snowmobile had taken a beating, but both still clung to the driver.

Maya and Hellcat dismounted, shaking with fear and cold. Figg helped Lopez stand, bent around the icicle in her shoulder.

Maya stepped closer to Trix and me.

"You're okay now," I said to Maya. "We're safe."

Maya smiled, unconvinced. Trix moved closer to our crew. Lopez grimaced in pain, but we could help her now. The outpost would have a sick bay. Figg could stitch up our commander.

"We're not safe." Lopez raised her eyes at the building closest to us.

About fifty men exited the raised level of the building, dressed for the elements in camouflage grey-and-white snow-suits. They fanned across the outer perimeter of the building, staring down at the barracks' entrance where we stood.

This was no research station, a fact that was confirmed when all fifty men pointed their guns at our crew.

We had escaped the alien attack, only to land somewhere more dangerous—in the middle of an armed barricade on the edge of a forgotten land.

―――――――

The men who'd dived away from our skidding snowmobiles found their feet and aimed automatic weapons through the open gate.

"Close the bloomin' gate!" Fari yelled, and two dazed grunts worked together, winding the heavy mechanism beside the gate. The massive doors winched closed, thudding as the two halves met, locking the storm outside.

The wind roared beyond the two-storey walls. Flurried snow blew around the courtyard, thick and sharp as hail. I leaned against its force.

Our crew faced the military men pointing guns at us from above. This was survival, not negotiation.

I grabbed Maya's hand. She wasn't used to a full-on military assault and seemed overwhelmed. I was used to violence. A Northies rat had to look over their shoulder to survive. But the worst violence was always outside. My childhood home was a walk in a perfumed rose garden compared to the battlements we'd landed in.

"Fari, we're harmless." Lopez appealed to our saviours-turned-enemies. "Search our ship. We crash-landed here. We need to return to our people."

"So you can share intel about this outpost?" Scarface growled, spitting in the snow at our feet.

"We don't know anything," I said. "There's nothing to tell."

"Please, let me tend to our injured," Figg said.

"They won't make it." A man with a grey moustache, nonchalantly carrying a steaming thermos, stepped onto the balcony of the building above. "Here, if the elements want, they'll take you."

"We'll take something else for ourselves," Fari snarled. "How about your alien friend?"

"I wouldn't advise that," I said. "She's dangerous."

"You've given us the best reason to kill it."

"She," I said. "Her name is Trix."

"Why name a rabid dog?" Fari shoved Trix and me away from the snowmobile.

"Why did you rescue us if you're only going to kill us?" I kept my tone conciliatory.

Our crew huddled closer together. Would it be better to stay inside the compound or take our chances in the storm?

The grey-moustachioed man casually sipped the liquid from his steaming thermos. He lowered the flask, never taking his eyes off Trix.

"Wait." I stepped forward.

The grunt next to the moustachioed man sent a string of bullets towards my feet, snapping into the snow. I jumped back, hands in the air.

"You walk when I say you walk," the man said, his grunt reloading his weapon. "And if I don't say squat, you stay put!"

"Yes, sir, no problem," I squeaked.

"I take it you're in charge?" Lopez said evenly.

"The name's Khan," he said.

"Pleasure to meet you. I am Commander Lopez." She pointed to the satellite dish on the roof of the building. "At least let us contact our people. Our comms were down, and our satellite phone can't breach the storm."

"Who are your 'people'?" Khan stared shrewdly at Lopez.

"We must contact Prime Minister Pollins," Lopez replied, taking in the man's greedy stare. "I'm sure he can strike a deal. It could be lucrative."

"You hear that, boys?" Khan turned to his men. "We've got ourselves a direct line to the leader of the Remaining Northern Countries. It's payday!"

Khan motioned for his men to surround us, and they crowded in, gun muzzles pushed into our backs. They marched us towards the barracks.

"We have demands," Fari said.

The men laughed, a greedy glint in their eyes.

"Warm up the blower," Khan said to someone hovering by the inner door. "And say exactly what I ask."

"Do what they say." I said to my crew, controlling the terror in my voice.

"Commander," Hellcat said, with a rigid set to her jaw. Her eyes were full of panic, but she kept her voice steady.

Figg looked ready to pass out. For once, she wasn't in control of the scary armed men.

Lopez nodded her permission.

I said, "Let's talk to Pollins."

Pollins was the last person I'd thought would be our saviour, who could help our crew escape this frigid ice shelf.

Fari's men stabbed the muzzles of their guns into our backs, pushing us towards the barracks.

The storm squalled, the wind biting hard into my cheeks. We stomped up the wooden stairs in our thick moon boots, careful not to slip on their icy sheen.

We stepped through the wide doors on the balcony into a mess hall filled with long tables and metal chairs. Khan nodded to Fari and Scarface, who shut the mess hall doors against the blustering weather outside.

The doors were locked, keeping us safe from the elements. The mess hall was warmer from the body heat of the crowding men.

A TV sat on one side of the cramped rec area. Along the far wall was a kitchen area with a steel bench. Walkways led deeper into the complex on either side.

Khan motioned down a dark corridor, and we followed, single file, with Fari and Scarface aiming machine guns at our backs.

We entered a cramped comms room. The desk contained electronic equipment and three large touch screens. A microphone sat on the side, and cabinets lined the far wall. A scrawny man with a braided beard sat at the desk, awaiting orders.

Scarface and Fari crowded into the small room, jostling and

chuckling. I felt like we'd just increased morale for a remote military installation that didn't get support from the outside world. Scarface had already made eyes at Lopez. I was glad for Trix's strong arms beside me.

"Pierre, get us a link," Khan said.

The braided-beard man pressed touch screens and warmed up the comms.

Pierre lifted his eyebrows to me in apology.

"You're not quite a research station," I said.

"Not so much." Pierre's unenthusiastic reply matched the unfriendly atmosphere.

He established a grainy, blue-screened video link and stood back, waving Lopez forward.

"Just punch in your digits," he said.

Lopez did as instructed. I was thankful for our astronaut training. We had memorised key operational information, including the number to the comms room back to Earth.

The video link rang, connecting.

"Make it short before the weather hits," Pierre said, the tip of his braided beard trembling with anticipation.

Fari closed in, his breath foul in the cramped space. The particular notes of body odour reminded me of Northies. Showers out here were optional. We didn't smell much better.

The comms synced, and a distorted, glitching face appeared on the other end.

"Jackpot!" Khan said. "It's our man, Pollins."

Pollins's pale face stared back, confused by the men photo-bombing the stream.

"Lopez, thank goodness you're alive. Where are you?" Pollins said.

"Antarctica. You can follow our ship's black box, if it's still intact. We're at a base about eight kilometres southwest from there."

"There are no bases at those coordinates." Pollins's eyebrows raised.

"You're looking at it," Fari said.

"Our mission didn't go as planned." I bustled in front.

"So, no cure then?" Pollins asked.

"But we have the crystal," I said.

Pollins couldn't hide his pleasure. I had him now, and played my only hand.

"But we're not bringing it home until my family is safe."

Pollins shot a shrewd glance my way, and I realised he was back in his war bunker, the map of the world on a large screen behind him.

A map with a tonne of blinking red lights above the Remaining Countries.

Did that mean we were under attack?

Before I could ask, Khan pushed in front and addressed the video link.

"We haven't met, but I know who you are," he said.

"And who are you?" Pollins evened out his voice.

"I'm Khan. And I'm in charge of this base, which means I'm in charge of your people."

"Of course, I understand," Pollins replied. "What do you want?"

"What do I want, says the leader of the Remaining Countries. Only you're not the remaining countries. Not by a long shot."

"I ask again, what do you want?"

Khan considered, then replied, "An apology. For the attempted genocide of our people. So, a very *public* apology."

"We just want our crew back. What do you really want? Supplies? Weapons? Food?"

"I want you on record, apologising for the war against our people," Khan said, coming closer to the comms and shoving a gun at Lopez's temple. "Or things go sideways for your crew."

Lopez barely flinched, but a film of sweat appeared on her forehead, even in this ice-box room. She maintained a neutral expression.

"I don't know what you mean."

"Aren't these your Northern Alliance rebels eliminating our people?"

"We have no forces south of the equator," Pollins replied.

"Yes, it messes with your identity; you are called the Northern Alliance. Being here is treason to your side."

"Please, there are no rebels."

Khan dug the muzzle of the pistol deeper, pressing a white dent into Lopez's skin.

"Are you going to keep up that charade, *Prime Minister*?" Khan's eyes narrowed.

"Ah, let's be reasonable." Pollins's chin wobbled.

But he didn't deny it, which meant that he already knew. Lies upon lies. How would we be rescued now?

Pollins hadn't confirmed that my family was alive.

"They may be," Trix said.

Do you know if they are? I thought.

"I have seen your possible future back in Cookham East."

In a vision?

"Yes."

But is my family safe?

"I cannot see."

Maybe I could. My focus landed on the map of the world behind Pollins.

More than London was at risk. The red-blinking war zones took over. Pollins was losing the battle.

The entire world could be destroyed; this might be my last chance to save it.

Save my sister, save my friends, save the world.

It was no longer enough to think about the ones I loved. Humanity teetered on extinction. Space aboard the Ark was limited. My sister couldn't go, which meant neither could I.

This planet was all we had.

I knew what to do. *Get ready, Trix.*

CHAPTER 28

KHAN DUG the barrel of his gun into Lopez's forehead, shuffling in the cramped comms room. Fari guarded the door while Scarface hung out behind us. Pierre was next to the comms desk, farthest from the door.

Our crew was alert, eyeing the exit back to the mess hall. We were trapped, with nowhere to run, unable to dodge point-blank bullets.

But a bunch of outlaw humans wouldn't stop our progress.

We do not surrender to these men.

"I'm ready," Trix said.

Lopez flicked her eyes upwards in acknowledgement.

I slapped Khan's gun away from Lopez's temple.

Trix swiped Khan's shoulder, catching him off balance. He let go of Lopez and fired his gun into the ceiling. The shot rang clear in the cramped space.

Part of the ceiling collapsed, and pre-fab sheets and insulation fell on Lopez. Dust clouded around us, and we squinted through the gloom, choking on the thick powder.

Trix, however, didn't breathe, so was able to slam her fist into Khan's belly. He doubled over, gasping for air, choking on the dust particles.

Lopez rallied, stomping on Khan's boot. Khan dropped the gun. It skidded over the smooth, insulated flooring underneath the comms desk.

Pollins shouted, "Hang tight, we have dispatched—"

Pierre banged his fist on the touch screen, shutting off the comms.

Scarface muscled in, grabbing Trix in a crushing tackle. They fell into the wall, denting the pre-fab with Trix's scaled back.

Trix punched the muscled Scarface on his arm, having the height advantage, but Scarface head-butted her neck—the highest part of her he could reach—and spat into her eye.

Trix didn't blink, because she didn't have eyelids. She wiped the spittle from her eye, unshaken.

Scarface hesitated, then punched her in her belly.

Trix grunted and slapped the sides of his head with her hands, stunning him. Scarface lost his balance and slammed into Khan. They both hit the ground.

Hellcat leaped onto Pierre's back, pulling his braided beard until a clump of frizzy hairs broke free. Pierre roared and struck out, dislodging Hellcat from his back. He slapped her on the cheek. Hellcat retaliated and swapped punches with the petite man. The blows landed heavily. Hellcat stepped back, the last punch grabbing her breath.

My middle throbbed like an engine revving before a drag race, sending nerve-jarring pain through me. I leaned against the rear wall, rallying my strength. Would I see the fight's end?

But I wasn't dead yet.

Pierre was closest to me, his braided beard scuffed and bloody.

A glint shone in his ankle holster—the blade of his knife. I snatched the knife, slicing the back of his parka. He twisted to face me, and I ducked his blow, landing on the floor. I hacked out, slashing his Achilles.

He screamed and fell over, clutching his ankle.

His good foot pedalled on the ground as he scooted away from my reach.

Fari wrestled with Hellcat, and I crouched low, holding my insides still, willing the pain to ease. Fari stepped back to avoid a jab from Hellcat, and I stabbed Pierre's knife into Fari's boot. The knife pinged as the blade hit the steel-capped toes below the leather.

Just great. Doing zero damage. It only annoyed the tall man.

Fari lifted me by the scruff of my space suit, shaking me, shooting blackout pain into my middle. He threw me against the wall, and I slid to the ground. Slumping over, I hung onto consciousness, my energy spent. Not even the adrenalin could keep me upright.

Maya scooted under the comms desk, grabbing the gun.

Fari left me on the ground and went to help Khan, who was scrapping with Lopez.

"Secure the crystal!" Khan said, pinned behind Lopez's blocking stance. "If Pollins wants it so badly, it must be valuable."

Scarface landed a blow that cracked Lopez's jawbone.

He grabbed Lopez's still-frozen icicle spear, sticking out the back of her shoulder, and twisted it. Lopez screamed in pain as Scarface wrenched her to the floor.

"Give me the crystal, Commander." Khan pushed his face closer to hers.

"I'll shoot you." Maya's hands trembled as she stood from below the comms desk. She pointed the gun at Scarface, then Khan.

Scarface sneered back. "You won't."

"No, but I will." Figg snatched the gun from Fari's second holster.

She fired a shot.

The gun's crack in the confined room deadened all sound. The blast's shock was overpowering. Who was hit?

Then, dark blood seeped into Scarface's torso. It spread across his grey-and-white camouflage jacket, staining the fabric, the blood seeping like a spilled black-red dye.

Scarface pressed his hand to his belly, then leaned his bloody hand against the wall. The blood left a handprint as he slid to the floor.

Lopez stomped on Fari's boot. Fari flinched, towering over the more compact Lopez.

Figg aimed the gun at Khan but couldn't get a clean shot. Lopez and Hellcat were in the way.

Lopez kicked out at Fari, bowling over Khan. Pierre hopped to the comms desk, grabbing his Achilles with both hands. Scarface was done, crumpled on the floor, nursing his gunshot wound.

Was it bad that I didn't mind if they died? What if these grunts captured the crystal? They were already preparing for war. The crystal would be destroyed, obliterating everyone I loved.

But I saw an opening. The way to the door was clear.

Lopez grabbed her shoulder, steeling herself against the pain. She pushed out of the comms room, and Maya and Figg followed.

Hellcat scrapped with Fari, each holding the other in an armlock.

Trix moved her intimidating bulk forward to help. She towered over Fari, tall as he was. He fumbled backwards, lost his footing, and bashed his head on the corner of the comms desk. He fell to the floor like a tumbling of bricks, out cold.

That left the scrawny Pierre limping around his injury, his fight extinguished. But Khan wasn't afraid. He had taken everything in, assessing Trix's threat.

Khan's calculated gaze flicked over Trix. Then he stooped, pulling Scarface into a seated position. Scarface grunted in pain, searching his leader's eyes. Khan's immediate henchmen were out for the count.

I expected Khan to charge after us, but he tended to Scarface, pressing a hand to his gunshot wound to staunch the blood. Hellcat pushed past Pierre, who no longer resisted.

Trix and I followed Hellcat.

Our crew crowded in the corridor outside the comms room. There was the way towards the mess hall and Khan's men. Or the way forward, deeper into the barracks, and potentially a dead end.

The crippling pain was familiar now. I stood taller, fighting its lure.

"Come on." I led us back to the mess hall, towards the exit.

Maya still had her gun, although I wasn't sure she could use it. I tossed my knife to Hellcat, who held it in front of her, slashing forward. Figg had Fari's gun. Lopez staunched the blood flow on her shoulder. Her icicle spear had melted in the warmer building.

The lights flickered as the roaring wind lashed outside.

We pushed into the mess hall.

Two men appeared and shot off rounds from their handguns.

I fired easy shields at the bullets. We were caught in my moving time-stop, running towards rescue.

I dropped my shield. To the men, it appeared as if the bullets had magically fallen to the floor, which I guess they did.

The surprised men backed up, shuffling against the chairs and tables of the mess hall.

One uprooted a table onto its side like a barricade. Metal on the concrete floor screeched above the squalling storm outside.

Several men dove behind the tables, taking up defensive positions. The first grunt fired a string of bullets through the gaps.

Trix and I alternated our shields, protecting our right flank. I eyed the exit.

"Go," Trix said.

I flicked my eyes to the door, in full view of my crew. They didn't hesitate.

"Fire!" The men squeezed off rounds towards Trix.

Our shields enacted. We protected our crew's right flank.

"Get to the exit!" I gritted my teeth. My shield's warmth was welcome in this freezing place. The greens melded with the electric, cracking yellows. I dropped my shield as Trix enacted hers.

Wave after wave hit our shields. I gritted my teeth around the pain, not able to stand upright, concentrating on the bullets.

Just the bullets.

Keeping us safe.

My lightning-fast shield alternated with Trix's stronger force field. I moulded my being to sing with the bullets, anticipating their angle and thrust.

Soon, our shields were solid, keeping time open on our side.

"We're almost there," Lopez said, in the next time-stop.

My attention misdirected, as I thought we could be safe. We may go home.

A bullet squeezed through my shield.

The thwack of the bullet punctured Maya's space suit.

"Maya!" I shouted, forgetting the attack.

She twisted from the force of the bullet. Blood seeped from her left armpit. She hit the ground.

The bullet could have penetrated her ribcage—right into her heart.

Hellcat heaved her from the ground, throwing Maya's arm over her shoulder.

"Keep going," Hellcat said.

Maya was in shock, she didn't react as if the pain registered. She seemed confused.

Trix heaved into a last shield, the one to end the mess hall grunts. She forced the bullets back in one massive push of energy.

The bullets shot back at our attackers, popping holes through the table barricades. Men shouted in pain and shock. They scrambled farther back into the mess hall.

The distraction was all we needed.

We rushed outside into the heaving storm.

Outside, plunging temperatures kicked the wind right out of my chest, making breathing difficult.

The advancing men were better dressed for the frigid temperatures. Bitter air whacked my senses, freezing now that the storm was on top of us.

It was as if my legs waded in mounds of rubbery foam in this space suit. How many shields did I have left before I succumbed? I was on my very last wobbly legs.

Didn't Figg say I had a couple of hours at best? And I wasn't the only one needing a hospital. Adrenalin kept us going, but Maya's injuries could be serious.

Maya's head drooped as Hellcat dragged her along.

I rushed over, helping Hellcat keep her upright. But I only tore fresh pain into my side, as if a giant had ripped me in half with its bare hands.

"I've got her," Hellcat said, determined.

Mini-guns peppered fire from the turrets beyond the barracks' outer gate. Who were they firing at? Was it Pollins's men rescuing us?

The storm swallowed men's screams, and dull gunfire echoed and fell. Pain was silenced.

Khan's soldiers concentrated fresh fire on the enemy and didn't notice our crew limping from the mess hall. I hoped they didn't fire on our rescue party.

We stomped down the stairs to the courtyard below. Standing on the lower level, I squinted against the snow-thick air.

Hellcat propped up Maya, who was unsteady. Lopez grabbed her injured shoulder, open with fresh blood. Figg held Lopez steady.

Trix's energy waned, the curl on her head flat now, without the sun's recharging radiation.

"We have to return to the shuttle." Lopez winced as her icicle wound dripped blood into the snow.

Visibility was down to a couple of metres, but Lopez pointed to three snowmobiles parked in front of the lower buildings. Snow covered their black frames like white packing foam.

Wrapped and ready for our escape.

"Hold on, Maya." My vision dimmed a little. Was it just the storm closing in?

Maya stooped around her ribcage, dripping lines of blood down her white suit and creating a red pattern in the ice. Thrashing snow devoured the blood.

"Get the gate!" Lopez yelled around the mini-gun fire.

Figg ran to the gate winch, but it was too heavy to operate by herself. Hellcat leaned Maya against the snowmobile and joined Figg. Despite that, the gate stuck, as if welded shut.

They thrust their backs into the winch, giving it everything they had, desperately shoving.

Trix sloped over, her sludgy feet sticking on the ice. But she pushed forward.

Hellcat and Figg heaved into the mechanism, and Trix added her force. The gate creaked open, catching the closest gun turret guard's attention.

"They're escaping!"

Hellcat, Figg, and Trix ran back to the snowmobiles.

Trix fired up the closest one and waved me on. "Let us go, Ofelia."

An explosion rattled the area outside of the barracks.

Then, a rocket fired overhead. The missile arced downwards towards the building we'd just exited.

An explosion unfurled in black, smoking flame.

The rocket eviscerated the building, landing on the roof of the mess hall, carving a crater in the structure, and sending a fireball high into the air.

We ducked as debris shot out—shattered roofing tiles, steel beams, boxes of machine guns. A water barrel smashed into the icy courtyard, liquid spilling out and freezing as it touched the ground.

A second explosion rocked the building as the flames caught fresh ammo.

Metal tables from the mess hall shot into the air, heading for our crew. I turned just in time to enact my shield and held the tables while our crew scooted out of the way. I deflected the dented mess, throwing the tables beside the gate.

The skirmish distracted the turret guards, who returned fire outside the barracks.

Khan limped out of the mess hall doors, which hung at an angle. They were otherwise intact, clinging onto the collapsing frames. The doors detached and fell through the second-storey balcony.

Men fled the building, screaming, their clothes on fire. Two grunts flung themselves off the balcony into the snowdrifts beside the stairs, dousing their flaming clothes. The stench of singed hair and exploded gasoline added to the polar storm.

The rest of the building behind Khan was demolished, spewing carcinogenic smoke and collapsing into the bottom storey.

Like the spires of Trash Mountain caving in the squalling winds. I knew demolition and decay.

Men screamed and begged for help as our crew found their feet.

Khan yelled above the wind, "It's over!"

Perhaps it was over, and our luck had fizzled into a spent firecracker in this hell of a wet, frigid storm.

"Let's go." Figg fired up her snowmobile as Maya settled on the back. Hellcat started the next one, with Lopez holding on with her uninjured arm.

I limped over to Trix, slid into the seat, and held her middle. I didn't even feel our electrical fizzle this time. Everything seemed distant, like an unending dream. Nothing mattered.

And yet, everything mattered.

Trix kicked our snowmobile into gear, and we shot out of the gates.

Straight into a war zone.

CHAPTER 29

Our crew sped away from the burning barracks on our snowmobiles. At first, I thought Pollins had dispatched his troops to take us home. But the approaching army, in black snow jackets, didn't stop for introductions.

I waved. Bullets sang past my ear.

Holy heck—too close.

"We're on your side!" I yelled as the military advanced.

The new squad's insignia—a sinister, mottled black and blue snake winding around a fist—differed from the Northern Alliance.

"Not your army," Trix said.

"Yeah, I got that." My voice was sucked away by the wind.

Mini-gun fire peppered the ground from the turrets at the barracks. The bullets swerved between our escaping snowmobiles, carving hot missiles into the ground. Snow clouds kicked up behind our vehicle's skis as we sped along the path, past the barricades on either side.

Hellcat and Lopez's snowmobile leaped over the barricades, landing on the other side. Hellcat swung inland, drawing the mini-gun fire away from our other two snowmobiles.

The fist-and-snake army and Khan's grey-mottled force

were locked in deadly skirmishes. Neither side was friendly. More black-clad personnel swarmed into our path, between us and the way towards the shuttle.

Figg's and Maya's snowmobile straggled. Figg's driving was less than expert. Maya barely hung on with her good arm.

"We have to help them," I said to Trix over the din of our engine as another explosion rocked the barracks walls.

"You must go forward," Trix replied.

"Not without them."

But Trix sailed us over a chunk of ice. I winced as we landed roughly.

Figg and Maya's snowmobile caught the line of mini-gun fire, swerving in the snow, avoiding the dance of deadly rain.

"Maya, no!" I projected my shield towards the path from the barracks, holding Maya safely inside.

The bullets hit, and I held the shield, moving time forward for us and stock-still for the attack. We sped away, gaining ground on the warring faction ahead.

Out of the frying pan, into the sizzling, burning battlefield.

More snowmobiles scattered from the barracks behind us as the compound exploded. The turrets gave way. The mini-guns ceased. A long alarm sounded. The walls collapsed, but their men pushed on.

We crested a rise in the snow, and the storm cleared, revealing the battlefield below. Ahead, black snowploughs with reinforced bullet-proof panels carved a path for the approaching army to follow. Men crouched behind the snowploughs, whose treads packed the snow as they crushed forward.

They were between us and the burning carcass of the wrecked shuttle. We had to reach the shuttle to the beacon aboard so Pollins could locate us, which meant dodging the encroaching army.

Bullets, rocket fire, and grenades blasted around us, shredding the snow into icy missiles.

A bomb exploded on the ground to our right. Men screamed as they were tossed high into the air, sinking into the crater. They didn't move.

Another bullet shot a hole through our front left ski.

Return fire from in front. Screams of the injured. Pleading from the fallen. Was that my crew or the feuding armies?

A black-clad soldier threw a grenade at our snowmobile. It exploded in front of Trix and me, blasting a crater into our path. We swerved to miss it.

But Figg didn't see the crater.

Their snowmobile caught the crater's lip. Flipped. Landed on its side and careened into a ditch, throwing Figg and Maya clear.

The snowmobile's gas tank caught fire.

"Trix, we have to go back!" I searched the white terrain for their space suits.

Trix twisted the snowmobile into a tight circle and slowed as we searched for Figg and Maya. On autopilot, I fended off a string of bullets while scanning the blasted terrain.

I spotted the blue patch on Maya's shoulder, a small token in the white mess. She lay face-down in the snow.

"No, no, you're okay..." I jumped off and struggled through the drifts. Kneeling beside her, I forgot my injury. I had to save my friend. "Gotta get up now, Maya."

I turned her body over. Her face seemed grey in this light. I dusted the snow from her cheeks. "It's me, remember, your worst roomie ever?"

Maya didn't respond, her eyes unfocussed. Figg limped over, assessing Maya's condition.

"We're not going to make it," Figg said.

"The hell we're not." I shook Maya. "We're getting you home to your family. To Sumati, to your Aajee."

The light returned to Maya's irises.

It was the light of survival.

Hellcat and Lopez joined us.

I motioned to the two remaining snowmobiles. "Figg, go with Hellcat and Lopez. I'll go with Trix and Maya."

I helped Maya onto our snowmobile, and she grabbed on tight. Trix kicked us into gear. We sped forward, jolting so hard I thought Maya would fall off. Grabbing her with one arm, I wound my other around Trix's middle.

"I've got you." I forced my attention ahead.

The massing black-clad army advanced, revealing their stock of grenades, rockets, and an impenetrable line of vehicles. Behind us, Khan's grey-mottled rabble escaped from the compound, hemming us in.

We floundered in a war more deadly than the Kaseath force. Humans were always the most dangerous threat.

Black smoke rose from our shuttle's shell on the far side of the approaching enemy. That's where Pollins would come to rescue us. We had to evade the army before us.

Sinister snakes flapped on the enemy's flags, snowploughs carving the way. We raced across the battlefield.

Men appeared on the ice beside us, in front, and behind.

"I cannot create shields and drive," Trix said.

A bullet whizzed towards us, and I enacted my shield. Time stopped, but our snowmobile kept going.

I forced the power outwards, keeping the bullet ahead as we sped forward. As we rocketed on, I caught several more bullets against the shield.

The edges of my consciousness were fading. The pain finally dulled. I couldn't feel my body. Was it the cold? Or was I dying?

Maybe we wouldn't make it.

Would I see Imogen again? Was this our last minute on Earth before the crystal destroyed our planet?

"Do not despair, Ofelia," Trix said.

Not while I still had breath—I had to protect my crew.

We swerved around the advancing army, which clumped beside our thin path on the edge of the drop-off into the ocean. I glanced down—the fall was not survivable.

I roared and pushed the shield back, shooting the bullets at our attackers. The energy dissipated, and I clung to Maya and Trix as time restarted for the men in front.

One of my bullets hit a soldier beside our path. He fell.

Another threw a grenade at us. Trix batted it away. The man's scream was lost in the storm as the grenade exploded.

Men swarmed our snowmobiles. We'd found the middle of the battlefield. Soldiers approached from in front, hollering at those behind. A collective roar sounded, and the fist-and-snake army advanced. Trix slowed our snowmobile, heading for the frontline.

We were caught like deer wandering into a slaughterhouse. And these soldiers were starving.

Soldiers bashed shoulders as they surged forward to attack —Khan's men behind, the fist-and-snake armies in front.

The inland elevated section was too steep for snowmobiles. Our crew was trapped between the inland hills on our right, the sheer drop-off to the ocean on our left, and the armies in front and behind. There was no escape. My shields couldn't deflect attacks from both directions.

I dismounted and helped Maya off. She knelt in the snow, her head bowed, breath heaving.

Lopez, Hellcat, and Figg fought through the snow on foot.

"Over here," I said in the squall.

Lopez trailed Trix's faint glow, the only beacon in the

gloom. Our crew regrouped, huddling together against the approaching enemies. We formed a circle, warding off the forces intent on killing us.

Bullets pinged off an approaching snowplough's protective panels. It bore down, its whine overpowering. One of Khan's soldiers knelt, holding a wide tube aimed at the snowplough.

We were in the way.

"Duck!" I hit the deck.

The rocket fired, kicking the man in the shoulder with the force. It was like slow motion. Then, the missile sped towards us.

Figg stood, dazed, and I yanked her to the ground.

The rocket whooshed overhead, landing in the driver's compartment of the front snowplough. The snowplough exploded—its treads came loose, the cab crushed inwards, and a reinforced panel flew towards us.

I caught the panel on the other side of my force field.

The explosion ricocheted as I restarted time. Figg picked up the panel, holding it protectively in front of her. She had her own shield.

The man with the rocket launcher stooped, re-loading.

A thunderclap shuddered the air. Off to our left, a massive chunk of the ice shelf cracked. Its deep fissure scattered fractures in several directions. The source of the break deepened until the entire ice shelf spasmed in a terrible earthquake.

Shaking ground knocked our crew over. The burning snowplough fell into the crack.

A section of the ice shelf beside the ocean crumpled inwards, an elegant, terrible carving that fell away into the sea. Ice shards disintegrated, no longer stable.

Fingers of cracks teased the ice beneath us, and we steadied our footing. Maya was beyond the fracture in the ice. I pulled her closer.

Just in time.

The ice shelf beside us dropped away.

I took a breath, terrified. The elements had almost taken us. If the armies didn't swallow us, the sea would.

The ice shelf dropped in a chaotic line, fanning into the distance. The sharp cracks were louder than any storm.

We huddled on the stable part of the ice.

Further away, our shuttle dropped with the disintegrating shelf. The black smoking shell slipped away, devoured by the sea. The shuttle's rescue beacon disappeared into the bottom of the ocean. How would Pollins find us now?

There was no way through. It was the end.

As the remaining ice shelf stabilised, I slumped into the snow next to Maya. The approaching armies roared around us, slogging through the snowstorm. I was separated from Trix, reaching out my hand...

To Demi. It was finally here.

Death comes for all of us, an inevitable end.

The battlefield surrounded us in either direction, around the rugged inland terrain and the drop-off from the ice shelf into the ocean. I slumped into a deep crack as the ground slipped. Lopez grabbed me with her uninjured arm and pulled me closer.

We huddled on the precipice of the ice shelf.

Nowhere to run.

The army's numbers were too many. Dodging bullets proved impossible now. The military forces whacked heads, shot off rounds, and blew each other up. Our crew ducked into a snow hollow. Cresting the trench meant death.

My energy waned, and Trix's soft-cone droop on the tip of her head was flat. She was depleted, too.

A fresh line of men appeared, hollering and shooting off rounds from their machine guns. The spurting fire cracked at the ends of the barrels, sending eerie yellow-red flashes through the snowy air.

Khan roared to his men. They kamikazed into the fray, their ranks cut down by the gunfire.

Our group ducked low as the fighting advanced.

Khan turned and noticed me peeking out of our snow trench.

"There's nowhere to go." He threaded weary steps back to our group.

Lightning slivered the dark clouds over the sea, illuminating the charcoal blackness beyond, proving his point.

I shivered so hard my teeth chattered, and I couldn't feel my body. These guys didn't even have to shoot us. We'd freeze solid in minutes.

Khan approached, pointing a gun at our group.

Fari caught up to his leader, grinning and barging into our ragged group. He clocked Lopez on her injured shoulder.

Lopez grunted in pain, her eyes resolute, staring back.

"That's for knocking me out." Fari punched her again, his knuckles whacking her jawbone. "And that's for my latest scar."

He pointed to his bloody chin. An explosion rocked the ground, but Fari didn't flinch.

Lopez fell forward, stunned by the blow, and the crystal chain peeked out of her breast pocket.

The glowing purple light shone in Fari's greedy eyes.

Lopez tried to tuck the crystal back into her pocket, but it fell into the snow.

The mesmerising, perfectly cut crystal sat in the snowdrift, its chain winding around Lopez's fist. Lopez clenched her hand tight but couldn't ward off Fari.

He whipped the crystal from her grasp. It glowed in the dull light.

Trix grabbed Fari around his chest, crushing the breath out of him. She wound her other arm around his neck, and his eyes widened.

"We have your man." Lopez waved at Khan.

Khan whipped out a handgun, aimed a shot, and fired straight through Fari's forehead.

Fari slumped in Trix's grasp, then fell to the snow, stone dead.

The shock spooked our crew.

"Why did you do that?" I bent to check, but Fari was dead. I closed his still-open eyelids. "That was senseless!"

Khan moved forward. "He was planning to double-cross me and take the crystal himself. And I need to win this war. Too many of my men have died."

I hid the crystal from Fari's limp hand behind my hip.

Lopez turned to Khan. "Your actions could destroy everything."

"What do you call this?" Khan gestured at the surrounding battle. "It's the end either way."

"The commander isn't joking," I said.

Khan turned his head to the side. "Hand over that crystal your leader wants so badly, or I'll shoot you and take it. Pollins might appreciate me returning it. He might even end this war."

I reached out to Trix. Her warm touch rippled through me, but our powers were weakened.

"Commander," I said, "I'd rather die than give him the crystal."

But men swarmed around us—Khan's men, in their grey-mottled jackets, meeting the black jackets advancing from our shuttle's direction. We were caught on the battlefield. I stumbled as rockets shook the ground.

The enemy sides clashed, aggression and pain following.

Khan's men jeered as they joined the fray—ten, twenty, thirty strong, spewing from the army's defensive line. More men than Trix and I could handle with our shields.

Leaping into the ocean would be a cleaner death.

"We will not die today," Trix said.

Three fist-and-snake soldiers attacked Khan, who whipped out his handgun and shot a black-clad soldier point-blank. He slogged the other man on his shoulder, sending him tumbling over the drop-off into the ocean. With one more soldier to dispatch, Khan ducked a rifle butt and slid a knife into the soft parts between the man's ribs.

Khan eased the man to the ground and shouted to his men.

"Forward!" His men turned their guns away from us and onto the enemy army.

Khan sauntered towards us, taking his sweet old time. He stood before me, grinning underneath his snow-crusted moustache and stepping around the freshly cracked ground.

He held out his gloved hand.

I sought Lopez's permission. This wasn't my decision to make.

"You've got one breath, recruit," she said. "What do you do?"

My mind flashed to the training sim at Space Camp.

I understood now.

I would be the one to *destroy* the world, not save it.

Things would always end this way. An end to suffering, war, and pain. An end for humanity. Including everyone I had ever known, everyone I loved, hated, or tolerated—my friends, my foes.

Everyone would meet the same fate.

My throat choked as I hoped Imogen would forgive me. We would meet in whatever came after. I silently apologised to Maya, wishing she heard my thoughts—she was also innocent.

Now, her pain would cease.

Khan reached closer. I handed him the crystal, flicking open the cap at the top.

The liquid inside glowed a deeper purple, sloshing at my touch. Khan grabbed the crystal.

He held it to the diminishing light still filtering through the clouds above the ice shelf. His eyes drank in the crystal's power.

As he lifted it higher, a tiny droplet of liquid escaped.

Time elongated as the anti-matter fell to the ground.

It landed in the snow, spreading, staining the ground purple. I enacted my shield, circling our crew, keeping a snow ring safe beneath us and catching Khan inside my circle.

Purple spread outwards from my time-stop, the stain creeping underneath Khan's men.

The ground shook, and Khan stumbled off balance, leaping closer to our safe area.

I sent the force field high into the air, wrapping it around our crew. Our bubble of shooting greens and blues. The anti-matter whipped like a hurricane around the shield. Fierce winds hurled debris, lifting the snowploughs into the air.

Then, the ice exploded upwards, throwing the snake-and-fist men in the air like tufts of soot.

"Now, Ofelia," Trix said.

Trix combined my last desperate shield with hers.

I held the shield, my face burning from the heat, my middle's searing blades severing it raw. The shield absorbed the energy, and Trix and I created a sphere, keeping our crew safe —the last bubble of hope.

Neutralising anti-matter would be near impossible. It exceeded Trix's and my powers. But we had to try.

My final act before global annihilation.

The ground around our ice spire collapsed, engulfing everything in its purple-stained path. Anti-matter sucked under the military base, the armies, the snowmobiles, their vehicles, and barricades—absorbed into the earth itself, an earthquake of energy.

The thrashing sea washed around our pillar, devouring the ice shelf.

A hole in space and time appeared, spreading a purple path back towards the shield's green sphere, keeping us safe.

The hole was infinite darkness, a purple inevitability.

But we weren't dead yet. I infused the powerful sphere with hope and love. Maybe we didn't have to die today. Maybe there was a future for our planet.

The air shimmered and shattered, turning black like the void of space. Reality broke apart, and my sphere was the only thing remaining. Our little bubble would destroy everything.

An overwhelming purple light flashed. Our crew cowered from the heat and energy. I crouched on the ground, no longer able to stand. The weight of the universe's matter pressed down.

We would obliterate all life if Trix and I couldn't contain this energy.

A purple fireball erupted from the earth. The crystal shot skyward.

Khan crawled towards the edge and grabbed the crystal. As he did, he lost his footing and fell into the crevice.

I screamed with the effort of concentrating, of blocking out the pain that tore my body in half. My scream turned to a roar, and I gave it everything. All of my life force, all of my love for my family. Rejecting all the times I hadn't kept my family safe. Then, I drew on my one goal—to see my sister one last time. This was for Imogen.

"I've got you, Limpet," I grunted, regrouping beside Trix. Our fireball shield thrashed around us, the sphere threatening to break space and time, warding off the purple gash in the universe.

My hair flew about, my cheeks crushed like the g-force of a launching rocket. I squinted into the wind of the hurricane. My body thrummed, vibrating in frequencies unknown. My being was breaking into atoms.

Time folded in on itself outside of the sphere. It fused and blended with the beings around us. I held time, past, present, and future—all existence, all consciousness. Trix and I melded our minds, sharing this colossal force containing every possibility of every moment.

I carved a way through time, seeking its tunnels and navigating its twists. Which reality did I seek?

The one where everyone survived. The one where I didn't explode the anti-matter, and Earth along with it.

I dissected time as painfully as Figg's surgical incision. Until I found the thread I sought.

The protective globe twisted about, unpredictable and weakening. I held onto every moment, yet time was scarce. That thread was our last chance.

I seized Trix's arm. "On three, we blast this bastard into hell. Ready?"

"Ready," Trix replied, her voice softer in my head.

"One, two... three!"

I struggled with every effort like nothing else existed except for me, Trix, and our shield. My eyes glowed in the purple barrage beyond our shield, the anti-matter encroaching on our ice island that hadn't imploded.

Warding off our most dangerous threat yet—a terrifying intensity that could engulf us all.

This was the end of the world.

How long could we hold on?

I entwined all thought, all concentration, all feeling into our shield. I didn't have to count down.

Trix and I were one.

We let it go—all our force—creating a massive whirlwind overhead, our crackling shield exploding all energy above us.

More terrifying than the blackened storm, as inevitable as a cataclysm. The world's future was in my hands.

The purple of the antimatter collided with the green of our shield. Both colours, both energies, fused and diluted each other.

The purple sucked into the green, its power diminishing.

A fiery red implosion devoured everything. Reality bent, distorting like static. And then we let our ultimate force loose.

Massive enough to destroy the planet.

CHAPTER 30

Our crew huddled on the tiny island of ice-covered earth. Residual storm clouds whipped around. A tremendous abyss had consumed the armies and the entire ice shelf, leaving our tiny platform alone in the cold sea.

The drop was not survivable.

Anti-matter dissipated into the surrounding air. It crackled with latent energy and then shot above the clouds into the atmosphere beyond.

We cowered on the remaining ice spire, teetering in the wind.

"I have you." I smiled at Maya.

"Not bad for a Northies rat." She settled back in the snow, blood from her bullet wound staining the ice.

I shuffled forward and hugged her close. "It's for nothing, anyway. The world's literally been sucked away. Our shuttle is at the bottom of the ocean. And that means so is the beacon. Pollins has no way of locating us."

"We won't make it home?" Maya said, her eyes glistening.

"At least we're together."

"Help!" a man shouted, just audible over the wind.

"Khan." Maya rolled her eyes.

I peered over the lip. Khan held on by his fingertips, clutching at one tiny handhold of ice. His feet scrambled for purchase on the slippery, sheer ice wall.

Hesitating, I considered my next move. Letting him perish in the ocean with his men would be easy.

But I was still human, after all.

I lay on the platform's edge, my head and torso hanging over. Trix grabbed my feet to stop me from plunging off the ice spire. The cold beneath my stomach dulled the pain.

Khan's gloved fingertips shook with the cold. Or with fear? He lunged with one last effort, and I caught his hand.

His glove slipped, and he almost fell into the frothy ocean peaks below. But then Lopez helped, grabbing his elbow.

We struggled to hang on. Nobody but our crew would know if I pushed him into the abyss. But his eyes held a new terror. He had seen the crystal's power.

We heaved him onto the ledge and lay on our backs, panting from the effort.

My last worldly act was saving one man. And not a nice one. But most people never have that chance.

Did that compensate for the other casualties? I tried not to think about the lives I'd taken today.

The ocean swilled around our ice spire, its waves crashing into the thin, last-remaining island.

Beneath us, the spire cracked at the bottom, listing to the side. The ice crunched, and our platform angled, threatening to tip us into the ocean below.

"Hand it over," I said to Khan.

His hangdog expression was contrite as he offered me the crystal.

"It was all for nothing. We'll die anyway," Figg said, terror in her eyes.

"Maybe that's for the best," Lopez mused, cradling Maya to keep her off the frigid ice.

'Words gone wrong' started wars, and my words had failed us.

"I let us down," I said.

"Do not despair," Trix said.

The wind flattened our hair, the force settling onto the ice platform. Had the storm returned, one last fury from nature?

The overhead wind caressed my face as a shadow passed.

Trix's fighter ship hovered just above us. It lowered to the height of the ice platform.

"You can apologise later." Maya sat up. "Trix has us covered."

The canopy opened at Trix's touch.

Maya grinned at me, and my elation caught up. We may not die today after all.

The ice cracked beneath us, sharper than a thunderclap. We were running shy of time.

Trix climbed into the canopy and discarded boxes of supplies, anything that added bulk to the ship. She ripped out the cockpit seats, tossing them into the ocean like an offering, making room.

"We're too bulky in our suits. We won't fit," Lopez said.

Our crew helped each other disrobe, tossing our space suits into the sea, freezing in our undershirts and pants.

I tugged my space boots free and tossed them over. We couldn't hear the splash above the bluster of the fighter's engines. My toes curled on the frigid ice.

I hung the crystal on its chain around my neck.

Trix lowered the cockpit to the platform's height—one large step for a human.

Maya went first, climbing inside and flattening against the rear compartment. Then Figg, then Lopez. They crammed in, making room for Hellcat and me to follow. Trix settled into the cockpit area, now devoid of her seat.

Khan, the last puppy at the rescue shelter, stood on the ice. He wiped a bloody gash on the crown of his head.

"He's not worth it," Hellcat said.

I reached out. Khan hesitated, and then the ice spire split, losing its integrity.

He leaped up as the ice dropped away. Khan dangled on the canopy's side. I helped him crawl in.

We made room for our last passenger. It was rush hour in the most crowded of public transport, and we shuffled to fit inside the canopy.

I breathed in Maya's hair gel, Khan's sweaty undershirt, and Lopez's iron-tinted bloody wound.

For a split second, I smelled the undertones of Griffin's blueberry bubble gum.

That made me smile.

The fighter listed, unused to such a heavy load. Then Trix closed the overhead canopy. I leaned against my crew.

The deafening sound of the engines angled us away from the disappeared earth.

We had made it.

Our crew settled uncomfortably for the ride back to London in Trix's fighter ship. We were muted, shell-shocked, and relieved to return home.

Supposing a home still existed. Had the anti-matter obliterated the world?

I glanced out of the glass canopy past Trix, who concentrated on flying the ship. We couldn't talk, because she controlled the fighter with her mind.

Trix brought the ship beneath the clouds. The ocean lay in sparkling grey blues beneath us.

Had the anti-matter wiped Earth clean of land?

Our crew scanned the scenery below. Relief followed as Maya pointed to something brown and hazy on the horizon.

As we approached, the line grew into a solid object until there was land beneath us, its contours of greens and browns beside the blue oceans.

This part of Earth, at least, was intact.

There were no comms aboard the fighter since the Kaseath didn't communicate out loud, but I worried about making it home.

"They might assume we're the Kaseath," I said.

"Only some of us are." Trix regarded me.

"What about the sat phone?" Maya pulled it from her pocket.

"That could work." Lopez sat straighter, grimacing at the pain in her shoulder. The melted ice shard had left a grim gash about a knuckle-length wide.

Maya handed me the phone, and I tossed it to Lopez. She turned it on and waited for the signal to pair.

Signs of civilisation appeared. Buildings, houses, roads, and vehicles. Surely we shouldn't see human habitation here? Pollins said civilisation was limited to the northern alliance of countries and its enemies up north. Pollins hadn't been truthful about much. Khan and his men were proof of Pollins's ignorance—or deception.

"How much longer?" Maya asked.

I wound my arm around hers, holding her steady.

"Not far." I smiled. But Maya's face was tinged with grey. I wondered how deep her bullet wound went. She wasn't out of danger.

I couldn't go on if she died. Not Maya. She was my anchor,

validating what I'd been through—because she'd also endured the horrors of Elditch.

She knew what Figg was capable of.

Hurry, I thought to Trix.

Trix responded, pushing the fighter into a couple of g's as we sped forward. The ground became a mass of browns amongst the swirling oceans. Then she slowed as we approached a smaller island, its contours familiar. We'd spotted the view from a much higher vantage point in space.

London wasn't far away.

"This is Commander Luz Lopez of Valentina One," Lopez said. "Request safe passage to land."

Bullets arced around our canopy.

"What the—" Lopez said. "Stand down! Friendly craft approaching."

Bullets embedded into the fighter's side.

Two fighter planes wound around us in tight formation.

"This is Commander Luz Lopez. The Kaseath ship is friendly!"

The planes twirled higher, rounding for another pass.

A voice crackled on the other end. "Commander Lopez?"

"Yes! Who is this?"

"This is Sebastian at Mission Control. Is it really you?"

"Yes, Dr Wood," Lopez replied.

There was a pause. I hadn't thought I'd ever be glad to hear Sebastian's voice.

"What's the status of your crew?" he asked.

"Mostly intact," Lopez said.

"Clear for landing, Commander. We have you at the north runway. It will be a bumpy ride. Good luck."

The fighter descended, and the partly destroyed buildings of London lay below, with the greenery of the suburbs visible in the distance. Black smoke twined up from massive fires dotted around the land. Reds and yellows flowered, tiny explosions off to the side. It seemed harmless, even beautiful.

War had come to London.

Was my family safe?

Two more fighter jets whizzed past, and Trix ducked our ship to evade the collision. The planes twisted in the sky as our fighter prepared for landing.

I noticed the insignia on the plane—the black and red snake winding around the white fist.

The same enemy who was fighting Khan's men.

"That doesn't make sense..." Khan said.

"I guess you weren't fighting Pollins's men," Lopez said.

"Maybe they used to be," Khan said. "And they turned against him."

The fighters returned, aiming gunfire around our ship. Trix struggled to keep us steady, following the yellow and blue runway lights in the gloom. The plane's fire looped around us, skimming the top of the canopy.

Their bullets destroyed another fighter behind us I hadn't even seen. We were just in the way.

The enemy fighter went down, a disintegrating mess exploding into a derelict office block.

The runway appeared, revealing skeletons of bombed aircraft and other debris. The Mission Control building was intact, a beacon off to one side. Shells had damaged the surrounding buildings—Space Camp, the barracks, the supporting aircraft hangars and warehouses. A hole in the closest aircraft hangar revealed men repairing several fighter jets.

Trix lowered our fighter, bringing it down and angling it towards the runway. The ship hovered above the ground, slowing from its descent. Then it halted, hovering while a landing apparatus folded out. The fighter settled on the ground.

Two fire trucks wound onto the runway, lights flashing.

There was no need. Our ship was intact, with a couple of holes and some weary crew.

An explosion rocked the sky to our left, but the fire trucks kept going. A man leaped from the cab. Its driver circled, and the other fire truck halted.

The man approached as our canopy opened at Trix's touch.

"It's not safe here," he yelled. "Proceed to the farthest hangar, 12-B."

Trix nodded and lifted the ship again, limping us through the debris to a large hangar off to one side.

As we progressed, two enemy aircraft took aim at the fire trucks. One of them shot the truck's wheels. Two drivers exited, rescued by another man's truck. They left the other fire truck sitting on the runway.

Trix navigated to 12-B as the fighting raged around us.

We entered the massive doors, the hangar gaping overhead, and they winched closed.

Shutting us into darkness, our cocoon of safety.

Pollins greeted us along with a medical team, who helped us from the cramped craft. I noticed Pollins's haggard, worried expression. But he wasn't concerned about his crew. His eyes sought Lopez.

"You have the crystal?" Pollins asked.

"We're fine, thanks for asking," I said.

It was always about control. Pollins cared more about wielding the ultimate power.

Lopez nodded her approval to me.

I took the crystal from around my neck and held it by its chain. Pollins's eyes glowed with its purple energy. A smile teased his lips. It was a greedy smile—the smile of men in power.

I handed Pollins the crystal.

"I'm happy you all made it," Pollins said, as an afterthought, as he tucked the crystal into his fist.

"Not all of us," Maya said. "Not even close."

Pollins grinned, all business. "Let's get you all seen to."

"Our families?" I asked. "Are they okay?"

"For now," Pollins said.

My breath puffed as relief flooded my mind. My lips trembled, and my chest squeezed with tension. I cried in a furious burst, my tears blurring everything around me.

My family was safe.

Khan stepped from behind Trix, and Pollins nodded briefly. Khan's jaw clenched, and he broke eye contact first.

The medical team settled Lopez, Maya, and me into wheelchairs. Two ambulances parked with their back doors open, and paramedics helped Figg, Hellcat, and Khan over for assessment.

Maya wheeled next to me, and I reached out my hand. We squeezed tight, and tears flowed with shock and overwhelming emotion—a release of tension over the entire mission.

We'd made it together.

But it was time to return to our families.

CHAPTER 31

ONCE THE MEDICAL team made their assessments, Maya headed to theatre to have her bullet removed, and Lopez followed so her impaled shoulder could be stitched up.

I lay in the imaging machine to be scanned for internal injuries, with the terrifying sensation that I was back at the research facility. Had I ever left? The tests, being locked in a cell. The isolation and desperation. For a moment, my insecurities took over.

Scavenger. Northies rat. Lab rat.

Why should I board that Ark?

A sliver pushed into my mind, doubting I was worthy of survival.

A flash overcame me—I visualised Valentina One crashing. The battle. Those men dying like that.

All because of me.

I must have wriggled, because Sebastian said, "Hold still, please."

The visions wouldn't stop. I reverted to a helpless kid, experimental fodder.

But then, I had also met Maya and Trix. My life had

improved. We'd stuck together and helped each other. I was stronger because of my friends.

This wasn't my end. I had to get my family aboard that Ark.

The scan ended, and the bed slid out from inside the machine. I sat up, rubbing the scales on my stomach.

Once the machine stopped humming, Sebastian approached. I glared at the man who had given his DNA to make me. But he was not my father.

"You've avoided damage to your organs." He ignored my hostility. "There is still an internal bleed. However, it seemed to heal as we conducted the scan."

"Must be the genes, Doctor Wood," I said.

He reddened, then said, "Not from my genes. Now try to rest."

But there was no time to rest. Sebastian had said it himself. I was a freakin' healing miracle. Now, I clamoured to return home.

He left me with a technician. The television in the control room caught my eye.

News reports flashed images of war, broadcast relentlessly, all with Pollins's spin. The Alliance fighters fought the attack on our city and the Remaining Countries. We'd pushed back the offensive. But we were losing, despite the cheery news reports. I recognised the bombed-out areas.

One of those areas was the familiar shacks in Northies. The people I'd grown up with, co-existed with, survived with.

The area was a burning crater now, with wily scavengers picking the bones.

The technician helped me off the bed.

"I need to call my sister," I said.

"Sorry," she said. "They've locked down the base. That means no communication."

I pulled the IV cannula from my arm. "I'm going home then."

"You're not cleared to leave." The technician pushed me back towards the bed. A flash of muscled orderlies from the research facility strobed against my retina—a glimpse into a past hell.

I batted her arm away. "I'm cleared to do whatever I want."

The technician blocked the exit. Huffing like an insolent teenage delinquent, I entered a staring competition.

Trix arrived like a defensive football player. Her imposing bulk towered over the technician.

The technician backed up, freaked out by the large Kaseath in her medical bay.

"You can tell Doctor Wood we left by force," I said evenly.

"Honestly, I don't care." The technician stepped aside. "The base might not survive through my shift."

Trix and I left the imaging room, searching the medical bay. We found Maya and Lopez in beds beside each other, recovering from their surgeries. Hellcat sat slumped in a chair, keeping a worried vigil.

Figg was missing, probably already blasting off for the Ark, saving her skin as usual.

"Let's get out of here." I helped Maya from the bed as Lopez sat forward, checking the sticking plaster around her shoulder.

"And go where?" Hellcat said, glancing at Maya.

"We need to go home."

Khan joined our remaining crew in the medical bay. He wore a bandage over his jaw, and his eyes were bright with adrenalin.

"Time to move. The base is under attack." He trained his eyes on the deserted hall.

Where had the staff gone?

Maya removed her IV lines and wires from the beeping machines. I held her arm, keeping her steady. Lopez seemed okay on her own. Trix and Khan stepped into the hall, scoping out the base's workers.

Panicked doctors ran along the halls, their rubber theatre clogs impeding their progress.

"This way," Khan said.

"We're following Khan's orders now?" I asked.

Khan's presence reminded me of what I'd done.

All those men...

"I'm on your side, Ofelia," Khan said, and I believed him.

But also, he messed with my morality. He was our enemy, and he'd killed Fari in cold blood. He was the opposing force in a bloody war. But Khan and Pollins fought the same fist-and-snake rebels.

I couldn't put his memory in a box and keep going. He was proof of my guilt. I'd obliterated those men to return to my family.

"I've seen what that anti-matter can do," Khan said. "Pollins shouldn't have the crystal. Let me help."

"We have to leave," Hellcat said.

We followed Khan and the fleeing doctors, our rabble under-dressed and alert.

The overhead lights dimmed, then flickered. Then the ceiling shook, and grime dislodged, showering us.

We ran on, our hair dusted grey.

One panicked doctor in green scrubs fled through an emergency door, and we followed him outside.

The sky was purple-black, the sunset orange on the horizon. Lights dotted Space Camp and the surrounding damaged buildings. Mission Control was lit only on one floor. Smoke tainted the air, and sirens wound up and down, signalling fresh danger.

The parking lot was chaos. An explosion bloomed a while away, near our old barracks at Space Camp. It lit up the night sky and the medical bay we'd just exited.

Lopez pointed to a military-grade Humvee, its passenger door ajar.

"I'll drive." Hellcat's eyes lit with excitement.

"Didn't you crash your ship?" Khan approached the vehicle. "I'll drive."

We piled into the Humvee—Lopez up front, Khan driving, Hellcat and Trix in the backseat, and Maya and me huddled in the rear jumpseat.

The keys dangled from the ignition. Someone had abandoned this truck in a rush. Khan grinned, fired us up, and backed onto the service road. We passed the fleeing doctors, who waved for us to stop. But Khan was relentless, pushing through the staff, guiding us onto the straight road beyond the runway.

"Turn right at the next intersection," Lopez said.

"Or I could just do this." Khan yanked the wheel, driving us over the decorative concrete barrier, right through the flaming guts of Space Camp.

Khan drove past the Mission Control building. Then, the training hangar, its roof gaping like a half-peeled orange. Unfurled, with the training sims sitting there, abandoned. We had spent so much time there. But our training was over.

Two sentries by the wooden boom gate waved for us to stop.

Khan planted his foot on the accelerator.

The men shouldered their weapons and aimed them at our truck. Khan played chicken, keeping the vehicle at top speed.

The men fired, and bullets pinged off the bulletproof exterior. Khan didn't slow down. The men dove out of the way.

We smashed through the flimsy wooden gate and into the ravaged streets, our vehicle speeding ahead.

Life was worse out of the base.

It was anarchy.

The streets were full of people fighting, smashing windows, and throwing broken bottles. Some huddled behind hastily constructed barricades.

It was the Northies rabble.

Their home was destroyed, and now they fought for survival. They were out on the streets. My heart broke anew, but I couldn't help them. They couldn't even help themselves.

Khan forged through the rubble, shifting barricades with the Humvee's front grille. Citizens attacked our vehicle. Somebody bounced against the outside of the cab.

A familiar figure stood on an upturned Dumpster, his long coat's bullet holes backlit by the flaming barrel behind him.

It was Shifty Pocks, Figg's henchman, who ran Northies. His thugs gathered on the upturned Dumpster as Pocks addressed the rabble, who cheered.

Pocks pointed to our car, and the mob turned, focussing their attention on our escape.

Something cold slipped into my heart as Pocks recognised me from the car window. This was his jam. Anarchy fired him up. And he hated me more than anyone else in Northies.

"Get this thing going," I said.

Khan punched the accelerator, but the Humvee was slow. It was compact and durable, but sluggish.

We headed through the thick rabble surrounding our truck.

"Don't stop." Lopez eyed the crush of people.

Khan struggled not to hit the surrounding bystanders. The car slowed, unable to avoid the mass in front.

We crawled forward, then stopped. Pocks thudded into the dust on the ground next to the upturned Dumpster, pointing a shotgun at our vehicle.

A flaming bottle exploded, rocking the side of the road. The crowd fled in all directions. Away from the road's exposure and our Humvee.

Khan hit the accelerator, and we cleared a path through the rabble, leaving Northies and Pocks far behind.

The streets were dark, the streetlights out, as we sped onwards. I gave Khan directions. We raced on to Cookham East.

We rode along the smoother roads, approaching the gated suburban area of Cookham East. But someone had welded shut the barricaded gate at the entrance. There was no way through.

"I know another way." I directed Khan to reverse and approach the circular road above the park on the hill above the suburbs.

The streets were dark, and the park was a gloomy, flat break in the surrounding buildings.

"We'll go on foot from here," I said.

We exited the Humvee. Khan locked the doors and tucked the keys in his pocket. I led our group down the slope, past the children's playground. The swings creaked in the wind, an eerie sound. Would kids play in this new future?

The roofs of the suburbs spread beyond the tall perimeter fence laid out below. Except the houses were dark, the streetlights extinguished. The electricity must be out.

We passed the lake and approached the slope's base. The gate's scanner wasn't working, which meant it was unlocked. It squeaked open as I pushed through.

Maya and I exchanged worried glances. What would we find inside? Maya had just as much to lose. Her family lived next to ours.

"It could be dangerous." Khan scoped the cul-de-sac as we crept through the gate.

The moon appeared through the clouds, casting sinister, muted lighting over the dark shapes around us. Cookham East looked like the back lot of a horror movie set. Manicured lawns were overgrown with tall weeds, and the houses were dark and abandoned, sitting on the rise above their driveways.

The front door of my house was ajar, like a missing tooth. Someone had left in a hurry. My family was no longer there.

My guts dropped, and worry took over. Where was everyone—had they moved elsewhere? How would I find them?

Maya's house was next to mine and also dark and empty.

Hellcat pointed down the hill to a house farther away. It was Aze's.

A streak of light filtered through the window. That meant people were about!

We headed to the house, slowly advancing. Our group gathered on the decorative path, between the overgrown, weedy lawn.

We huddled on the front porch. Trix stood behind us, hanging back.

Muted chatter rose inside—an argument. Were they the people who'd barricaded the gate? Were they outsiders or the original residents?

Imogen could be inside; that was all that mattered. I tried the locked door handle, then pounded my fists against the front door, seeking answers to this place.

The chatter inside stopped, and the light extinguished, throwing the porch into inkiness.

The hallway floorboards creaked as someone approached. They opened the door wide enough to peer outside.

I recognised those eyes and furrowed brow.

It was my step-dad, Roland.

Trix remained outside as the rest of our group pushed into the house. Roland, my mum, and Imogen gathered around.

"Limpet, you're looking better!" I said as my family crowded around for hugs.

"So are you," Mum said.

Imogen wiped away tears of happiness. I clung to my family. Earthy fragrances overpowered—Roland's aftershave, Mum's coconut shampoo, Imogen's freshly washed t-shirt—the scents of opulence.

A dream that was never my reality.

I turned to Imogen, tears flooding my eyes so I couldn't see. My throat choked up.

"I'm sorry, Imogen. There's no cure."

I flung my arms around my sister, sobbing into her shoulder. My one mission was to keep her safe, and I'd failed.

"I'm feeling much better," she said as Mum stroked my hair.

For now, I thought to myself. But it wasn't forever. One day, her body would succumb to the plague. One day, she wouldn't be able to fight back. And she couldn't board the Interplanetary Voyager Ark. No cure meant no ticket.

Mum and Roland consoled me. Guilt weighed my bones.

I would survive, but my sister would die. My curse was loss. My deepest wound was guilt.

I was responsible for all of us, and I had failed.

The Cookham East residents huddled in the living room,

standing in small groups or sitting on chairs reserved for older adults.

Exhaustion settled like I was short a week of sleep. But my family had to know.

I heaved a breath and said, "We need to talk."

Mum nodded as my crew filtered past to join the neighbourhood throng. Maya touched my shoulder as she passed, reuniting with her family and hugging her little sister and parents.

After the conversation settled, the neighbours gave me their attention.

My face reddened with anxiety, but we had to be straight.

I told them everything—the journey to the Kaseath, our failed diplomatic discussion, and returning without the cure. The residents didn't seem to mind, but it was Imogen's death knell, and I couldn't meet her eye.

Taking a breath, I told them about stealing the alien tech and hot-footing it home. Even though Pollins maintained that everyone south of the equator had perished, I described the battle in Antarctica. I said that the crystal was dangerous anti-matter. Finally, I mentioned our crew's last stand and being rescued.

"We came straight here," I finished.

The residents seemed shell-shocked at first. They argued amongst themselves, and the chatter swelled into anger, fear, and panic.

"It's time to stop fighting each other," I said as the residents turned towards me. The room quietened. "It's time to leave for the Ark."

EPILOGUE

I sat with Imogen in a quiet corner of the house, stroking her hair while we rested in each other's company. The chair was soft underneath, vacated while the adults slept. My sister and I didn't have to speak. I blamed myself, even if she didn't.

"I'm sorry, Imogen. We thought we had the cure. I didn't intend to lie..."

"It's okay." Imogen sat up, her face bright. "It was a long shot."

"But I thought I'd saved you..."

"I don't need saving," she said, her eyes downcast.

My lip trembled, and I fought the pinpricks of tears that clouded my vision.

I hugged her close, breathing in her soapy scent, stroking her hair, holding her fragile frame.

Maya hovered across the room, chatting with her little sister, Sumati.

"At least we're together," I said as Maya hugged Sumati.

Mousie and Aze approached shyly. That wasn't their style.

"Hey," Mousie said.

"Hey," I replied.

"So what was the QyronNexa like?" Aze's face filled with awe.

"Hot," I said, then grinned. Tension left my body like a vast sigh.

"We're glad you made it." Mousie ruffled a hand through her short, spiky hair. It had grown to a decent length.

Families gathered in the room, catching up. My mum spoke with a neighbour, but Roland looked uncomfortable. He'd never make it with the suburbs folk, but Mum was a natural. There were advantages to growing up outside of Northies.

The night's earlier arguments had given way to hope and eager conversation.

Maybe we'd escape Earth after all. Perhaps we had a chance.

The chatter became claustrophobic with peppered laughter. There were too many people, I couldn't concentrate.

"Imogen, I'll come see you soon." I nudged her from my lap.

Despite her death sentence, she nodded and joined Sumati —just another kid.

I approached Mousie and Aze and said, "I'll be back."

They grinned, but tension edged behind their smiles. Cookham East was no longer safe, and we were far from boarding the Ark. My friends understood the risks. Like me, they had to fight their way through Northies. They knew the worst of humanity.

Was I considered part of that—the worst of humanity?

It was all about perspective. One side won, the other lost— the duality of being human.

I left the chatter, and Mousie locked the front door behind me.

Outside, the wind shifted, the air thick with smoke. Smog

obscured the moon, and everything took on a surreal edge, a dangerous tinge.

The suburban streets were deserted, the chatter inside the house inaudible. The houses' windows glared back from their shuttered gloom. I imagined an enemy Kaseath standing in the dark, peering at me. The windows were accusatory eyes into my soul. Was my heart already black? Or was there hope for us?

I trudged up the hill. The hum of the streetlights was absent. A loose gate banged in the wind. The houses were faint outlines, like dormant bears in a thousand-year sleep.

I trudged to my house on the top of the hill, up the sloping driveway. Through the open door, into our house's shell.

The couch was more grey than white. The television was a ghost's image, the kitchen bench menacing.

But the house didn't interest me. I pushed through into the backyard.

The former grass was now a knee-height, weed-strewn lawn. The back fence was still sturdy, and the plants at the perimeter were overgrown and scraggly.

Demi's sapling had grown into a slender tree.

Ashes fell all around, the air thick with advancing smoke, covering the green and brown weedy lawn.

I reached out to the trunk, which was thicker than before the failed mission. It was cold to the touch, its bark smooth. Its branches pushed higher than I remembered, its limbs thin and young. It wasn't yet fully grown—a partial memory.

Closing my eyes, I remembered Demi from Trash Mountain on the day Figg had snatched her. I hid like a coward, letting Figg take her.

"I'm sorry, Demi." My voice caught—just another scared kid without power.

Scavenger. Northies rat. Lab rat.

Sinking to the ground beneath the tree, I knelt on its roots, which dug into the soil. Winding my arms around the tree, I interlocked my fingers on the far side.

Holding my sister close.

I sat at Demi's tree, taking a moment. The ashes in the air fell, landing on me like gentle snow, their grey catching in my hair and dusting my clothes.

Burying me alive.

I yearned for that oblivion. The struggle, the pain. And now, the guilt. It consumed me. I'd lied to Imogen and my family, given them false hope.

There was no saving any of us.

Daybreak peeled into the black sky, the first pinpricks of dark-violet light teasing the horizon. The sun rose, sending an orange smoke haze through the clouds. The silent morning grew loud, with sirens rushing around the perimeter of Cookham East. Then, two fighter jets shot by, reminding me that this was all temporary. I'd have to leave Demi for good.

I settled against the trunk, watching the sun rise above the suburbs' rooftops. A helicopter thudded on the park's other side. Two more fighter planes shot overhead, their sonic boom catching up after they disappeared.

I closed my eyes.

Her small breath caught on the way out—a familiar sound.

I opened my eyes. "Hey, Limpet."

My sister sat beside me, her back against the spindly trunk. She said nothing. Just put her head against my shoulder.

And that was when I let the tears flow. An outpouring. A messy, undignified sobbing. I bawled my eyes out while my sister sat, letting me cry.

My nose ran, mixing with my tears. My head hurt, my eyes stung, and my chest felt like a narrowing vice had crushed it to paper.

I couldn't stop the tears, and I grabbed Imogen, holding her, willing the pain to stop.

Would it ever stop?

I cried until my eyes were gritty, my head aching. I wiped my face with the back of my sleeve. Imogen didn't say a word. Just let me grieve.

I felt empty, as if a massive weight had lifted from my chest. From inside my being, deep where my heart sat, beating slowly.

"I can't go. I can't leave you. You have no place on the Ark."

Guilt overrode the sadness. I couldn't look Imogen in the eye.

"You can ask for whatever you want." She hugged my middle weakly. "You're Pollins's link to the Kaseath."

"Yeah, just another one of his weapons."

Maya stepped through the back door.

"As long as we're breathing, there's hope, right?" She joined Imogen and me at the tree.

Maya hugged us both.

Overlapping sirens filled the air, along with speeding cars on the highway beside our gated community. Daybreak sent the sky into a hazy blue around the ever-present smoke.

Mousie and Aze stepped into the yard, smiling at me. Then Trix joined us, holding Maya's little sister's hand.

Figg was right about one thing. This was bigger than me and my sister. It was bigger than every suburb combined, every person I'd known and loved.

I decided. The thought was inevitable.

"We have to board the Ark." I glanced at Imogen. "All of us."

"Heck, yes." Mousie grinned.

"We're with you." Maya wound her arm around her sister's.

My friends settled beside me, lost in their thoughts.

I gazed up at the tree one last time, noticing fresh green buds, tiny shoots, on the tips of the smooth branches. Unrelenting, new life burst through.

As my friends gathered close, I squeezed my sister's hand. I reached out to the nearest green shoot on the tree, caressing the bud with my fingertip and thumb. It was fragile beneath my touch, but resilient. Soon, it would unfurl and find its unique strength—a persistent life, surviving in the toughest places.

There was hope for,a new beginning. We just had to escape our past.

Would you like to continue the adventure?

When your enemy holds the key to survival... how far would you go to protect the ones you love?

The fight isn't over. It's only just begun.

Humanity's last hope lies in starting again on a new world.

But the Kaseath's powers are more terrifying than anyone ever imagined.

In the final battle to escape annihilation, alliances will fracture—and only those who dare to evolve will live.

Coming soon: *Final Resistance*, Book 3 in The Kaseath Chronicles.

Want to be the first to know when it's released?

Join the pre-release notification list at:

jackiemccarthy.com/sign-up

Love The Kaseath Chronicles?

As a thank you for reading, I'd love to gift you a free prequel short story!

Maya's United Nations dives deeper into Maya's adventures before she met Ofelia (don't worry—no spoilers!).

You'll meet familiar faces and new ones, and I think you'll really enjoy the extra glimpse into their world. Plus, you'll get early updates on new releases, behind-the-scenes notes, and more.

Grab your FREE short story:

jackiemccarthy.com/prequel

Enjoyed the book?

If you have a moment, I'd love for you to share your thoughts wherever you prefer to leave reviews.

Your feedback helps new readers find their next favourite story—and it means more to me than you know.

Thank you so much for being part of this journey!

Strong female characters and quirky, empowering tales.

Jackie is an award-winning author of Young Adult (YA) & New Adult (NA) fiction, with a speculative twist. If it's dystopian, futuristic or magical, she'll happily take you there. She stuffs as many strong female characters into her books as she possibly can, for your enjoyment.

Her novel "The Hybrid Cure," Book 1 in The Kaseath Chronicles, was runner-up for YA Science Fiction in the 2025 Incipere Awards.

Jackie has worked in publishing and the media for over 20 years, in both London and Sydney. Her debut novel, "The Ghost Mothers," is (very loosely) inspired by her time on "The Australian Women's Weekly Magazine," many moons ago.

If you would like to be notified of new books as they are released, you can join the readers' group at

jackiemccarthy.com/sign-up/

You can find all of Jackie's books on her website:

jackiemccarthy.com

Happy reading, and thanks for stopping by!

ALSO BY JACKIE MCCARTHY

The Hybrid Cure

(The Kaseath Chronicles, Book 1)

jackiemccarthy.com/books/the-hybrid-cure

The Ghost Mothers

(Standalone Novel)

jackiemccarthy.com/books/the-ghost-mothers

Visit the website for all current and upcoming titles at:

jackiemccarthy.com/books

ISBN (ebook): 978-0-6486942-4-3
ISBN (paperback): 978-0-6486942-9-8
ISBN (hardcover): 978-1-7640939-0-3